Women

The Ownership Manual

Logan Alexander

American Taboo Press
New York - Los Angeles

Table of Contents

Author's Note

The spirit of this manual is guided by the fierce urge of a man to possess a woman in the profoundest of ways. For some, a normal human connection devoid of the extreme polarities of emotional, psychological and sexual experience that merge in dominance and submission play is akin to a death sentence of relationship mediocrity. "*I cannot date vanilla ever again,*" they profess again and again in their outcast-flavored turn of the tongue. He wants her body and soul so completely that he yearns to make her his actual physical property. She wants to be craved so badly that she longs to be made his absolute possession.

Unlike outdated patriarchal notions of a man controlling a woman's destiny, in this post-feminist world we live in, free thinking women chose to be owned and open-minded men want to own their women in new radically deviant ways. They reject traditional relationships and long for a kind of fanatical completeness with one another which transforms daily life into rituals saturated with kinetic connections and kinky thrills.

So just what does it mean to own and to be owned? It means him making her such a grand priority in his life that the feeling of absolute trust in him lets her go completely and obey his most outrageous demands. It means her acting intentionally bratty so she'll get fucked into submission with a firm hand on her throat and her sweaty body sliding violently back and forth on the kitchen table. It means being marched out of a restaurant, bent over the car, skirt pulled up, panties pulled down, bare ass spanked hard and then taken back inside to finish eating dinner. It means waking "daddy" up early in the morning by grinding her ass against his body so he'll wake up and take what belongs to him. It means being treated like a beautiful princess but pounded like his dirty little slut. It means him locking a lustrous silver collar around her neck which can never be removed. It means making love to her with his mind before he ever even touches her body. It means him whispering in her ear on a frigid rainy evening when nothing else feels like it's going right: *"You'll always be mine, babygirl."* It means what happens when a man's dominating strength acts as the wildest aphrodisiac on a woman's heart, mind and body all at once.

This manual is written primarily as a freewheeling guide for men seeking to own a woman and for women seeking to be owned by a man within a certain creative space of the BDSM realm. It is not a general relationship guide for every Dominant-submissive couple in the so-called "scene". It is inspired by the same masculine visionary energies that gave rise to confrontational works of art and ancient traditions of phallic worship. It is but one subjective vision of living an inspired life of dominating a woman. It includes both broad strokes and extremely particular ideas.

Yet, it also serves as a source of inspiration for men and women in any relationship as the desire to possess and be possessed is universal, even if it is only a small compulsion within the complex dynamic of a normal relationship. Regular people have always fed on the excessive proclivities of those on the fringe of society and reality. The style of this work is in part formal for it is meant as a thought-provoking source from which to draw ideas and inspire fresh deviance. The narrative personal accounts, in their part, are highly informal and delve headlong into the kinkiest sexual worlds. The details of specific sexual training processes take up the final chapters. This book is not, though, a how-to-guide on sophisticated rope tying techniques, proper etiquette, advanced sexual positions or other technical BDSM skills. Additional resources for such subjects are listed throughout the book and in the appendix. Real world experiences are included from first-hand experiences and direct conversations with men who own women and women who are owned by their men. The practices are meant as ideal extremes of ownership to be used as one so desires in the dynamic reality of an individual union.

Chapter 1: The New World Order of Kink

"I do not think, sir, you have any right to command me, merely because you are older than I, or because you have seen more of the world than I have; your claim to superiority depends on the use you have made of your time and experience." —Charlotte Brontë

"One must still have chaos in oneself to be able to give birth to a dancing star." —Friedrich Nietzsche

The postmodern world we all live in is a de-centered chaos of anything-goes. The traditional structures of society, personal relationships and sexual preferences are in a constant state of disruption and ever-changing flow. Even as each person attempts to find his or her place in the mix, new ideas and fresh perspectives challenge their ability to hold firm to one singular conception of what a personal relationship means to them. In the online hemisphere, the most perverse pornographic videos exist side-by-side with the most tight-lipped conservative ideologies. There is also a vast trove of BDSM writings and photostreams on websites, blogs, apps and social media sites that is perpetually growing into an untamable mass of info-visuals from which it is nearly impossible to separate fantasy from reality. The online geography of kink allows like-minded strangers who are thousands of miles apart to connect, but also serves to further exacerbate the difficulties of any long-distance connection in a potential relationship.

Furthermore, any man who wants a serious relationship with a submissive woman must be prepared to navigate through the sheer complexity of modern female desires to find what works for his own personal vision of dominance.

The same is obviously true for any woman seeking a dominant man.

There are major differences between traditional views of female submissiveness and the contemporary realities of women who possess strong submissive tendencies. The traditional conceptions of submissiveness and dominance focus on establishing clear roles for the man and the woman from the very first encounter. She has affirmed to herself that she is a "submissive" and she seeks a "Dom" to train her. It becomes her personal identity. At the extreme, she lives through him. She is his. Her identity exists in relationship to him. Her own individual pursuits and personal relationships are lived with an awareness of his command over her. She becomes thoroughly proud to be his possession. It enthralls her and frees her like nothing else ever has. It becomes second nature to conceive of herself as *his* woman and to always ponder what he would think of her actions before she even acts.

Traditional submissiveness still thrives in the contemporary world but women in the twenty-first century are often much more complicated. The undeniable compulsion to submit is tied up with strong urges to assert their own individual identities in gender roles, in their work lives, in their domestic lives and in their sex lives. Submitting becomes much more problematic. A woman still thoroughly craves to be made a dominant man's possession, but the journey to complete submission is more dynamic. It is not simply a static identity. It becomes a process of discovering and creating a unique Dominant/submissive genesis. The journey to ownership travels through the same difficult waters as any couple striving for a serious relationship. Each man must make his own unique world of creative dominance for the woman if he wants to bring her to a place of sincere and complete submission.

Dominance and Submission

The act of "owning" a woman is the extreme end-all and be-all of a Dominant/submissive (D/s) relationship. To seek out such a connection opens the doors of perception to the interplay between complete domination and ultimate surrender. To say one "owns" a woman means to formally assert that a woman is a man's personal property. The term can also be used as a *general* affirmation that a man is in dominant control of the overall relationship dynamic. And finally, it can be used in a raw sexual meaning, as in: *"I own your pussy, baby."*

Yet, the deep urge to possess a woman exists in nearly every connection between the opposite sexes. Sometimes a man wants to sexually conquer a woman and make her his. Sometimes he wants her as his muse and she feels desired simply by profoundly inspiring him. Sometimes he wants her as the submissive backbone of a marriage so he can be free to ambitiously navigate the larger world without worrying about any unnecessary difficulties at home. Sometimes he just wants her plain and simple, down and dirty, and she thrives on being wanted in those heavy handed ways. And that's enough…at least for that night.

The underpinnings of any Dominant/submissive relationship are created in the eroticizing of power and the transformation of personal identity. At the heart of this power, a thousand threads of emotion and desire get wrapped up with deeper longings for love and tendencies towards infatuation. While every relationship in both the "vanilla" and kink realms begins with mutual attraction, in D/s the attraction is infused with the assertion and exchange of power. On the surface, this means the man wields his power and influence over the woman, and she in turn yields to it. Yet, the deeper reality of any dynamic is entangled in endless complexities and saturated with the infinite possibilities of how that power is exchanged. A true Dominant/submissive relationship, meaning one that goes beyond kinky trysts, involves cultivating consciousness at the most profound levels of personal trust, sexual force and existential awareness.

All Dominant/submissive relationships start with two strangers who do not know anything about one another. In the beginning, there is no trust at all. It must be gained by the dominant because he is the one pursuing and the one demanding submission. From the outset, he must be aware of the limits, the emotional vulnerabilities and the negative triggers of a submissive woman if he is to gain her sincere faith in him. The man thrives in his role as active controller of the relationship and the woman thrives in her role as the one who is receptive to his control. Yet, in reality, this can play out in immeasurable ways. The path to power and control is different for every man and every woman.

For the man, power is the awareness of knowing how to use both control and seduction, and knowing when to use each one. A dominant must continually seduce eager consent from a submissive, even if he is harshly demanding it. His presence, his manner, his words and his actions are the precursors to the actual physical, mental and emotional domination. For a submissive woman, his direct presence and his vocal delivery are the keys to her heart, her mind and her body. A dominant man is not putting on a mask or enacting a character. He is being himself. He is letting the strongest components of his character naturally guide every moment he is with her, as the perfect aphrodisiac for any submissive woman is a man's genuine and unshakable self-confidence.

A submissive woman wants to be in an emotional, mental and physical space where she instinctively serves the dominant. She desires to feel that she is *his* and craves to be even more *his*. She feels his awareness of her at every turn of her thoughts. He knows her because he is the right man for her and he sees her for who she really is. Her submission is not simply physical attraction to his power. It is an overwhelming desire to surrender in intense erotic moments *and* at deeper levels of consciousness where she lets go of fundamental ego attachments. She longs to be free of the lonely struggle of doing everything on her own in the face of society's overwhelming pressures to fill a hundred different roles. She wants reassurance of her personal worth at the very core of her being as a woman. She wants to feel true love in being owned by that one man who appreciates and desires her completely.

Women come from very different places before they arrive at the submissive mindset. Some women become thoroughly engaged in the online BDSM realm or go to events/play parties, while others have no inclinations to become part of the "scene". Each to his or her own. Others are introduced to it by boyfriends who desire to treat them in a submissive manner. There are women who have discovered their submissive inner nature on their own, and then seek out the kind of dominant men who are a good fit for their various needs, their kinky desires and their relationship visions. Other women have a more complicated conception of their submissiveness. They might have their own streak of dominance in their personalities, they might resist any kind of simple-minded submission or they might only want to be dominated in very particular areas of their lives.

When a woman discovers or is introduced to the submissive world, there is usually a long process of feeling-out what she really likes and wants. A boyfriend might suddenly spank her and she is shocked by how much she likes the physicality of it. She might realize that she keeps dating guys who are very aggressive or are "Alpha male" types. She might have had experiences early in her life that made her crave being controlled or dominated. Perhaps she ventures online and suddenly discovers the wild world of perverse sexuality in all of its glorious deviance. She realizes that she is not alone. There are thousands and thousands of other very kinky people with similar thoughts and feelings. She starts interacting with men in a different way, both online and in the real world. The sparks begin to fly. She wants to do certain things which she had only previously fantasized about doing. The idea of submitting to a man, and him dominating her, is now a very potent part of what she wants in any sexual tryst or serious relationship…

Preamble: The Language of Sex and Power

Language itself is a means of asserting one's power and control. Whether you speak in New York street slang or in an Elizabethan dialect, you are attempting to control and empower the language, as well as its relationship to the world around you and to the world itself. Shakespeare is credited by the *Oxford English Dictionary* with the introduction of nearly 3,000 words. He not only had a great command of the English language, he also created his power by employing and inventing a particular use of his mother tongue.

The language and world of BDSM is at the nexus of this same will to power. Individuals who are heavily involved in the kink realm often have a great deal of their identity and ego tied up in defining, codifying and justifying their perversions. There is a general urge to separate what is labeled kinky or considered BDSM from the chaotic flux of life, sex, psychology and language in its entirety. One person's definition of dominance might not make sense as a definition to another at all. Readers should keep in mind that writers are always attempting to control the language and the knowledge that they are communicating, even if they are trying to expand upon or deconstruct previous definitions. In addition, words have long histories.

The word *"kink"* comes straight from the German heartland. A *"fetish"* is synonymous with foreign objects in Africa. Yet, the origin of *"to own"* resides deep in the English language, like other extremely familiar words such as *home*, *get* and *wife*.

The French philosopher Michel Foucault wrote a great deal about the power of language. In *The History of Sexuality* he states: "As if in order to gain mastery over it [sex] in reality, it had first been necessary to subjugate it at the level of language, control its free circulation in speech, expunge it… and extinguish the words that rendered it too visibly present." Foucault recognized the power that language holds over existence, as evidenced by his claim that sex had to be subjugated at the level of language. What he appeared to understand is that without something to define an idea, to place it within specific parameters of meaning, then the idea is left formless and cannot exist within the human mind. He claimed that a word to classify a thing, and definitions of such a thing, are necessary for the thing's existence.

A few definitions:

Vanilla *(noun)* origin: mid 17th century: from Spanish *vainilla* 'pod', from Latin *vagina* 'sheath'.

1. (*Oxford American English*): a substance obtained from vanilla beans or produced artificially and used to flavor sweet foods or to impart a fragrant scent to cosmetic preparations.
2. (*Urban Dictionary*): Unexciting, normal, conventional, boring. The opposite of kinky. Not in any way involved with BDSM.

Kink *(noun)* origin: Dutch, akin to Middle Low German *kinke*.

1. (*Oxford American English*): a sharp twist or curve in something that is otherwise straight.
2. (*Merriam-Webster*): unconventional sexual taste or behavior.
3. (*Urban Dictionary*): Foot-sucking, rubber wearing, pee on me, fruit-fuckin', candlewax drippin', long fingernail scrapin', tossed salad eatin', multiple partner havin', she-male, oil-drenched, chocolate sauce, whipped cream covered, vibrator usin', dress-up, banned in 30 states type of sex.

Fetish (*noun*) origin: Latin from *factitious*. Originally denoting an object used by the peoples of West Africa as an amulet or charm.

1. (*Oxford American English*): an inanimate object worshipped for its supposed magical powers or because it is considered to be inhabited by a spirit.
2. (*Merriam-Webster*) a need or desire for an object, body part or activity for sexual excitement.
3. (*Sigmund Freud*): The displacement of desire and fantasy onto alternate objects or body parts in order to obviate a subject's confrontation with the castration complex.

[*Museum of Sex*: A **kink** enhances partner intimacy and a **fetish** replaces the partner and the intimacy.]

To Own (*verb*) origin: Old English *agnian*.

1. (*Oxford American English*): to have something as one's own; possess.
2. (*Merriam-Webster*): to have power or mastery over. To have or hold as property.
3. (*Urban Dictionary*): to beat an opponent while displaying a high degree of skill and style.

BDSM (Bondage Discipline Sadism Masochism) *or* (Bondage Dominance Submission Sadism Masochism)

Bondage (*noun*) origin: Middle English from Anglo-Latin *bondagium*.

1. (*Merriam-Webster*): the tenure or service of a villain, serf or slave.
2. (*Oxford American English*): sexual practice that involves the tying up or restraining of one partner.

Discipline (*noun*) origin: Latin *discipulus*.

1. (*Oxford American English*): the practice of training people to obey rules or a code of behavior, using punishment to correct disobedience.
2. (*Merriam-Webster*): training that corrects, molds or perfects the mental faculties or moral character.

Sadism (*noun*) origin: French/*Marquis de Sade*.

1. (*Oxford American English*): the tendency to derive pleasure, especially sexual gratification, from inflicting pain, suffering or humiliation on others.
2. (*Merriam-Webster*): a sexual perversion in which gratification is obtained by the infliction of physical or mental pain on others (as on a love object).
3. (*Marquis de Sade*): "The Marquis proceeded to harangue her with the most vile and degrading insults. To Testard's horror he also began to engage in the most provocative and blasphemous acts, including masturbating into a chalice, referring to the Lord as 'motherfucker' and inserting two communion hosts into the terrified young woman before entering her himself, all the while screaming, 'If thou art God, avenge thyself!'"

Masochism (*noun*) origin: Slavic/*Leopold von Sacher-Masoch*.

1. (*Oxford American English*): the enjoyment of what appears to be painful or tiresome.
2. (*Merriam-Webster*): a sexual perversion characterized by pleasure in being subjected to pain or humiliation, especially by a love object.
3. (*Leopold von Sacher-Masoch*): "I imagine the favorite of this beautiful despot, who is whipped when his mistress grows tired of kissing him, and whose love only grows more intense the more he is trampled underfoot."

Dominance (*noun*) origin: Latin *dominans*.

1. (*Oxford American English*): power and influence over others.
2. (*Urban Dictionary*): When a man lets the girl know he's in charge.

Submission (*noun*) origin: Middle English, from Anglo-French, from Latin *submission-, submissio* act of lowering, from *submittere*.

1. (*Oxford American English*): the action or fact of accepting or yielding to a superior force or to the will or authority of another person.
2. (*Urban Dictionary*): A move made by a man on a woman to subdue her for strictly sexual purposes.

Dominant/Top: The partner in the relationship/activity who is the physically *active* or *controlling* participant.

submissive/bottom: The partner in the relationship/activity who is the physically *receptive* or *controlled* participant.

Master (*noun*) origin: Latin from *magister-* chief, head or director.

1. (*Merriam-Webster*): *(a)* male teacher, *(b)* a revered religious teacher, *(c)* a worker or artisan qualified to teach apprentices, *(d)* an artist, performer or player of consummate skill, *(e)* a great figure of the past, *(f)* one having authority over another, *(g)* one that conquers, *(h)* one having control, *(i)* an owner especially of a slave or animal.
2. (*Urban Dictionary*): The dominant person in a D/s or BDSM relationship.

Daddy (*noun*) origin: "of the actual origin we have no evidence" (*OED*), *dada* originates in infantile speech.

1. (*Oxford English Dictionary*): the father. Used mainly by children or when speaking to children.
2. (*Urban Dictionary*): A name used by a significant other, fuckbuddy and/or hot guy. During sex, a girl may scream out "Daddy!" when he's beating the pussy up. It's a huge turn on for some and it's mostly used by those who like it rough or just for those kinky little shits.

Sir (*noun*) origin: from the honorific title *sire*; *sire* developed alongside the word *seigneur*, also used to refer to a feudal lord. Both derived from the Vulgar Latin *senior*.

1. (*Merriam-Webster*): a man entitled to be addressed as *sir* — used as a title before the given name of a knight or baronet and formerly sometimes before the given name of a priest.
2. (*Urban Dictionary*): The proper way for a submissive to greet a Dominant.

Babygirl (*noun*) origin: slang, chiefly African-American Vernacular.

1. (*Wiktionary*): friendly or intimate term of address for a woman.
2. (*Urban Dictionary*): A nickname for only the most rare and unique girl out there. There are many qualities that can be associated with a babygirl. For instance, they are funny, sweet, cute, outgoing, proud, sexy, spontaneous, adorable, trustworthy, honest, sincere, loving, wifey-type, babymama-type, giggly, cheesy, dumb, soulmate, attractive, wonderful, beautiful, and amazing. Just to name a few. She will make your heart beat fast and cause you to get tongue tied all the time over the phone.

Slave (*noun*) origin: from Old French *esclave*, from Medieval Latin *sclavus* "slave" (source also of Italian *schiavo*, French *esclave*, Spanish *esclavo*), originally "Slav"; so used in this secondary sense because of the many Slavs sold into slavery by conquering peoples.

1. (*Merriam-Webster*): (a) person held in servitude as the chattel of another, (b) one that is completely subservient to a dominating influence.
2. (*Urban Dictionary*): Someone who is willingly owned as property by a master or mistress. Slaves have a very deep need to please and serve a Dominant person, and doing so is the only way they can feel truly happy and complete. Not to be confused with a bottom or submissive. *"Ignorant people often think owning a slave by mutual consent is abusive, not understanding that they want and need this."*

24/7: A dominant/submissive relationship in which the power dynamic extends 24 hours a day, 7 days a week, as opposed to the temporary set and setting of a "scene" or "play" time. It is also used as a term to distinguish relationships that incorporate elements of BDSM in a "part-time" dynamic from those that exist "full-time, 24/7".

Safe, Sane and Consensual (SSC): A formalized term for practicing BDSM activities in good faith. Risky activities are made as safe as possible. Interactions should be on the rational side of the sanity line, meaning using sincere judgment to avoid damaging the mental or physical health of the participants. Lastly, everyone involved knowingly consents in advance to what is going to happen, what is not going to happen and how each person is going to stop something bad from happening.

RACK (Risk Aware Consensual Kink): A formalized term expressing the agreement between BDSM participants that there is inherent risk in the activities to which they are consenting. The difference between SSC and RACK is truly defined by each individual, but to generalize, RACK is focused on making everyone aware of the risk and SSC is focused on eliminating any unsafe and insanely risky elements.

Negotiation and Consent: A formalized term expressing the explicit discussion of and agreement to any BDSM activity by all participants, in advance of that activity. This may or may not include a "safe word" that allows either participant to stop the activity.

Case Study 1.1

"One Complicated Woman's Extensive List of Turn-ons"

Mara

A kiss that can unleash the demon inside me, no holds barred animalistic sex, *"I want to lick your mind."*, being petted until I fall asleep, *"I'm not asking, I'm telling"*, foreign accents, sex in the kitchen, a bite is a kiss with more feeling, *"I want to fuck that foul mouth of yours"*, a damn good fucking, *"A little fight in you. I like that"*, a hand on her throat, getting aftershocks from intense orgasms, *"I love you, but I will hurt you"*, 'a lady, a woman, a little girl....all in one'.

Being more complex than an anonymous list of fetishes could show, a leather glove over your mouth and nose, a man that could throw me on the bed, a man who knows how to take control, a man who sees a strong woman as an asset, a predatory grin that says *"Run, I dare you!"*, a room full of books, *"Babygirl needs her daddy, doesn't she?"*, angry sex, *"Beginning to regret your misbehavior?"*, arousal by smart people, auralism, back against the wall hand on the throat hot breath in the ear.

Batting eyelashes and pretending I'm innocent, *"Cum for me, baby"* whispered in my ear, being a dirty slut in a pretty dress, *"Grind on daddy's lap, babygirl."*, vintage disciplinary implements, being a priority, not an option, *"I didn't do that! Oh...that? That I did do."*, being a total slut for someone worthy, *"I may not win...but I won't back down..."*, being both gentle and strict with you, being bratty until you get fucked into submission, *"If I catch you, I'm going to fuck you"*, being deliciously sore, being fucked four or five times a day, *"If I find you, I'm going to fuck you."*

Lingerie that gets him uncontrollably aroused, being fucked so hard it hurts for days, *"My fantasy? Whatever your fantasy is."*, being naked except for my heels and collar, being groped from behind while cooking, *"Teach me how to fuck daddy"*, being held down and fucked, *"We might get caught"* sex, being held down while panties are ripped down, *"Why don't you come over here and find out?"*, being his Betty Crocker and his Bettie Page, *"You belong to me!"* whispered in your ear, being licked through my wet panties.

"You disturb me. I like that in a person", being ordered to *"spread your legs"*, being pinned against the wall and fingered, *"You're a filthy little slut, aren't you?"*, being pounded from behind, being pushed up against a wall in a passionate kiss, being put in her place, being rewarded with *"good girl"*, being treated like a beautiful princess but fucked like a dirty little whore, being whispered to during rough sex, bending you over the couch for a sudden fuck.

Spontaneous role-playing, biting the sweet spot where the neck connects to the shoulder, blindfolds, breath play, burlesque, caught with your lover in a rainstorm, choking you while you cum, combining aggression and tenderness, sending naked pictures via text message, consensual nonconsent, cuddling up to daddy and falling asleep, cunnilingus, cursing like a motherfucking sailor, dirty sex on the hood of the car, discreet pleasures in movie theaters, dogging in seedy back alley cinemas, doggy style rough and hard.

Dominants who love strong women, talking dirty in secret at formal events, embracing the darkness within, erotic photography, exotic women of color, fear, fingering, fucking good girls like dirty little sluts, fucking to music, gentlemen who are not necessarily gentle men, getting off on you, getting off on me, girls who sit on my lap and flirt with me, grabbing her pussy and asking, *"Who owns it?"*

Having pretty panties pulled to the side, using random household items for completely perverted purposes, hot steamy sex in a raging thunderstorm, *"I can still smell you on me, and I like it"*, *"I say 'no' but I mean 'yes'"*, *"If you make me"*, *"I'm sexy and you know it"*, *"If you want to fuck me, just tell me"*, intelligence, kissing the back of the neck, knowing sex is more mental than physical, sex in the dressing room, looking innocent but having a dark side, looking sweet, fooling everyone, making love in the form of rough violent sex.

Going braless in broad daylight, men who love to eat pussy, morning sex, then going back to sleep, mutual masturbation, nice girls with a well hidden slut inside, *"No games, just say what the fuck you want"*, panties, passionate kissing while being taken, people who make me laugh, think and cum, predator/prey, pussy worship, role play, rough sex, rough violent fucking, seduction, sensory deprivation, sensualism, sex in abandoned buildings, sex in cars, sex in public, sex in the shower.

Sex outdoors during a thunderstorm, threesomes, sex so good the neighbors need a cigarette, she whispers *"I need to suck your cock"*, skirt up, panties down, bent over, and fucked, sliding your panties aside and just fucking you, someone worth chasing and pouncing on, sophisticated dominant men in suits, *"Spread those legs, I want to devour you"*, taking you without warning, whenever I want, talking dirty, *"This is a bad idea. Let's do it."*, treat her like a lady, fuck her like a slut, treating you like a princess, and fucking you like a whore.

Trust that allows you to let go completely, using my knife to cut off your panties, violence, voyeurism, waking daddy up by grinding my ass against his cock so he'll wake up and take what belongs to him, waking her with my tongue in her pussy, well spoken and gentlemanly dominant men, where my flesh becomes your flesh, whispering naughty things in my ear in public, whispering softly in a low, menacing voice this close to your ear and making you so hot you can't stand it any longer, women of color, women who love to watch men cum, writhing in his arms and struggling as he whispers everything he's going to do in my ear.

Chapter 2: Submissive Women

"I do not want to be the leader. I refuse to be the leader. I want to live darkly and richly in my femaleness. I want a man lying over me, always over me. His will, his pleasure, his desire, his life, his work, his sexuality the touchstone, the command, my pivot. I don't mind working, holding my ground intellectually, artistically; but as a woman, oh, God, as a woman I want to be dominated. I don't mind being told to stand on my own feet, not to cling, be all that I am capable of doing, but I am going to be pursued, fucked, possessed by the will of a male at his time, his bidding." —Anais Nin

"Keep me rather in this cage, and feed me sparingly, if you dare. Anything that brings me closer to illness and the edge of death makes me more faithful. It is only when you make me suffer that I feel safe and secure. You should never have agreed to be a god for me if you were afraid to assume the duties of a god, and we know that they are not as tender as all that. You have already seen me cry. Now you must learn to relish my tears." —Pauline Réage

Signposts and Signals to Submissive Women

The first consideration in beginning a dominant-submissive relationship is determining the extent to which a woman wants to be "owned". Men and women are like animals roaming the prairie, honing their natural instincts to advance their own lot in Darwinian ways. Every woman is born with the instinct to attract and the desire to be taken with some degree of passionate force, whether she is an Upper East Side princess, a trailer park slut or an accomplished astrophysicist. Some women outright seek to be owned as personal property and place their profiles on alternative or kink-oriented websites. Some of these women have extensive experience in these types of relationships while many do not have any at all. Other women wander out into the good night or stroll into Sunday church service seeking companionship with an authoritarian flavor.

It is important to determine if a woman who overtly seeks to be owned is truly serious about what she wants and is realistic in what such a life entails. Being "owned" is wrapped up in a world of fetish and many women might simply be looking for a certain sexual kink as part of a vanilla relationship. Other women seek out Dominant/submissive relationships because either they haven't found what they are seeking in the vanilla world, or are even on the rebound from a bad relationship and believe D/s is the cure to their pain and loneliness.

In any case, every man and every woman seeks very different things. Open communication is vital. Do not be eager to assume the world about a woman's personality. Some women are very highly educated and desire to be owned in a very sophisticated manner. Other women have simpler desires and idealize being kept at home in a cage like a pet. Some women want both extremes. Some women crave to be aggressive leaders at work and submissive sluts at home. Whether a man is browsing online profiles, on a first date or out randomly at a bar and meets a woman who flirts with hints of submissiveness, he should thoroughly interrogate her to determine if her submissive desires are genuine and fit within the realm of his own cravings.

Rarely do relationships work if both people aren't of reasonably similar educational and socio-economic backgrounds. That is just the painful fact drawn from the real world data. The exception to this is if the man is seeking an inferior-type submissive or a slave such as a poorly educated woman from a third-world country. Anything is possible in love and relationships, but one should be grounded in reality.

Women who thrive in submissive roles and sex-play run the gamut, from CEOs to unemployed students. Though it might seem like everyone is online these days, don't expect women who must closely guard their public image to post profiles on popular kink sites. The same is true of men. This might include individuals in politics, in high-level executive positions, in law enforcement, in the military, in the legal world, in the entertainment industry and in many other image-conscious professions. Though online dating sites geared toward the world of kinksters have been a godsend to meeting like-minded perverts in semi-private settings, don't make the mistake of believing that it is the end-all and be-all of the entire pool of submissive women.

Whether people are aware of it or not, everyone is in dominant-submissive relationships at work, in their political persuasions, in their participation in the power structures of society, in the relationship between their bodies and those of others and in their everyday rapport with strangers. Every woman has dominant-submissive persuasions, whether they are made up of mild fantasies or extremely kinky urges. That power-tripping marketing executive in leather boots who maintains the iciest demeanor at a business meeting might just be craving to be made to crawl on her hands and knees as she is gagged and repeatedly whipped every moment she is behind closed doors. One never knows. Life often works to conceal its true self.

It should also be noted that there tends to be a significant number of females with submissive inclinations who have had some type of traumatic experience in their lives. While there is certainly a countless array of kinky women who grew up perfectly balanced in loving environments and have never even been at the receiving end of a single dominating tryst, a man should keep in mind that there are many females on the opposite side of that spectrum. The very potent bond of love and desire that D/s relationships can kindle also attracts females with abusive childhoods, victims of emotional, physical and sexual violence, girls with self-esteem issues and women who were adopted as children and have serious difficulties with trust and feeling loved. The same can obviously be said of dominant men. Every human is different, but it is important to remember that they *are* human and they come with their own personal histories, eccentricities and emotional triggers. While the idea of owning a woman might seem like a fantasy come true, be careful what you ask for as you just might get it, as they say. All relationships come with the good and the bad, and one should be prepared to embrace both.

The Submissive-Seeking Dominant Man: Illusions and Delusions

Whether a man is looking to meet a woman online or out in the regular ol' physical world, or even if he is not explicitly looking at all, every avenue begins with *personal awareness*. He must be thoroughly self-aware, knowing what he is seeking and not seeking, as well as be extremely perceptive to his own strengths and weaknesses. Equally important, though, is the fact that he must be aware of the nature of a woman's unique heart and mind. While some element of awareness is born, it is largely a matter of cultivation. It is the practice of listening and looking- *really* listening and looking. A dominant man who is supremely aware is worlds away from a brutish aggressor who thrives on immediately forcing a female to physically submit to him.

Any man should bluntly ask himself these five fundamental questions:

1. *"Am I truly dominant or just selfishly controlling in what I want from a woman?"*

2. *"Why exactly am I attracted to submissive women to begin with?"*

3. *"How is my vision of dominance different from other men's visions of dominance?"*

4. *"Am I dominant because I am trying to compensate for certain insecurities or lack of control in my own life?"*

5. *"What do I give to the submissive when I am telling her I am going to take everything?"*

Unless a man enjoys wasting his time in awful drama-ridden relationships, before he even begins to date much less get heavily involved with a submissive-minded woman, he should honestly consider his own agenda and his underlying integrity. The phrase "*Know Thyself*" was carved into stone at the entrance to Apollo's temple at Delphi in Ancient Greece for a reason.

Knowing oneself is about how much applied introspection to one's personality has been taken and to what degree one can witness one's own strengths and weaknesses. The beginning of wisdom of any kind, including knowledge of oneself, is acknowledgment of the infirmity of our beliefs and the paucity of our knowledge; the fact that opinions we have might just be opinions. The disparity between the confidence with which people express their opinions, on one hand, and the negligible ability they have to back them up is astonishingly common. Thinking that confidence is an indication of one's degree of correctness is nothing more than hubris. A man should acknowledge his limitations. Own up to them and own them.

Secondly, having empathy, or knowing how to see things from another person's point of view is crucial. It also allows a man to see himself more effectively. It gets one to realize things difficult to see from the first-person perspective. Empathizing with others who know you well might, for instance, help to understand why they describe you as they do.

Awareness in general comes with life experience, and relationship experience in particular, but it is truly about how one learns from those experiences. It spans from the idea of being present in the moment to developing a rich trove of psychological and physical observations from which to draw. A man should be able to read a woman based on what she says and what she writes as well as from the physical cues in both her subtle and blunt reactions to him. He should use the full depths of his intuition while filtering out egotisticallyinclined perceptions and gut feelings that are really erroneously derived from previous bad experiences. This is further elucidated in the fourth chapter of this work.

Types of Submissives

There are two fundamental *"archetypes"* of submissive women:

1. The Pure Submissive: She freely acknowledges the inner nature of her deeply submissive identity. She is eagerly ready to completely surrender to the right Dominant man who she can trust unequivocally. She searches for her true master as she wards off phony aggressors. She actively accepts her place as the receiver of the Dominant's total control of her life. She does not seek any kind of power struggle. She basks in knowing her place as a woman and fully inhabiting it. She rarely needs punishment because she is so ardently trying to please her man. Her daily focus is on pride in service, obedience, sacrifice and giving pleasure. She finds her personal worth in making her dominant happy and feeling irreplaceably *his*.

2. The Enforced Submissive: She thrives on being made to actively submit. She loves to be vigorously dominated with sexual force, physical power, discipline, mental control and emotional strength. She wants active power play with her dominant so she can feel his presence in subduing her, controlling her and ruling her. Her submissiveness is more of an evolving dynamic than a static identity. She fights back so she can separate her own strengths from his. She finds much of her personal worth within a relationship in being actively desired and dominated like no other woman in his life.

The first rule about judging a woman as belonging to a *type* of submissive is that a type is not a real human. It is only a type. Never think a woman is simply a type because individual personalities always exceed generalities. Although some women like to be put in a real cage, very few like to be put in a box. Some women, especially younger ones, are blatantly oblivious to the fact that their personalities are nothing more than a generic psychological pattern, but there is little point in telling them so unless one is looking to be sadistic, or just bluntly honest. Yet, more importantly, no one's entire personality can fit any one type. There are always particularities, differences, idiosyncrasies and nuances that make each woman unique. Focus on these and use the categories out there as a personal guide.

What can be said about types, though, is that they are always some combination of one's nature and one's nurturing. Some women are just wired in a very particular way. Secondly, many submissive traits often come from fundamental experiences growing up or from early romantic relationships. For example, a woman might consciously know that she is a typical recovering Catholic school girl with a guilt complex and traditional disciplinary fantasies, but there is nothing she can do about the reoccurring images of being sternly spanked by a father-figure type that keeps coming into her thoughts. There are almost as many types as there are women. They can vary greatly and they can be constructed according to scientific study, personal experience or sheer intuition. Most women, just like most men, are a blend of many different types.

It is a good idea to have any potential submissive take both a basic personality test and a BDSM personality test. Well-established objective psychological assessments can be difficult to swallow but they are also extremely valuable. Any man who has not already done so should do likewise. There are many available online. Overall personality tests include the MOTIV personality test and the Myers-Briggs test. BDSM personality tests can be found on such sites as FetLife and OKCupid. These will at least give a man a good idea of her basic tendencies and help him determine if she is a possible good fit for him.

The following categories are meant to stimulate the realization that every woman is different and a man should not assume that the person in front of him is there just to fulfill his own particular domination fantasies.

The Vanilla Submissive

She is part of the largest group of submissives out there. She is the *Fifty Shades of Gray* reader. She might inhabit the BDSM scene or she might be entirely turned off by its pretenses and language, but she knows that she is aroused by a man who takes charge of her. She might be aware of the full depth of her proclivities or she might not. She often tries to balance meeting a "normal" man and finding one who will naturally indulge her specific desires, be that engaging in rough play, being spanked, being tied up or participating in any other irrepressible kinky act. She usually envisions part-time BDSM play behind closed doors, usually with a man of financial means and romantic substance. How open she is to the extremes of being an owned woman will greatly depend on the character, desires and abilities of the man she really falls for.

The Online Introvert

She is shy, has a vivid imagination and avoids stressful social situations. She seeks partners almost exclusively through online dating sites. She has difficulty being herself at first, but once she feels comfortable, she often lets her freak side come out to play. Sometimes she goes for strong extroverts while other times she likes fellow smart introverts who share her closet perversions but are on the dominant side behind closed doors.

The Pretty Money Dreamer

She has dreamy visions of a tall, dashing, financially successful man coming to sweep her off her tired feet. She'll submit to and do anything in the world for him so long as he provides her an abundance of security, love and luxurious amenities. Deep personal chemistry is not as vital to her as a whirlwind romance and being cherished for who she is and what she can give to a man. Provide the life and lifestyle she envisions and a man can own her body and soul.

The Feminist Controller

She has strong feminist principles which have guided her throughout life. Some realize that have been only wearing a social mask as a feminist while others realize that they are diehard feminists who secretly want that dominating man at home to tell them what to do so they can just let go. She is usually unrecognizable as a submissive upon first meetings and often comes across as more dominant. She likes to control all the details of her life, wants a dominant man who is either her intellectual equal or just old-school manly. She insists on testing a partner as a kind of hard-fought courtship to see if he both respects her *and* wants to meticulously whip her. 1950's lifestyle to her is more a matter of private fantasy and secret escape than conforming to patriarchal rule.

The Kinky, Kinky Kinkster

She is extremely sexual at the core of her being. The most perverse, kinkiest fantasies enter her mind all the time. She might describe herself as "like a guy" because she feels the need to explain the fact that she constantly wants erotic stimulation. She might just call herself a hedonist. She loves to fuck. She loves to be called a good slut. She is highly sensual. She is open to many types of guys, but she truly craves a man who doesn't judge her for being such a diehard pervert. She might have an atypical body or facial appearance that is not considered beautiful in mainstream society. Her body might also be highly sensitive in certain places or she might have atypical physical reactions during sex.

The Smart-Assed Masochist (SAM)

She is a "bratty" submissive and a sarcastic/naughty woman in general. She loves to talk back, act disrespectful and be disobedient. She usually knows that she is doing it because she likes to get the attention of the dominant and to be disciplined for her behavior. She might have mild masochistic tendencies or she might be a total masochist. Disciplining her can be problematic because she likes pain so it is not really punishment for her to receive it. Punishment often requires not giving her the attention she is craving when the man does not want to reward her for her behavior.

The Life Lover

She craves to experience life in all its infinite dimensions. She is submissive to sensual experience in an Anais Nin sort of way. It is an extension of her being. She eagerly seeks to have relationships of authentic honesty, but the men she truly craves are generally dominant-tending leaders and creators. She is most likely accomplished in what she does for a profession, but feels incomplete without a certain kind of powerful male presence. She can tame solitude to a certain degree but she would rather throw herself into the experience of submitting to a fellow life-loving man, or at least one who sees her as an erotic muse.

The Complicated Woman

She comes with a thousand contradictions. She has strong fantasies about being dominated and ultimately wants a dominant man, but getting her to submit is a real fight. She wants to be thoroughly respected for who she is and she is turned off by arrogant displays of dominance. She has a world of strong interests both in the BDSM world and outside of it. She really needs to fall hard for a man before she submits to him.

The Masochistic Doormat

She needs to feel small and has an uncontrollable emotional need to be humiliated and trampled on. She loves abrasive, tough-talking men who put her in her place. She consents to being slapped across the face for talking back. She gets turned on by being manhandled. When she is emotionally humiliated, kicked out of the door and paddled until she is black and blue, she still eagerly spreads her legs for her man and loves when he takes her with force. Pain makes her wet. She does everything he tells her and when she feels that he is not attracted to her, she will be naughty just so he disciplines her.

The Dominate-Me Woman

She is enthralled by being dominated but doesn't really act submissive in the traditional sense of wanting to submit and serve. She is very controlling in her own right. There is often a psychological gap between her sexual fantasies of being dominated and being dominated in a real relationship. She likes to "top from the bottom". She might not even be capable of being "an owned woman". She will continually express her submissive desires but will always try to control the details of how she submits. She requires extreme trust to let go and, even then, will try to fight any ultimatums she is given.

The Primal Woman

For her, the extremes of dominance and submission are simply expressions of the same primal force. She can get uncontrollably aroused by her own willingness to take the sexual reins from a man who is not as existentially capable as she is. She lives a life of unashamed morality. The dominant man is the one who takes her to her emotional and psychological limits, knows her depths and makes her thoroughly understand that he takes what he wants. Her irrepressible desires make her highly sexual and she must be subdued with both raw and divine force.

The Damaged Goods

She has suffered serious emotional, sexual or physical abuse growing up or in previous relationships. She has an incredibly difficult time having any "normal" relationship. She might have to go to therapy to keep from resorting to harmful and self-destructive habits. As a young woman, she typically ends up in abusive relationships with bad-boy dominants. As she grows older, or more enlightened, she gravitates to men older than her who provide her guidance, to fellow sufferers who keep her in check in a healthy way or to "regular" guys with a dominant streak to make her feel like just a normal loved girlfriend. She often needs the cathartic extremes of BDSM play to connect her to old feelings to either reclaim them or to irrationally relive them. She might be a "mindfuck-girl", endlessly compelled to the destructive side because she thinks that a regular human relationship will never make her feel complete.

The Artistic

She is more of a free spirit but craves the restraint and precision of a disciplined life. She used to practice ballet or piano or some other demanding art. She feels drawn to dominants who are strict, safe or controlling in order to keep her balanced. She loves to be kept in a tightly-laced corset, made to assume difficult positions as part of discipline and have a set daily schedule so she can feel free to express herself.

The Caged Slave

She tends toward the dramatic and the extreme. She might even be diagnosed with some kind of personality disorder because she just doesn't relate to people in casual ways. She desires to be striped of her humanity and kept in a cage like an animal. She needs absolute rules and absolute commitment. She desires to submit to the idea of a real slave who exists solely for her owner's use and pleasure. Her vision of being owned is very physical and she dislikes the mediocrity of mainstream society.

The Ethnically Dominated

She thrives on the perceived or real physical superiorities of other ethnicities/races. She might be Asian and she endlessly longs for tall, strong white men. She might be white and nothing gets her wet like a well muscled black-skinned man with a huge cock. She might be black and loves the contrasting exoticism of a blue-eyed white guy and the extremely taboo idea of being his slave. Most of these mixes follow the historical precedent set by invading, dominating countries. There are also women who thrive on being specifically dominated by a man from their own ethnic/racial/nationalistic background, such as an Indian woman who needs a strict Indian man or an Arab woman who is kept traditionally-clothed and thrashed for any disobedience. The line between subjugation and willfully enslaved can be very thin.

The Raised to Please

She grew up in a traditional household in which female and male roles were clear. She wants to make her man happy, she thrives on the "cult of domesticity" and she nearly always has a pleasing smile on her face. She is more likely to be from the South or the Midwest in the U.S. or from countries with distinct social classes and strong traditions of gender roles. She might have rebelled against her upbringing and then later realized that she wanted to willingly embrace her submissive role. She loves the idea of pride in service, giving a great blow job and dressing to attract his attention.

The Loved and Beaten

She either grew up with corporal punishment, or even abuse, or she experienced rough play in an early romantic relationship. She associates being loved and desired with being treated in a rough, physical way. She loves to be slapped and spanked in harsh ways. She might have issues getting into a relationship involving domestic violence with the wrong kind of man. She needs to learn that she must openly communicate her needs and set limits.

The Precocious

She is too smart for her own good, she learned how to get men's attention at a young age and she gravitates toward wiser, old-soul types. She gets bored with vanilla sex and dumb men. She craves a man who is extremely detailed in his demeanor, is demanding and is highly aware of her crafty ways. She wants the full spectrum of BDSM play to truly feel alive in every pore.

The Lifestyler

She spends an inordinate amount of time on BDSM websites and frequently attends local gatherings such as *munches* and play parties. She is very comfortable being herself within the kinkster community. She likes activities to be very well-defined. She has most likely completely given up on vanilla dating. She is a strict adherent to the rules and terminology of the BDSM establishment.

The Daddy's Girl

She has a thing for men who are caring, controlling Daddy-types. She longs to be a real "Daddy's girl" who is deeply cared for in a paternalistic type of relationship. She might have been raised being very spoiled and either wants something similar, or the polar opposite in which someone frequently tells her "no". She also might not have had the presence of a father growing up and can't let go of that craving for it in her adult life. She likes rules, limits and the safety of someone to look after her and keep her in line. She probably craves discipline as punishment and for pleasure.

The Intellectual

She lives inside her head, thinking way too much. The physical simplicity of being dominated makes her feel grounded and really turned on. She is good at rationalizing everything in good and bad ways. Strong-willed men make her weak at the knees. She might be the nerdy science-minded woman who desires a dominant man with fearless social skills and a high emotional IQ. She needs someone who is her intellectual equal in ways, but she craves someone who puts a leash on both her thoughts and around her neck.

The Ambitious Female

She is extremely ambitious in her profession and works long hours to either be more successful or because she is a perfectionist. She might have a job that requires her to be always in command or even aggressively dominant. She craves a man with whom she can just completely let her guard down and submit to. She might like to just mentally let go in his presence or she might need stern domination that subdues her desire to be in control at all times.

The Attention Needy

She loves male attention and the feeling of being totally dominated and owned is the natural extension of this. She might be on the exhibitionist side or a bit of a flirt. She is open to being shared by her man in a committed relationship. She might like to make a man jealous. She might like wardrobe control. She gets off on feeling men really desire her physically. She might like to prove how addictive she is by perfecting her cock sucking or fucking skills.

The Uncontrolled Who Long for Control

She grew up in some kind of dysfunctional household or perhaps didn't have anyone that restricted her spoiled ways in any capacity. She might have had crazy divorced parents, an absent father or simply a chaotic childhood. She had to create a world of control around her as a young adult in order to gain some stability and to function in the world. Deep down, though, she intensely longs to surrender to the right man who is consistent and loyal, but still perversely kinky. She might think that she never wanted a man to dominate her, but now she realizes it is what she wants more than anything else. She might envision him as this supremely stable presence who always does what he says he's going to do but still takes her into the dark chaotic world of domination fantasies.

The My-Submission-is-a-Gift Submissive

She conceives of her submissiveness as a precious gift which will only be given to the right man who she can trust absolutely with all her heart. She probably likes some kind of old-fashioned courtship or at least a lengthy show of sincere interest in her that goes beyond sexual kink. She might have endured many bad relationships with men who she felt did not appreciate her and she now longs for the absolute commitment that Dominant/submissive relationships require.

The Absolutely Submissive

She has come to a crystal-clear realization that she loves be outright submissive. She has no need for a power struggle with a dominant man. She knows her place and likes to be kept in her place. She thrives in her role of giving, pleasing, looking up to her man, basking in her submissiveness and providing a total balance to the man's dominant role in the relationship. 1950's lifestyle is a perfect fit for her. She loves to feel needed and wanted. She strives to know him and be ever-present for him. She is always trying to figure out what he truly wants. Career ambitions are not high on her list. She wants a man who makes her his wife.

Note: The following case study is only a condensed snapshot of two lives coming together and only the broad strokes of the relationship are revealed. Because the other elements of this book tend to center on the mental, emotional and intellectual aspects of D/s, the sexual dynamic is more of the prime focus here. Each story could be expanded to a book of its own if one were to expound on the full details of the relationship. This is true of all the samples in this book.

Case Study 2.1

"Finding Love in the Online Kink Jungle"

Roman and Katrina

Roman: Before I ever even starting messaging Katrina online, we had both gone through our own heavy share of dominant/submissive nightmares. I had dated one woman who started methodically hitting her head against the wall like some kind of mental asylum patient after I had given her a sound spanking. Katrina had gone out on a first date with a guy who practically tried to rape her in an alley outside of the French restaurant where they had eaten dinner because she had nonchalantly told him that she craves men who dominate her sexually.

Thinking back to that long hard road to first meeting her and the equally long road to truly getting to know one another, last night's memory of her cooking an impromptu feast from recipes she had slyly garnered from far-flung sources, wearing only a starched white apron, a pair of red sequined heels and a stainless steel collar, feels as if I have already reached relationship nirvana. I don't know if good things come to those who wait, but I've learned the best things come to those who endure.

So pardon me for detailing the practical nuances of dominant man meets submissive female, but I feel like my late night efforts of figuring out how to bring all my urges for kinky love and rough sex and soul mate-vibrations into a until-death-do-us-part romance is worth something.

I had only ventured into the online world after I realized I had strong dominant inclinations in my previous relationships. I had always avoided online dating as it felt totally phony to me. There was nothing like the flesh and blood spontaneity of meeting that girl in school or that woman out and about in the working world when random conversations and the meeting of eyes and beliefs ignited everything. But I came to a point where I was watching all my friends from school and work fade away with some significant other, whether it was for better or worse, and it struck me that I wanted something entirely different.

At the time it seemed like wading through the online waters the only option. I felt like I couldn't tell a woman in the regular dating world that she needed a good hard strapping and a rough fuck whenever I wanted one. I knew my animalistic impulses didn't fit into proper society's game plan, not that I'm some kind of Neanderthal. Plus, I had begun to dread wasting my time going out only to have a bunch of formulaic chit chat with women wanting a life that looked like an Instagram post.

Yet, I found the online kink world to be the polar opposite. Almost everyone advertises their litany of fetishes right on their virtual foreheads as if it were their official political affiliation. Both women and men there are a different breed of sex seekers and relationship pursuers all together. The vast majority also seem to check their non-kink personality at the door, as if it doesn't matter in the least.

Not only was I completely unaware of the vast subculture of people into BDSM, it never occurred to me how starkly different each person is in his or her deviant disposition. Yet, they all seemed to be searching for some kind of idealistic perfect match for their very particular laundry list of turn-ons. At one end, I met women who just wanted a normal connection with a man who takes charge exclusively in the bedroom, and at the opposite end, I met women who didn't mind getting punched in the face or being put in a cage for days at a time. It was crazy. It wasn't like going to an online bar. It was like going to a dark basement party filled with strangers from a thousand different bars all chaotically jumbled together.

It became obvious to me that a woman calling herself submissive could mean very, very, very different things. Most were looking for some particular kind of fetish fix in their partners while I wanted a real woman with all her complications who just happened to be as submissive and kinky as fuck.

After trolling around and casually dating like-minded matches for a number of years, it finally occurred to me that I needed to take a starkly different approach. The online world is saturated with so many people creating a make believe world for themselves or simply of the type who is in their comfort zone in front of a screen. The first thing I did was to let my profile do the work for me rather than waste time aimlessly slogging through the online wastelands. I realized that just making a simple description of what I was looking for didn't stand out in the least, and even then, women would interpret it in a hundred different ways. If I seriously wanted to find someone to get serious about, I needed to put in the effort in presenting myself with the same amount of vigor as I would if I was going out on a first date with a woman I had secretly loved for years.

That was my essential mundane epiphany: Put in the work to bring the online world of women to my in-the-flesh reality. I don't know if it was my military background that instilled a kind of "seek, identify and secure" mindset into me, but that's how I went about it.

For me personally, it was all about creating a sense of the kind of man I am in both images and words, not only in the BDSM world but also in the broader scheme of life, and depicting the kind of relationship which I was seeking. We live in a world in which reality is partially a giant online fabrication and I needed to do some fine fabrication. I actually spent a whole afternoon trying to transform the basic description on my profile into some kind of literary magnum opus of my character.

As far as pics, I never posted a basic face photo due to privacy concerns with my career. Instead, I created a kind of visionary slideshow and of who I am and what turns me on...shots of my clothed body in my finest threads, a pic of my broad bare chest in old school black-and-white, nicely curated selections of kinky fetish photos that aroused me and, most importantly, a slew of non-kinky images of things I love to do or that I believe in – outdoor adventures, exotic travel, riveting books, compelling quotes and so on. In retrospect, I only did this on my online kink profile, but I should have done it with all the dating apps I was on. I learned that not presenting oneself in a way that profoundly stands out is by far the biggest mistake both men and women make in the online world. People waste years of their lives chasing women or looking for the right man online without the slightest realization that they look like a lazy slob or sound like a generic kink robot.

Secondly, it occurred to me that any woman who would be interested in me would probe deeper into my profile on her own. There was no need to chase. Most of these dating and kink sites, or any social media sites for that matter, have places where you can post your opinions about anything and everything. I could simply post how I felt about any particular subject in the exact articulate words I wanted to use and let my forceful persuasiveness do the work.

Sometimes it was something sexual or relationship-related. Other times it was something that didn't have anything to do with kink at all, like a good novel or a new restaurant started by a chef with who I had gone to school. It was like the online equivalent of saying something intriguing or witty at a bar or party while knowing that a woman you were interested in standing nearby could hear everything you said. Women would casually post something about the same subject or even message me directly. They were intrigued by what I was all about and they let me know it in their sly feminine ways.

Katrina just happened to read a post I had written about kinky European films such as *Double Lover* and *Belle de Jour*. She posted a comment right after mine, I checked out her profile, I messaged her and things just took off from there. We clicked right away both online and in conversation. A few days later, I asked her out to dinner. It happened so fast I practically forgot about all the work I had put into making it so easy.

From her profile and our conversations, it was clear that she desired to be submissive in a very general way, but didn't have a set agenda of what kind of relationship she really wanted. I liked how open she was to the possibilities and how she gave an abundance of room for spontaneity to do its magic. She was very much a sensualist in her submissive leanings but also liked "to be told what to do."

A couple of hours before we we're supposed to meet for our first date, I decided to be a bit audacious and see how open she would be to me from the beginning. I was at a point in my life that I felt that everyone is so mortal and insignificant in the grand scheme of things that you might as well wake up every day and just bare the chest you got and go for it. So, I sent her a text that read: "I don't like to dominate a woman I've never met, but if we do become serious, you will definitely not be allowed to wear a bra and panties without my permission. Take that as you will. I won't consider it disobedience if you decide to wear them tonight."

All she sent back was a raised eyebrow emoji.

I was waiting outside the restaurant when I spotted her walking toward me. Even from twenty feet away, I could see that she was wearing a silky white button-up blouse and her round breasts were casually bouncing up and down with each step she took toward me. When our eyes met, I felt a deep emotional jolt and I almost felt guilty for starting things off in such a sexually demanding way. She slyly eyed me from head to toe as if she was making a snap judgment if I was her kind

43

of man. She smiled deviously when I complemented her attire and I tried to hide my own ravenous grin.

She wore her chestnut brown hair delicately pulled back in a metal clasp and she had provocatively large white earrings on that seemed to suggest something I couldn't quite comprehend. Her full bare pink lips and the crisp flutter of her eyebrows as she stood in front of me drove my insides wild.

I was already outrageously aroused before she had even said one word to me.

The evening passed like a relaxing seven course affair. There was a nice balance of flirtatiousness and casual conversation about our lives. She is one of those women who always seems alert and tuned in to the person she is talking with in a very animated way. It was as if there was an electric vivacity in the movements of her face. Her sheer ability to notice everything is absolutely precious. She told me that she had a hectic work life and liked the idea of a man controlling some aspects of it in order to give her more balance. She was definitely open to being dominated in and out of the bedroom.

She worked in the music industry and had to spend a lot of time out and about. She lived through music but as a career she felt like she got sucked into the commercial demands and was always "going, going, going." She expressed a need for someone to set rules for her and to guide her without being an absolute controlling prick about it. Deep down, I wanted to own every part of her right there, but I didn't say it. I could already feel a sense of how our diametrically different personalities complemented each other. Her floundering whirlwind of energy seemed to just be begging for a heavy dose of my fierce unyielding desire to direct and command.

The only blunder I made, if you can call it that, was during the meal when the waiter accidently dropped a dish behind me. I franticly jumped out of my chair when I heard it crash loudly on the floor, knocking over a water glass in my panicked reaction to the noise. Katrina asked me if I was alright and I just brushed off my spastic response. I should have told her then why the sound startled me so badly but I didn't. It was something I would have to confess to her later.

Toward the end of dinner, I thanked her for following my first rule. She blushed softly and self-consciously ran her fingers through her crisp brown hair, swaying drunkenly to one side from the handful of cocktails she had imbibed. I asked her if she liked asking for permission to do things. She thought about it for a moment and said, in a very alluring way, "Maybe." Our eyes locked. We were sitting in a back corner of the restaurant and the lighting was fairly dim.

I glanced around to make sure no one was looking, and then told her: "Ask me permission to show me that you followed my rule." She looked back at me as if I was joking. "You heard me. Ask me right now," I calmly ordered her.

She struggled to swallow for a moment and then straightened herself in her chair. She replied uneasily, "May I show you?"

I ran my hand around the back of her neck, drawing myself closer to her, and then whispered into her ear: "Be more precise in exactly what you are asking for." I glared at her sharply. "Always," I told her. I could sense she was getting excited by the exchange.

Her eyes darted about before she spoke again. She cleared her throat and then deliberately mouthed each word very slowly: "May I please show you my cold bare breasts right now?" She grinned at the kinky sound of her own question. I nodded in pleased affirmation.

She turned a bit toward the wall to conceal herself and then she casually reached up, undid the top few buttons of her shirt and spread it open ever so slightly. I ogled the curve of her naked chest and her exposed cinnamon-colored nipples. I gave her a devious grin and told her she could button back up. An uncontrollable smile spread across her face. She loved the natural thrill of it. It was only a simple exchange, but it was more about the meaning behind it and her willingness to dance with my dominating urges. We finished dinner, I gave her a casual kiss on the cheek, I wished her a good night like a gentleman and we parted.

There was no doubt about how undeniably attracted we were to one another. We immediately began to exchange endless text messages and talked on the phone a couple of nights over the following weeks. I'll never forget a particular moment that passed between us during this time. It was altogether out of my usual character. We met for a quick drink after work one day. Both of us had pressed schedules but we wanted to see one another again face to face.

It was a hurried conversation but in the middle of it, I told her in a casual point blank manner: "I think I'm in love with you, but I'm not sure because I've never really been in love with anyone." The moment I said it I felt almost foolish, but I didn't let her sense that. It was a crazy thing to say, but I uttered it because I wanted to make it clear what meeting her had done to me. She didn't know how to respond and I adeptly diffused the moment by joking with her that I must have accidently ordered an Absinthe off the drink list. Her eyelids fluttered but she was obviously taken back as well as slightly wary.

We went out a few more times and quickly got to know one another. The way I began to dominate her just happened organically. I knew she longed for control and I desired to control. The idea of asking for permission was instilled in our very first encounter and it set the tone for how we interacted.

We went out on many more dates and there were always some kind of kinky foray. We went to see a movie one night and I made her keep her hand on my thigh just at the edge of my cock for the entire length of the film. I harshly slapped her hand once when she unconsciously moved it and she glared at me in the dark with a ribald smirk.

Another time, we met at a museum and I had her wear a short, pleated black skirt with no panties on underneath. As we strolled around eyeing the artwork, I would whisper dirty thoughts into her ear about what I was going to do to her. I then made her sit face forward on my lap on a granite bench and slyly fondled her underneath her dress while she pretended to stare at the Brancusi sculpture in front of her. I told her to orgasm for me right then and there, and after about 20 minutes of clandestine touching and fingering, she clenched up and let out a deep climactic exhalation.

We went out to dinner another time and I told her that I would be ordering every single thing she drank and ate. She was relieved to let me take control in these minor moments. Sometimes, we would just hang out, be ourselves and have riveting conversation about people or politics or whatever. Other times, things got more deviant. Once when she came over to my house, I made her strip down completely naked before she entered and put a ball gag in her mouth. I told her bluntly that she was not there to talk, that she was there to get fucked like the dirty little slut she was.

I made her lay across my lap while I watched a movie as she stroked me. I paused the film once to fuck her as she bent over with her hands splayed across the floor, her taut haunches bouncing up and down on my cock. I paused it a second time to pound myself into her again, this time on top of the dining room table, the legs wobbling so hard that I thought it was going to crash to the floor. And after it was over I thrust myself into her a third time in the hallway just before she left, only taking the gag out once she was outside my front door. I think it was at that point that she fully realized the strength of my libidinous nature.

Beyond the erotic play, though, things grew more complicated. I thrive on being in control and was unconsciously bringing this into her life. I had spent a few years in the Marines during one of the worst times in the Middle East conflicts before I found my direction in life and had seen more dead friends and foes than I would ever get over in ten lifetimes. A sense that I had control over reality brought me a feeling of peace, even though I knew deep down that nothing was ultimately controllable. I always had to know that things were going well to an almost paranoid degree. This was something I brought into my domination of her that needed to be reconciled.

After dating for a handful of months, I told her that I wanted to know her exact schedule to get a sense of how she spent her day. I instructed her to send me a text message each morning when she woke up to wish me a good morning, to call me at lunch for a casual conversation about her day and to send me another text at bedtime to wish me a good night.

I had her write down her daily schedule but it changed often as she had to go out randomly on many different nights. I told her then that she needed to ask me permission for any nights she went out. She protested that she was uncertain about giving me that kind of control as there were some nights that she had to go out for work purposes.

I explained to her that I had no desire to get in the way of her career, but I needed to know where she was at and why. I let her know that I expected her to perform to her potential in her career but that I needed to make sure that she wasn't excessively tiring herself out or simply going out too much. She cautiously agreed but told me she might have difficulty following that order. I told her that I wasn't giving her a choice. I told her that I would take responsibility for what was best for her, but she would need to ask for permission no matter what.

After a couple of weeks, I realized that she was not only working way too much, but she would sometimes go out after work with colleagues with no real goals in mind. From then on, I limited the number of times she was allowed to go out each week and required her to explain her specific aim each time she went out. At first, she protested that she couldn't do it and she would still venture out with the same directionless mindset. Finally, things came to a head when she went out one night and confessed afterward that she really hadn't gotten anything done and that she was utterly exhausted.

I told her that she wouldn't be going out at all for the rest of the week until she took stock of her daily awareness of what she needed to get done. She threw a fit. Then I told her that she would be coming over to my place that week instead to have her mind trained.

"Trained?" she exclaimed. "I am not your pet," she yelled at me. She refused to have any part of being trained. I told her then that she would be disciplined until she was willing to change her bad habits.

When she didn't come over to my place, I sent her a text message that she wouldn't be seeing me again until she learned to accept a simple rule that was made for her own good. I told her to call me in a week to ask me for permission to have her schedule controlled as I saw fit.

During the week, she sent me numerous text messages, but I simply ignored them in frustration. At first, she half-heartedly apologized for needlessly going out. Then she protested that she had to go out that week. She asked if we could talk, but I didn't respond. A couple days later, she said she would agree to my rules. Still, I didn't respond. It drove her crazy. She sent me another late-night message that she really did want the control and she apologized again. She went through all sorts of emotions and reactions during that week that we didn't have any interactions.

After a week had passed, I called her to ask her if she was ready but she did not answer the phone. She did not return my call that day or the day after. Now I was the one being driven crazy. Finally, she returned my call and told me she was having second thoughts about everything. I asked her to just trust me and agree to my rules to see how things turned out. After some deliberation, she agreed to come over even though I could tell by her tone that she didn't know what she was agreeing to. When she got to my place, she started to try and explain herself. I sat her down in a chair and told her I was going to literally make her beg for me to control her schedule. I raised my voice for the first time with her and told her that she had three seconds to ask me permission to be disciplined.

She erupted and demanded to know what exactly was driving me to want to control and dominate her to this degree. She said she had to know more from me if she was going to move forward with all this. I suddenly realized that I must have seemed like a brute of a control freak to her right then. I needed to be more forthright with her about myself. I was lost for words for a moment and hesitated to say anything.

I paced around the room. I had already casually told her about my time in the military but she had absolutely no idea how much traumatic stress I buried deep inside me every day. I began to describe some of my experiences and nearly choked up in tears on the spot. The floor of our Humvee filled with blood, my naïve excitement of combat that descended into a terrible war in a 24-hour haze, screaming at a kid not to move or I'd shoot him, the blast waves from the IEDs that ripped through my organs and tore up my memories on the spot….it was all too much to talk about once again. She was taken aback.

"That's why you jumped out of your chair that time at the restaurant," she confirmed to me.

"Yes," I confessed. "Loud noises spook me. It happens all the time but I just conceal it."

"I've noticed how jumpy and on edge you often seem, but I was never convinced that it was just your personality," she said.

Katrina noticed absolutely everything I would learn over time. It was her gift.

I confessed that I had tried therapy and meditation, and even medication, but the sweat-inducing thoughts and memories never went away. I knew that in some way I was substituting my inability to control what had happened to me in those times of war with controlling her life. I suddenly felt like a phony, that my motives had been revealed for what they really were. Yet it was so much more complicated than that. My urges to dominate were practically born into me and what happened in combat simply threw it all into confusion. I tried to convey to her that I had done a lot of soul searching when I came back home, and after a few disastrous relationships, I had made a reckoning with myself.

I came to the realization that it was the healthiest way for me to deal with the everyday trauma that ran through my mind. These thoughts were never going to go away. I had learned that as long as I was aware that my control was not harmful to the person I was controlling…that in fact it was a beneficial process for both of us…that this is what I needed and wanted in any meaningful relationship with a woman.

She told me that she understood, but she wanted to understand more. There was a sense of relief on her part that there was something tangible to my compulsions, but she also asked that I return to meditation and perhaps try yoga to work through the pain on my own. I agreed I would. We both took a deep breath and she seemed more at ease.

There was a lull in the conversation after my heavy owning up to my behavior. All of these things I had already mulled over a thousand times in my mind and I understood that only time was going to do the real healing.

"Now that I've bared my soul to you," I began to tell her in sudden change of tone, "It's time for you to bare yourself."

The gauntlet suddenly swung back toward her as she was the reason I had told her to come over. I gave her a stern lecture that she wouldn't be going out at all for a week, that she would be coming over to my place immediately after work and that she would learn to appreciate the effort I put forth in controlling her schedule. She was reluctant to agree. I asked her if she wanted a second week added. She quickly said that she didn't and agreed to be disciplined.

That week, I taught her to focus on giving up control and learning to not feel as if she always needed to be doing something. A lot of her punishment was accomplished merely in not allowing her to go out as she desired. Yet, I also drove home the fact with physical discipline and teaching her to ask permission for every single thing. As soon as she got to my place, I told her to ask me permission to get take off every piece of her clothing. I wanted her bare and exposed. I wanted her to feel that she had no control over herself at that moment and be open to the simple changes she needed to make.

At first she was reluctant and unsure of moving into this territory, but she slowly got into it. She asked to take off her shoes, and then her shirt, and then her jeans, and then her shirt and finally her panties. I made her stand there and ask me permission over and over to be allowed to be naked in front of me. She repeated such phrases as: "May I always be stripped bare for you?" and "May I change my old ways for you?"

Then, I got a chair and made her bend over the back of it. I took a handful of my suit ties and fastened her wrists and ankles to the chair so she couldn't move. At first, she began to panic but I calmly told her that she needed to relax and I placed my hands on her to relax her body and her mind. I instructed her to focus on doing nothing and eased her into letting go with the most soothing words I could muster.

Halfway through her time tied to the chair, I would come up behind her and tell her to ask me for permission to get spanked with my strap. She reluctantly asked permission. I told her to ask me permission to be disciplined for not following the rules. She cautiously asked permission. I gave her a good twenty lashes with my leather strap on her bare butt, and between each stroke I would make her ask for permission to follow my rules again and again. Stroke by stroke, I made her consciously shift the focus from doing what she wanted to do to doing it with my permission foremost in her mind. The spanking was really just to wake her up. The real training was on teaching her to let go of old instincts to always be doing something in order to reach some phantom goal.

As the week went on, I left her tied to the chair for increasing lengths of time. On the first day it was only an hour, but by the end of the week she was left there for several hours. She began to get better and better at letting go and doing nothing. She would eagerly come in and ask to take her clothes off, and then willingly wait over the back of the chair until I was ready to tie her up. It was her first experience with me at really entering "sub space" and she really began to see it for what it was.

Later on, she got so heavily into being tied up and restrained that she needed it like an addict. I hog-tied her, twisted her about in elaborate rope bondage and even confined her with metal shackles bolted to the walls, but she could never get enough. I had unleashed a needy feign. I eventually allowed her to meet up with rope "riggers" that would tie her up in elaborate configurations and hang her by her limbs from the ceiling. It was something rather beautiful and more than I ever imagined would come out of my initial disciplining.

Anyway, the next week, we went back to our regular schedule. The physical experience of being restrained and disciplined evolved into a more conscious dynamic between us. Ever so slowly, she began to trust me. She realized that I was not controlling her just to control her, but because she needed and wanted to relinquish her own forced control. I was focused on what was good for her and I was also very consistent in my demands.

She learned to actively consider her work agenda every time that she went out and to willingly ask for my permission. She became much more attentive and slowly she realized that she both liked and needed to have each and every day controlled to some degree. She longed for that touchstone. I suddenly felt the extent of the power I had in her letting me take over her life like that. It was a bit scary for her and it made me realize the responsibility I had in making sound judgments.

Our relationship began to progress in all sorts of ways with the specific focus on her asking for permission to do anything and giving me more and more control over her life. I increasingly became aware of how her mind worked, what she was looking for in a relationship and how she viewed her work life. She confessed that she had been hurt in previous relationships in which she gave too much of herself and was wary of getting hurt like never before. We had a lot of late-night conversations about the typical emotional baggage that we both were carrying into this new territory of our lives.

She confessed, though, that she did crave the control I took with her. It really grounded her and put her in a state of feeling younger and carefree and safe on a deeper level, she expressed to me.

"And when you dominate me, that always gets me wet," she added with a smirk. "Is your dominating me part of your need to control?" she asked one night.

I told her no, that I've always loved to physically dominate since even in my early high school relationships. I explained that I was deeply aroused on a sexual level by using dominating force, but I also felt that there was so much wild energy that was generated in the creation of a real dominant-submissive bond that didn't exist in a regular relationship. It exposed each person to very raw feelings inside that we could let out without any fear. When I said that to her, she gave me a look that told me she was mine. She was ready to be taken to whatever depths I wanted to take her.

From then on, our relationship became a combination of me controlling nearly every last detail of her life and the two of us just spontaneously experiencing our kinky time together. As I learned more and more about how she viewed her work life and what she wanted out of it, the more I understood that her instinct to be constantly going was burning her out at work.

She confessed that she no longer loved music the way she use to because being so deep in the industry made listening to it feel like an obligation half the time instead of it being a wonderful inspiration all the time. Her instinct to always be doing something at every moment had been instilled in her so long ago and that she was her own worst enemy when it came to setting lofty expectations and envisioning some perfect career and future.

"Now I just wish I could do it when I wanted to, like as a freelancer or a consultant," she told me.

I thought about it for a bit.

"Well," I replied to her jokingly, "you can be a music industry executive part-time and be my sex slave the rest of the time."

She laughed and glared at me deviously.

"I'd like that," she purred, her eyes glaring at me suggestively.

Suddenly what was just a joke became a serious idea to ponder. We talked for a while about her options for quitting her full time job and working for herself. I made it clear to her that I would take care of any financial shortfall if she decided to go for it. This was just what she was waiting to hear.

I began to transition her from the perspective of being "a music industry executive" to being my woman who works in the music industry. I held her accountable for reasonable career goals, I limited her time she spent at work, I insisted she bring me exhilarating new music each week and I became her bona fide new boss.

I had my own career to think about but the time we talked about her work was very directed toward a new stage of her life. She knew what she had to do and she knew that I was guiding her in the right way. We had certain nights that we talked about work, other nights that I forbade her to speak of work at all and other nights that the two interacted.

At that point, the majority of our time we spent together was on weekends. Friday night was my downtime and I didn't want to hear anything at all except how she was going to please me. Saturday was when we spent deviant time together at home or having kinky liaisons on some excursion.

Sunday was about lounging and letting go of any hardcore dominant-submissive demands and just chilling out.

A lot of the time, she would have to be out working on Friday nights at events. When she did, I would sometimes meet up with her at the venue. She knew that even though she was working that it was my time to dominate her and her time to serve me. I enjoyed watching her doing her thing, but I loved to spontaneously summon her and order her around in the most extreme ways. She would be talking to some musician and I would casually motion her to come to me. I would sometimes tell her to go take off her bra and panties while she worked. Other times I would slyly hand her a remote controlled vibrator and tell her to go put it in. I watched her try not to squirm uncontrollably as she was speaking to someone as I ramped up the vibrations from across the room.

Sometimes I would whisper in her ear that she needed to remember that she was "my slut" and that she needed to bring me the drinks while she worked. I would make her go to the bar, order a cocktail that was filled to the very brim of the glass and then carry it all the way to my table without spilling a single drop. If she let one bit of it fall, I would discipline her. Sometimes this meant taking her outside to the far end of the parking lot and spanking her bare ass. Other times this meant making her come over to me every 30 minutes and asking me: "Can your naughty little slut try again, please?" I think I was as much turned on by watching her go right back into business mode as I was at anything that she said or that I did to her. Many times we ended up going off somewhere when she could take a break and fuck like wild animals. Deviant games like this really became absolutely entrenched in her days and nights at work.

Our erotic connection and the deeper personal needs in our relationship became very interconnected. I have learned to truly understand what drives her at a profound level as she has with me. I taught her that any relationship is mutual but that the guiding force of ours will always be the dominating one. At times, moments and situations were very intense. At other times, we just fell into the rhythms of any relationship. There is a vast mode of possibilities between the simple act of dominating in the bedroom and a woman identifying as a total slave with zero will of her own. Karina dwelled willingly somewhere in the middle of it all.

There was this gradual and natural movement toward her being my woman in a very possessive sense. At first she liked it and then she loved it. Everything else just grew from there...the obedience training, the kinky role playing, the speech restrictions, the wardrobe control...all the individual D/s elements were part of the greater love affair. The trust has kept growing deeper and things have just continued moving along in a state of wild and kinky bliss.

One evening she asked me about the time when we first met and I told her that I thought I loved her. I said to her that I didn't remember that night at all. That drove her mad, but she chalked it up to my PTSD. But I remembered exactly what I said. I simply wanted to tell her how wildly I was in love with her in my own terms, in my own way, at the most unexpected moment.

Chapter 3: Introducing a Woman to Domination and Ownership

"Attraction is not a choice." —David DeAngelo

"It is the woman who chooses the man who will choose her."
—Paul Géraldy

Introducing a woman to domination and the idea of being "owned" can be a very different process for each man. It not only depends on one's definition of domination, but also on the woman's previous experiences in the Dominant/submissive landscape of relationships. The spectrum is vast. At one end, a woman might only have the barest of inclinations toward submissiveness in the greater vanilla world. At the other end, she might be in the midst of an ambitious quest to be an owned woman within the most extreme traditions of D/s identity.

For any man, what is vital is keeping an open mind and a maintaining a razor-sharp level of awareness of the emotional, mental and sexual possibilities in any woman he meets. The essential thing in starting a D/s liaison is connecting with the right woman on a level of natural mutual attraction while always keeping in mind the true compatibility of his major kinks with those of hers. Do not project ideas of your dream woman onto any woman you meet and avoid woman who do the same to you. You will accomplish nothing but wasting time. See and listen to the woman in front of you for who she is and what she is telling you she wants.

The path from the beginning of a relationship to a full-on ownership dynamic should be an organic process. It is directed by the man but it should not be forced. One should focus on creating a one-of-a-kind dynamic and not on fitting the woman into some kind of preconceived idea of what a D/s relationship is supposed to be.

Dominating the Woman vs. Sincere Desire for the Female

The nexus of any Dominant/submissive relationship is found in that exceptional place where the masculine desire to subdue and dominate meets female longings to feel irresistibly wanted, to be taken care of and to sense genuine security. Almost any dominant man thrives in the physical pursuit of and the raw sexual command over a woman, yet true dominance lies in creating a bond that is immensely more potent than simple carnal force. An authentic ownership-type relationship is achieved by fusing a man's dominating urges with his sincere interest in caring for a woman in a very heartfelt way.

This balance between dominating aggression and sincere care must be kept in mind from the very beginning of any D/s connection. Masculine sexual urges come in a million different forms in the realm of kink. Men want to grab, spank, slap, tie-up, penetrate, control, order, punish and dominate a woman in endless ways. And a true submissive woman loves every moment of it. Yet, whether one is in the throes of a lustful tryst or is involved in a serious relationship, to honestly dominate a woman involves understanding what makes her tick.

The path to possession is generally not a direct one. Every woman requires a man to travel a unique route through her mind before he takes her body. Her very being is wrapped up in layers and layers of sensitivity that can be very different than a man's uncomplicated hunger for pleasure. She might have the same deviant urges, but she will invariably insist that he pull her emotional triggers to unleash their full strength.

Attraction begins with basic instincts, yet the interaction that follows lays the groundwork for the end of the night and the beginning of any relationship. The erotic realm, whether it means a hard fuck or intricate rope bondage, is the pathway to the deeper dynamic of a long-term dominant presence demanding constant surrender from the submissive woman.

Kink Play Beginnings

Kink play is often the starting point for both men's and women's interest in Dominant/submissive relationships. Unlike most vanilla dating situations and websites, Dominant/submissive connections are almost always intertwined with hardcore desires for very particular erotic pleasures. Men want to do things to women such as tie them up, spank them, fuck them roughly, deep throat them, keep them naked, objectify them, humiliate them, teach them to obey, bind them in spreaders or put them in cages. And women *want* such things done to them...or at least they fantasize about such things being done to them by the right man. It is the grey, grey realm of discovery. A man or a woman is putting himself or herself out there and experimenting to see what happens. It can take place in a controlled setting with like-minded kinksters, on a first date, in a developing affair or in a long-established relationship.

There is a stark difference between a man and a woman meeting for BDSM play and meeting with the expressed hope and desire for a long term ownership-type relationship. If one's predominant intent in connecting with someone online or at a kink event is to engage in play, both people should fully communicate and be mutually aware of what they are getting into. Perhaps a man or a woman simply wants to experiment with or experience a certain type of kinky activity to see what it feels like. They might want to play with rope bondage, get punished with a cane, have rough deviant sex or engage in a very particular kind of edge play. There is certainly nothing wrong with pursuing dominant and submissive play as long as both people know that it *is* play. BDSM play exists on its own *and* as part of a relationship, but one should never confuse the two.

When engaging in a scene with someone who you don't intimately know, it is paramount that there is an explicit discussion regarding the specific activities you are going to engage in. Limits should be set, past history should be put on the table, the full spectrum of details should be negotiated, verbal consent should be given, a "safe word" should be created that allows either person to stop the activity, aftercare should be discussed and sincere communication should guide the entire process. A spanking session with a stranger might be the beginning of a torrid love affair, but it is worlds apart from the act of grabbing your submissive girlfriend/wife without any notice, bending her over the back of the couch and strapping her to tears for being disobedient.

When done online, kink play can simply be a matter of experimentation or getting easy sexual gratification. There is a wealth of kink-specific websites and forums to be found. On sites such as FetLife, there are also groups tailored to every imaginable fetish out there. Online play and discussion is a great way for both men and women to discover what really turns them on and serves as a means of helping them understand the deeper reasons as to why it might turn them on.

Real live kink play can happen with a partner who one is already dating or with a stranger who is seeking like-minded activities. Before a man sets out for any kind of serious relationship, he should gain some basic experience in dominating and experimenting with his particular kinks or fetishes. When creating a personal profile on the major BDSM dating sites, one should clearly state that he is seeking kink play in order to experiment or gain experience. Be sincere and open-minded. There is no point in being deceptive as trust is vital to good interactions. The major BDSM sites also provide calendars for local events such as munches, play parties and workshops. There is also the option of going to a BDSM studio/dungeon where professional submissives will accommodate your wildest fantasies, minus any real sexual interactions. If one longs to sort out the complicated desires beneath his fetishes in more clandestine ways, there are online venues such as SeekingArrangement, Ashley Madison and Craigslist.

The most optimal situation for play is with a woman who shares multiple kinks with a man. It can serve as the beginning of a real relationship or simply be a matter of deviant-minded fun and experimentation. Some people might just get off on fetish-focused activities such as handcuff bondage, old-fashioned corporal punishment or exhibitionistic public play. As previously mentioned, proper negotiation and consent is vital to having a good experience. Typically, though, the best kink play is between two people who have a sincere interest in getting involved in some kind of serious relationship and want to meld deviant desires into the deep core of their dynamic.

An overview of the endless assortment of kinks and fetishes is presented in later chapters.

Introductions and First Dates

The fundamental rule for meeting submissive-minded women: Don't put on obnoxiously obvious pretenses of being a dominant man. One is not a caveman looking to drag away his cavewoman by the hair. One should be oneself and seek natural human connections with a woman. The dominating force is always present, but it knows when to show itself and when to remain hidden. This is not the 13th century. While there are many women who want very traditional relationships and to be kept in their place, there are just as many women who seek a balance between being a powerful female *and* a controlled submissive.

The beginning of a Dominant/submissive encounter is ruled by the art of conversation and the creative force of action.

Conversation can only be cultivated by education and experience. To speak well, one has to listen well. One can purchase a book on the art of conversation or one can simply engage in as many conversations as possible to learn what works and doesn't work for his personality. Also, nearly every submissive woman arrives in front of a man with certain tendencies, stories and emotional triggers dancing around in her head. The second element is all about action. Submissive women generally aren't looking to meet neurotically-inclined babblers. They want a man who is a doer. Yet, the art of action is grounded in both the willingness to confidently take risks and the skill to do things creatively. A good dominant invents his style of dominance.

An important fact to keep in mind is that every submissive woman is looking for someone to do something *to* them. They come to a conversation or a meeting with a whole array of needs, wants and fantasies. While some may be more on the passive side, many more love to push buttons, have their fantasies fulfilled, get their needs met, trigger instincts, inflame your emotions and test your character. A good rule of thumb is to not react to a submissive's words or actions without thinking things through. There might be ulterior motives, deeper reasons, desires for serious power exchange or sheer deception underneath it all. Play your cards well.

At the outset of any first encounter, a man should keep in mind that there is a craft to dominating-style seduction that revolves around his self-confidence.

He knows who he is and he is there to discover the woman for who she is in a meaningful way. It is a matter of balancing his dominating magnetism with a show of self-restraint. He doesn't simply pounce on her, yet he skillfully leads her to a state of being that makes her utterly crave to be pounced upon. He is there to begin to show her how he's going to have his way with her, but he is absolutely patient and sincere. He takes her when he knows she is open to being taken, even if this openness creates a wild play of aggression, negotiation and consent.

But there are many early practicalities to consider…

If a man is looking to meet a woman online, it is important to cut through any deceptive ploys and make sure the woman understands who he is in real life. Be original and truthful. While in person, one's eyes may be the window to the soul, online it is one's use of language. Be direct without getting annoyed by the limits of online interaction. Interrogate how a woman has described herself to make sure she is not lying about her personal situation, her physical attributes and her desires. Inquire about any general "issues" she has brought as emotional baggage into past relationships. Get a sense of her reoccurring fantasies and her key fetishes. And most importantly, connect with her on a real level of mutual interests, both in BDSM and outside of any kinky realms. Get a feel for each other's sensibilities. Conversely, a man should also express all his own basic desires, issues and fantasies. There is no point in trying to disguise one's true self behind a veneer of simplistic dominance.

In the online world, it is always very difficult to get a true sense of someone's personality. Don't bother trying to dominate a woman online. It comes off as weak and contrived. A man should be himself and let her speak openly, but he should control the tempo and feeling of the conversation. A woman should get a subtle sense of the nature of a man's strong character.

The online kink world can also be a very frustrating place due to the sheer physical distance between people who might connect on the cyber playing field. A man might meet a woman who seems like his perfect kinky soul mate, yet she lives 1,000 miles away. Long distance relationships are rarely a good idea unless there is a very clear path to meeting in person along with realistic possibilities of eventually moving to the same city. If a man is serious about meeting the right woman without any consideration as to where she lives, he should possess the financial means to arrange for regular weekend visits and for eventual relocation expenses. Long-distance relationships might also be the only possibility if a person lives in a small town and it is the only viable option to meeting the right person.

If a man finds a woman he might be interested in, insist on talking on the phone or meeting in a public place. Do not bother in long drawn-out conversations online. They are not only a waste of time but people are very different in real life than in an online chat room or in a text exchange. A man who understands how to control things in general knows that he should be efficient even in personal relationships. He knows that some things must be left to just happen but some other things need to be made to happen. It is also vital that a man seeks a real human connection with a woman and not simply try to match his kinky interests with hers. D/s ownership is not a jig-saw puzzle that must be put together. It should rise naturally from an organic human connection with the other person.

When meeting a woman for the first time, there are a wide variety of ways to set the tone and circumstances of the date. One should not run headlong into "controldom", as there are the typical uncertainties of meeting someone for the first time. A woman is going to be naturally cautious and fearful of meeting a stranger. If she is more of a submissive with a strong dominant streak, she will not even consider taking an order from a man she has never met. Just enjoy the jousting.

A dominant man wants to dominate, but a vital part of making a woman surrender to him is reading and understanding what she herself seeks.

It is a delicate balance. The dominant force should set the tone of the dynamic but he knows that there must be a deep mutual interaction of desires and needs. It is his responsibility to use his intuition to know if a woman is right for him. He should sense if what she wants coalesces with what he wants. If she is the woman for him, his manner of domination should naturally integrate into the flux of conversation, whether the topic is the meaning of a hard spanking, the latest political happenings or their tastes in movies.

That being said, some women need to reach a certain level of trust while others long for sensual adventure at the outset. Early commands are all about the vocal delivery of the order. One can hint at or suggest an idea to gauge her interest, or one can simply order her to do it to see how she responds. He can tell her to meet him at an exact place of his choosing and tell her what to wear or what not to wear. He can choose a destination or adventurous activity that suggests what he's all about or that can lead to naughtier interludes. That can be anything from brunch at a culinary hotspot, a wine tasting jaunt out-of-town, an art gallery opening, an outdoor expedition hiking or skydiving, a food festival or a road trip in a swanky rental car. The essential idea is to take her to a place in which you are in your strongest element and your dominance naturally reigns supreme.

There are a number of kinky avenues to take in the spirit of making a good first impression. It depends on the extent of rapport already developed and how aggressive and adventurous the man likes to be. He can tell her what he likes to drink and that she is to have a drink ready for him upon arrival. A man can tell her to be scantily clad or ask her to wear a particular outfit that she thinks would please him. In early interactions, it is important to keep directives playful. If a man has already conversed with her long enough for her to enjoy basic orders, make her wear something kinkier such as a plunge dress or a tight shirt without a bra. Never forget that the verbal delivery of an instruction counts for everything.

If a man wants to be more cavalier and take it in an especially sexual direction, he can tell her not to wear any panties underneath her skirt or leave some risqué lingerie in a gift box with the hostess or bartender of the meeting place. He can tell them to give the box to the woman upon her arrival or text her instructions to put them on before he arrives. Or, he can tell her nothing at all and be focused on developing a sincere personal connection to determine the degree of relationship potential there is. Men are generally much more sexually and sensually aggressive on the outset, but are also prone to the weakness of seeking physical trysts before an undeniable emotional and psychological attraction is developed. One only gets one chance to make a good first impression. That first impression will also, if things go well, become the first memory of a couple's livelong love affair. You don't want to force things but you also realize that you only live once. Why be boring if one doesn't have to be?

There are limits to how much a man can dominate a woman he has not yet met, but first impressions are important.

It is also pleasurable simply to venture into a world of controlled play with strangers. It is a ritualistic tit-for-tat to determine if the man's means of control are meant for the woman. A man and a woman might not hit it off, but a woman should understand that he is there to begin to dictate the broad strokes of the relationship. A submissive woman craves to be desired from the onset but wants to feel it is just for her. Some men like women who are immediately promiscuous while others prefer that women remain properly restrained until a deeper personal connection is developed.

On early dates, a man should compliment what he truly likes about a woman without being exaggeratedly flattering in his speech. It is best to err on the side of reserved coolness in conversation and demeanor. It not only makes a woman understand that a man is not there to simply get a quick sexual fix, but it draws out her genuine interest in him. She'll yearn to say or do something that gets his attention because she wants to feel desired and because she wants to see what is behind his relaxed facade. One should also make appropriate eye contact. It should be reasonably brief but calm, direct and frequent. In general, make more eye contact while listening, but a little less while talking.

Two people are getting to know one another and if things are meant to be, some sparks should fly. There should be something particular about the woman's way of submitting that arouses the man's desire to dominate in his way. She arrives with her own list of desires and needs in her mind and these have to be met with real answers and true character. Every D/s relationship begins in a world of sensual play as each person searches for the signposts to serious attraction. One should be aware of how the two forces intermingle and not confuse one for the other.

It is never too early to set the tone for a man's style of discipline. Some men prefer not to have a punishment dynamic at all. They seek women who are eagerly submissive who they don't need to discipline. Others thrive on using discipline to make their point in following rules, as negative reinforcement for bad behavior and as a fundamental element of domination. For them, early disciplinary action is important for setting the tone. If she arrives late, he can make her write down on a piece of paper or a napkin that she will be spanked for her tardy arrival at a later date. Make sure she writes the exact day and time. Tell her to keep the note in her purse until the time it will be rectified.

If a man has already conversed extensively with the woman and she has said something displeasing or acted like a brat, arrive with a disciplinary element in hand, such as a strap or ruler. Hand it to her and tell her to go wait outside the men's restroom for her punishment. Take her inside, make her bend over the sink and spank her. Note, there is a fine line between the excitement of spontaneous domination and negotiated consent. A woman does not want to be forced to do something, yet she also doesn't want a dominant man who feels like he needs to ask permission for every act he does. A man should know when a cavalier command to a woman is called for and when there is a risk that she is simply feeling disrespected.

A man can create any sort of specific first impression or simply arrive and be himself. A man who is prepared to own a woman knows not only that time is precious but that even a one-time meeting should be embraced with a creative love for spontaneously controlling the moment without forcing anything that is not meant to be forced.

The possibilities are really endless, depending on what has already been discussed in conversation. The entire dynamic should be a mixture of control and play. A woman should know that a man is in charge from the very beginning but that he does not need to control. He creates the control through his personality, his imagination and his physical demeanor, but he is at ease in his power. He decides on where they sit, when they order and how the conversation moves without anything feeling strained, even if he seems to allow her to decide everything. He knows the art of control and makes sure she understands that. He lets her protest, act out and resist his demands willingly. He basks in her feistiness and her urge to resist the will of a man she does not know. He wants to see her feminine strengths. He wants to know what she is made of so he can envision the kind of submissive he will make.

If a man is simply out and about in the world at a bar, a restaurant, a party or anywhere else, meeting submissive women who have dreams of being owned becomes more complicated.

More often than not, dominant men will meet women who will need to be introduced to the idea of being owned. A man does not need to advertise on his chest that he wants to own a woman. Certain women are naturally attracted to the men in a room who command respect and make themselves felt as a dominating presence. A truly dominant man can simply be himself and let his eyes do the work. He can survey a room full of people the way a military commander surveys a potential battlefield. He can sense what women might be seeking what he is seeking.

Submissive women who desire to be dominated crave it intensely. They will often wander over toward a man who exudes confidence. They want to project the idea that they are open to be taken by a strong man who takes what he wants. They are not offended when you tell them to finish their drink before the one you are ordering for them arrives. Or if they are offended, they will provide subtle hints that you need to show your respect for them first before ordering them around. They might object, but they don't walk away. Their eyes reveal their longing to be possessed in a more definitive way than your average woman. They look around a room trying to sense a strong presence. When they make eye contact, the visual connection speaks volumes about their depths. They might nervously take a drink, run their hand through their hair, fidget with their panties or try to sense if he is one of *them*.

A man who is meant to own a woman approaches her simply, commands her presence and seduces her without forcing anything. He lets her know he is going to have her without even saying it. His confidence is pure. Without being overtly aggressive, he communicates that he is going to ravish her at some indefinite time in the future and she knows it. She wants to see what he is made of and test his character. She wants to pretend to play the game so he will make the rules. She wants to resist and struggle to see how badly he wants to subdue her.

Some women have submissive tendencies but have not been exposed to the full realm of BDSM culture nor have they opened their minds to consider such ideas and actions. A woman might need to be guided through the stages of deviant "self awareness", in which she realizes she has desires related to BDSM scenarios and decides to be open to participating in them. Some authors call this an "internal coming-out." Most women realize early on in their adult life what they like but this is not universal. Two separate surveys on this topic independently came to the conclusion that 58 percent and 67 percent of the sample respectively had realized their disposition before their 19th birthday.

It is vital for a man to let a woman know what he truly wants.

If a man connects with a woman and he senses she longs to submit in deeper ways, he should simply tell her how he envisions a relationship. He should tell her early in the relationship, in his own words, that he eventually wants to own a woman completely. A casually submissive woman will feign shock but deep down, or at a later point in time, she will be intrigued by the idea of being a man's "property". She will be enthralled to know what it really means to be owned by a man. A man can choose to tell her everything under the sun or only the broad strokes. Some women are more receptive than others and a man should speak accordingly.

In any situation, a man should let a woman know in subtle physical ways that he is going to begin to control her. He can rest his hand on the small of her back as he speaks to her. Once she becomes comfortable with him, he can move his hands anywhere he wants. Run a hand through her hair and grasp it tightly so she feels it. He can casually run his fingers along the line of her panties and give them a subtle tug. He can hold her by the back of her neck. If sitting down opposite each other, a man can let a woman know that she is his by the relaxed firmness of his stare. A woman should feel a man's pure confidence in getting what he wants.

In BDSM-speak, the term "negotiation" means creating a space to talk about one's needs, wants, fantasies, limits and negative triggers. If a man is meeting a woman in a BDSM setting for "play" or to do a "scene", this is the best way to go. In real life, negotiation happens in the flux of conversation. It is a matter of being honest and open, disclosing real desires and fears and getting to know someone's true self. It is a matter of communication without deception. It is resistance and seduction. It is confronting one's fears but demanding a certain level of trust. A dominant man must earn a woman's submission and a submissive woman must earn a man's deepest desires.

He always controls the conversation even if he lets a woman speak freely for hours on end. She is made to understand that she is telling him things because he wants her to tell him. He can let her speak openly the entire evening or a he can suddenly tell her not to speak unless she is spoken to. The creative dynamic of control should be set by the man and the woman should thrive on the nature of his verbal domination. When he speaks, she should feel his intellectual caliber and the firmness of his beliefs. A dominant man is always passionate about what he does and has a strong vision at the core of his work. It should be made clear to a woman what her role is to be in both the relationship and in her work situation. An owned woman can be anything from a slave kept at home in a servant role to an ambitious leader at the head of her own company. A man should make clear what his own beliefs are concerning work and family. An owned woman is meant to be owned by a man and not by society's beliefs.

In getting to know a woman on the first few dates, the man should set the tone for the sexual nature of the relationship.

A man should not try to force his advances without having built a basic level of trust and having communicated his sexual proclivities. STD tests and strict adherence to safety is paramount. A dominant man should have already had detailed discussions with his doctor and researched the latest documentation on STD's.

That being said, a woman who longs to be owned longs to be sexually taken by an assertive man. A woman should offer real and sincere reasons if she refuses sensual entreaties at the onset of a relationship. If she does, he must respect those reasons. If she does not, the man should take what he wants while being keenly aware of her limits and emotional needs. There is no domination if one does not dominate, but the submission must be earned. He does not want to pressure her, but he still wants to push the envelope of risky behavior and assertive gestures. For every woman, this is different.

A submissive with her own strong tendencies to control, and a high IQ to match it, longs for serious seduction from a seasoned dominant. For such a woman, his confidence must come from the core of his being and from his experience in life. She will quickly identify phony or half-hearted dominants. He must understand the depths of human psychology, be supremely aware of her own demanding needs and be a true connoisseur of power play. The conversation might be intensely intellectual or psychological. It might move wildly through politics or art or sex or business or anything else, as she tests his caliber on every level and he asserts himself deeper and deeper into her mind. Conversation becomes foreplay, the power exchange feels almost palpable and emotions get riled. It might carry over into the first few dates, or they might both be so intensely into each other that they begin the relationship with a kinky tryst in the riskiest of settings.

Other women crave the most simplistic forms of domination and every aggressive gesture he makes produces instant, uncontrollable arousal. If he tells her to go the restroom in a restaurant and take off her underwear, he expects her to go to the restroom and take off her underwear. If he tells her that he is going to take her home at the end of the night and fuck her, she should understand that if she goes home with him, she will be getting fucked that night. If they meet in private and he tells her in advance that she will be made to strip off her clothes to be examined, she should be ready to strip off all her clothes. If they are in a bar, after several dates, and he whispers to her that he likes his cock sucked, he should expect her to ask him how he likes it to be sucked.

Other women like to take things very slowly. They have come to the self-realization that they are submissive, but they are very cautious about jumping into the deep waters of domination. They know that the same masculine tendencies that create an erotically-charged submissive experience can unleash the worst violent behavior of a controlling psychopath. They are aware of their desire to trust a man completely so they don't surrender easily.

In the addictive world of control, power and domination, a man should never forget that "no" always means no. A woman's feelings might suddenly change or something happens that she didn't expect to happen. In fact, it is a good idea to tell her at the outset of a relationship to that she is completely in charge of when to tell him "no". Another option is using a "safe word" that is agreed upon in advance as a cue to stop all activities. A dominant man knows not only that rape and physical assault are crimes punishable by prison time, but he knows not to get caught up in the nasty emotions of certain women who don't like to play fair.

The possibilities of early sexual play are endless but in any situation in which there is true potential for a relationship, the man should thrive on getting what he wants and the woman should thrive on giving it to him, even if she insists on making him fight for it. How this plays out will depend not only on the raw attraction between a man and a woman, but also on the man's sheer abilities to dominate and on the woman's urge to tease, resist and joust for respect. Some women love the fight and play of power itself, but in the end, they want to be subdued and controlled by a stronger force. Other women long to be objectified and are excited by the thought of serving like some kind of naked animal.

A final key element in initial meetings and dates is the tone of discipline instilled in a couple's interaction. The rules of any relationship, D/s or otherwise, are generally set within the first two weeks of being with someone. Owning a woman means molding her into your woman. The molding is a life-time experience but it does not happen on its own. It often requires strict discipline. Some women need to be disciplined often while others embrace total submission. A man should discuss a woman's experiences with being disciplined. A man should make an immediate example of what she should expect in the future as soon as the woman has earned it. This could mean a bare-handed spanking, a formal paddling, verbal humiliation, a writing assignment or anything else that is meant as negative reinforcement. A man does not have to reveal his full repertoire of disciplinary control with a woman he has just met. He should simply set a precedent for a future life together.

The Psychology of Ownership

The psychology of owning a woman is layered with a thousand different conceptions and emotions. To own a woman means to physically own her like personal property, yet it also means to own her psychologically because she trusts him with her entire life. She craves to be owned in the simplest and in the most perverse ways. She wants a hand guiding her by the neck, a hand that harshly slaps her across her bare ass and a hand that holds her tenderly. She daydreams about having a man who protects her as his own in all circumstances and at all times. At moments, she fantasizes about being used and treated like a slut. She needs that completeness and she is ready to do anything for the right man.

It is important for a man who seeks to own a woman, though, that ownership comes after there is a deep connection. Any man can't own any woman. He should understand that there must be the same dynamic web of mutual attraction and desire that transcends the basic instinct to possess. The urge to own a woman is a desire to control her but it cannot be based in egocentricity and megalomania. It cannot be a negative instinct to use and abuse nor even a compulsion to feel that her feelings or opinions do no matter. A man meant to own a woman has a strong self-awareness of his desires. He wants to own a woman but he does not need it so badly that he loses his perspective or makes bad judgments about a potential woman. He ascertains if a woman desires to be owned because she feels unwanted or unloved, or if she wants to be owned because she craves the totality of emotion bound up in such a relationship.

To own a woman is to unleash the full spectrum of masculine desire from the basest urges to the loftiest aspirations. He knows at a very crude level that he is made with a cock in order to penetrate a woman's body. His physical and psychological make-up demands that he pursue a woman and subdue her. He knows that his seduction of her is grounded in his raw will to dominate her and have her for his own pleasure. A woman meant to be owned understands this in very deep ways. At a crude level, she wants her cunt filled and overpowered with his force. She wants to be uniquely desired with pure masculine energy. At a mental and emotional level, she wants to please him so ardently that no other woman could ever replace her. She wants the world beyond sexual conquest. In giving up her own strong will to live for herself, she wants to feel overwhelmingly needed and loved by him in everything she does for him. He wants to make and create her and she wants to be made and created.

The Practicality of Ownership

The full and total ownership of a woman is far from being an easy or convenient process. All relationships require "work" and a D/s connection involving total power exchange between the man and the woman is certainly no exception. In a 2003 study of 24/7 BDSM relationships, the author Bert Cutler found that the "perfect match" where both in the relationship shared the same tastes and desires was rare, and most relationships required both partners to take up or put away some of their desires. The most reported issue amongst respondents was not finding enough time to be in role with most adopting a 24/7 lifestyle wherein both partners maintain their dominant or submissive role throughout the day. Such a study reiterates the importance of the man to prepare himself mentally, physically and financially so he has the freedom to own the woman in the way he would like. Furthermore, a man with a well-trained mind understands that there is no perfect match and his desires naturally adapt to realistic ends.

If a man begins to become seriously involved with a submissive woman, he should understand that a "24/7 lifestyle" can mean many things. It does not necessarily have to entail a women being kept as a bound slave, wearing exactly what he wants her to wear, doing exactly what he wants her to do at every second of the day and night. Her work life may come with its own demands or she might have serious family obligations such as children from a previous relationship. The focus of 24/7 should be on the mental and emotional connection at the core of the relationship. She might be overloaded with endless stress at her job, but she knows to do such tasks as check in with her man via text messages, wear what she is told to wear underneath her work attire, ask to orally service him when she gets home and meditate on his demands and desires when they are not together. A man should use his creative instincts to work around the inevitable obstacles.

Secondly, a man should be fully aware of how a woman conceives of her own submission. She will inevitably have very particular ideas and fantasies about what being dominated entails. Communication is vital. A woman will not want to be dominated by a man who does not care at all about her own visions of submission and her own particular kinks. Also, as one grows older, the nature of the D/s connection will inevitably grow beyond immediate sexual play. One should always be mindful that there is a true D/s connection underneath the fulfillment of erotic scenarios. A serious relationship cannot simply be based on fantasies of spankings, bondage and rough sex. The dynamic should come from the reality of each partner's personality and not be external realities imposed on the relationship. A dominant-submissive bond can be an extremely powerful connection from which a couple can explore a thousand other erotic scenarios and controlling elements that might not be possible without that bond.

Endless Fantasies and Basic Realities

Any Dominant/submissive relationship begins and evolves at the intersection of fantasy and reality. The challenge is to constantly embrace the realm of fantasy while still being mindful of living in reality. The endless kink fantasies that exist in one's mind cannot be the basis for a complex relationship between two people with complicated desires. At the same time, a relationship that falls into routine patterns devoid of any spontaneous engagement in fantasy can become as dull as the worst vanilla marriage in the world.

The impulse to search out and enter into a D/s relationship often begins with basic desires. A man or a woman might want the security of a very *defined* relationship in which personal identities are made crystal clear. He or she might also long for the extreme emotions brought out by a total power exchange with another person. All relationships involve an exchange of power, but in a D/s relationship this exchange is transformed into conscious feelings and actions. The man knows he is dominating and the woman knows she is submitting. The natural spectrum of emotions succumbs to singular expressions of power. Constantly shifting character traits are made subservient to fixed affirmations of extreme personal identity.

The basic urges that lead men and women into any relationship are the same in a D/s connection. People long for companionship over solitude. They want the safety of a long-term partner over the risks of engaging life on their own. They want to fall in love and to be loved. They want to feel desired and needed. Sometimes, all these urges take the same form in a D/s relationship. Other times, many, if not all, of these desires are amplified to disproportionate degrees by the forces of domination and submission. One should understand that the world of D/s is not an escape from the normal difficulties of finding and being with a significant other. A relationship involving dominance and submission is not a goal. It is, like everything else in life, a journey of experience.

Case Study 3.1

"Trials and Tribulations of a Babygirl"

Gabriel and Addison

Addison: It's slightly embarrassing to say, but Gabriel was one of my professors in college when I met him during my freshman year. He was still just an associate professor then and was not *that* much older than me, but he definitely brought out my daddy issues. I use to torment myself for a long, long time with my daddy issues, but not anymore these days. I love my daddy issues. Please issue me heaps and heaps more of them. Now I bask in my freakdom side whereas before I use to hide it like a case of incest.

Anyway, I'm really just a weird country girl from nowhere, Ohio and I already felt out of my element and out of my league at that prestigious east coast school with all its pretensions and its nepotistic herds. My parents were very strict with me growing up, but they had gotten divorced while I was in junior high school. It had completely shattered my sheltered view of family and relationships and life and all that heartbreaking shit. It didn't help that I was an accident child and partially blamed myself for their separation. I developed a terrible anxiety complex and dealt with most any difficulty from that point on by throwing myself into schoolwork and books when I wasn't masturbating to taboo porn I found online. It was the one ironic blessing of the ordeal as my stupendous grades got me out of the culture-starved tedium of the rural Midwest and into one of the best colleges in the good ol' U. S. of A.

I had randomly enrolled in an introductory course in American Literature that happened to be taught by Gabriel. I say Gabriel now, but it was only much later on that I called him that, and even then it was rare for me to address him by his first name. At that point he was Professor Rossi, or just Professor, or at the onset of things simply "sir."

There were indecent sparks between us from the very beginning, and from the very beginning I mean the very first time I walked into his classroom. We exchanged glances and my heart nearly ricocheted right out of my body. His very presence made me so anxious that I swiftly slipped into one of the back seats of the classroom to hide the goose bumps radiating across every inch of my flesh. He seemed larger than life to me and he definitely dressed the part of some kind of movieland teacher with his charcoal colored tweed jacket, his perfectly starched white shirt and his stiff designer jeans. The sound of his hard leather soles of his dress shoes clacking against the floor as he walked back and forth behind the podium made me shudder in sensuous revelry.

He spoke in such an ardent and intensified way about whomever he was lecturing on that it felt more like a Pentecostal tent revival than any sort of typical collegiate instruction. Yet, as much as I was mesmerized by him from the outset, I was at first terribly nervous about being called upon to speak. I managed to make it through the first class

81

and practically ran back to my dorm room to pour over every page of the required reading for the course. The first book was *The Scarlet Letter* but I felt like I was really the doomed woman that Professor Rossi would be interrogating for answers. I even dreamt that night of being locked in wooden stocks, only I dreamt I was some Puritanical handmaid dressed in a theatrically stiff red satin dress which somehow made me feel utterly fertile.

By the next class, I had not only read the book from cover to cover, I had digested a pile of critical works on the novel which I had found in the school library. This time, I perched myself at the very front of the classroom and eagerly waited for him to ask for responses to his questions. When the time came, I raised my hand and rattled off a symphony of opinions that I had gleaned from my research. He stoically thanked me for my analysis of the book but he seemed less than impressed. I was a bit crestfallen.

I always had a tendency growing up to overcompensate for my insecurities by convincing myself that I was absolutely right in every way in my beliefs and facts. And usually I was. So, the next time I had a chance to speak, I was utterly determined to get his attention. When he was speaking to us about the main character of the book, Hester Prynne, I raised my hand once again in the middle of his lecture.

"Yes, Addison," he inquired. "You have something to add?"

"Yes, I mean…well, I don't think you fully understand Hester's predicament at all," I started to pontificate. He glared at me with an amused look. A couple of the other students turned their heads toward me. I rattled off every opinion and half-thought I could possibly muster up in my quest to show him how much I knew about the work.

"That's a very interesting perspective," he replied. "I see someone has been doing some deep reading at the library. That's from Professor Peytons' study he published a few years ago isn't it?"

My face must have turned stark red from the embarrassment of him knowing that I was just reciting someone else's research with which he was all too familiar.

"Yes, I believe so," I stuttered.

"Thank you for bringing that view to the class, Addison. I do like it when students go above and beyond with what is required of them in the course," he added.

I wasn't sure if he was complimenting me or relieving me of my feeling of humiliation. He went on with the lecture as I took note of his every word and tried not to stare into his entrancing brown eyes. I spent the rest of the class trying to make up for my initial outburst with even more comments. By the end, my attempt at showing him my intelligent insight had crumbled into inflammatory jabs and even scorned sarcasm.

As I was walking out of the room feeling like a silly girl, he told me that he would like to speak to me. I could instantly feel the sweat bead on the palms on my hands.

"Yes, Professor Rossi," I responded, half paralyzed.

He waited for the other students to leave.

"Addison, I just wanted to commend you on your eager curiosity," he began. "I sincerely admire students who take the reading seriously."

He looked over at me in a very direct way and my legs wobbled beneath me. I replied with a simple thank you.

"But your attention should be directed at the text," he told me. "Everything is in the text. Do a deep read of the story itself before you go off digesting a million critical opinions about it. Do you understand?"

He stared directly into my eyes with a firm but inviting gaze.

"Yes," I said.

He suddenly lifted his hand and placed it on my shoulder.

"Yes, sir," he uttered with a firm tone.

"What?" I replied in utter confusion.

He smiled warmly at my reaction.

"You are to address me as sir when I ask you if you understand," he clarified.

"Yes, sir," I immediately replied, even though I was bewildered by this unexpected order.

"Addison," he went on in an abrupt change of tone, "you not only interrupted my lecture multiple times today, but you talked over nearly every other student who was trying to speak. It seems you might have an issue with self-restraint and respecting other people's viewpoints."

I could barely swallow. Throughout high school I had always been very vocal because I believed I was right in what I said and everyone let me have my say, especially since most of them didn't give a shit about books. No one had ever called me out so bluntly on it though.

"Ok...I'm sorry, I just..." I began to explain.

"You don't need to be sorry. Just don't let it happen again. Is that clear?"

"Yes," I responded.

He grinned as he ran his hand down the length of my arm.

"Until it is clear to me, you will address me as sir. Proper respect is important to me. Is that clear, Addison?"

My heart was beating frantically from this unusually stern exchange.

"Yes, sir," I replied hastily.

His smile broadened as he clutched my hand for a moment and then let go.

"Good girl," he commended me.

I beamed with an inexplicable thrill.

"You may go now," he told me, opening his hand toward the door before he turned and walked back to his desk. I swiftly scuttled out.

That night I masturbated repeatedly to every moment of the conversation and to a hundred other fantasies in my mind. I had never had anyone speak to me in such a way. He had an undeniable grip on me that I couldn't even fully explain to myself.

The next few weeks of class I did exactly as he asked, only focusing on reading the required books and not obnoxiously interrupting the class. To my chagrin, though, he only offered mild compliments to my responses and tepid comments on my essays. By the sixth week I was going absolutely mad with his lack of attention. I was adamantly obsessed on getting him to call me aside once again.

The following class I made sure he took notice of me. I took my usual seat at the front of the room, wearing a short pleated skirt that revealed the full length of my bare legs. When he took roll, I watched his eyes dart toward my thighs and then back to the sheet in front of him. As he began to lecture, he remained sitting at his desk while he spoke. I, in turn, started to fidget in my chair, letting my legs sway slowly back and forth as I pretended to not be aware that I was revealing more and more of my thighs. When I straightened out the front of my skirt, I saw him sneak a glance toward me. He quickly looked away but I knew that he had seen that I was not wearing any underwear. I pretended like I was just an eager young student ravenous for his knowledge.

When the time came for responses, I raised my hand repeatedly until he called on me. I voiced my opinions about the book we were discussing in even stronger tones than I did on the first day of class. He listened to me in indomitable amusement as he strolled in front of the podium. He glanced every which way except at my slightly spread legs, but I knew had gotten to him.

"Thank you, Addison," he said. "That's an interesting take on the text. Anyone else have something to add?"

After the class ended, just as I was about to leave the nearly empty room, he told me that he wanted to talk to me.

"Yes, sir," I playfully grinned.

He told me though that he wanted to talk to me privately outside. I asked him why but he simply directed me to walk with him out to the courtyard. When we got out into the fresh air, he turned and asked me very directly if I would like to join him for dinner that night. I was shocked that he

85

was so abruptly personal with me. I had expected him to talk to me about my behavior in class but he seemed to be asking me out on some kind of date. It suddenly occurred to me in the starkest light that my fantasies could be something real.

I stuttered for a moment while I tried to figure out what to say. He reached down and took a hold of my wrist and I stopped mumbling. He simply ordered me to be ready at seven. I nervously agreed. He told me to give him my phone number and I quickly rattled it off as I glanced around to see if anyone was listening. It unexpectedly felt so illicit. Before we parted, he told me to make sure to wear something that would please him. I glared at him in disbelief, astounded that he would be so presumptuous. I instinctively made some sarcastic remark about his demand but he gave me a cutting look and repeated his command. His eyes locked onto mine.

"Yes, sir," I nervously replied.

As it got closer to seven, I received a text message about where we were to meet. I responded with a question about what exactly he expected me to wear. He replied that I seemed to know exactly what to wear in class so he guessed I would figure it out and that he'd see me at seven sharp.

When I got to the restaurant, he was waiting for me outside. I wore a very provocative sleek dragonfly-blue pleated dress with a plunging neckline that tied around the back of my neck, and absolutely nothing underneath it. My nipples were visibly poking against the front of it. He said in an approving manner that it was a very nice choice. He reached over and kissed me delicately on the cheek, wrapping his hand around my back. I was taken aback his immediate intimacy but deep down I was utterly aroused by his forwardness. It all seemed a bit surreal now to be going out with my professor. It was entirely new territory for me to be in this position. I had only gone on dates with boys, but never a man. It felt like I was entering into a ritualistic initiation.

We sat down to eat and quickly launched into various conversations about school and life. We actually connected unusually well and I could feel that he knew I liked that he was older than me. Plus, even though it was technically a first date, we had already been slyly interacting for most of the semester so I think we felt comfortable around each other. I asked him a thousand questions about all sorts of highbrow subjects and I could feel myself eyeing him in a kind of fawning way while he spoke. He knew that I was feeding his ego, yet I was also getting visually aroused by his enthusiasm for all the intellectual worlds he was guiding me through.

Halfway through dinner, though, I began to get a bit sarcastic like I did when I was in class. I couldn't help myself. It's one of my issues from growing up. It was as if I couldn't stand the fact that there was no tension in the feeling between us. I needed conflict and affirmation of some sort that this was real. He told me that I needed to watch my attitude and I immediately challenged him, asking him what he was going to do about it. He casually reached over and wrapped his hand around the back of my neck. He leaned his head toward me and whispered into my ear that if I made one more sarcastic remark that he would give me a good hard spanking for it.

My face must have turned a thousand shades of red at the shock and thrill of his threat, especially after only the short amount of time we had spent together. I hadn't been spanked since I was a child. There was an awkward moment of silence as I thought about how to respond. At first, I was carefully watching my words, but I just couldn't help myself. I wanted to test his ultimatum.

Towards the end of dinner, just as the waiter was clearing the table, I intentionally made another remark. He gave me a stern look but didn't say anything. He asked for the check and he excused himself to go to the restroom. I took a deep breath, but then I realized that he had immediately returned to the table and I looked up at him for an explanation as to why he had come back so quickly.

He ordered me to get up. I asked him why. He glared at me and repeated his order. I cautiously stood up. He swiftly dropped a few bills on the table to pay for dinner and then grabbed me by the arm. I audibly gasped as he led me roughly to the back of the restaurant. A couple of diners even glanced over at us in concern when we passed. It was as if he was forcing me to go, but at the same time I was also willingly enjoying being made to go. It was like I was watching myself as a stranger would. When we got to the men's room, he opened the door, took me hastily inside the single room restroom and closed the door. When I saw him shift the metal lock sharply into its place, I asked him what he thought he was doing.

He replied bluntly, "What did I tell you about your mouth?"

I didn't know what to say, but he didn't really give me time to respond. He grabbed me forcefully around my waist and bent me over the sink. I kept asking him what he was doing in a frantic tone as he lifted up my dress and immediately began to spank me with the palm of his hand. He noticed right away that I was not wearing anything underneath at all. It must have further incited him.

He spanked me so hard that when I glanced back I saw that my bare cheeks had quickly turned a bright shade of red. I struggled in his arms but it was a half-hearted struggle. I honestly loved the fact that he had the bold will to just take me into the gentlemen's room and spank my bare ass. I continued to protest and plead to him that I didn't mean to be so sarcastic, but it was like it was all a charade. I really did long for that physical contact and he gave it to me. It was as if it wasn't even discipline. It was just a very fierce physical way of starting our relationship.

After it was over, I turned around to face him as I straightened my dress. There was such an extraordinary intensity between us. He ordered me to go wait outside for him. I huffed and puffed like a brat, but he knew I was loving every second of it. He got his car from the valet and ushered me into the passenger seat. I thought he was going to take me home, be he turned the opposite way. I couldn't believe this was happening. For a moment, I wondered if this had happened with any of his other students, but I was so entranced by the intensity of our connection that I casually dispelled any such notions. On the way to his house, I sat there in his car seat pouting still as if I were sincerely upset.

He nonchalantly reached over and started fondling me while we were driving. At first, when he ran his hand from my inner thigh up my dress, I grabbed it and asked him again what he thought he was doing. He ignored my question and ordered me to spread my legs. After a few seconds of holding my thighs tightly together, I slowly parted my thighs. I was trying to feign outrage but I couldn't deny how horny this was all making me. He slapped me firmly between my legs and told me to spread them wide. My body jerked from the shock of his palm striking my cunt but the wincing sound I made obviously sounded more pleasurable than painful. I spread my legs as wide as the car seat and he fondled me all the way to his house. By the time he pulled into the driveway, I was writhing in pleasure and completely wet.

I looked over at him.

"Can't you get in trouble for doing something like this?" I asked.

His expression suddenly turned very serious.

"Don't you dare go there, Addison," he replied. "If you're one of those kinds of girls, it's over now. If you have even a single vindictive fiber in you, it's over this very second. I'm not one of those guys. Not now, not ever. Would you like me to take you home right now?"

That was the last thing I wanted.

"No," I said.

He raised an eyebrow at me.

"No, sir."

The long drawn out foreplay leading up to the act was almost as good as the sex itself, but the sex was like nothing I had ever experienced. We had intense intercourse on his living room floor and that was the inauguration of our relationship. There were tender moments but it was truly raw and rough. It wasn't like any of the short, awkward trysts I had experienced with boys my own age. He held me down by my hair and fucked me long and hard from behind right through my own orgasm, and then told me he wasn't through with me, and went on to give me another. Afterward, we just laid on the floor and he held me gently in his arms. I kissed him all over his face and chest like a gleeful supplicant while inhaling the earthy scent of his lean body. I was in ecstasy.

It irrevocably set the tone for the marrow of our relationship.

He told me the following day that he wouldn't be so easy on me the next time I mouthed off to him so sarcastically. He had seen with his own eyes how much I enjoyed getting spanked and told me that it didn't serve as punishment in the least. I realized later how much he was cued into my bratty streak and was cued in to the fact that slapping my ass aroused me uncontrollably.

I brushed off his threat, though, and when I did it again, he ended up whipping me later that week with a thick old leather strap so hard that I was begging him to stop. I was in all seriousness frightened when he was blistering my butt so badly that I was sweating and shaking on my feet. I hadn't felt anything remotely as agonizing since I was a kid. He lectured me about immediately setting boundaries between pleasurable spankings and disciplinary spankings as he wasn't about to have me getting rewarded for acting like a brat. He had found where my pain threshold was and began to mold me with his special brand of discipline.

He also had figured out that I loved to test the person I was with to make sure he was genuinely into me. He began to give me rules to abide by from the outset and I loved it. Each morning, he made me go on webcam before I left for class and get approval for my entire outfit. Sometimes, he would make me change two or three times before he was satisfied and let me leave.

He ruled my academic performance with dictatorial strictness, requiring me to get straight A's on every paper, making me spend a certain number of hours studying in the library in my schoolgirl uniform and ordering me to report to him after every class with oral summaries of the lectures. Any shortcomings in his expectations resulted in my ass cheeks being thoroughly spanked with a wooden paddle he kept hung in his den. When I performed to his approval, though, he would reward me with nights out at primo restaurants and kinky lovemaking all over his house that would sometimes last into the wee hours of the morning.

I absolutely loved every second of it. While all my friends were off with their silly immature boys at some keg party, I felt like I was living a naughty hidden existence that was all together more thrilling. I adored how much attention he paid to me and it seemed like he could never be strict enough. Yet even with the firm domination over my life, I would still try to get away with things or sneak off when I thought he wouldn't notice.

Apart from the discipline and the nights of sweaty sex, we actually connected quite well despite the age difference. When I wasn't getting spanked for acting so bratty, I loved to just cuddle in bed with him and ask him a million questions. I realized then that I definitely adored being treated like a babygirl and had probably always been attracted to older men. I felt like he was this strong wise presence and he welcomed taking that role. I knew that he really did care for me beyond the kinky aspect of it, and we were certainly both very kinky.

One weekend morning, I came out of the shower and flopped on his bed next to him.

"You look so irresistible. I'd do anything for you, daddy."

He immediately jerked his head toward me.

"What did you just call me?"

I smirked devilishly. It felt strange and illicit for me to even say it, but it had been on the tip of my tongue for a while.

"Daddy. Aren't you my Daddy?"

"I don't think you asked for permission to call me that," he replied.

I snuggled up to him and whispered in his ear: "May I please, please, please call you Daddy? And can I be your naughty babygirl?"

He laughed at my playful overtures but didn't say anything for a moment while he contemplated it.

"You may. But only if you're a good girl," he told me. "Otherwise, it's to be sir. And *always* professor in public. Don't you tell a soul about what we do together. Is that clear?"

"Yes, Daddy," I replied in mock seriousness.

I wrapped my thigh across his and began to grind against him, kissing his neck.

"Babygirl needs it doggie style in a bad, bad way," I teased him.

He couldn't resist my entreaties. He grabbed a hold of me and had his way with me for the rest of the morning. Afterward I cooked him fresh eggs and crispy bacon the way he liked it, and added my own special recipe of berries layered on top of crème fraiche and a thick dollop of honey. I wanted our time together to last forever.

I adored the warm almost make-believe cocoon we inhabited. I would lounge around his house in the afternoons like a kitten waiting for him to come back from his class. He'd open up the front door to see me on my hands and knees on his living room floor, completely naked except for the leash around my neck. I'd be lapping at a bowl of warm milk and he'd just smirk at me while he strolled over and took me by the leash and lead me to his bedroom. It was pure bliss.

A few weeks later, I was taking a hike by myself in the picture-perfect rolling hills near the school. It was a crisp sunny day and the New England autumn leaves were falling in an orgy of color. My mind was full of smiles.

On my way back, I began to ponder over how I even ended up in this relationship. I knew some of the reason was due to how I grew up but I wanted to believe it was much more than that. Before my parents had separated, my father was very strict with me. I had firm rules to abide by and couldn't do anything that my friends were allowed to do. I was grounded and spanked often and hated the lack of freedom I had. Yet, after my parents divorced, I lived mostly with my mother and she let me do almost anything I wanted to and she forbid my father from ever spanking me again. It was wonderful at first but then I got completely out of control toward the end of high school. I would do rebellious things like drink wine before school and sneak out in the middle of the night to meet boys.

It was strangely ironic that I now longed for that strict paternalistic discipline in my life. But it was different. It wasn't so utterly stifling like it was when I was a kid. I also still yearned to be carefree and do whatever I wanted to do. In my mind, I had grand plans for my life and career, and still saw myself as a strong young woman who wouldn't take shit from anyone. It was such an oddly magical and transformative time. I adored being the little girl who felt protected and looked after, and loved to kiss and cuddle under the covers like a romantic, and at the same time, I was enthralled in being the woman engulfed in a whole new world of raw manly sex and endless conversations that flowed through the whole spectrum of humanity.

It was all so intense from the first day I walked into his class and the future only got even more intense. There were so many unforgettable moments that I don't even know where I would begin. Let's just say that I have one fond memory of being made to sit in the front of his class in a short skirt with my legs slightly open and no panties on. He had gotten me pierced and I was wearing a little metal clit ring with a dangling attachment etched with the words "good girl". It had to be visible to him from the beginning of class until the end. When I would politely raise my hand to ask a question, and he would see that naughty little thing, I would watch him get so aroused. His lectures would turn into Beethoven-like performances.

I call this a memory because now that is what it is. I should have known that the intensity was bound not to last and would eventually fade. But I was so young that I only imagined things would always be like they were between us. When the inevitable day came later in the year when I saw him excitedly chatting with another female student from across the courtyard, I sensed in the back of my mind that my mind-altering romance might only be a transitory exploration in his already deeply experienced life. Yet, it was far from clear at that point.

I demanded, of course, to know what they were talking about. He brushed off my paranoia and told me she was just some entitled rich girl whose father had donated enough money to have the Arts and Sciences building named after him. He was only indulging her in case he ever needed a favor from him before he got tenure. I wanted to know right then and there what exactly our relationship meant to him. He laughed off my jealousy and swore that he had never met anyone like me. I kept prodding him, asking if he had been with any of his other students in the past and if I was just a passing fling to him.

"Addison, just relax. You're turning this into such a drama. You're so young. Just enjoy what we have together, okay?"

He clasped his arm warmly around my shoulders, which was about all he could do in the middle of the courtyard where we were standing. He was already running late for one of his classes so he promised we'd talk more later when we were alone. I stood there watching him briskly strut away down the tree-lined walkway in his brown tweed jacket and stiff blue jeans. I knew I was in love with him but I didn't really know what that meant.

I was trying to picture what a life would be like with him but it was hard to see very clearly beyond the small kinky world we dwelled in at his house off campus. In the back of my mind I imagined us together for years and years and had even fantasized about having a family with him. Yet, it was nearly the end of the school year and I already had secured an internship in New York for the summer. I was now beginning to wonder where everything was all headed.

We had a long discussion that night. He confessed that he had been with a couple of other students in years past but insisted it didn't mean anything at all. I wanted to know if he loved me and if he ever pictured us together married. He was entirely overwhelmed by my insistence for absolute commitment.

"Addison, let's just take things as they come. I have strong feelings for you but all of that takes time," he admonished me.

"No, it doesn't," I argued. "You either know or you don't."

He just kind of laughed at my fervent demands. In retrospect, I realized how young and immature I was at the time, but there still is a part of me that needs to have a kind of black and white commitment from anyone I feel strongly about. I don't do well in any relationship I am in if it is not extremely defined in its terms and feelings and understandings.

I told him at that point that I needed some time apart to think about everything.

"What?" he asked me incredulously. "What are you talking about? Everything is going wonderful between us. What else could be better about it?"

He just didn't understand my need for him to want me completely and to there to be no doubt that I was his babygirl and would always be his babygirl. It was so silly of me to ask so much of him at the time, but I had never been in such an intense relationship. Plus, after he had confessed to me that he had been intimate with other students in the past I suddenly felt like I would eventually just be one of those other students in his past. He was completely right that I should have been more patient and let things evolve naturally. I was simply incapable of doing that. I needed all or nothing.

After that day he called me several times but I didn't pick up. We had one more conversation the next week but neither one of was going to change how we felt. I finally decided to just end things. He was still in utter shock and kept asking me to just give it time, but it wasn't about time for me.

I left for New York at the end of the school year without even saying goodbye to him. When I returned the following semester I made it a point to avoid taking any classes near him. I started to date guys my own age and started to develop more friendships. It was so strange I realized that my entire first year of college was filled with nothing but memories of him. I hardly even spoke with the girls in my own dorm or the other students in my class.

Toward the end of that semester, I received an email from Gabriel letting me know he had received a job offer for a full time position as a professor at another university and was going to take it. He asked me how everything was going and wanted to know if I wanted to get together before he left. I sent him back a message and wished him well but told him I couldn't. I knew I still had feelings for him and couldn't bare saying goodbye to him again. I had to bury everything so deep inside me after we stopped seeing each other. There must have been months and months that I did nothing but go out every night of the week and get drunk or hook up with some random guy. It was only after I knew that he was no longer at the school that I really was able to move on. I was done with the past, I told myself.

Yet, years later, after I had graduated and was living in New York, the past abruptly announced it was not yet done with me. One spring day, from completely out of the blue, I randomly ran into him on the street. Our eyes locked and I nearly collapsed on the spot. He looked almost exactly like I remembered him when I first walked into his class. He was as surprised to see me as I was to see him. He casually asked me how everything was going "out here in the big city". My legs wobbled and I could barely talk to him. Even after the time had passed, I knew at that moment that I still had feelings for him.

"I'm doing very well. I love it here," I stammered. I started to ask him how he was doing and for a second I almost called him "daddy".

"How are you doing, Gabriel?" It might have been the first time I even called him that and it sounded so strange just hearing myself address him by his first name.

We sat down on the stoop of the adjacent brownstone and talked for a while about what we had been doing over the past few years. He was teaching at a university a couple of hours north but told me the he spent quite a few weekends in the city.

"Just look at you," he suddenly exclaimed. "Babygirl is all grown up into a full-fledged woman."

My heart swooned just at the sound of him calling me that. I noticed he was nearly getting a bit teary. Apart from a few thin wrinkles at the corners of his eyes, he had barely aged at all.

"I don't even really think of myself as a woman, yet," I countered. It was true. I was barely into my twenties and still felt more like a girl. Now that I was out in the working world, I was already beginning to avoid all the responsibilities that came with actual adulthood.

We sat and talked for nearly two hours about anything and everything. It was all quite surreal. When there was a lull in the conversation I glanced over at him and our eyes met. I couldn't stand it anymore. I reached over and wrapped my arms around him. I wanted to tell him how much I missed him but I didn't say anything. I just went on hugging his warm body for what seemed like an eternity. I finally let go and stood up.

"I should go," I stuttered. "I need to get home to walk my dog."

He stood up next to me and wrapped his hand around my wrist just like that first time in the school courtyard.

"Am I going to see you again, stranger?" he inquired humorously.

I didn't know what to say. I was still reeling from the unexpected meeting. It seemed so utterly serendipitous that he felt like fate calling.

"Yes," I just blurted out, my eyes nearly swimming in tears. "I'd like to. That is if you do."

"Yes, I definitely would like to catch up on things with you," he told me. "To make sure you're keeping on top of it all like a good girl," he joked.

We laughed.

I gave him another hug after exchanging numbers and we went on our separate ways.

We have begun to start seeing each other again now. He comes into the city nearly every weekend just for me. A few times I have taken the train up to his place. I really don't know what is going to become of it. There is not the same intensity between us compared to when we first met, but all the same feelings are there. I think I have just grown a bit older and am hesitant to throw myself into it again. Ironically, he is more interested in settling down and starting a family now, while I am just in the throes of figuring out what I want to do with my life.

The one thing that occurred to me after that unforeseen meeting on the street is that I could suddenly no longer imagine him not in my life. During all those years apart from him, in my heart of hearts, a part of me was still his babygirl. All I can say for certain at this point, though, is that time certain makes kinky weekend sex much much fonder.

Chapter 4: Self-Control

"He who controls others may be powerful, but he who has mastered himself is mightier still." —Lao Tzu

"We all have dreams. But in order to make dreams come into reality, it takes an awful lot of determination, dedication, self-discipline, and effort." —Jesse Owens

"Class is an aura of confidence that is being sure without being cocky. Class has nothing to do with money. Class never runs scared. It is self-discipline and self-knowledge. It's the sure footedness that comes with having proved you can meet life." —Ann Landers

The most important preparatory step for a man who desires to truly own a woman is to assert full control over his own life. It is the hard truth that hardens a man. There is little sense in trying to dominate another person to any serious degree before he has dominated his own fears and insecurities. It is a waste of time for a man to pursue a submissive woman if he doesn't have a vital base of self-discipline. Many men make the mistake of trying to gain a sense of control of their own lives by controlling a woman's life. It might make for good emotional drama but it is destined to fail. Once a woman submits to his initial control, she will learn that she does not respect the lack of control he has in his own life. It will make her feel unsafe. She will intuitively sense the weakness, causing her to seek strength elsewhere or from another man. The man will also sense his own inability to control his own life and take out his feelings of failure on the woman. Many dominant-tending men are caught up in frustrated work lives, or simply have inferiority complexes, and seek to have a sense of control of their lives by controlling a woman.

No matter how dominant a man wishes to be with a woman in his personal life, the fact is that most submissive women will naturally gravitate to men in power, to men who have mastered their own personal lives to a certain degree and to self-made leaders. Sexual dominance in the bedroom is a very different thing than dominance in the larger world and dominance of a woman's heart and mind. One can, of course, be a kinky dominant pervert as much as one wants and for as long as a woman will indulge him and take part in it. Yet, an authentic dominant man who is both dominant in life *and* in his perversities will at the end of the day have the woman he genuinely wants as his lifelong possession.

A woman will endure the severest of pains and sacrifices if she believes a man is in control of his destiny and she feels safe submitting her own future to him. She wants security, inspiration and adventure in every capacity. Depending on the kind of woman a man wants, it doesn't matter if he is a CEO of a Fortune 500 company or a roughneck prize fighter if he commands respect due to his proven inner strength and his real-world ability to execute his personal vision. At least 95% of the process of meeting and making a woman want to be owned by a man happens before he ever makes the slightest effort in doing so. It is akin to a fighter who makes sure the fight is over before he ever steps into the ring. All the work is done in the preparation. The woman will come to him because she knows he has the capacity to own her with her deepest intuition.

Self-discipline is built over time from the cultivation of the mind, from dedicated practice in one's chosen working world and from the making of sound life decisions. At a basic level, this could mean education at an elite university, superior achievement within a company, a relentless drive as an artist or success in venturing out on one's own in a self-made entrepreneurial capacity. At an internal level, it means control over one's own emotions and fears. A man should cultivate a deep inner confidence in who he is which is not simply a quest to appear strong.

A dominant man is not easily swayed by other people's attempts to undermine who he is and what he believes in. He knows himself and his limits, but he is also always growing and yearning for more knowledge. He does not run from his fears but he confronts them. He understands that fear is natural and he uses those fears to advance his understanding of himself. This could be in a physical confrontation, during an intellectual argument or at a crucial decision point in any environment.

Grace under pressure is the kernel at the core of domination whether you are a bull fighter or a newspaper delivery boy. The maintaining of inner calm when there are great external threats and overwhelming demands is the key to growing stronger as a person. A woman wants to ideally feel that she is with someone who can handle any situation due to that person's experience and understanding of his own capabilities. Self-discipline can be cultivated in innumerable ways apart from the work place. Good avenues include the practice of martial arts, the serious study of powerful books, debating issues with others who have strong minds and acquiring skills in areas which you are weak. Yet, it really all comes down to hard-earned life experience.

A woman might be looking to be owned and to completely submit her will to a man, but she is not looking to be owned by any man. It is somewhat of a paradox. A man who wants to own a woman is generally aggressive, demanding, controlling and dominating. He wants what he wants and will take a woman with his full psychological and physical force. Yet, women are always being bombarded by aggressive men. They want to by subdued by a man who already knows how to subdue the world around him and takes her with natural ease. They want to be taken by a man who knows how to take.

Apart from the true strengths of one's personality, the most essential physical asset garnered by living a disciplined life is sufficient financial resources to live the life one envisions. A man does not have to be extremely rich or overly materialistic, but women in most societies are nurtured to desire a certain level of comfort and leisure. Most importantly, they envision settling into a home that fits their expectations of living well. In the most extreme circumstances, they want the finest fashion, dinners at the best restaurants, an immaculate home envied by other women and vacations in exciting destinations. Yet even in typical circumstances, they don't expect a dominant man to be struggling to pay his own bills. At the very minimum, it costs money to have a woman give up any of her time spent in her own working world to serve a man's personal desires.

A submissive woman might not desire anything extravagant at all, but she will almost certainly desire to be taken by a man who can provide some of these things over a man who cannot. A woman who wants to be enslaved typically imagines herself as a slave in secure and/or upscale surroundings. It is the simple truth of survival of the fittest in a capitalistic society. A woman cannot necessarily be bought, but she is typically willing to overlook many faults of a man and give herself to him if she can imagine a life of wealth that frees her from the daily struggles of making it on her own.

That being said, not everyone can be wealthy and each woman has a different perspective on what is enough to satisfy her basic needs and to quell her materialistic fears. Secondly, a man who leads a truly disciplined life led by self-control, or has a certain creative mastery of the domination psychology, can overcome almost any materialistic shortcoming. He will learn how to both inspire and control a woman's perspective on how much she really needs in life. He understands that he is the capitalistic underdog and makes the most of what he has been given. He might not give a fuck about the money disciples of the world and does whatever he wants to such extreme degrees that he commands respect for his fearless nerve.

The final element of one's own person that should be cultivated before he seeks to own a woman is social aptitude. Most women generally do not like loners, recluses and men with social disorders. They seek a man whose dynamic personality and sense of humor makes him the natural center of attention among his own friends. Cultivating friendships, and making use of the broad spectrum of acquaintances, personal alliances, casual friends and true friends that are part of one's world of personal relationships creates an aura of desirability around a man before he ever says one word to a woman. Other men generally want to be around people who are charismatic, optimistic, successful and witty. They want to see themselves in their friendships. Yet, once again, considering the contrary existence, certain loners and recluses have the balls and fortitude to do things on their own terms apart from the social flow. They don't give a damn about society's mores. They are too busy conversing with the universe at large and living their lives with thoughts of personal mortality front and center. They might simply be antisocial because other people can be such hell to do deal with day-in and day-out.

A sense of humor not only adds to one's life-loving outlook, or amplifies life's utter purposelessness, but it also makes others believe that you don't take yourself or the entire world too seriously. It is a sign that your inner confidence is real and you are not afraid to find comedy in your own place in life. It connects you to other people no matter who you are or who they are.

A dominant man should never try to cover up his flaws or hide his weaknesses. He willingly embraces his faults. He affirms that he is human and tries his best to improve himself. He listens intently. He devoutly respects a submissive woman's strengths. He can easily laugh at himself and not feel like he is undermining his dominant core. A man should not become a prisoner of his own domination, feeling like he needs to play the dominant role every moment of the day. There should be a balance with the natural flow of life, the dynamic flux of a relationship and the casual play of regular conversation.

The last details that should be taken care of include cultivation of one's body and one's wardrobe. Though both should come naturally to a man who follows a general path of self-control and personal achievement, one should never underestimate the power of an attractive physique and good taste in clothing. They are basic requirements that a woman who desires to be owned will notice. First impressions are vital. A woman should feel like a man is made to take her for his own by his mere physical appearance.

Some dominant men will naturally follow a path of self-discipline while others must develop it. In the end, it is important that a man simply be himself. He is confident in who he is and what he wants. When he sees a woman who he desires, he wants her completely for his own. It excites him on the deepest level to possess a woman entirely. He understands the extreme dynamism of owning a woman and controlling her life. He is aware of the total trust he demands from her because he is aware of the depth of his strength.

It is erotically thrilling to train her mind and body. There is a sexual charge to controlling her life and feeling her serving him. The extreme nature of the relationship takes the man and the woman into their own created world. It goes to depths that normal relationships only hint at. It makes each person feel alive in the totality of their desires and actions. A man who is truly meant to own a woman is invigorated by his training of her and finds endless, creative ways of asserting and maintaining his possession of her.

Effective domination within the dynamic of the relationship and in the moment of dominating itself comes from a man's power and grace. He cultivates a profound awareness of himself, the world around him and the woman in front of him. He knows when to turn on the dominance and when to turn it off. He understands when it is the submissive actively choosing to surrender and when he is demanding her to surrender. He is aware of the consequences of his decisiveness. Acting with intent will always produce emotional fallout and he stays aware of those effects. He strives to be one with the moment and embraces everything about each experience.

Demanding Pleasure vs. Giving Pleasure

Every man is guided by erotic stimulation. No matter how sophisticated he is, each man knows that he is hardwired to get turned on by the mere sight of an attractive woman's body displayed in the right way. To embrace the dominant impulse means to channel these sexual urges in the direction that he wants to channel them.

There are two ways of sexually dominating in a D/s relationship: direct sexual domination and indirect sexual domination. The first one is the obvious one. The man acts as the sexual aggressor in everything he does. He uses conversation as an aphrodisiac to make her want to be aggressively taken. He grabs her by her hair and kisses her forcefully. He picks her up and spreads her legs. He makes her get on her knees. He thrusts his cock deep into her mouth and tells her to suck it. He commands her to strip off her clothes and bend over a chair. He roughly pounds himself in and out of her in total abandon until his sexual urges have been satisfied in every way he wants them satisfied. He thrives in his domination of her and she adores being dominated. He likes to take and she adores giving. Such domination fantasies can be played out in endless scenarios.

Indirect sexual domination is about maintaining the balance of pleasure between the dominant man and the submissive woman. A man should understand that a woman has both simple and deep desires to be pleased herself. He should understand that the ways she likes to be pleased can be very different than the ways he likes to please himself. And most importantly, a man should *want* to give pleasure to the woman he is with. He should be with a woman who naturally stimulates him to sexually turn her on in the way she likes to be turned on. A true dominant man is not a selfish brute addicted to simple-minded aggression. He realizes that he is in a relationship with a complex woman and that if he wants her sincere trust and her eager willingness to submit, he must maintain awareness of her real sexual desires.

Indirect sexual domination is more natural for some men than it is for others. Some men know what turns a woman on because they have strong intuition and are good listeners. Others must actively ask the women what she likes and fantasizes about, and then figure out how to make it happen. The important thing for any man is to be aware of the balance between taking pleasure and giving pleasure. Giving pleasure can be anything from delicately embracing a woman during a romantic stroll to licking her pussy until she is writhing in orgasm.

It is about being in touch with a woman's desires and understanding what makes her tick. It is about knowing her erotic triggers and knowing how to turn them into real fantasies. It is about knowing her body. It is about knowing the right words and actions that will get her truly excited. It is about whispering deviant thoughts in her ear in front of her friends. It is about fondling her clit in the right way. It is about sucking her nipples until she squirms in pleasure. It is about kissing her neck passionately and asking her if her pussy is wet. It is about touching her cunt in the most pleasurable of ways, taking her to the brink of a climax and then making her beg like a naughty slut to let her cum.

Case Study 4.1

"A Woman with a Well Hidden Slut Inside"

Jacob and Brianna

Jacob: When I happened to cross paths with Brianna, she was in her twilight twenties and it seemed as if she was ravenously ambitious straight out of the womb. She was not only sharp-witted and aggressive in her demeanor, but she practically looked like a dominatrix in the way she dressed. Tall dark heels and contoured haute couture skirts were her unofficial work attire. I met her while we were both attending a high profile business conference in Aspen. She worked for a prestigious asset management firm in New York and was at the event solely to land new clients. I was there with a couple of hedge fund colleagues but we were honestly more interested in finding pristine snowfall to ski in than sit through a bunch of mostly mediocre investment presentations.

We personally met at a hotel bar at the end of the third day of the conference but we had noticed each other on the first day. She was responding to questions after she had given an impeccable pitch about her company's portfolio and our eyes just happened to connect. It was a very subtle vibe but I could just tell the way she hesitated for a moment when she looked at me that there was more to her than met the eye.

We ran into each other again as we were exiting a reception. There was that same complex exchange of glances. I introduced myself and gave her a firm all-business handshake. We traded observations about the event we had just attended, yet both of us kept a very professional demeanor. We chatted a bit about our backgrounds and there was this feeling of reserved respect for what each of us had done in our careers, even though it was obvious to me she was on her way to far surpassing anything I would ever accomplish. She was that boldly driven.

As we were passing the bar on the way out, I stopped for a moment and turned to her. She paused in her place and looked up at me. I said to her in a very calm, simple manner without the slightest insinuation, "Let's get a drink."

She tried to read my intent and then casually insisted that she was tired and needed to get back to her room. I sensed that she was not turning me down as much as testing the waters to see if there were more than business purposes in my motivations. I looked directly at her, lifted the palm of my hand warmly toward the entrance to the bar and repeated the invitation with just a hint of stern intonation: "Let's get a drink."

I watched her fidget for a moment and struggle to respond.

"Ok, let's get a drink," she affirmatively countered.

In the bar, our conversation was intense and combative. She put up a hard exterior but it began to wear away after the first cocktail. The liquor loosened both of us up in fact. After our third drink, we had started to subtly flirt with each other but she was getting slightly emotional about it. She confessed that it had been a long day and that she was really tired from "putting on a show". There was something so provocative about how professional and vulnerable she was in the same moment. I could tell that she was trying very hard to keep the veneer of the ambitious businesswoman, but underneath there was something extremely different.

The conversation began to turn more and more personal. We each spoke of past relationships and inadvertently mentioned intimate details of sex that turned us on, yet it was still in a very formal, emotionally-protected sort of way. I casually began to brush up against her and make overtly salacious remarks. I could tell that I was getting to her, yet she was still slightly coy about it.

There was a lull in the conversation and we both took a sip of our drinks.

"We should have dinner tomorrow," I proposed.

She eyed me curiously. "Should we?"

"Yes. We most definitely should. Does seven o'clock work for you?"

"Well," she mused, "we should have dinner but I'm afraid my schedule is completely booked up for the entire conference."

"Is that so?" I responded, trying to read her.

"Yes, it is so," she explained warmly. "I'm not trying to put you off. Not in the least. I just have so much work to get done over the next three days. In fact, I really should be in bed right now resting up for my morning meeting."

"In bed?" I replied suggestively. "Yes, you should definitely be in bed."

She was still flirtatiously eyeing me. I sensed she was getting fatigued by all the talking but she turned to me and asked me another question about business. I responded by asking her if I could tell her something in secret. She glared at me, wondering what I meant, but then she smiled and nodded in affirmation.

I leaned over to her and whispered in her ear in a serious, deep voice that she needed to stop talking about work. I told her that she has already done more in her career than I probably ever would and that she was finished doing work for the night. She leaned her head back and raised her eyebrows at me. Her eyes began to move rapidly from side to side as she tried to read me.

"I'm finished doing work?" she responded in mock outrage. I nodded to her. She asked what that meant. I told her that we both know what it meant. More rapid movement of her eyes. The attraction suddenly became unexpectedly intense.

I looked at her for a moment and decided to just make a move. I slipped my hand into my jacket and took out the key card for my hotel room. She watched me as I reached around her back and slid it underneath the waistband of her skirt. She jerked her head around frantically to see if anyone was watching. Her cheeks flushed. I glided the tips of my fingers down the top of her skirt so I could make sure that it was lodged beneath the thin string of her panties.

"What exactly do you think you're doing?" she asked me in a state of confused shock.

I leaned over to her and told her in a calm but blunt tone to shut her mouth, go up to my room and wait for me on her hands and knees on the bed. She laughed drunkenly, briskly brushed back her hair and glared at me like I was utterly crazy.

"I don't even know you," she exclaimed.

"Well, it wouldn't be very thrilling if you did, would it?" I asked her.

I casually grinned at her and waited for her to gain her composure and let my abrupt lewd demand sink in. We were standing at the end of the bar so there was no one behind me. I drew myself closer to her and held her with one hand around the small of her back.

"I don't mean to be disrespectful in the least," I told her, "but I'm not asking you to go to my room. I'm telling you to."

I subtly pressed myself between her legs as I told her bluntly what I was going to do to her. I could feel and see her growing increasingly aroused as I spoke. Her dominating working-world strength was giving way to explicit personal sensuality. I knew and she knew that she was uncontrollably turned on.

"I'll take your wetness as consent," I remarked brashly.

She raised her eyebrows at me. "You have definitely rattled me," she responded in a tone of sharp amusement. "But you're lucky that I like that in a man."

She once again glanced around to make sure no one was watching, and then out of the clear blue, she reached between my legs and firmly grabbed a hold of me. I quickly flinched but held my ground.

"Are you sure you know how to handle a woman like me?" she asked. "Because the only thing I ever consent to is a man who is not only well endowed, but knows how to use his endowment."

I was aghast at her audacity. She had turned the tables on me in the most cutting of ways. She had my thoroughly aroused cock in her grasp and seemed to be sizing it up. I let it grow rock hard in her clutch, waiting for her to feel its full girth. I didn't make the slightest show that she had gotten to me.

"Like I said," I replied firmly, "you are done working for the day and need to do what you are told."

I knew that there was the possibility that I had completely overplayed my hand, but I figured the risk was worth it. If she turned me down, I knew she wouldn't be able to get the thoughts out of her mind. She was still eyeing me as if she was calculating a million considerations inside her head.

She slowly unclasped her hand.

"This never happened," she stated in a sharp matter of fact tone. "I have a reputation and I'll ruin you if you turn this into some kind of boys-in-the-locker-room story. Is that clear?"

"Crystal clear," I responded.

She gave me a slow, determined nod. She gulped down what was left of her drink, gave me a piercing look, turned from the bar and hastily strutted away. My heart was beating wildly and my cock pressed stoutly against the front of my pants.

When I got up to my room, the door was left slightly ajar. I opened it and immediately saw her figure on the bed. She was not precisely on her hands and knees though. She was on her knees with her hands held behind her back and her face turned sideways on the bed. Her skirt and dress shirt were off, revealing this exquisite lingerie ensemble that was some kind of black leather garter belt and body harness that crisscrossed her thighs and body. It was utterly elegant yet almost gothic. She had not taken off her heels either. What really put me over the edge, though, was when I saw the shiny crimson object between her ass cheeks. She was wearing a plug. I couldn't believe it. I wondered if she had been wearing it all day long. Was she that much of a kinky little freak? It was such an amazing sight and so fucking erotic. She really knew how to strike a devastating pose.

She turned her head to look back at me.

"Well, what are you waiting for? Don't you know how to manhandle a lady?" she chimed.

I shook my head in disbelief and walked around the far end of the bed just to get a good look at her from head to toe. She turned her head toward the other side so she could follow me. I told her that I had asked her to get on her hands and knees. She gave me a sly smile and lifted herself to her hands as she arched her back. She told me that she didn't want to give me the wrong idea about the kind of woman she was. I responded by telling her that I knew exactly the kind of woman she was and she just giggled in deviant laughter.

I continued to pace back and forth around the bed as she patiently waited in her kinky position. Finally, I kneeled behind her and slid my fingers between her legs. She was already extremely wet. When I fondled her clit, she started to moan. She was very vocal. As I rubbed her cunt in every direction, I could feel her body tense up in pleasure. When I slid a pair of fingers deep inside of her, she began to moan even louder. I quickly began to enjoy how much noise she made and told her to do it even louder. I had never been with a woman in which things became so sexual so quickly.

When I began to really thrust my fingers in and out of her, the sounds filled the entire room. I'm sure that even the other hotel guests on both sides of us could hear. I knew then she had a quite a gargantuan freaky side to her. I kept telling her, though, that I wanted to hear her getting finger-fucked and she would moan even louder. I started to forcefully thrust my fingers in and out of her while I fondled her clit with my other hand. Her legs started to shake as she neared an orgasm. The whole time I was just kneeling over her while I ogled her erotic figure perched on the bed. Just as she was about to climax, I suddenly pulled my fingers out of her. Her legs stopped shaking and she looked back at me. She begged me not to stop.

I reached over her back, grabbed her by the hair and pulled her around toward me. I told her to take her hands and grasp the heels of her shoes. She didn't even hesitate when I gave her the directions. She obediently twisted her arms around and took hold of her heels. Her body was contorted like a bound animal and she struggled to lift her head to look at me. I calmly unzipped my dress pants and took out my cock. I told her to open her mouth and she opened it. I told her "wider" and she opened it wider. I held my erect cock straight out and slid it deep into her mouth until I heard her gag. I pulled it back out and then did it again. I continued to push it in and out of her over and over as she gagged again and again. Saliva trickled out of her mouth. I commanded her to take it all the way in and she tried her very best to deep throat me. No matter what I told her to do, she did it. She loved every time I gave her an order.

We must have spent hours having the kinkiest sex. Every position I told her to put herself in, she did. Every movement I told her to make, she did. Every sound and word I told her to say, she did. Brianna completely thrived on submitting to me wholeheartedly, especially after the long day of her needing to be in total control at the conference. She was all about working hard and playing hard. After we exhausted ourselves, we were laying in bed talking. She asked me how she knew that she liked to be dominated. I told her that it was just a calculated guess but I had no idea she was such a little freak. She laughed. I confessed to her that I had typically been dominant with almost all the women I'd been with in some way, but most of them were more naturally submissive in all aspects of their personalities. She was the first one who was kind of an Alpha female outside the bedroom.

We spent the next two days at the conference making repeat performances of that night. I watched her command a room full of multi-millionaire investors during the day and crawl to me on her hands and knees at night. She was exactly my kind of rare breed of woman I had always longed for. I loved her intelligence and strength as much as her eagerness to serve me like an ingratiating sex addict.

When we got back to New York, we began to see each other right away and the same dynamic was set. We talked about what we both were looking for in a relationship. She confessed that she had a tendency to micromanage every last detail at work and to constantly try to outperform every other colleague. When she got home, she wanted to completely let go and just submit to her partner. I told her that I was dominant in most of my relationships, but that I really desired to take it to another level of completely owning a woman. The idea didn't shock her in the least and she asked me what I envisioned exactly. I explained to her that her work life was hers to dominate and control, but the moment she got home, her decisions, her will, her mind and her body was mine. I wanted absolute submission. I would be her dictator. When I told her that, a warm mischievous smile spread across her face.

"No woman can resist a dictator," she chided me.

She would typically come over to my apartment on the Upper East Side after she got off work and it was a given that there was a strict separation between work and home. Our dynamic was more about having a psychological and sexual release. I thrived on having a woman I could totally tell what to do at the end of a long work day and she thrived on totally letting go. I began to give her rules that transformed her more into an obedient submissive to me.

On some weekend nights, she would cook and serve me extravagant dinners while I fondled her pussy ceaselessly. I would grope her from behind while she cooked, make her spread her legs between each course so I could finger her deeply and then fuck her on the living room floor after we ate dessert. When she walked in, she would have to remove all her work clothes, put them in the closet next to the front door and change into various outfits I would have her wear. They started out as various cocktail dresses, maid uniforms and tight corsets, but I made up one in particular that she wore the majority of the time.

It began with a vintage sterling silver collar I had bought at an auction. It had a little ring on it for a leash so I added a silver chain that dangled down her back. Later, I discovered these really kinky metal anal hooks sold at BDSM stores online. They looked so animalistic. They were like meat hooks. I got one and added it to the outfit by connecting the necklace chain to the end of the hook. It forced Brianna to walk around with perfect posture with her chin held high. The final touch was a custom waist cincher made of black leather and studded with small diamonds. She loved feeling totally constricted like that as much as I loved to see her going to and fro in the get-up.

Most of the time, she was forbidden to speak about work. As far as she was concerned, she was my household slave and any conversation had to concern pleasurable topics such as movies, the news, entertaining me and serving me. At the beginning, she had difficulty letting work go when she came home and I had to discipline her for it. She absolutely hated cleaning and was usually incredibly tired after work, so it was unbearable punishment for her when I made her clean my whole apartment with a scrub brush on her hands and knees. After an ordeal like that, she quickly learned to not even think about work once she stepped into my apartment. It was a very healthy balance for her and very pleasurable in every way for me. All in all, it was the beginning of a wildly unique relationship.

I had never met anyone like Brianna before. She isn't needy or clingy in the least. She likes that we each have our separate lives and then come together to have our needs fulfilled at the end of the day. Sometimes I don't hear from her at all the whole day and often she is engaged in the evenings with business meetings. She is so well-balanced that I practically envy her in her ability to be so heavily driven in her career and then come home and transform into my little wild nympho. I do, though, always require her to wear something naughty to work every day, be that an anal plug or some obscenely exquisite lingerie. Yet, to be honest she is so kinky she would probably wear something anyway. The fact that I tell her to simply gives the act a loving personal completeness.

We talk at points about the future and desires for family, but we are both content at this moment in our lives with what we have. She is such a special woman and the connection we have is irreplaceable. The fact that we can engage at so many other levels apart from sex just makes the sex all that much better. My "ownership" of her is really something that is unsaid, expect for all the times when I tell her that I own her in deviant ways. She loves when I spank her clit over and over and tell her again and again that I own her pussy. Or when we are out strolling at night with my hand on the back of her neck guiding her and I remind her that she is all mine. Even an act such as that quickly evolves into some kind of naughty tryst in a public place.

I can't imagine things not becoming more and more serious between us, but who knows? For now, all the naked cooking and the edge play and the choking and the strip teasing and the rope bondage and the spreader bars and the endless role play is more than enough for the both of us.

Chapter 5 – Mental and Emotional Ownership

"If you wish to know the mind of a man, listen to his words."
—Chinese Proverb

"One man that has a mind and knows it can always beat ten men who haven't and don't" —George Bernard Shaw

"I know but one freedom and that is the freedom of the mind."
—Antoine de Saint-Exupery

"A mind that is stretched by a new experience can never go back to its old dimensions." —Oliver Wendell Holmes

"It's hard for an educated woman to turn her head off. That's part of the joy of being a submissive. None of the decisions are yours. When you can't refuse anything and can't even move, those voices in your head go silent. All you can do, and all you are permitted to do, is feel."
—Cherise Sinclair

The Bare Basics of Training a Woman

Training a woman is the formal regimen of guiding a woman into full submission and emotional ownership. Although it begins the first moment a man makes contact with a woman, its full thrust is not possible until there is a strong natural attraction and a basic level of trust between them. It is an active, never-ending process of nurturing her to act, speak, think or exist as a dominant man wants her to act, speak, think or exist. It is not changing a woman's core personality. It is bringing out the best of her personality and molding her to identify as a submissive in relation to her dominant owner.

117

A woman who has urges to submit has urges to be trained. Training a woman generally happens as a man gets to know her. Her basic attraction to a dominant man brings out a simple willingness to be trained by him in the smallest of ways. As she grows closer to him, she begins to see the world through his eyes. She wants to be desired by him and to make herself desirable according to what turns him on. On a mental and emotional level, she yearns for his approval and guidance. She craves the security, strength and the love that he eagerly wants to give to the right woman. When she opens herself up to him, his deeper nature comes out to reveal itself in return. He actively *gives* his dominant training with sincere intentions and clear expressions of undeniable concern for her.

Although it takes time to evolve, a relationship should reach a point in which a woman wants to be trained so fully that a deep transformation of her mind and her emotions takes place. She will want to serve him, please him and sacrifice for him like never before. She will be both erotically aroused and feel deeply connected as she is trained day-by-day, month-by-month and year-by-year to be his woman.

The Mental and the Emotional

What does it mean to own a woman?

A man wants a woman in extreme ways. The woman wants to be wanted in extreme ways. Each one has a unique vision of a life together in an intense dynamic of sex, control, love and desire. It happens in a place where the kinks, the fetishes, the power, the domination, the submission, one's daily life, the desires for long-term commitment, the power play, the edge play and one's personal issues all come together. He imagines dominating her in endless ways, both in the bedroom and everywhere else on the planet. She wants to feel his presence at all times, whether he is there or not. He might want to control the broad strokes of her life or he even might want total power over every last detail of her existence. He thrives on the intoxicating acts of his power – being the one she looks to for guidance, ordering her to do demanding tasks, telling her exactly what to wear, taking her roughly whenever he so desires, spanking her over the kitchen table when she is naughty, ruling her personal life with total authority and so on into ownership ecstasy. She wants to need him. She might want to turn off everything in her mind that makes her feel uneasy or fearful, or causes her unnecessary emotional and mental agony. There is no boredom in his presence because he is doing something to her or she is serving his desires. There is a kinetic energy between them. They feed off one another. The pain of solitude seems as far away as humanly possible.

Mental control is the force which binds a man and his woman. If a woman is mentally stimulated by a man's intellectual capabilities and psychological strength, and she can trust him, she will immediately open herself up to submission. She will be erotically charged by his intellectual force. She will want to be engulfed by the same mental velocity with which he thrusts into the world around him. A woman does not want to hope that he is stronger than her nor feel that her own mental energies are intimidating to him.

Mental strength is also very different than intelligence. It comes from experience being tested, strength under pressure, the ability to persevere, life wisdom and the awareness of how the mind works. A true dominant also synthesizes the mental strengths of the woman into the relationship. He does not feel threatened by them. He loves her fortitude and her unique intelligence as much as he is enthralled by her fragility and tenderness. He subdues her not only to assert his authority over her but to assert his belief in her own mental strengths.

Intelligence can be on a mental level or an emotional level. A submissive woman might even have a higher IQ, a better education and a more demanding job than her dominant partner, yet still feel an uncontrollable desire to be dominated by him due to his emotional intelligence or his mental fortitude. Power comes in many forms.

Emotional intelligence is the capacity to be highly aware of emotional states and to use that awareness to enhance thinking. It is the ability to recognize the meaning of emotions and their relationships to other parts of the brain, and to reason and problem-solve on the basis of them. A person with a "high emotional IQ" knows who or what pushes his buttons, knows how it happens and knows how to take control of these situations. It allows a person to remain flexible and open-minded when faced with strong emotions that might be overwhelming.

This can mean knowing how to react when he or the people around him are in a good mood or a bad mood. It is about knowing how to relax and have fun in order to enhance positive performance. It is about having social awareness to know how to react to the emotion behind other's actions. It is about sensing when to stop doing something and take stock of what you are feeling and doing. It is about knowing what excites someone's emotions and knowing when and how to use that excitement. It is about knowing how to speak to someone without making them feel inferior and harshly criticized. It is about remaining calm and focusing on the real goals, whether that's a woman's career choices or reaching a more powerful sexual climax.

A dominant man with a high emotional IQ uses his intense awareness of people's emotional states and his own experience reacting in highly charged situations. He becomes the emotional foundation for the submissive. He is the person who guides her when she becomes angry, gets discouraged, is overly self-critical, makes bad decisions, gets fearful over trying new pursuits, has difficulty in stressful social situations, falls into bad behavioral patterns or becomes bored with her life. He sees the connections between her daily behavior and her personal history. Erotically, he senses how to dominate her with the right feelings and teaches her to become aware of his own emotional demands. He knows when to softly slip his hand between her shirt to fondle her nipples, when to give her a hard spanking without warning, when to restrain her to teach her to relax, when to fuck her roughly to take her mind away from her problems and when to order her to get on her knees to give him oral servicing when she thinks of herself too much.

No matter what the personal connection between two people, a dominant's power in a D/s relationship resides in his having a certain mental, intellectual or emotional strength that provides balance and invigoration to the submissive's life. Opposites attract in the most extreme ways in a potent dynamic. The physical realm, with all of its endlessly kinky possibilities, is the playing field where everything becomes intimate and clear. Feelings and fantasies are literally fleshed out.

A woman who desires to be owned can be of many different types. Some submissive-tending females desire to be the servile housewife who is there to endlessly please her man. She is not the type to challenge him or to question him, or perhaps not even to see herself on the same mental level as him. He is the man of the house and she does what she is told because it is what she likes or it is how she has been raised. These are the easiest women to own and training them can be uncomplicated and trouble-free. Some men love these types of extreme submissives as it makes them feel in charge from the very first minute. Their work lives are stressful enough and they don't want to have to work at home to make the woman do what she needs to do. She stands ready to be fully molded into the woman he wants her to be.

Other women fall at the other end of the spectrum. They are feisty, challenging and prone to question everything. In their own right, they are very controlling themselves. They want things done in a very particular way and will seek to order other people's lives. In the end, though, they want a man who is stronger than them and controls the depths of their lives in a fundamentally powerful way. If left to their own free will, their urge to control will make them feel out of control. They need to be taken charge of and constantly tamed. They are challenging in conversations so they can feel their own mental vigor, but still want to be subdued or even ordered to be silent. They might act out just so they will be whipped. They feel balanced when they fully submit. They cry out inside to be taken control of. They struggle physically so they will be held down and fucked. They want to hold hands tenderly at times but might long to be slapped across the face or swatted on the bare butt when they are disobedient or during a rough session of sex. They want to feel the domination in every fiber of their being. They want to know that the man has thoroughly worked to own them. They might require harsh discipline and they love extreme control.

No matter what kind of woman you long to own, mental control requires that you get into the depths of her mind. A man must know what makes a woman tick. He must know why she longs to be owned and what triggers her emotions. He must pry into her past and make her reveal her insecurities, secrets and perverse desires. A man must not only know the subtle ways a woman does what she does, but he must comprehend the larger feminine principles that govern attraction. A woman will go to all ends of the earth to make a man want her and need her. As she grows older, she will generally want the security of commitment, money and family. A man who owns a woman needs to not only understand these desires but set the rules for how these desires will be fulfilled. There should be open communication from the beginning about the kind of life they both seek. There should be parameters about what will be discussed and what he is open to changing, if anything.

In the end, the desire of the man is for the woman, but the desire of the woman is for the desire of the man. Women are driven by a different kind of passion. It lies inside of them always. At times it is sleeping and waiting, tinged by a feeling of being unwanted. When the passion stirs, it speaks forcefully to them, guides them, rules them and makes them obey its call. Women adore the joy of love, the clarity of pain and the ecstasy of uninhibited pleasure. A man must understand the passion principle that makes nearly every woman feel alive and act the way she acts. Before he officially owns a woman, a man must understand how she is different from other women and how to embrace the opposing qualities she embodies. Some collaboration has to take place in the mind between the woman and the man before the art of ownership can be accomplished.

There are so many kinds of men, types of women and varieties of Dominant-submission relationships that is impossible to provide a cut-and-dry path from the first moment to the sunset of one's later years. The beauty of an extreme Dominant/submissive relationship is that it is a creative dynamic. There are always other realms of domination to explore and deeper layers of surrender to discover. A trusting bond might happen immediately or it might take years to form. There are many conceptions of "owning" a woman, but the ultimate ownership does not come from a singular use of force. It is the application of a dominating presence in perpetuity, even after she has willingly opened her submissive side in the deepest of emotional ways.

Trust

Trust in the lynchpin of any serious relationship. A dominant man wants to train a submissive woman in endlessly self-satisfying ways, yet he must gain her serious trust in order to gain her constant surrender. People trust their partners only when they assess that there is a little or no risk of rejection or betrayal involved in getting closer to him or her. Trust happens over time and the nature of it is different for every couple. Fundamental ways of establishing it include:

1. Be consistent over time. Do what you say you are going to do. Discipline her accordingly when she is disobedient. Reward her when she deserves it. Don't drastically alter the way you do things without proper communication. A woman will develop trust based on the faith she has in a man's show of love, his emotional closeness, and his demonstration of character. If she thinks a man is just putting on a show in order to get what he wants, she will become less willing to commit herself to deeper submission.

2. Be there for her in a time of real need. If she is sick, take care of her. If she is having family problems, be there to help her solve them. If she is having issues at work, help her resolve them. If she has some kind of emotional crisis, lead her through it or get her adequate counseling. Show her that you'll be there for her no matter what. Make her understand that you want more than just kinky sex.

3. Listen to her. Discuss her past personal history and ask for her side of the story following confrontational situations. Finding out her fears can go a long way toward recognizing when a man's actions or words trigger those fears and cause her to lash out or distance herself. Ask her to reveal only what she feels comfortable revealing. A woman who has been hurt in the past may still have her guard up and choose not to tell her whole story to you immediately for fear of risking vulnerability. Secondly, the emotional patterns people develop in childhood typically resurface throughout their lives. Analyze her emotional patterns as well as your own. Learn to recognize each other's emotional makeup and work with it. Lastly, ask her about her most deviant sexual fantasies. Try to understand the emotions that are behind them. Show her that you are willing to try things that you might not have been previously willing to try.

4. Be honest. Don't try to be someone who you are not or trick her into thinking a relationship is going to be something that it isn't. It's vital to establish a pattern of honesty with a woman, even with the smaller things. If she finds out that you lied about where you went with your friends after work or where you were when she couldn't get a hold of you, she might wonder what else you're hiding from her. Open communication is essential. If she has been hurt in the past, she will already be judging the risk of growing closer to you on a regular basis. Be forthcoming with everything and show her that your intentions are transparent. Demonstrate that you're honest, open and loving instead of judgmental or closed-minded.

5. Reveal yourself to her. Tell her about your own past traumas and about your deeper reasons for wanting a D/s relationship. If you show that you trust her with your private thoughts and feelings, she will learn to trust you with hers. Open up your world to her. Get to know each other on a level of friendship. Evaluate when it is appropriate to push for greater intimacy and make it happen. In a D/s connection, the man is often approaching things with aggressive urges that are tied up with his own interactions with the larger world. The woman is often approaching things as a loving fighter or survivor who will push a man away with her full force until she feels like she can trust him in an irrevocable way.

6. Show her your desire and appreciation for her. Tell her how good she looks and how much she turns you on. Give her genuine compliments when she does something which you feel deserves sincere recognition. Thank her when she goes out of her way to do something special for you. Be grateful for her sacrifice.

Difficulties, Downsides and Disconnections

Any Dominant/submissive relationship comes with the same challenges and difficulties of any relationship. The particular emotional and sexual potency, though, of controlling a woman and her submitting to being controlled often triggers particular problems that specifically relate to this intense exchange of power. A few of these include:

1. The woman who looks for a man to solve her issues. Many submissive woman have complicated personal histories of dramatic upbringings or traumatic past experiences. Sometimes, a woman seeks a man who she envisions as the solution to all her psychological issues and unresolved personal conflicts. She believes that if she just surrenders herself totally to a man, he will tell her what to do, love her for who she is, solve her problems and everything will be alright. While Dominant/submissive couples can compliment each other's deep needs and desires, it is never a solution for dealing with one's own mental health. If a woman has serious psychological issues that she knows that she is dealing with, it is in her best interest, and in the interest of any man she is dating, to seek proper therapy.

2. The man who wants instant submission. The impulse to dominate and control can be misinterpreted in endless ways. A man might think he is "Alpha" so any woman who wants what he's got should understand that she should do what she's told from the first moment. Most of the time, these men have psychological issues of their own such as low self-esteem, a need to control what they can't control in their own lives or very simple-minded ideas of domination that center around physical force. While it is certainly in the realm of real possibility that a woman can be made to submit in certain ways from the first second they meet, when the connection feels uncomfortably forced, a woman should just walk away without a second thought.

3. The woman who is looking too hard to be in a relationship. Some women, both in the BDSM world and in the vanilla world, feel like they need to be in a relationship or they will be viewed by their peers and society as unwanted or undesirable. Just as women get married just to be married, there are women who want a "Dom" or master or owner so badly that they get involved with men who are not right for them for the long term. A woman should follow Socrates advice to "know thyself" before she commits her life to another person. She should focus on meeting the man for her and not get entangled in chasing the relationship fantasies in her mind.

4. *The sheer amount of time and energy required in a D/s relationship.* Dominating a woman and submitting to a man can involve an incredible commitment on many levels. Gaining a woman's trust can involve many months of dating, romantic entanglements and intense disciplinary sessions. Submitting to man's control can involve changing major aspects of a woman's life. Enforcing a simple rule can result in triggering serious emotional drama. One should be aware that a relationship should be more about pleasure and happiness than about unnecessary drama and endless fights. Although there's nothing like angry sex, a relationship shouldn't require never-ending argument for simple things to be communicated.

5. *The miscommunication of what dominance and submission means to each person.* Everyone has a different idea of what dominating, being dominating, submitting and being made to submit means. Don't be eager to assume that the other person is looking for exactly what you are looking for. Put yourself in the other person's shoes, ask yourself what they are really seeking and be honest with your expectations for what the Dominant/submissive dynamic is going to bring to your life.

The Road to Ownership

Each man's and each woman's road to sincere ownership has its own unique twists and turns. Each person has their own level of comfort as far as how fast things move and how committed they are to a serious dynamic. A Dominant/submissive relationship should evolve like in other relationship. Things grow more intimate. People are more honest and forthright about their fears and insecurities. The newness of early sexual trysts begins to be replaced with the slower rhythms of a serious relationship. The man discovers aspects of the woman that he did not see during early encounters, and vice versa. They talk about a future together as they try and envision their separate lives as one life.

The most important aspect of moving forward to a greater commitment to each other is that it feels natural. A man should not look to own the woman he is with simply because he wants to own a woman. And a woman should not look to be owned simply to satisfy her basic needs and desires to be an owned woman. Greater dominance over a woman and greater submission to a man should happen organically. He takes greater control, institutes more rules, makes greater demands, asks for deeper trust, and he gives more of himself all along the way. She learns to let go, to abide by his rules, to meet his expectations, to seek his approval and to surrender more and more of herself. She has a greater desire to give and not take, to serve and not demand and to trust and not fear.

The second most important aspect of moving forward is keeping things kinky and spontaneous. A Dominant/submissive dynamic is always infused with a heavy amount of eroticism and that is a good thing. Sex *is* holy and a couple should never let their sensual connection become boring and repetitive. There are endless ways of training a woman how to sexually gratify him and there are always fresh ideas for deviance anywhere one looks.

Ownership is...

———

"I can't stop thinking about him all the time. I ask myself -- What would he do? Would he think I look good in this? Am I doing what I know I should be doing? Should I text him and ask him? How can I surprise him tonight? Am I thinking about him too much? Am I becoming too clingy? Does he want more personal space? I need to just ask him. He'll make it clear. He's always bluntly honest with what he wants. He won't tell me something just to control me. I can trust him. God, I'm really horny right now. I should text him a naughty photo so

he'll be completely aroused when he gets home. Maybe he'll make me do something really perverse."

———

"I said keep it tight"
"Fuck you. It is tight."
A slap across the face.
"I'll tell you when your cunt is tight enough for me. Spread your legs wider."
"Why?"
"Because I'm going to spank your pussy. Hard."
Thighs slowly spread.
"Wider. As far as they will go."
Legs taut. He slaps his fingers quickly against her bare, wet cunt. She flinches. He spanks it again. And then again. A flinch and another flinch. She gasps at the acute pain.
"Keep it tight."
"I am."
Raised eyebrows, gives her a stern look.
"Yes, Sir. I'll keep it very tight."
"Like a good slut?"
"Like the best slut."
Smiles.

———

"The first time I casually said something to him like 'You can...' and he smiled at me and said 'Thank you, I know what I can do' and I realized.... Oh, God, he can do anything, because I belong to him, and I realized I could no longer imagine when he didn't have that level of control over me."

———

"I'm going to speak to your ballet teacher and if she mentions the slightest thing about your attitude, just plan on being put on cane

reminder for the rest of the week. That means twenty strokes nightly, bare-bottomed, on your tippy toes for the full twenty, while you recite your optimist mantras. Is that understood?"

———

"I gave up everything I owned. Every piece of furniture, all of my clothing, memorabilia, things I'd made over the years, all of it. Thirty some years of accumulated life. All I got to keep was my laptop with family photos and my dog. It had a hugely stripping down effect on me. A bit wrenching, but in a way, kind of freeing too, in that it left me feeling hugely exposed and vulnerable, and in a way, more open to entering his life completely on his terms."

———

"She always had to be on top of everything at work. A part of her thrived in being in control, in managing others beneath her and in the pride getting things accomplished ... At home, she didn't want to have the slightest urge to think about telling anyone what to do about anything. If he told her to strip down and put on a little apron, she just acted. There was no thought about why she should put in on. She just put it on."

———

"I was always submissive to him, but over time I started calling him Master every once in a while (sometimes just joking with him). When we moved in together I started serving him all the time, and making an effort to please him. Soon after that I considered myself owned by him. We eventually started talking about collars, and then he got me one. I know there were moments when I thought all I wanted was to take care of him, and to be his and to make him proud, but I can't put a specific time to them. I think I just grew into the role as we grew closer in our relationship."

———

"I found something online," he tells her.

"What's that?"

"Antique wooden stocks for sale. Like the Puritans used to punish naughty women. Hands and neck restrained in thick pieces of wood."

She looks at him, bites her lip and doesn't know why the image is already turning her on.

————

"A cumulative realization that I was bending all of my decisions based on what would make him happy/not mad...When I started seeing patterns/rituals/chores that I was doing to please him before he could ask. When I started asking periodically if there was anything I could do or get him. When I made choices based on his schedule/preferences."

————

"We were having a rather heated disagreement and I opened the door to walk out, keys in hand and he quietly said, 'Turn around and sit. We are not done here.' And I did."

————

"I wanted a hair cut and it dawned on me that I no longer had the right to make that choice on my own anymore. Prior to that, I would ask permission out of respect for our D/s dynamic, but I still felt like my body belonged to me and I could technically do as a chose. One day, I all of a sudden realized that my body just wasn't my property anymore."

————

"The dynamic for us, is organic. I grow, I feel independent, and then something will happen and I realize, that even as I work hard and do well, I am still owned, still taken. Just as romantic relationships are *about falling in love over and over...so, for me, D/s relationships are about realizing you are owned over and over."*

Case Study 5.1

"Natural Born Slave"

Matthew and Rebecca

Matthew: By the time we met, Rebecca and I each had Homeric histories of relationships that just never made it across the threshold to the place we really wanted to be in a lifelong union. She would invariably let the affair go on too long in hopes that he would change for her. I would cut them all off at the earliest moment I sensed any kind of weak commitment towards a substantial kinship of love and a desire for having a family.

We came from such disparate backgrounds that no one would have ever envisioned us coming together. She was from a well-to-do old Philly family and sent to the finest schools. I was practically born in the Pittsburgh gutters and had to fight for everything I ever got in life. It forced me from an early age to not bother with trivial matters and focus my energy on what was absolutely essential to survive and thrive. I've learned that training one's own mind to not become distracted and cultivate a Spartan-like calm under pressure is paramount to getting what one truly wants in this world.

I've been dominant in all my relationships and I've always preferred to be with submissive-leaning woman on a very simple, but deep level. Over time, my preferences have only gotten more extreme. Generally, I call the relationship as one of master and slave, but the words really don't really matter. It's about unconditional power and complete surrender working beautifully together. It's about the need for defined personal identities, about making her your women in bed and in life, and about being that man who does what he says he's going to do in an undeniably strong, consistent way. Some people just need absolutes and I'm one of them.

It's the same with most of the heavily submissive women I've been with who have a borderline slave mentality. It's almost like they have a religious mindset. They need that overriding order and structure on a very deep psychological level. For some, I think it's often because something bad happened to them when they were younger. For others, I think their minds just can't find an easy balance with the big, bad confusing world. It's too much for them and they need to have a stronger grounding force to order and guide them. They want a man who they can surrender to completely for the long haul of life. They want a man who totally values their deep commitment to him. They want to give so much of themselves that they envision their life purpose is almost wholly derived from how happy they make him.

Rebecca's personality is one of hyperactive sensitivity to the world. I can only imagine how she experiences reality to be honest. She tells me that she has memories so vivid that she can practically taste them. A doctor suggested she might have what's called synesthesia, a condition that causes senses that aren't normally connected to merge together. It is her gift and has always guided her to pursue artistic studies and creative work. The only downside is that sometimes gets such sensory overload that she just shuts down. Her mode of being has naturally become intertwined in our relationship as I act as the terra firma to her turbulent storm of emotions.

My senses are just senses to me, and I would have never been able to survive in my work life if they had gotten overloaded. Just out of high school I had gotten a job as a drill rig operator in the oil fields in the Marcellus shale. It was tough work, but satisfying, though the boom and bust cycle sent the company into bankruptcy. I decided to entirely shift gears and I enrolled in the police academy. I was barely out in the ranks though when I got offered a management position by another oil company run by my old boss. I was to oversee security services in their exploration division abroad and I immediately took it. The position sent me all over the world to countries like Nigeria and Libya.

It was in Libya that I met up with an outfit that did private military services in dangerous places such as where I was working. The work paid extremely well so I took a job with them and spent several years on assignments that were akin to near warfare operations. There was one incident in which there was an attack on one of the oil fields we were hired to guard and had a co-worker friend right next to me get shot multiple times. He ended up dying and it completely threw my view of life into a new light. The company had a Marine-like mentality of leaving no man behind and I came out of it understanding how absolutely vital it is to be able to trust the person next to you. I'm sure I brought that mentality with me into my personal relationships. I couldn't not have.

In any case, when I returned to the States, all I was thinking about was settling down. Many of my past relationships had ended because of the long-distance strain on them. I couldn't make any real demands on my significant other when I wasn't there to cultivate the bond. The women would be attracted to my dominating nature and my inclinations toward rough kinky sex, but I just wasn't able to be there when they needed me to be so I would cut it off. When I started dating again, I knew what I wanted and didn't want. I must have gone on dozens of dates and had hired multiple matchmaking agencies. None of them worked out and I was on the point of giving up when I met Rebecca completely by chance at a birthday party for an old friend. Life's strange like that. One finds what one wants when you aren't even searching for it sometimes.

With Rebecca, she thrives on the feeling and knowledge that she is my possession. Her disposition was already oriented toward being submissive and she had had relationships with several dominant men. None of them had worked out she told me because she felt like they we're not able to properly fill the dominant role or because they had difficulties controlling their own lives. She also had been deeply hurt by one of them who lied to for a long time about all sorts of things without her knowing it. This made her very wary of getting emotionally involved with me at the outset.

When we met, though, we bonded immediately. She loved my adventurous background and how I was bluntly honest about what I wanted in a relationship. I was intrigued by her wild artistic spirit and how astonishingly perceptive she was. She can read people's personalities so well and so instantaneously upon meeting them, it feels as if she is a kind of bona fide psychic. It is uncanny, and for some reason very arousing. Her passion is in painting but she had been forced to take a number of unsatisfying jobs for years now. She was ready to get out of that situation.

Our first real date was a short road trip to this beautiful state park a couple hours from Philly. It was in the middle of summer and hot. We were flirting with each other the whole ride there and by the time we were on the hike, I was ready to devour her. She was wearing these tight light gray hiking shorts that revealed more and more of her cheeks the harder the trail got. I made her walk in front and slapped her ass every time she slowed down. Eventually we ended up going off the trail to a cluster of rocks and I just started stripping off her clothes. She didn't resist in the least. I bent her naked body over a huge sandstone boulder and tied her hands behind her back with a piece of climbing rope. I had my way with her for nearly the whole afternoon, only resting for water and lunch. Our chemistry was absolutely magnetic.

I had had previous submissive women in my life, but with her, I took it to a whole 'nother level. When I told her I was going to make her my slave, she just smiled and asked me if I was going to lock in her chains. There was really a very short period of getting to know each other. We were both ready for total commitment and we just happened to meet at the right time. It was more about making sure that we could trust in each other in the way that we wanted to trust in each other.

We went out for a couple of months and quickly realized we were into many of the same things. We liked the same music, had similar views on family and liked to spend quality time at home just lounging round or working on projects. Plus, she loved to sexually please– blow jobs while I was driving, riding me on the back porch in the evenings, begging me to fuck her first thing in the morning…. I couldn't resist pleasing her in return. She adored my ferocious lickjobs while I held her above me against the wall and when I took her out wearing only a collar and a plunging v-neck dress to show her off before I manhandled her in some dark nook of the city.

At the beginning, she was working at random jobs while trying to focus on her painting. I had started my own consulting company after I left my previous position abroad. We had already started to see each other every day and had discussed moving in together with a full D/s dynamic in mind. I spoke with her and told her that she should quit her job and paint full time. She could help me manage my home life and I would begin to train her as my slave. We talked a bit about expectations and limits, but it was a fairly short talk. We both wanted the same thing and we were undeniably attracted to each other. There was no doubt that we were making our real intentions very transparent. We had both reached a certain level of maturity and we knew what we wanted for the long-term.

As soon as she moved in, I created a very strict schedule for her along with a list of household rules. I have a three-bedroom house and each room has its place. There is the master bedroom for me, the slave quarters for Rebecca and the studio room where she paints. I have always had a hard time sleeping and I didn't want someone else's nighttime quirks to aggravate the problem. Rebecca sleeps in a separate room, though we often pass out together after intense nights of kinky sex. Otherwise, she is always required to go to bed after I do and wake up before me. Some mornings I like to be woken up with a fresh cup of coffee in her hands. Other times I like to be woken up with my cock in her mouth. Occasionally, I like her to surprise me in her own way. Sometimes this means whispering dirty thoughts in my ear to wake me or sliding on top of me to give me a morning fuck.

She is generally required to be naked while at home. She sleeps naked, cooks naked, paints naked, sits next to me naked while we watch TV and, apart from when visitors come over, does everything else completely stripped bare. I like a slave who knows her place. When she is out doing errands such as grocery shopping, she is required to dress 1950's style. It was something that she had introduced to me and I liked it. She generally wears cute dresses that fit tightly to her waist and sexy high-heeled shoes, but her wardrobe has grown to be quite elaborate. When she goes out with me for business purposes, she generally dresses in something similar. When we go out to dinner or to an event, usually she is usually expected to be very scantily clad is something tight or revealing.

I rarely have to discipline her. She is such an avid pleaser that she goes to incredibly lengths to make sure that things get done the way I like them to get done. Occasionally, if she repeats a mistake such as not returning calls she is supposed to return or forgetting to finish her to do list, I will scold her. The punishment for her is more about disappointing me and not meeting my expectations. Afterward, she will get gloomy and try to sulk about it, and I'll have to chastise her to put her smile back on and get back to work at the painting. She loves the fact that while I am gone most of the day at my office, she is pretty much entirely free to do her artwork.

She has really got into the whole 1950's lifestyle thing as well. She loves to bake like crazy and she has even put together a whole cookbook of my favorite dishes. When I get home, she is expected to have put down her brush, be fresh-out-of-the-shower clean and have a welcoming drink waiting for me. She really seems to have boundless energy a lot of the time. I don't know how I would ever be so motivated at work and in life without her. I'm usually exhausted after working all day but she thrives on the time we have together in the evenings and on the weekends. She's always searching for new movies that I might like or finding music I might be into. Although she is my slave, I really do feel like she's my better half sometimes.

The trust we've developed between us has just happened over time. The more she tries to please me, the more I appreciate her for how she's learned to understand how I tick, and vice versa. We have occasional disagreements but it is usually over minor things. She understands the deep reasons for why I like order in my life and how I can be a total control freak. She accepts my dominance wholeheartedly as it allows her to let go of her hypersensitive thoughts that would previously cause her to mentally shut down at times.

She sometimes needs to be reassured of her incredible worth. Every now and again she will get down on herself because her negative thoughts will still start to create a world of their own. She'll get anxiety attacks or stressed about something insignificant or will simply feel like she isn't attractive enough. I make sure to watch out for her change in mood and when I see it, I'll sit her down to talk to her. I'll reassure her in every way I can and remind her that I am there for her no matter what and will always be. That always brings her back to a state of calm and keeps her centered.

The balance we have in our relationship is very clear and neither one of us has ever done anything that would cause mistrust. We tell each other everything and we like it that way. We're at that point in which we're more than ready to start a family. I'll come up behind her while she is cooking away in the kitchen stark naked as usual and whisper in her ear all kinds of thoughts about "breeding" her. It gets her so wet and I always end up fucking her every which way all over the kitchen. It will be the one thing I will miss when we do have children. I guess we'll have to find a larger house with a nice soundproof basement that I can turn into her slave quarters.

Case Study 5.2

"The Bull of all Bulls"

Xavier and Elizabeth

Elizabeth: First off, before I detail the intimate pornographic details of our liaisons, I want to preface this personal account with just a few words about myself. I'm not a submissive female in the least bit when it comes down to who I really am as a woman. In fact, most of my relationships have been of the Femdom flavor and I've been ruthlessly dominant in my career ambitions. I've worn the pants in my private and public life proudly. That being said, life has a way of taking you on its own hairpin turns and I've always been open to the unexpected. But I never expected someone like Xavier. Never.

Sometimes I think that he is an entirely different species of man. He is a bull among bulls and utterly enigmatic at his core. I'd like to say that I have some say in him owning me, but I really do not. I could say no at any time but I do not want to and it wouldn't even matter. My mind and my body completely betray me when he wants to have me. I never thought I would be in such a relationship with anyone like the one I am in with him. It's on all counts outside any norm of anything that would be considered a regular affair. I mean it's not even monogamous. He's owned me through three different boyfriends and he'll go on owning me as long as wants to. And I wouldn't want it any other way. He releases something in me. It lets me go to a space inside myself that only I know about. He invigorates me on whole 'nother plane of physicality and consciousness.

The stark irony, like I mentioned, is that I was never the kind of woman who sought out anybody remotely like him. Friends have always told me how on top of things I always am. They say I am so put-together, so feisty and so opinionated. I mean I'm a criminal defense attorney and I'm use to getting my way both inside and outside of the courtroom. I'm not the sweet, shy submissive type at all.

I met Xavier through a mutual friend at a party. My first instinct was that he already had been with that friend and I wanted no part of it. But it didn't matter. When we started conversing, there were fireworks in all directions. Some of them were the beautiful kind that burst in eloquent explosion in the sky, but other were they kind that ignite in the warehouse and burn the whole place down.

Xavier is built like an Ancient Greek warrior. He towers over me. His broad chest and hefty legs are statuesque. He is overwhelmingly on a physical level just to be in front of in conversation. I thought he might even be military by the look of his tightly cropped hair and the scar on his temple of his head but he wasn't. His black suit and white dress shirt gave him an air of aristocracy but he wasn't of that ilk either. In addition, I swear when I met him I could make out the contours of his enormous cock even beneath his pants. I expected him to be a dull brute of a man on the intellectual side but it was entirely the opposite.

From the very first words, he casually interrogated me like the most curious person on earth. He wanted to know absolutely everything about me from what I did to what I was like when I was growing up in Brooklyn to why I preferred Brahms over Tchaikovsky to who put the chip on my shoulder. It was like I was suddenly the center of his world. Yet, even in the midst of his swarming interest in my life, there was always a slight feeling of detachment in his tone. This drove me wild. It gave me the feeling that he was wholeheartedly into me, yet there was this space that I didn't quite cross that led into a territory of being authentically impressed and aroused. It was almost a veneer of arrogance but more that he was simply envisioning something that transcended random casual exchanges.

I was so intrigued by him but I barely managed to extract even a semblance of his origins and his true character and any details from his work life. He told me much more later on, but that night I can only recall fragments...born in Croatia...mother was a war refugee who had immigrated to East Texas of all places...vague business dealings in California and an investment in a cyber security firm that left him free to enjoy life for a bit of time...

I could barely make sense of it all and the cocktails only made it more enigmatically riveting.

After passing half the evening in discussion and fierce debate, there was a sudden lull. I was nearly exhausted from the conversation. He stopped speaking and simply eyed me. He remarked how elegantly restrained my hair was. I believe I had it pulled back tightly and clasped in a silver clip. I don't remember exactly. What I do remember is that he next asked me if I was ready to go.

"Ready to go?" I replied with an arched eyebrow.

"Yes," he said. "Are you ready to go?"

"Ready to go where?" I responded quizzically.

His eyes shifted away and then turned directly at mine. It was as if he was incredibly eager to ravage me on the spot but at the same moment content with whatever came of our war of words.

"Yes or no?" he calmly asked me, delicately wrapping the tips of his fingers around my waist.

Suddenly, any expectations of flirtatious small talk and romantic negotiations had been consciously brushed aside. With any other man, I would have instantly turned him down or at the very least been much more combative or questioning of his true motives. But he put me in a kind of emotional trance and his physicality entirely took over me.

"Why don't I just give you my number?" I asked him, as if I were the voice of reason itself.

He just stared straight at me with a look of utter calm and confidence.

"Yes? Or no?" he repeated in a slow thick voice.

I'd never met a man who I felt was uncontrollably attracted to me but at the same time make me feel like he could just walk away and never wonder about seeing me again. It was infuriating. I fidgeted and stamped my feet.

"Fuck you," I burst out.

"What?' he replied in confusion.

"Yes," I said in a kind of highly aroused daze. "Yes," I said again as if I were confirming an appointment.

We were out the door and in a taxi before I even came to my senses. He had given the driver an address in SoHo which I assumed was his place.

"You do this often don't you?" I asked him.

He glanced over at me and wrapped his hand around my ponytailed hair.

"No," he said. "I rarely do anything often. Do you?"

"No. I mean I don't at all. In fact to be honest, I just started seeing someone," I confessed.

He nodded slowly up and down as if that was an insignificant fact. He wrapped his hand around my head and turned it toward him. His grip felt colossal. He lowered his mouth to me and kissed me.

"Are you going to tell him how roughly I manhandled you tonight?" he asked, utterly cocksure.

His words outraged me and I suddenly felt a pang of guilt.

"I don't know," I replied in a fluster of emotion.

I watched as he reached across me and took my purse from my side. Before I could ask him what he was doing, he casually unzipped it and then leaned to whisper into my ear.

"Pull your panties off and put them in your purse. I want that cheating little cunt of yours bare for me."

No one had ever spoken to me like that and gotten away with it. I laughed in disbelief and turned away to look out the window for a moment, but he firmly gripped me by my hair and turned my head to face his. The taxi had stopped and I realized that we were already at his place. He slid his other hand up my dress and took a hold of my underwear. I tightened my thighs around his hand but he just stared at me. My mind was somewhere between nervously panicked and inexplicably aroused. He firmed up his grip. The cab driver glanced back at us, waiting for us to get out. I asked myself for a moment what the hell I was doing, but my body was saying something else.

"Alright, alright," I told Xavier.

I slid my hands up my dress and pulled them off for him. I slipped them in my purse and zipped it closed. We got out and he took me by to the hand, leading me into his loft building. He glanced at me with a smirk on his face.

"What? What's so damn funny? I asked him.

"You should have seen that look on your face when I told you how I wanted your cheating little cunt," he chided me. "You sure do get easily rattled for being such a badass prosecutor."

"I should slap the shit out of you," I replied in a rage.

We were already at his door and he swiftly pulled me inside.

"Go ahead," he tempted me, sliding his one hand around my ass and pointing with his other hand to his face. "Go ahead and slap me."

Without a second thought, I whipped my palm across his cheek. He grinned. It had hardly budged him. I slapped him again and again and again. His face reddened from the flush of blood, but it was like trying to hurt a stone monument. When I went for him again with my full force, he blocked my hand and whorled me down to his feet. I suddenly felt myself being dragged across his hardwood floor by my hair and then picked up and flung onto his bed.

I looked up at him as he was beginning to undress. It was as if I was a piece of war booty trying to sort out her romantic allegiances for her own survival. I glanced around to get my bearings. His expansive loft was virtually barren, apart from a few pieces of artwork on the walls and an enormous shelf of books. When I turned back toward him my eyes adjusted to the sight of his massive phallus. It was like staring at a mythical satyr.

"My God," I pleaded deliriously, "I can't take that inside of me."

Xavier just grinned slyly, basking in all his naked largesse as he swaggered toward me.

"Take off your dress."

Before I could even respond, he reached down and grabbed a hold of my ankle and dragged me across the bed, turning me over and putting me on my hands and knees. He pulled down the zipper on the back of my dress and it was swiftly slipped off my body and tossed to the side. I felt his heavy thighs press against my ass. He grabbed a hold of my hand, pulled it through my legs and wrapped it around his thick shaft. I couldn't even get my fingers all the way around its girth.

"Stroke it nice and slow, then slide it in deep," he calmly ordered me.

I glanced back at him over my shoulder. His muscular torso cast a shadow over me.

"Don't you have protection?" I asked insistently.

"No. I only fuck bareback. I'm absolutely clean," he brazenly told me. "And I can tell you are too."

Before I had a second to respond, he slapped my ass firmly and pulled my thighs wider apart.

"Get it wet and stroke it hard, or I'll bulldoze you to the hilt right away."

No one had ever uttered such words to me. I felt engulfed by his physical authority and it made me so inexplicably angry and horny at the same time.

I gripped his huge cock and ran the head of it up and down between my legs and across my clit.

"Oh, my God," I moaned.

I was absolutely soaked and pushed back against his thighs while pulling his full length along my cunt until it was just as wet. It was so long the tip of it nearly touched my breasts. I took hold of it with both hands and swirled them around it vigorously, moving them all the way from its tip to its base over and over and over, and then reaching back deeper to fondle his huge hanging balls.

"That's it, Elizabeth baby. I'm going to make a size queen out of you before it's all said and done."

I honestly could have stroked it and grinded it against it for hours. I couldn't get enough of it. It felt as if I was with some preternatural animal. He glided his fingers along the curves of my body, sending shivers through me. He took hold of my hair, wrapping it around his wrist, and with his other hand deftly fondled my clit until I started to moan. I felt one of his fingers push into me. And then another. I stroked him like a jackhammer as he slide one more into me, stretching me wider and wider, then teasing my g-spot until I started to uncontrollably squirm.

He pulled back and pressed the tip of it into me. I clinched up.

"Slide it in deep," he commanded me.

"There's no way," I pleaded.

"Relax, baby. Breathe deep and just let yourself go."

He pushed the head in and out, in and out, until I reached back and took a hold of it again. I pushed myself back toward him, my breath heaving in and out, as he eased himself in and out of me deeper and deeper. I was stretched to the extreme and he made a slow thrust even deeper into me. I let out a birthing-like moan and jerked forward. He tugged me back by my hair.

"Right here," he told me, taking a grip of the base of his cock. "You can take it to right here. I'll have to break you all the way in over time."

145

It was as if I had no say in the matter and he knew that I was aware he was giving me no say. I eyed him and his hand around his thick phallus for a moment but he forcefully pulled me toward him and slid himself back inside of me until I felt the back of my thighs touch his hand. I left out a sigh of relief that he had filled me just to the brim.

It felt like days and nights passed as he pulled me toward him over and over with a forceful grip of my hair as if I were just a human rag doll. When he wanted me to thrust harder against him he would twist my hair tighter around his wrist and tug me back and forth. I felt my cunt strike against his hand again and again. I couldn't even imagine taking his full cock inside of me.

The slaps against my ass stung and I moaned loader and louder as he kept pounding himself deep into me. Just as I was about to climax, he pulled out.

"Oh, God no. Please don't stop," I pleaded.

He slipped his fingers into me and glided them acutely across my g-spot, sending shivers of pleasure through me.

"Beg that God for it," he enjoined me.

He kept on sliding his thick fingers inside me, slowly skimming them so perfectly across my erogenous interiors.

A vibrating jolt ran through my entire body.

"God, please. Please finish me off," I begged.

He slipped his fingers out of me and ran them delicately around the insides of my thighs and softly between my legs.

"Beg harder," he told me. "Beg like a slut. Beg for me to fill you up."

I pushed my ass against his thighs and squirmed in agony. I was delirious. I felt his fingers slide back into me.

"God, please. I'll do anything you want," I implored. "Just please fill this naughty slut up."

His curled-up fingers ran faster and faster into me and I began to moan in a craze of pleasure. Just as I was veering toward a climax once again, he suddenly plunged his thick cock deep inside of me. I gasped and then bawled out a flurry of curses and grunts and sighs.

He pulled both my hands behind my back and began to pound me over and over and over, stretching me out and filling me up with more cock than I have ever taken. I wailed in orgasm but he did not stop for a moment, nor did he stop for many, many more moments as he had his way with my body for several more orgasms, and not even stopping when his gush of warm cum pulsed into me, and only easing up to a decrescendo of shallower moans and thrusts until finally my body went limp in his hands.

It was early in the morning when I awoke and came to my senses. It was barely dawn and the previous night was still a whirl of snapshots in my mind and confused emotions. I woke him up and told him that I needed to go. He told me to write my number done on the pad next to his bed. I couldn't believe I was even giving my number to a man after I had slept with him. I kissed him on the cheek and went to slip out the door.

"Wait. Come back here," he implored.

I stutter-stepped back to his bed.

"Kneel down for a second," he said.

I absentmindedly bent myself to him.

"You were utterly beautiful last night," he told me. "Really. So open," he went on, glancing up at me with his tired eyes from the bed. "Open heart. Open cunt. Open mind," he went on. "That was something rare."

I didn't know what to say. I was spellbound but also just wanted to just get out of there and regain my senses.

Afterward, I felt so terribly dirty and guilty for what happened, despite the mind-altering pleasure of the sex. I told myself and I assumed on his part that this was a one-time thing that would never happen again. I didn't tell a word of it to my new boyfriend. How could I? It was so unlike me to do anything like what I had done, much less doing it when I was involved with someone else.

But as the days passed, the slow realization came over me that I would never be the same person sexually after that night. It was not simply that it was that pleasurable. It was

Xavier. It was what he did with my body and my mind simultaneously. He unleashed this primal urge in me that no one else has or no one else probably ever will. He's physically so unbelievably endowed, yet every man I had ever met along those lines was just so unstimulating that I quickly grew bored with their bodies.

Not only that, I had been with a couple of men who had large cocks, but never one quite the size of Xavier's and never had I been with a man who knew how to work it into me so well. Usually, I longed for one that just fit perfectly with my anatomy, but I was so aroused by him that I wanted to feel wholly engorged by it and filled absolutely to the brim. It was animalistic. It was honestly like I had been taken into a dark forest of my unconsciousness and impaled by some kind of centaur.

I couldn't tell anyone about what had happened. I didn't want any of my friends to know how I just let him manhandle me and how completely I submitted to him like some slut. It was unlike me at all. Plus, like I mentioned, I had assumed it was only a one-night stand kind of a thing and I would simply go on living with my life as I had been doing before it happened.

Yet, I was just deluding myself. About a week later, Xavier sent me a message telling me he was taking me out to dinner that night. I wasn't even sure how to respond so I told him I already had plans with my boyfriend, which was actually true. He immediately messaged me back informing me that he wasn't asking me, that he was telling me. The nerve of this asshole, I thought at that instant, and then wished to myself that he really was just a typical male asshole who I could dismiss. He messaged me again with the name of the restaurant and the time, and then followed up with another that read: "So I'll see you then?"

I just shook my head in utter frustration. I couldn't see him again I told myself. Where was this even headed? Was I just some booty call to him or was he actually looking to get involved? I kept telling myself over and over that I couldn't do this. And then I cancelled my plans with my boyfriend and asked Xavier what I should wear.

"I'll send something over," he texted me back.

A few hours later, just as I was finishing up some work in my office, a pair of packages arrived. Inside one was an elegant red dress with a white ribbon design around the collar. I glanced at the label and wondered how he could possibly know my tastes that well. I locked my door and slipped it on. When I looked in the mirror, I suddenly felt as if he were dressing me like a gift to be unwrapped. I opened up the other package and my mouth dropped open. It was a clear glass anal plug. My first instinct was to text him and tell him there was no way I was going to wear that to meet him. But, a few words into the text I just dropped my phone back on my desk.

"I have no say," I said out loud. "He'll just bull through any protest I make. I have absolutely no fucking say." A laughed in delirious frustration and sat down for a moment to think about what was happening to me. I glanced down at the dress and then at the glass object. I was suddenly so damn horny. All of this felt so illicit. It was not that I was doing this behind my boyfriend's back. It was that I was cheating on myself. I was secretly being the naughty little slut that will do anything a man tells her to do.

"This isn't me," I uttered out loud once again. "This is some other me."

When I walked into the restaurant to meet Xavier, my body was tingling with arousal. I was still getting use to taking steps laden with that glass object plugged deep inside of me. I was utterly paranoid that I'd run into someone who knew me but at same time feeling like life was moving at a trillion beats a second.

Xavier greeted me in the most nonchalant manner, as if this was some casual business meeting.

"You look wonderful, Elizabeth. Our table is all ready. Right this way," he stated as he wrapped his arm around the small of my back and led me to my chair.

We fell directly into heavy conversation as if we were picking up where we had left off at the party where we had met. We rambled straight into anything and everything, from politics to our personal lives to the financial markets to my work situation, and on and on as we ate and drink the evening away.

"Oh, I wanted to ask you if read that article that was going around about the brain and the universe being structured in the same way," he suddenly inquired.

I had not read it but there was something about the question that took me back and made me once again wonder what this all was leading to.

"Wait, wait, wait," I stuttered. "I just need to know some things."

"Things?" he said.

"Yes. What the fuck is this? Who the hell are you? Is this supposed to be some kind of affair or what?" I demanded to know in a fury of emotion.

He grinned at my outburst.

"Listen Elizabeth, I don't want to deceive you in any way," he began. "But I do want to be absolutely forthright in how I feel about you."

"Which means?" I responded, still completely perplexed.

"You're an unbelievably rare woman. I've never met anyone who is so strong willed and yet so open to the private worlds beyond whole the social routine. I want to be with you in a way I've never wanted to be with any woman," he declared in a heartfelt flurry of persuasion.

My mind reeled and my pulse quickened.

"But I'm not the marrying type and you are a woman set to be the matriarch of your own family."

His matter-of-fact statement bathed me in a sea of confusion.

"What?" I said dumbfounded. "I'm not looking...we've only just met," I stuttered. "Why would you say such a crazy thing?"

"Like I said, I don't want to deceive you. I'm not trying to play you. I'm just not conventional or even normal in that way. Trust me. I was institutionalized as a child. I've served time in prison. My morals will break your heart and drive you mad."

I was trying to wrap my mind around all of this.

"But why talk of marriage?" I pressed him.

"Marriage, boyfriend girlfriend, life partner...whatever you want to call it. It is a foreign country to me. And you. You were born to lead all of your relationships. One day, you will be the dominating matron of the most beautiful family. It is what you want. Let's not deceive ourselves," he implored.

Xavier certainly knows how to lunge straight into the heaviest of considerations. I sat there for a moment and let his words sink in. He was right about what I wanted. It just never entered my mind that someone like him would get to me.

"So this is some kind of affair? A wild fling?"

"It is what it is."

"Which is?"

I watched him lean back in his chair for a moment to think and then lean toward me again.

"You don't feel what it is?" he questioned me.

"Feel?" I responded. I felt like I was speaking a foreign language.

"Listen, Elizabeth. I'm going to have you anytime I want to have you. There's nothing you can do about it. There's nothing I can do about it. You do things to me no one else does. And I take you to a place only you know about. And that will always be true unless you say no to me. Once you say no to me, it is over."

I could barely swallow. I could feel my eyes darting about. I didn't even know what I was trying to figure out. It was far from what I expected to hear him say.

The waiter passed by and he casually asked him for the check.

"Are you ready to go? I have a bottle of champagne at my place that I am going to drench your naked body with."

He smirked. I nearly burst into maniacal laughter.

"By the way," he added. "You do look stunning in that dress. Is it your taste?"

I guffawed in disbelief. I could hardly speak or think straight at that point.

"Yes. Yes it is," I muttered.

"And your body is primed for me?"

I couldn't even respond to this.

This was how things always transpired between us. Or I should say, this *is* how things always transpire between us. To this day.

Each time I met him, the further I was drawn into his world until the point came that I didn't even question his outrageously presumptive demands. There was never really a point that I didn't want to be part of his unyielding madness. I use to question myself over and over how this happened. The only acceptable answer I ever found was that my own dominating urges allowed me at the outset to recognize the sheer force of his. The fact that his body was naturally dominant beyond any other man I had ever met and that his mind fearlessly took things to such extremes made me accept his natural superiority over me in some terribly arousing way. He became the private dictator of my body and I never said no to anything he told me to do, even if he only wanted to meet for an afternoon of conversation.

At first, I tried to balance the relationship I had with my current boyfriend and my wild liaisons with Xavier, but the decently good sexual relations I had previously had with the boyfriend had been annihilated into sessions of downright sensual tedium. I ended things with him and stayed single for quite a while after that.

For weeks and weeks I pondered not only my personal vision of what I had expected a serious lifelong relationship to entail but also my very conception of relationships. I had grown up in a generation with a sense of renewed female empowerment and was naturally assertive from my earliest years. Practically every relationship I had had up to that time consisted of me being the stronger authority directing things in general and making the day-to-day decisions in particular. I had been, at times, overbearing and even controlling, but it is what I wanted. It is still how I want the dynamic in my serious relationships to be.

Yet, Xavier blew apart every notion I had assumed about monogamy. Not only had I never cheated on a single boyfriend in my life up until him, every vision I had of a future life with a husband was one of two individuals so deeply in love that it was the ultimate end-all and be-all of personal kinship. There was never a third person involved. Never. I couldn't even conceive how such a thing would even work.

For a time, I told myself that Xavier really didn't mean what he said about it not being possible for the two of us to be together as some regular couple. I deceived myself into believing that he would change or I would change him, but he was absolutely correct when he said it would just drive me mad. I don't want to delve into the particulars but there were several feuds and skirmishes between us that finally made me understand what he meant. I genuinely did want to be in charge of my man. It is not only who I am but it is also what makes me feel the most grounded in being with a man day-in and day-out. I love when a man realizes how much of an indomitable woman I truly am and just lets me take the reins.

My deep flaw in all of this is that I can't help but crave men who possess their own undeniable prowess in life or in character. I want a man of substance and strength who submits to me. My conundrum at that point was that Xavier's colossal sexual prowess was beyond any man I'd ever meet, yet his substance was the diametrical opposite of what I wanted from any man in a serious relationship.

The grand bestial expeditions with him were more than enough at that point to keep me satisfied despite all the nights I longed for someone to just cuddle with and be myself. It's not that he ruined me for any other man. It's just that each time I am with him is so intoxicating because he makes me feel like I am the absolute center of attention with his dominating ways. It is as if I am the only that exists when we're together. And he always takes things to the extreme in the most perverse manner.

After our initial fling, each rendezvous was another step further down the road to my one and only experience of total submission. We invariably would meet before we had any kind of sexual play, but his heavy-tongued conversation acted as such a potent aphrodisiac for me that by the time it came for him to have his way with me I was already soaked in arousal. He introduced me to cock worship without even making it a formal thing. There were nights that I just bobbed and licked and choked myself on his huge phallus until I was drenched in my own saliva like some pornographic freak. Sometimes, we would just by lying there watching TV and I was compelled to hold it in my hand, to stroke it, to suck it and to repeatedly test how far down my throat I could take it.

His sway on my mind unhinged any bodily resistance I might have had with anyone else. I was utterly pliable in his hands, whether he was clutching my neck, manhandling my ass or fingering every hole of my body until it was gapping open and begging to be filled.

I don't know how long it took, but his fingers worked themselves deeper and deeper into me over time and there was finally the day where I miraculously took his full cock into me. To this day, I'm still not sure if it was my body or my mind that was expanded to greater dimensions to take his entire prick. All I know is that with each crazed liaison, his words kept unraveling me, his fingers kept probing heavily into all my holes and my cunt kept salivating uncontrollably. When I unexpectedly felt the edge of his thick thighs touch against my own during one of our trysts, I heaved in a chaotic mixture of pleasure and pain. Then every fiber of my body let go in a kind of deliverance from physical tension and

Xavier deep-fucked me for hours and hours on end. I was his, and his, and all his.

As time has passed, I have been in and out of relationships, but I feel like where I am at now could possibly be something that truly lasts. When I first started to date again after I had met Xavier, I would never tell the guy about him. How could I possibly bring it up from the onset? I would simply become involved with a man like I always had and Xavier would remain this secret world that only the two of us ever knew about. Yet, the inevitable conflicts grew more and more difficult to handle.

First off, there were the times that he would text or call me to order me to meet him somewhere or to come over to his place. There were instances in which I would be with a boyfriend when this would happen and I would have to make up some lie that I needed to go take care of something at work. After Xavier would absolutely ravage me, I would come back home as if I was completely wrecked by the job demands when the truth was I was completely wrecked by Xavier. At times it was utterly thrilling to meet for one of our rabid interludes, but at other times the guilt became unbearable. I would just end up ending the relationship because I knew it could never work out right.

My second attempt at making my relationships work was when I would outright tell guys that I was already seeing someone on the side and had no intention of stopping. A few guys wanted no part of it but there were others who were intrigued by a woman who did such things. Yet, almost all of them would end up being of the cuckold disposition and got off on being humiliated by women. They would love to be emasculated in some way and then I would instantly lose interest in them. Even though I wanted my man to ultimately submit to my authority, I still wanted him to be a manly man about it.

Then I met Philip. He was the first man in years who I was authentically taken by from the very beginning. He is a commanding presence in his own right yet he yields to my bossy impulses after the initial combative struggle. He is an attorney as well but was born in England and had a rather privileged and eccentric lifestyle growing up. He is just my type, yet in the back of my mind I began the relationship once again assuming that Xavier would remain my clandestine freak of a lover.

Yet it was one night when I was out at a bar with Philip when that all changed. We were standing there with our drinks when another man blatantly started to hit on me right in front of him. I told the man I was taken and sent him off, but out of the blue Philip began to tell me how arousing it all was. I asked him if he was serious and he went on to tell me that watching another man flirt with his girlfriend had always been one of his biggest turn-ons. I acted a bit surprised and took a slow sip of my drink as I pondered what to say next.

"So what if it went beyond flirting?" I cautiously probed.

"You mean to you acting on it with someone else?" he asked me unequivocally.

"Yes."

"I would love it. I'm a pure bred stag when it comes to that," he confessed.

"When do you mean by stag?" I replied.

"I mean if it's something you're into, I would totally encourage you to be with other men," he said.

"But isn't a stag on the dominant side of things?" I asked in confusion.

"Well, yes. I guess you could say that. I mean I would want to have some control over the whole thing," he explained.

I thought about everything he was telling me for a moment.

"But what if you had no ultimate control over it?" I inquired.

"What do you mean?" he asked.

It was then that I just decided to tell him all about Xavier. Everything. He leaned against the bar a bit shocked that I had been seeing this man for years now but at the same time undeniably thrilled about it all.

"My God, woman. You certainly do like to have things your own special way don't you?"

I shook my head and laughed at the reality of it.

"I never expected it. It just happened."

There was a moment of silence between us.

"So when you say I would have no control over it you mean he always comes first?" he inquired.

"No, only physically," I replied. "I want to be with someone who I really do love completely and who I can be honest about all of it with. But he does own my body and I wouldn't want it any other way. He physically dominates me beyond anything you could ever do. Apart from that, I want a real man who understands where he fits in the scheme of my life."

Philip gave me a sharp look and then turned toward the bar with his drink. He pondered the idea for a couple of minutes and then lifted his drink and clinked it against mine.

"I think I'm game. I don't know what the hell I'm getting into, but I'm game," he roared in delirious declaration.

And that was how it all started. I explicitly tell him whenever I go to meet up with Xavier. It drives him wildly jealous but when I tell him the intimate details he gets astonishingly aroused. He actually loves to have sex with me while I whisper all the naughty things Xavier just did to me. At one point, he expressed interest in watching me in the act itself. I was really apprehensive about this but Xavier said he was fine with it. I tried to explain to him that Xavier wasn't at all like other men and that he should be ready for the unexpected, but he still wanted to go through with it.

It was about a week or so later on a quiet Sunday morning that there was a knock on the door. Philip and I were just about to eat breakfast, and I went to see who it was. It was Xavier, of course. He had stopped by without any notice. He was dressed in a casual suit. My heart skipped a beat. It was the first time that my two distinct, separate lives had come together.

I let him in and he immediately went up to Philip and calmly shook his hand like a perfect gentleman. Philip was taken aback by the sheer size of Xavier. It was like a professional linebacker had just come out of the dressing room and was now standing over the two of us. I only emphasize that fact as Philip is not a small man in the least and very well built in the normal scheme of bodies.

Xavier then simply reached down and took hold of my hand.

"Let's go," he uttered before leading into my bedroom as if this was all normal.

I looked back at Philip who was standing there a bit paralyzed. As Xavier took me into the room and started to undress me I looked over to see him standing at the doorway in guarded expectation.

"Sit down and watch," Xavier told him, motioning to an armchair in the corner of my room. He slipped into the chair apprehensively.

It was then that Xavier did what only he can do. He paced across the room and then stopped in front of Philip, his arms akimbo on his naked waist.

"I want things to be very clear. I don't want to get in the way in whatever you and Elizabeth have," he began. "I sincerely hope the two of you have something very special," he added in utter sincerity.

Philip glanced over at me, a bit mystified.

"But as far as Elizabeth is concerned, I own that naughty little cunt in ways you could never imagine. Day and night. Every waking hour for as long as I want it. It will never be denied to me. Is that clear?"

I could see Philip struggle to swallow. He was jolted by just how much of a wild bull he was in person.

"Yes, I think so," he affirmed.

Then Xavier turned back to me and began to freely manhandle my body. Philip was completely blown away with the rough way I let him treat me on top of the shock of seeing the sheer largesse of his cock. Yet, the whole time he was so turned on he was visibly hard beneath the running pants he was wearing. He restlessly ran his hand across his thigh and quietly watched him perform his Herculean sensual feats.

Xavier noticed me repeatedly glancing over at him and put his mouth to my ear.

"Tell him to take it out and stroke it," he told me. "And don't let me catch you looking away from me again or I'll take matters into my own hands."

His lifted his head up and his eyes locked onto mine. I knew not to test such a warning with him.

"Philip," I called out. "Take that cock of yours out and stroke it. I want you to savor every last thing he does to me."

Just as I noticed him pulling it out, Xavier grabbed me by the hair and fastened his heavy stare upon me. As he pushed deeper and deeper inside of me with greater vigor, I didn't dare look away from him. Ever so slowly I stopped being concerned with how Philip was taking it all and was drawn back into the heavy sexual bond that was always there with Xavier. I came to the point of climax and my senses were once again thrown every which way. For a few moments, my mind was so undone that I thought it was just the two of us there like it always had been.

When I came to my senses, I glanced over toward where Philip had been sitting. He had already orgasmed, left the room and was now standing at the doorway taking in the final moments.

Xavier quietly got dressed at the end of the bed and then went to leave. I watched as he stopped to say something to Philip.

"I can tell by how she looks at you that you're a very worthy man. Ironically, part of me wishes I could be you. But I can only be me," he lamented. Then he simply walked out the front door as simply as he had walked in.

After he left, Philip and I talked about everything. He told me he now unquestionably understood why I was so drawn to Xavier.

"I've never seen anything like him. I mean I was even turned on just watching his muscular buttocks clinch each time he pushed into you. It was like watching a heavyweight fighter in his prime," he said emphatically.

I was utterly relieved how smoothly it went and excited that he got so turned on just by watching. It meant that I could let go of any sense of guilt that I had previously carried with me when I would have to cheat on other men.

After that day, the whole triad of a relationship fell into its own rhythm. The vast majority of the time I will go off to be with Xavier on my own. He wants me for himself without any distractions. I always come home and tell Philip every detail as he repeatedly shakes his head in aroused disbelief. More importantly, we have our own vivacious sex life that is a nice mixture of provocative recountings of my wild flings and Philip's unique sexual bravado. He is a born pleaser and he licks me so damn well that I could sit on his face and smother him for days.

One night we were lingering at the dinner table when he said something that has stayed with me to this day.

"You know, Elizabeth, I should feel terribly humiliated. I should rant and hate myself for not being able to satisfy you the way he does. But I don't."

"And why don't you?" I sincerely wondered.

"That man....your man....your bull or however you want to call him, these moments are everything to him. He will never have the kind of life with a woman that he truly wants."

I mulled over the thought. There were half-truths on both sides. Philip's confidence in himself and in him being the man for me remains unaltered. He accepts Xavier's physical superiority and his claim on my body and mind, but I really have no idea if Xavier truly wants anything except exactly what he is getting. Yet, Philip knows that time is on his side. Like all human beings, Xavier's body and my body will eventually succumb to time and he will probably lose interest in his physical domination of me.

Yet, I am not in this life to simply grow old with someone else simply because we have a loving bond at this moment. For now, it is all working perfectly for the first time so I am basking in every second of it.

I have, though, grown much closer to Philip. He has persevered through so many obstacles in his own life before I ever met him and he always yields to my guidance. There is an inestimable worth he places in the belief that I know what is best for him. All we talk about, apart from the sexual escapades, is the future and the possibility of having a family and growing as we get older.

As far as Xavier, he has always been right about everything. He saw me as the loving matriarch before I ever met Philip. He still owns my body, and he probably always will up to some point, but time has tamed the ferocity of his desires. Our rendezvous are less frequent and his interests are more and more telescoped toward cerebral domination beyond the two of us. Yet, always unexpectedly, we will be together on some random day and the conversation once again escalates into a frenzied pitch and I end up on all fours like a conquered animal.

I wonder occasionally if I should have just let go of my youthful ideas about men and love and family, but the ironic thing is that someone like Xavier never tried to convince to do so. He takes his place in the universe and Philip takes his. I gravitate somewhere in between and am perfectly content with that.

Chapter 6 – The Ten Steps to Owning a Woman

"Most women set out to change a man, and when they have changed him they do not like him." —Marlene Dietrich

"Women who seek to be equal with men lack ambition." —Timothy Leary

"How wrong is it for a woman to expect the man to build the world she wants, rather than to create it herself?" —Anaïs Nin

While every woman is wired in a very particular way and arrives in front of a man with a unique history, there are some good general guidelines to follow on the journey to ownership. One should also keep in mind that the act of "owning" a woman largely happens as a natural consequence of getting to know someone over time within a Dominant/submissive dynamic. A submissive woman who completely falls for a man will want to feel like *his* in a deeply intimate, possessed way. One can either formalize the ownership identity with a contract, a ceremony or a serious discussion, or one can simply affirm its existence through daily action and constant awareness.

1. Prepare oneself mentally, emotionally, physically and financially.

Before a man jumps into the inevitably time-consuming search for the right submissive woman, he should make sure he has his own affairs in order. Don't make the mistake of trying to control one's own life by controlling a woman's. Be honest with yourself about where you are in the scheme of things. Evaluate how emotionally grounded you are compared to other people. Make sure you are financially secure enough for the type of woman you seek to own. Verify that you are in good health and free of any STD's. Fine-tune your physique to where you would like it to be. Focus on knowing yourself well enough to a point that a woman will not question who you really are.

2. Get to know her personally on an intimate level.

A man should approach a D/s relationship like he would any relationship. Focusing on erotic fantasies or particular ideas on how to dominate shouldn't get in the way of seeing the woman for who she is. Let feelings and interests flow naturally back and forth. A man should be aware of what he likes about a woman's submissive nature and what he likes about her overall personality. Be honest with both your serious opinions and your kinky desires. Sincere interest in a woman is always going to be caught up with sexual longings to do things to her. Erotic deviance should be fully embraced in every way, but make sure you are not just chasing fantasies. It is vital that you are into the woman on deeper levels.

3. Understand her strengths and weaknesses.

There are always fundamental reasons why a woman would seek out or be interested in being owned. Some women are reasonably balanced in their mental and emotional make-up and see D/s as simply an extension of their kinky desires. Other women want to feel that dominating presence there 24/7 in all aspects of their lives. Either they need the total emotional and mental security of that kind of connection or they desire the sheer emotional/mental potency and the erotic possibilities that can only happen in D/s ownership. A man should thoroughly get to know the feelings underlying her desires to be in a power-exchange relationship. Ask her what she thinks are her greatest strengths and her greatest weaknesses as in individual and in the context of a relationship. Try to get a feeling for the "part" of her personality that craves domination.

4. Determine if your vision of dominance will work with her.

Every man has different ideas about what it means to be in a power exchange relationship. Explain to the woman how you envision a serious relationship both inside and outside of the bedroom. Talk about the particular ways you like to dominate and the particular ways you see her submitting. Discuss what differences you are willing to negotiate on and what ones you are not. Get to know a woman's emotional triggers and ask her details about any past traumatic experiences.

5. Initiate the D/s dynamic with particulars.

Establish the basic rules, structure and feeling of the relationship. If you elect to create a punishment dynamic, tell her what she will be disciplined for and how she will be disciplined. Explain to her the expectations you have of her and what she can expect from you. Let the sexual domination dynamic take hold and discuss mutual feelings about it after each interaction. Focus on understanding how she ticks and then mold her within your sphere of dominance. Let one's own wild desires to dominate interact with a woman's yearning to submit and see what the raw aftermath looks like. Take stock of the aftermath to separate one's desire to dominate in general from one's desire to dominate the woman in front of you.

6. Embrace the kink.

There is always some element of erotic deviance that is interwoven into a D/s dynamic. A man should fully embrace all his kinkiest sexual desires and encourage the woman to do the same. Sensual fantasies will often lead to deeper realizations about oneself and about the connection one has with a woman. A man or a woman might discover that there are deep emotional conflicts hidden underneath their perversions which need to be brought to the surface. Two people might also discover that their attraction to each other really doesn't have much potential beyond the bedroom. Lastly, it is important for each partner to get a sense of the longer-term possibilities of their sexual dynamic. See if you can envision your erotic escapades as a fundamental part of a serious relationship.

7. Build trust.

The more submissive you want a woman to be, the more trust she will require in letting go. Dominating a woman sexually is very different than demanding absolute surrender in a long-term relationship. A woman needs to feel that she is truly cared for and that her submissiveness is appreciated. She needs to feel that she is being controlled and disciplined for her own good as well as for the benefit of the dominant man. Give her verbal affirmation following her submissive actions to let her know that she has made you happy. Make her feel that by doing what she is told to do that she is giving your life greater meaning. Be consistent in rewarding her for good behavior and in disciplining her for any defiance. Let her know how much her submissiveness turns you on and how much it gives your own life a greater sense of importance. Make sure that you are in a relationship with a woman who you want more than anyone else.

8. Take care of the woman in the woman.

While every submissive woman loves to be on the receiving end of a man's dominating force, sexual aggression and regular discipline must be balanced with the care of a woman's needs. On a simple level, she might have many erotic desires that a man wouldn't necessarily fulfill with his own dominant sexual actions. This might be anything from treating her tenderly in bed to giving her oral pleasure. Ask her about all the things that turn her on and tell her to communicate them as the dynamic evolves. On a relationship level, a woman generally needs to be cared for in more sensitive ways than a man does. She might need more communication about how you feel about her, about what you like her to do and why, and about her daily needs in feeling your dominating presence. Understanding her emotional requirements is vital to building trust and getting her to further submit to your will.

9. Create your own world of Dominance.

There are no ultimate rules on how to dominate or how to submit. A man can make a D/s relationship into exactly what he wants it to be with the right woman. He can create his own set of rules, his own protocol, his own way of disciplining, his own fantasies and his own household dynamic. The important thing is to keep things interesting and spontaneous while still being consistent in the level of control and authority. A D/s relationship can become just as boring as a vanilla relationship if it is not tended to. It is vital to live out the dynamic with a sense of adventure, an openness to new ideas and an embracing of maturity.

10. Take a step back and then ten steps forward.

After you reach a comfortable intimacy with a woman, take a step back and evaluate everything. Discuss the long-term future with her and decide where you see everything going. Consider all the possibilities of living a truly one-of-a-kind ownership lifestyle. Once you are deeply confident with the dynamic, embrace everything about it and move forward with all your heart and every kinky vision. Learn to trust each other with every fiber of your being. Create a realm of control, sex, intimacy, domination, surrender, desire and love that brings each of you to another level of consciousness. Stay constantly aware, be in love with life and do whatever you want to do in the way you want to do it.

Chapter 7 - Daily Rituals

The species that have evolved long-term bonds are also, by and large, the ones that rely on elaborate courtship rituals. . . . Love and sex do indeed go together." —Edwin O. Wilson

"Without cultural sanction, most or all our religious beliefs and rituals would fall into the domain of mental disturbance." —John Schumaker

"I firmly believe that with the right footwear one can rule the world." —Bette Midler

The process of dominating and training a woman to a man's deepest satisfaction is one of the most exquisitely enjoyable parts of owning a woman. It takes the dullness of the work day and charges every moment with an erotic intensity. One of the key psychological traits of men who like to own a woman is the urge to take the most basic actions and transform them into something extraordinary by controlling every last detail of what is being done. It not only gives new meaning to daily life, it reinvigorates the mind with a sense of constant awareness. A woman goes from just getting dressed for work with only the most basic considerations to putting on every last article of clothing on her body as if she is preparing for a performance for an audience of one who never leaves the show.

There is an endless variety of ways to control the daily habits of a woman in order to train her to his specifications. These include wardrobe control, speech restrictions, household rules, cooking requirements, etiquette training, social activity limits, eye contact restrictions, formal education and many other things.

Wardrobe Control

Deciding what your woman can wear and cannot wear is one of the most powerful elements in dominating a female. Women take great care in how they look not only for men but for other women as well. To submit to a man's clothing decisions and rules both at home and at work is a significant leap in trust for a woman. One would expect that the man already finds the woman's overall style and taste in clothing to his liking if he was attracted to her from the onset, but this might not be the case. He might want a total transformation to the way she dresses.

The precise rules and preferences for a woman's wardrobe are only limited by the man's imagination, his attention to detail and his level of strictness. Here are a plethora of ideas, styles and rules a man can use as a foundation or as inspiration for other directions:

Time and Place Rules- The woman must be appropriately clothed or unclothed according to the time of the day and where she is at. For example, she must strip down naked when she comes home, wear only an apron while cooking, be in a dress when she serves you meals and wear a metal collar when she goes to bed. She must have her work attire approved and has specific types of clothing that she must wear depending on where she is going. On weekends, she must dress in another way, such as being only permitted to wear skirts or wearing a corset at all hours.

1950's Style- The fifties lifestyle is both a fashion of dress and a way of living. After the war years in the U.S., traditional roles were reaffirmed. Men were expected to be the breadwinners. Women, even when they worked, assumed their proper place was at home. The social mores about sex were particularly restrictive, characterized by strong taboos, conservatism and an attitude toward prudish conformity. The female style of dress includes sweeping long skirts and outfits with a fitted waist, rounded shoulders and a pointed bust. Some of the clothing invented in those years included new interlining materials to shape the silhouette. Narrow pencil skirts and bullet bras are very emblematic of this style. There are also day dresses with fitted bodices, halter-top sundresses, cocktail dresses, houseboy pants and pedal-pushers.

This style can be particularly powerful in contemporary times when women think nothing of dressing down in sweats, loose jeans and guy shorts. A 1950's woman is generally expected to look her best at all times. Rules can include wearing a cocktail dress and heals at all times at home, attiring herself in traditional undergarments such as garter belts and form-fitting lingerie and maintaining a pronounced curve to her figure. A variation of the 1950's style is the "woman on the streets, slut in the sheets" philosophy in which the woman is required to maintain a very proper formal style out of the house and a very slutty fifties style at home.

A 1950's lifestyle can include establishing definitive gender roles in a household hierarchy. A woman focuses on the quality time spent together instead of her own materialistic desires and career-oriented ambitions. The man is the head of the household/relationship, works as the sole provider and makes all the major decisions such as where they live, what they do in the evenings, when they go on vacation and so forth. The woman serves and pleases her man, doesn't work outside the home, manages the needs of the house, prepares fresh meals, bakes from her collection of cookbooks, gardens, keeps the house spotlessly clean, does errands and serves as the perfect homemaker.

The allure of the 1950's lifestyle is that each person knows his or her role definitively. There is no power play or jousting for control. This might be very attractive to men who like women who are extremely submissive in their disposition, are service-oriented and love to please. It is a perfect fit for women who want to escape the work world and who thrive in domestic life. It can be a very alluring alternative to the chaos of the contemporary world with all of its endless work demands and its belief that men and women should both be ambitiously focused on their career accomplishments.

It is a tempting alternative universe where traditional mores rule strong and one can always defer to established values. The focus is on spending sincere time together, living within one's means and supporting each other. The challenge is integrating contemporary perspectives into this lifestyle, whether it is a BDSM-oriented 1950's way of living or not. A popular trend that fits within this lifestyle is the practice of living a more basic, close-to-nature existence that focuses on simple quality over heavy materialistic consumption. That can include making/consuming artisanal products and handcrafted wares, growing one's own food and being as self-sufficient has humanly possible.

Slutwear – One of the great pleasures of owning a woman is that you can make her look like a slut. Such items and styles include obscenely tight jeans, camel-toe leggings, thin shirts without bras, transparent skirts and dresses with slutty panties, short shorts that reveal her cheeks, plunge dresses, g-string swimwear, revealing torn holes on jeans and white summer dresses with nothing underneath. A good rule of thumb to give a woman is that it must be tight, revealing or transparent, or it shouldn't be worn at all.

Slavewear- There are both traditional slave attire made by BDSM manufacturers and untraditional slave wear that can be found anywhere and everywhere. Traditional slave gear includes ball gags, muzzles, collars made of leather, metal, vinyl, rubber and other materials, posture gear for the neck and full body, body harnesses, corsets and latex dresses, bras, stockings, pants and gloves. Non-traditional slave gear can be found in many unconventional places such as online auction sites, pet stores and hardware stores. These include authentic slave collars and shackles from the antebellum period, vintage dog collars, electric dog collars, equine gear, choker necklaces, industrial chains and GPS anklets. There is also servant attire such as maid outfits. Some men prefer to have custom outfits made for their women. These includes full body catsuits with holes for her mouth, cunt, breasts and ass, an anal hook that is chained to a metal collar and a chain that locks around her waist. Other men prefer that their slaves remain naked at all times.

Haute Couture- Some men prefer that their women always look as if they have stepped out of a catalog or off the runway. A man can either leave it up to the woman to present outfits to him to determine if he likes them or he can take her to the appropriate stores to pick them out himself. One variant of this style is the "superiority rule" in which the man requires the woman to always look as good or better than any woman at a certain place or during all occasions. If the man sees another woman who he thinks has done a better job with her appearance, the woman is to be disciplined immediately for her failure to look superior. Some men carry a portable disciplinary implement with them, such as a small leather strap, on such occasions.

Corsets- Waist-cinching corsets have always been a fundamental piece of attire worn by women to keep their figure bound in a certain shape and remind them of their place. There is a wide variety of corset styles and historical types. There are full figured, overbust, underbust and basic waist cinchers. Major historical types include the Victorian style, Edwardian style and the 1950's waist cincher. If a man is serious about adorning his women in a proper corset, or if he intends on tightlacing her to reduce the size of her waist, he should purchase a vintage corset made with real boning. There are also a number of custom corset makers who can manufacture original pieces according to the woman's measurements. Some of these items include Steampunk designs, Burlesque-inspired fashions, Nazi-style green leather, neo-Victorian designs, wedding corsets and other styles that synthesize every variant of fashion history with a contemporary flair.

Permission to Dress- Some men prefer to take the extent of their control to the extreme and require a woman to request permission any time she gets dressed or gets undressed. This typically includes sleeping naked or in a particular outfit, asking permission to get dressed to make breakfast, asking permission to get dressed for work, asking permission to get undressed from work and so on.

Dress to Please- Some men simply do not want to bother with worrying about a woman's wardrobe nor bother with picking out every single article of clothing she is to wear. In this situation, a man will simply tell a woman that she should always please him with what she is wearing. If she does not please him, she will be ordered to remove her clothing, disciplined and told to change clothes. If she has purchased any of these articles of clothing with his money, she should be doubly punished.

Work Life and Home Life

A man who owns a woman should establish the gender roles for each of them. Traditional gender roles that entail the man works and woman takes care of the household work well but generally need to be altered for contemporary living. Some men prefer that an owned woman work. A few even desire her to excel at her profession to an even greater degree than she would without him. It is rare, though, that a man does not want his woman to perform or manage some of the household duties such as cooking, cleaning, doing the grocery shopping or doing the laundry. At the very least, he typically wants her to manage over the service providers who do these tasks. To own a woman can mean that she is a man's servant and she should thrive on performing traditional household tasks.

Cooking

An owned woman is often expected be an excellent cook. If so, he should either be enrolled in cooking classes at a proper culinary school or be given particular directions as to the man's expectations. This could include course work, a list of culinary preferences, cook books and instructional videos. The precise demands placed on the woman can vary widely depending on the man's desires and his preferences for attention to detail. Example regimens include:

Menu preparation- The woman should prepare a daily, weekly or monthly menu for all meals. She should make sure that all ingredients are purchased in advance and have the meals ready at precise times. Some men desire that his woman create a physical restaurant-style menu and present it to him before she prepares each meal. It should offer numerous choices according to his specifications. It can also include daily specials that offer local fresh ingredients or spontaneous surprises.

Meal service – The woman should be properly attired to cook and serve the meal. She can be required to wear a servant's outfit, a cook's clothing, an apron or nothing at all. Some men prefer that she wear only an apron and maintain a stock of various styles to keep him continually pleased. The woman should set the table to according to the man's specifications. This could be laying out basic utensils or setting the table according to the extremes of English royalty. If multiple courses are desired, she should present and clear each course in the manner of a trained waitress.

Separate Eating Places- The woman can either join the man at the table or be given a separate place to eat. This can be either at a different table, in a separate room or at the same table but after the man has finished his meal. Some men prefer to go to more extremes and treat the woman in a more slave-like way. They prefer that the woman eat on the floor like an animal. She can either eat from her plate or be given a bowl like a pet. If this is desired, instruct her if she should be allowed utensils or eat directly with her mouth while on her hands and knees. Other men like to be sexually serviced during meals or between courses. The woman can be ordered to remain underneath the table to orally serve the man. If a man desires to take things to the extreme, the woman can be required to swallow his cum before she eats anything else at that meal.

Domestic Rules

A woman should understand that there are specific rules that must be followed in the household. These could include speech restrictions, eye contact restrictions, wardrobe rules, household chores, protocol requirements, disciplinary specifics, behavior modification goals and many other rules. A man should post these rules or have a list of rules readily available for the woman. An owner can also hang a chalkboard or an erasable marker board for adding specific needs or listing infractions that require discipline. Speech restrictions can be used on a temporary basis or a permanent rule. A man can forbid the use of profanity, complaining, bad speaking habits or many other things that require alteration. One can also use it in a disciplinary way such as forbidding the woman to speak at all for a certain length of time. This can be accentuated by placing a ball gag in her mouth.

The use of proper protocol is entirely up to the man's preference. He can insist on the very traditional use of "Sir" or "Master" and then specify when it is to be used to address him. He can require it to be said every time he is spoken to, only during affirmative questions that require a "yes, sir" or "no, sir", or only when the woman is being scolded or disciplined. Some men simply prefer to be addressed by their first name when asking his woman any questions.

Eye contact restrictions can be used in multiple ways. A woman can be forbidden from looking at her owner directly in the eye or be required to always look her owner directly in the eye. A man can also vary this to require a woman to look or not look at him only when he is speaking. It can be used as a temporary punishment as well. If desired, a man can forbid a woman from making eye contact with any other man when out in public, with or without him.

Any other household rules should be written and explained clearly so the woman knows what is expected from her and what will happen if she is disobedient. There are endless ways that a woman can be further trained in order to abide by the man's rules and desires.

If he desires a properly trained woman with "good social breeding", enrolling her in an etiquette course is an excellent idea. Etiquette training can teach the woman proper posture, elegant poise, hostess manners, correct pronunciation of words, the art of conversation, social manners, formal table setting rules, dining etiquette and many other skills to ensure she can handle herself in high society. There are also numerous traditional books on proper etiquette such as *Amy Vanderbilt's Complete Book of Etiquette* and *Miss Manners* by Judith Martin.

Other training can include professional massage instruction, secretarial coursework, accounting classes and fashion design school.

Work Life

A man should have a serious discussion with a woman about her professional work life. It should be determined not only what her goals are but what how her work life will integrate with her home life. There are innumerable possibilities of how the two worlds can co-exist. A man can agree to total freedom and independence for a woman within the sphere of her work. This can be an especially powerful dynamic as it gives a sense of balance to the two very different worlds. At the opposite end of the spectrum, he can also control and micro-manage every decision she makes regarding her professional life. He can even demand that she excel in her chosen profession and career path to an elite degree, or further than she had planned before being owned. Some men want the woman to quit her job, or work part-time, and focus entirely on her duties as an owned woman. Other men who own their own companies or are in positions of leadership prefer to take in the woman as an assistant, a secretary or even in a major leadership role. In the end, the man should decide what works best for him *and* for the happiness and health of the woman.

Case Study 7.1

"Clothes Make the Woman"

Colton and Kaylee

Colton: Kaylee knows that whatever she is wearing is to be worn to please my exacting tastes. It doesn't matter if it's at home on a lazy Sunday afternoon or at a grand public spectacle with paparazzi snapping away with their ravenous camera clicks.

Yet it's not just her specifically that brings out that urge in me to see her adorned in a particular way. I've always believed that a woman's wardrobe is her Kryptonian power when it comes to attracting men. It has invariably been the striking details of a specific outfit that draws me toward a random female as if she were strewn in magnetic fibers that trigger something uncontrollable in me. Of course in a relationship a woman's character, her intelligence and her loving nature are what matters, but she will also implicitly express a certain degree of these qualities in how she drapes her body out in the world.

Even as a man, it is vividly clear to me that fashion is a language, and so much more for women than it is for men. A man can dress like a bum, but if he is an iconic billionaire or a brash masterful chef or a writer with swaggering genius, his attire becomes nearly inconsequential. It is rarely so for women. There is still some kind of evolutionary twist that commands women to decorate their bodies to attract their soul mates and to satiate their need to feel desired to the nth degree. What a woman wears is how she presents herself to the world, especially today, when human contacts are so fleeting.

It was like an epiphany when I discovered this fundamental truth years ago. I was standing at a crosswalk waiting for the light to change when I noticed this woman standing behind a number of people. From my point of view,

I could only see her head but she seemed quite attractive. When the light changed and I caught a full view of her, I saw that she was wearing a very frumpy pair of sweats, an ugly t-shirt with holes in it and tennis shoes caked with dirt. She looked like she might have even been homeless. This might have been a superficial judgment on my part at that moment, but it spoke volumes to me how clothing can completely alter one's opinion of someone.

It made me realize that if she had been wearing a really alluring outfit, and had been cleaned-upped, I wouldn't have thought twice about flirting with her. The more I began to study women's appearance, the more I noticed how much of a difference it truly makes. I would see a woman who would not be considered especially attractive if she hadn't been wearing a particularly provocative outfit. I don't just mean dressing slutty, either. I mean dressing in a way that gives her a look of sexual charisma, or is even suggestive of her creative intelligence or her poise. I mean dressing in a way that is original at an elite level of the fashion world. I mean knowing how to show it off that makes a woman vividly stand out in a crowd.

I started to see Kaylee in a very casual way. A mutual friend had introduced us because the friend thought that she was my type. I had blatantly voiced my desire to be with women who liked to be told what to do. The friend told me that Kaylee is the type of woman who is always looking to satisfy her man and loves to get attention. She also mentioned that she's from the Deep South and she's as sweet as an aiming-to-please Georgia peach can possibly be. She knew I had a thing for Southern women.

I was very busy with work at the time, though, and we only had a chance to see each other a few times over the course of a month. I think, though, that it was because of the infrequency in seeing each other that made her feel compelled to get my attention. On our fourth date, she arrived at the restaurant wearing this ridiculously risqué dress. It was velvet black with a plunge style front that was made to be worn without a bra. She had on a necklace that was some kind of exotic aboriginal design with colorful painted wood trinkets. Her high heels matched the colors but in a very subtle way. The outfit was not only highly provocative, but her masterful sensibility was very enticing. She was definitely telling me that it was time to take notice or it might be the last time I ever saw her.

We had a great time that night, we flirted with each other the entire evening and I told her that I wanted to see her again the next day. When we met the following afternoon for coffee, she was once again wearing this very alluring outfit. I didn't even know the name for it, but she told me it was a type of "jumpsuit". The pants and shirt were made of a single piece of clothing and the light gray fabric was just tight enough to subtly accentuate every curve and crevasse of her body. The thick belt that cinched her waist made it even more visually stimulating.

Over the next few weeks, we began to date and we grew to realize how much raw chemistry there was between us. Our tastes seemed to mesh absolutely seamlessly, from general viewpoints about men and women to a shared appreciation for all things vintage and venerably old-fashioned. In and out of the bedroom, she loved when I ordered her to do things. Sometimes it would be something simple like telling her to go down to the corner store to get me a newspaper or ordering for her in a restaurant. Other times it would be something very sexual like summoning her to my office at lunch to give me a stealth blow job underneath my desk. I would always take command of her in bed and I began to dominate additional aspects of her life.

A few months into the relationship, I made a second realization about how women tend to dress. Kaylee showed up to my apartment one day wearing a very casual pair of jeans and a loose t-shirt. The outfit was not attractive at all. It occurred to me that she had subconsciously thought that we had reached the point in our relationship in which she didn't need to really dress up to get my attention. I immediately asked her what she thought she was doing coming dressed like that to see me. She gave me a perplexed look, and then asked me jokingly if she was supposed to be dressed to the nines every moment she was with me.

I glared at her and blatantly told her: "Yes, you are supposed to be."

It was then that it occurred to me how much it really turned me on every time I saw her primped up in a new outfit. She immediately objected that she didn't have enough clothes to wear something new every single day. I knew she was right, but I didn't want her to think that I hadn't already considered that fact. I chastised her again, gave her some money for a new outfit and told her not to come back until she was properly dressed.

By the time she returned, I had begun to formulate this elaborate set of wardrobe rules for her. First, I explained that from that point forward, there would be strict expectations of appropriate attire for every moment of her day. I specified the initial categories but added to these as time went on. At first, it began with work attire, sleep attire, at-home attire and going out attire, but I found it more and more interesting to divide things into more sophisticated divisions. I started to require specific attire for when she was cooking, cleaning, relaxing, working out, spending time with her friends, going out formally, going out casually, going on vacation, going to the beach and just about any other way I could make her dress for me in a new way. My fascination with how women dress had swiftly intensified and proliferated into a dictatorial madness with her.

She also absolutely loved everything about it, from the parade of compliments she received every time we went out to the endless moments that her provocative outfit drove to me ravish her at that very moment.

I had required that she never wear the same outfit twice without my permission, but I quickly realized I could not possibly afford to buy her such a gargantuan sized wardrobe. I solved the problem by having her enroll in basic fashion design courses that would give her the skills to make nearly any outfit I wanted to see her wear. After a couple of months, she had a strict new schedule that practically revolved around her clothing.

On the first Sunday of each month, she is required to sort through a half-dozen different fashion magazines and tear out the pages featuring outfits that I might like. Once I approve of the specific apparel, she makes a trip to the garment district to pick up the necessary fabrics. I have a spare room in my apartment that was converted into her design room where she can sew away on certain nights like my little sweat shop girl. She often trots back and forth from the room to get my approval on her works-in-progress before she adds the final touches to the end designs.

She has now amassed quite a sizeable wardrobe-hundreds of dresses, skirts, panties, jeans, shorts and shirts of a seemingly infinite variety. On a typical day, she wakes up in her skimpy sleepwear, strips down bare naked to go her wardrobe room and them puts on one of her aprons to make me breakfast. After she showers, she changes into her work wear, goes to work, comes home, changes into her appropriate home attire, waits for me to decide what we will be doing that night and then changes accordingly for going out, cooking or serving me take-out.

She has literally hundreds and hundreds of the most imaginative and creative articles of clothing a man could ever want to ogle: sultry summer dresses, skimpy mini dresses, revealing short skirts styled in every variety from school girl plaid to clubwear slut vinyl, obscene skin-tight jeans that vary from full-length snug to profanely torn to cheek-revealing booty shorts, tiny panties and suggestive bras and lingerie ensembles of every naughty sort, see-through blouses, low-cut shirts, yoga pants of every ass-hugging and camel toe variety, fuck-me leather boots, thigh high boots, enough heels to fill a closet, elegant evening gowns, girly rompers, v-string bathing suits, classy ridding jodhpurs, haute couture dresses and nearly every other flavor and variety of clothing that gets me aroused. What she can't make, she simply buys with the allowance I give her. What a woman can do with a piece of fabric is absolutely endless.

Oh, and yes, our relationship apart from this diabolical endeavor is going swimmingly. On nights she needs a break from it all, she lounges around completely naked and we do something like listening to old jazz records and boozing it up on some 19th century cocktails and having heavy conversations about the history of the South and having sweaty sex all over our authentic Mies Van Der rohe leather sofa.

Chapter 8 – Breaking a Woman In

"You don't break these animals, you come to an understanding with them." —Phil West

"Every one may not know what breaking in is, therefore I will describe it. It means to teach a woman to wear a collar, and to carry on her back a man; to go just the way he wishes, and to go obediently. Besides this she is to stand still while the man speaks; and she must go fast or slow, just as her driver wishes. She must never start at what she sees, nor speak to other men, nor bite, nor kick, nor have any unbreakable will of her own; but always do her master's will, even though she may be very tired or hungry; but the worst of all is, when her harness is once on, she may neither jump for joy nor lie down for weariness. So you see this breaking in is a great thing." —The Alternative Black Beauty

Breaking a woman in is the process of aligning her own nature with what a man wants her to be. All women bring their own particular ideas of what a relationship should be and what their role within that relationship is going to be. Some women seeking a D/s relationship even have very controlling ideas of how they should be submissive and how the man should be dominant. When a woman is broken in, her preconceived ideas are dispelled, her way of thinking is altered, her body is forfeited and she begins the full process of being trained to be owned as property.

Before breaking in a woman, it is important to know all her negative triggers, phobias, past traumatic experiences and any other personal history that could come to the forefront when she is pushed to the edge of her emotions. Nothing should be hid. Most importantly, a woman must consent to be broken in. He must inform her of the precise process he will be using to break her in and she must desire it for herself.

The process of breaking a woman in should only begin once a couple has established a serious connection and their attraction to each other runs deep at multiple levels. There is no point in breaking a woman in unless a man is sincerely intent on owning her for a long period of time. A woman can either be broken in at the onset of a more serious relationship or further down the road. It is up to the man and what he believes will work best.

How a woman is broken in depends on the personality of the woman and what the man believes will work best to train her mind and behavior. A man can break a woman in over time using rules, rituals, training techniques, discipline and regular interactions. Some women require more extreme measures to break old habits and ways of thinking. A woman will often bring some kind of emotional baggage from past relationships that needs to be addressed in harsher ways. Most importantly, a woman cannot be turned into someone who she is not capable of being turned into. She might be shedding layers of her ego and her self-indulgent side, but the woman who she is being molded into should be a woman who is happy in her owned state. She should thrive in feeling that she is his being made his property on a physical, emotional and mental level.

The point of breaking in a woman is to ritualize the process of turning a relationship into a very serious Dominant/submissive commitment which will guide the rest of their lives together.

There are many ways a woman can be broken in. It can simply be an organic part of the relationship process in which a woman naturally becomes deeply submissive to the man as the connection develops. It is a good idea, though, to make it ritualized in some way to clarify that she is entering a new period of her life. The breaking in period is typically of a short duration in which certain activities, disciplinary regimens and behavior modification actions are intensified.

Its goal is to make the woman understand that she is purely his property. Her will and life are no longer her own. She thinks and acts for her owner. She is his possession. It comes only after a deep level of trust is established and there is a mutual agreement to enter a full D/s ownership relationship.

Some woman naturally adapt to being broken in during the early stages of the relationship. Others require an intense breaking in period of a week or a month. During this period, the man should use extreme techniques and harsh discipline to achieve the goal of fully transitioning the woman to a deeper sense of "slavery". The techniques should be a balanced use of positive and negative reinforcement. This could include removal of all clothing for consecutive days or weeks, writing assignments, intense sexual use of her body, cock worship, interrogation sessions, harsh discipline, intense labor, use of stress positions, cage internment, forbidding contact with friends and family and brainwashing sessions. The precise technique used depends on the nature of the woman and the goals the man aims to achieve.

On the more extreme side, brainwashing techniques include thought-stopping techniques such as repeating particular phrases, control of what the woman watches and reads, shaming or ridiculing a woman for undesirable thoughts or actions, giving her only black-and-white choices to eliminate undesired critical thinking on certain subjects and posting of images of the woman with desirable adjectives.

The underlying goal of brainwashing is to take control of the woman's mind while she relinquishes control of the core of her ego. It is the process by which individual freedom of choice and action is transformed by processes that modify perception, motivation, affect, cognition and behavioral outcomes. Its goals include conformity, compliance, persuasion, fear arousal, modeling and identification as an owned woman. When performed correctly, it creates a powerful crucible of extreme mental and behavioral manipulation, but it must be synthesized with charismatic love, authoritarian enforcement, transmission of dominant ideologies, extreme discipline and promised rewards.

Rewards should be given to the women when she properly meets desired goals. These could include expressions of love and desire for her, verbal reinforcement of her worthiness as an owned woman, sexual gratification of her choice and material gifts.

From the onset of breaking in to the finishing touches, a woman should understand that she is being made his property. The man should treat an owned woman with strict, caring love that nurtures her self-worth as his woman and encourages her overall health within his domain.

Writing assignments could vary from sentence writing to extended essays. Sample topics include:

"Why Ownership Makes me Happy"
"How I Envision Being an Owned Woman"
"Why I am Meant to be Owned"
"Behavior I Will Never do Again and Why"
"100 Ways I am Owned"
"How I am to Serve my Owner"
"Why I Might be Disciplined"
"How I Balance Being an Owned Woman with Regular Life"

Consensual Nonconsent

Consensual nonconsent is a formalized term in BDSM ideology. The concept is that the submissive is consenting to activities in advance over which she will not be given any explicit control. She will be forced to do things, for example, but she has agreed to the force in advance, and she will have no say over how much force is used. Such activities tread into very dangerous territory. They are part of the larger world of "edge play".

While this expression has been codified into a BDSM concept, its roots are in age-old fantasies and human desires. A woman wants to be taken, to feel out of control, to struggle against overwhelming strength and to be constrained until she is completely subdued and reaches a point of release. Yet, she wants all this to happen in the right way with the right man. In a play session, she doesn't want to be raped. She wants a rape fantasy that feels real but is not real. She wants her bare ass whipped until she feels completely *broken*, but she doesn't want her real human spirit to be broken. Sometimes a woman simply can't or is not willing to go where she needs to go and needs to be taken there by her man.

The concept, the details and the fantasies of consensual nonconsent should be thoroughly expressed in advance. In a way, the experience is another way of breaking in a woman. The process of breaking her in could amount to several scenes and processes of consensual nonconsent. The important element is that the submissive has agreed to be taken to places in her heart and mind that are completely decided by the dominant man. Knowing the ins-and-outs of a woman is vital as a man is completely responsible for her reactions and her aftercare. It must not be something done to feed one's ego. It is in the best interest of the health of the submissive and in the vitality of the relationship. He must be fully aware of the sub's sensitivities, as well as her physical safety, but he is taking a step forward with his own autocratic rule in mind.

Consensual nonconsent can include just about any activity that is taken to the extreme. In addition to the processes previously mentioned, it also can include such activities as severe corporal punishment, extended bondage, forced deep throat, vaginal fisting, total sensory deprivation, subhuman treatment, hardcore objectification and extreme use of her body. There are no real limits beyond one's own imagination, legal parameters and the safety of the participants.

Case Study 8.1

"Brute Love"

Hunter and Selene

Hunter: I used to feel awful about being mean to girls when I was younger and finally learned to suppress my unruly vicious urges in order to maintain "healthy relationships". Then I met Selene and all that changed. I didn't even know what the word sadistic really meant until she brought the very spirit of the Marquise de Sade out of me.

Yet, it was more than just my complicated chauvinistic feelings about women. I've almost always been jaded on life in general. Maybe it was because my father was a prick and took out his failures on me, but I think that was just the trigger. There was also religion. I was raised Catholic and sent to all these strict schools. It soured my spiritual side. But really I think that it is simply because I was born with an oversensitive slant and could always see past people's ostensible actions and claims straight into their true motives. All this nature-nurture mix just swelled into a larger fatalistic view of things.

To me, life is just a transitory sort of dream, most men and women endlessly chase childish notions that are outright ridiculous and anyone who doesn't wake up with the fact of mortality somewhere in their daily mindset is a sad fool. Don't get me wrong. I still have a warm life-affirming side as well. The world is a miraculous mystery and women are such enigmatic creatures that it mesmerizes me.

Anyways, I pontificate. So, Selene. That cute little bitch was brought for some unknown reason from thousands of miles away to end up my one and only true love. She is Korean but she was adopted and raised by white parents. Not only does she have issues of feeling truly wanted, but she

190

is an only child who was used to getting all the attention. I met her online, of course, and on a BDSM dating site on top of that.

She was very particular in what she wanted from the beginning. She not only described the precise things she wanted in a man as far as his dominant nature, she drew this elaborate picture of her ideal man that sounded like it was something out of a catalog. She detailed how she wanted him to look, his interests, the ways he would control her and even how they would spend their free time. She was very controlling for a young woman who said she was submissive and wanted to be dominated by a strong man. She posted various photos of herself that made her seem like the iconic petite, submissive Asian girl, but they all looked very staged. One had her posed in a plaid schoolgirl skirt with her toes pointed inward in a look of feminine meekness. In another, she covered her nude upper body with her arm and had a pink gag ball strapped in her mouth.

Meeting someone off a BDSM dating site is truly a strange thing. You don't know much of anything about the woman, but at the same time, she has already revealed these incredibly perverse desires to you. Selene had vividly described that she liked getting her face slapped, being spanked regularly and being taken roughly in all sorts of ways. She even said that she was curious about being humiliated and kept in a cage. These are very extreme things to know about a woman who hasn't even told you what she likes to watch on TV.

The first time we met, she acted very snooty. Her insecurities were really obvious and she tried to overcompensate by acting like a spoiled princess. She wanted to play the bratty girl but she also wanted to decide exactly how this bratty girl got disciplined. She was just out of graduate school and had never had a real job, but she thought she knew everything in the world.

Halfway through the first date, I didn't think I even wanted to see her a second time. Yet, she was very attractive in a myriad of ways. She was smart and had a strange inscrutable density to her personality. She was also physically attractive in the submissive sort of way I liked. Her black eye shadow was drawn to make her eyes appear seductively outspread and her cold nipples poked against her shirt. She physically had a rather fragile girlish constitution but she gave off this vibe that she saw herself as a strong, beautiful woman who was desired by all men. She had even recently gotten a boob job to try to cure her body-image issues. I could tell she was going to be a handful. There was something about her, though, that made me want to get involved with her. I like complicated women, even though many of them end up being so complicated that they are real basket cases.

While we ate dinner, I let her do most of the talking and just sat back and listened. I knew that she had very specific ideas of what kind of man she wanted and that if I didn't immediately try to dominate her in the way she had imagined, she would grow flustered. My air of indifference drove her crazy. She needed to feel desired on the spot, but I patiently nurtured the tone of the conversation and didn't even bring up anything kinky.

When she took a haughty tone with me, I just glared at her like it barely registered in my mind. Cruel desires had begun to simmer in me but I just let them be. I could tell she had serious trust issues and I knew that she needed to feel a strong sense of security in her life. Her desire to be controlled was much more about trying to gain a sense of control of her own life. She was about to graduate and she had never had to do things on her own. A lot of her sexual kinks were reactionary. She wanted to avoid her responsibilities and hated feeling alone. She confessed to fantasizing about being spanked every day and that she sometimes had masturbated for hours and hours instead of doing her schoolwork.

I'm probably making an over-generalization about Asian females, but from my experience what is of tantamount importance for them in a man is his sheer mental and physical fortitude, his ability to make her feel secure and his degree of personal success in life (be that in how he is perceived by society or just his sheer wealth.)

We went out three or four times before I made any attempt at all to dominate her. I wanted her to get to know me and for her to feel at ease around me so she would reveal more of her true character. I also wanted to discover if there was really something about her that truly made me want to consider her as more than a couple of nights of edgy conversation and me treating her like a simple fucktoy. I longed for there to be real engaging rapport and for her to get a sense of what her life would be like with me. I had her over to my house for a small party I was having and even introduced her to a few of my friends.

On the fifth date, though, the calm before the storm ended with a sudden outburst of torrential drama. She was mouthing off to me the entire time during dinner, arguing with every point I made to a ridiculous degree. It was like trying to deal with a know-it-all teenager and she was completely ruining the evening. It sent me over the edge.

I stood up and told her that dinner was over.

"Get your jacket and go wait outside for me, you mouthy little bitch," I told her.

She was shocked that I abruptly spoke to her like that. She huffed and puffed, and then stormed out while I paid the bill. When I got outside she was waiting by my car and demanded that I take her home. I grabbed her harshly by her hair and pulled her close to me.

"Shut that cunt mouth of yours up and get in the car," I angrily ordered her. I grasped her more firmly by her hair and turned her head so she was forced to look me in the eyes from inches away.

"Don't you ever talk to me like you did tonight," I scolded her. "No man wants to deal with that kind of childish bullshit. Is that clear?"

I grasped her by the hair even harder.

"Ouch!" she cried out, glancing around to see if anyone was watching. "Fine, can we just go?"

I opened the door and practically threw her in the car.

When she noticed we were going to my place instead of hers, she hardly reacted. Pushing buttons for her is natural. When we got to my place, I went into the dining room and grabbed one of the wooden chairs from the table. I brought it into the living room and set it down in the middle of the room. I told her to sit down. She nervously obeyed and looked up at me to see what I was going to say. I had kept a mental list of nearly every snotty remark and obnoxious objection she had made, as well as a tally of the obvious things that she was doing in her life that was just an attempt to avoid dealing with reality.

I explained to her that from this moment forward there would be strict rules that she would need to abide by without question.

"What kind of rules?" she pout-protested with a sneer. I told her that before I explained them to her that she would be spanked for every single rude, nasty and conceited remark she had ever made. She stood up and objected in a sassy outburst that she hadn't said anything. I told her that she needed to shut her goddamn mouth and listen.

She protested again and I casually moved toward her. I calmly placed my left on the tip of her chin and then slapped her firmly across the face with my other hand. She looked up at me in shock. It was the moment of truth.

"Sit down and shut your mouth," I told her.

She hesitated.

"Either sit your ass down right now you bratty little cunt, or you can leave for good this second."

She wavered for just a moment and I slapped her again.

"Do you understand?" I asked her.

"Yes, fine," she replied in a huff before turning to sit down in the chair.

It was a monumentally dramatic turn in how we interacted from that day forward. I realized how much she really craved fierce unyielding domination. She liked to buck wildly just so she would feel someone was there to tame her. I also realized how aroused I got from putting her in her place. It felt like it unleashed years of pent-up sadistic impulses in a split second.

I rattled off nearly word-for-word every comment she had made that displeased me. Unlucky for her, my memory is near photographic. There were at least 20 remarks in all. After I was done, I instructed her to stand up and bend over the back of the chair. She hesitated again and I grabbed her by her arm, pulled her to her feet and then roughly put her over the back of the chair.

When she heard me unbuckle my belt, she asked me if I spanked hard. I wondered then how many others had spanked her. I warned her if she didn't take what she had earned I'd whip her bare ass raw all night. She turned back and began to plead not to do it too hard and I shouted at her again to get over the chair. She cautiously leaned over the back of it and placed her palms on the seat. I lifted her skirt and quickly tugged her panties down to her thighs.

I explained to her that she would now repeat back to me every remark in the manner the she had said it. She protested to me that there was no way she could remember all the things I had just said. I immediately whipped my belt across her bare butt three times in quick succession. Her body flinched each time I spanked her. I told her to begin the list. In her first attempt, she only got six of the remarks. I responded by giving her 14 hard spankings, thrashing her repeatedly until she was on the tips of her toes. The second time, she got nine of the remarks. The third time, she got 11. I continue to whip the belt across her bare cheeks as they began to turn a bright shade of red. I could see the perspiration that had formed on her forehead from trying to withstand the pain. It soon began to trickle down her cheeks.

She appealed to me that she couldn't take anymore but I sensed that it was a half-hearted plea made to test my resolve to take her beyond anything she had received before. I had already discussed her limits in a previous conversation so I knew the extremes she craved to be subjected to. I told her that she wouldn't get up until she repeated all 20 remarks. She tried to stand and I grabbed her. I hand spanked her until she submitted to bending back over the chair. I decided to be a bit lenient with her and I repeated the remarks that she couldn't remember. It still took her two more attempts to finish the oral exercise and I spanked her with the same full force.

After she finally finished, I lifted her up and took her to the corner of the living room. I ordered her to stand in the corner for an hour without speaking and consider why she thought that acting the way she had with me would be an enjoyable experience for anyone. I lifted her hands to the back of her head and instructed her to keep them held there. I pulled her skirt and panties down to her ankles so her reddened butt was exposed. She put her nose to the corner of the room and began to pout. I knew right then how much she loved to feel like a disciplined little girl.

I left her there for an hour and she did not say a word. After her time was up, I told her to pull up her clothes and sit back down on the chair. I explained to her that from that point onward she would be spanked regularly for any disobedience to the rules I was going to give her. She asked what the rules were and I began to carefully explain each one. They included various speech restrictions, requirements regarding her career pursuits, limitations on her daily schedule and a prohibition against any sexual self-pleasure without my approval. I also outlined how she would need to ask my permission for going out with her friends or staying up past a certain time. It was like a sudden announcement that I was now going to be the ultimate authority figure taking over her life.

She protested and pouted again, telling me that she wasn't ready to trust me, but I could tell she loved every strict rule. I asked her formally if she agreed to the new restrictions on her life and she said she would have to think about it. I told her she needed to give me a yes or no answer right then. She gave me a sassy look and said "fine" in her typical sulky way. I grabbed her by the chin with my hand, gave her another slap across her face and told her the options were either yes or no. She feigned reluctance and then muttered a yes. It was very ritualistic the way it all happened. Later that night, I drove her home.

The next night when we went out to dinner, the sexual energy between us was outright palpable. She had texted me three times during the day to ask if she could touch herself. After we left the restaurant, we took a stroll down the street on our way to a nearby bar. We were passing this alley when I grabbed her by the arm and led her down it. Once we were out of view, I immediately took hold of her, pushed her back against the brick wall and started kissing her. She began to grind her body against me. She was even hornier than I was. We kissed each other deeply for a few minutes and then I pulled back for a moment just to look at her.

She was breathing deeply with excitement. I slapped her, and then again even harder. My true feelings were boiling to the surface. She glared back at me like an aroused animal. I wrapped my hand around her throat and held her against the wall. I slid my other hand up her skirt. She was already wet. I could feel her breath moving in and out of her. I held her neck tightly in my hand and looked her directly in the eye.

"You need to be taken home and have your naughty little cunt fucked hard right now," I uttered.

She just bit her lip and gave me a devilish grin.

I practically dragged her from the car to my front door by her hair. When we got inside, I shut the door, turned her around and pushed her against it. I held her by her throat and told her to strip. She was gasping for breath by the time she was naked. We fucked right there in the standing position. I picked her up and wrapped her around me, bouncing her up and down on me until my arms were about to fall off. It was just incredible good cathartic sex.

After the first spanking session, I had printed out the new rules on fine stationary and gave them to her to carry at all times. Our relationship began to evolve in other ways as a normal couple, but I always made it clear that the rules were the foundation for everything. I told her very presumptuously that she was my girl and she needed to be mindful of that at all moments. She said that she understood but there was an enormous transitional period. We got to know each other in deeper ways as a regular couple while doing typical things like going out to eat or binge-watching some show at my place or having long conversations in out-of-the way bars and cafes or going hiking in the mountains for the weekend or venturing to various events, but the power-exchange took time to fully be established.

The heart of our relationship became a very intriguing mixture of vanilla connections and hardcore BDSM. We would sometimes just hang out as friends and drink wine or watch a movie. At other times, she would be very combative and extremely sassy, resulting in a progression of face slapping, spanking, a verbal thrashing, bondage and rough sex. She had a difficult time finding any sort of middle ground in her life in general. She didn't have that many close friends and none of them had any clue that she was even mildly kinky. She preferred to appear as a very straight-laced young woman to everyone. With me, she had an extremely tough time letting her guard down, exposing her emotions and trusting me fully. She was kind of an all-or-nothing type of female.

On my part, I was really starting to fall deeply for her. She is the first female I have ever been with who makes me feel like I can completely be myself. I treat her sweet and lovingly when I am in the mood and she deserves the warm attention, and like a low-down cunt when she acts out. She loves to be put in her place. It has been my own inauguration into brute love. I no longer feel in the least bit guilty with her when I manhandle her physically or speak to her in the most degrading terms. In fact, it arouses me uncontrollably. Still to this day, nothing gets me going like doing something such as whispering to her in public that she is my little fuck pig and ordering her to pull her panties off right then and there.

In addition, she loves and needs it as well on a deep level. I mean she maintains a healthy and happy existence in her daily life, but there is another part of her that deals with all of her existential insecurities by finding a strange peace of mind in knowing that I consistently turn those insecurities into my own perverse pleasures. In her own twisted way, she loves that I have that power over her and treat her however I want to without the slightest remorse. The feeling of being humiliated or degraded or roughly handled takes her to a place she needs to be taken to again and again. Plus, every instance of it gets the both of us incredibly horny and wet like nothing else does.

About six months into our relationship, though, real things came to a breaking point.

She had repeatedly put off looking for a job in the slyest of ways, she failed to abide by several of the rules and she would purposely disobey me just to get a spanking. She really liked getting whipped so it became a fetishistic pleasure for her as much as it was painful discipline. After a number of months of enforcing the rules with harsher and harsher spankings, or other disciplinary acts, I decided there needed to be a change in the kinky, disciplinary power dynamic between us. We lived almost an hour apart so it was becoming increasingly difficult to stay on top of her behavior. She would tell me what she was doing, but she was very good at evading her responsibilities. She was the kind of girl that needed to be kept in check at all times. If I didn't clearly confront her, she would go do things in her own way just so I would put her back in line.

I sat her down and informed her bluntly that either she needed to move in with me or the relationship was over. She pleaded to me that there was no way her parents would understand her moving in with someone who she had met not that long ago. I was wholly shell shocked that she would even need their approval, but that is the kind of girl she is. I told her that she needed to talk to them if that was the case. She said she couldn't. I said that the relationship was over then. I wasn't going to waste any more time chasing her around. She started to cry but it didn't change my ultimatum. I knew she could only understand absolutes.

She left and we didn't speak for at least a week. Then, she called me and asked me if I would reconsider. I told her no again. The next day, she called again and asked me if I would speak with her father about moving in with me. I was completely dumbfounded why I would need to have a conversation with a grown woman's father about this. I asked her why I would need to do such a thing and she told me that I just needed to explain my intentions to him. She said that if her father was fine with me than she would do whatever I wanted.

My mind whirled with this whole crazy situation but it somehow made sense once I considered her personal history. She came into childhood as an orphan. The reasons why her own parents would birth her and then send her off thousands of miles away must have driven her mad inside. I wondered why her adoptive mother and father even sought out such a child. The explanation she had given to me about their Christian outlook on life left so many holes in what I consider genuine honesty.

She is definitely a daddy's girl in an altogether different way than I had ever even imagined. She has to feel so totally wanted and cared for by the people around her that that suspicious paranoia of being abandoned is utterly squashed in her mind.

Her parents lived Back East so meeting her father in person wasn't immediately possible. I decided to just call him and let things go where they were meant to go. We initially talked in heavy detail about my career and my educational background but then the conversation turned into a candid discussion about Selene.

I didn't mince words at all nor try to hide the basic tone of our relationship. I told him bluntly that she needed strict rules to move forward in a positive way with her life and that I needed her under my roof to make sure she abided by them. I explained unequivocally to him that she needed to be disciplined regularly to ensure she did what she was told. There was almost an uncomfortable suggestiveness about the way I said it, but he reservedly agreed that I was right. It was almost as if we were talking about his daughter like she was personal property. By the end of the conversation, he told me that he would like to meet me in the near future, but he was satisfied with my intentions. It must have been the oddest interaction I've ever had in my life.

I called Selene and told her about the conversation. She was very excited and she was suddenly ready to move in with me. I was upset, though, that she had not made this decision on her own. I felt like she was almost acting more out of a need for security than a deep desire to be with me personally. I wondered what would happen in the future if her family or something out of my control drove her to find a different world of assuring circumstances. I told her that because of this she would have to convince me that she truly desired to live with me and not just live under my roof. She was still unemployed at the time and I was a little paranoid that was simply envisioning being in a place that she could keep putting off personal responsibility. She asked me what she needed to do to prove her feelings to me, but I told her that she just had to sincerely convince me.

For the next few months, she acted like a perfect saint. She asked me permission for everything and managed to get numerous job interviews. My intentions, though, were not just to prove her loyalty. I had just got a significant raise at work and was now considering purchasing a new house. I wanted to be sure that if I found something that would accommodate the lifestyle I wanted, she would be there for good.

We had already spoken in depth about the kind of future relationship that we each envisioned. We both longed for the normalcy of a regular "vanilla" life, but still wanted to have a very kinky realm of our own behind closed doors. As she put it, she wanted "a white picket fence and a dungeon in the basement." She longed for these dual lives even more than I did because of the way she had grown up. She had always tried so hard to fit in to this idealized American world in her mind, yet she had deeply conflicting desires to see herself as an objectified female treated in a very physical way. I knew also that she craved a future of affluence and luxury, and I wanted to make sure I could trust her beyond this materialistic impulse.

I ended up deciding on a large four bedroom Victorian-style home in the suburbs. It not only had a large, private backyard but there was an enormous cellar. It was a perfect place to keep an owned woman.

I let Selene suffer in uncertainty for another month until I closed the deal on the house. I surprised her one day by taking her there and showing her the house. She put her hands to her face in disbelief. I knew that she would see the whole situation as her idealized dream come true. She felt like she was getting what she wanted to get from the beginning.

Yet, I knew I couldn't possibly reinforce the idea that she could control how she was controlled. I informed her that she would be allowed to move in, but she would have to earn her place as my girl. I would not tolerate her disobeying me and trying to go astray in how she led her life. She was so excited with the idea of living in this dream-like house and being owned by a man who authentically cared about her and loved her that she readily agreed without any questions.

I explained to her that this meant I would be breaking her in as I saw fit and that she needed to consent to whatever I thought was necessary. She wanted to know of course what exactly this would involve. I told her that she would need to accept in her heart of hearts that she my outright physical possession before we began our new life together in a full on

D/s relationship. We had previously had a serious discussion about "consensual nonconsent" as we were both into it before we had even met. We were equally aware that it could lead to venturing into some deep waters on both an emotional level and a physical level. She said she was a little fearful of what the breaking-in would entail but she was ready to just let go. I asked her formally then if she consented. She looked up at me with a strange, nervous excitement in her eyes and said yes.

By the next week, she had moved her possessions into the house and officially came to live with me the following weekend. It was then that she noticed that none of her clothes were in the master bedroom. She asked me why and I told her that they would remain in the moving bags for the time being as she didn't yet deserve to live in the house. I explained to her that she needed to earn my trust that she would be all mine through thick and thin and that she wouldn't be allowed in the house until she did. She asked me in total shock and confusion as to where she was supposed to stay if she couldn't be in the house. I glared at her in mild sadistic exhilaration over what I was about to tell her. She looked back at me and she knew that I had conjured up something wildly extreme. She frantically asked me again where she was to stay.

I calmly led her to the rear of the house where a large window framed the expansive backyard. I nodded to a small white structure at the far end and then casually told her as if it was the most normal thing in the world that she would sleep in the doghouse that I had built for her.

She just stood there for a few seconds practically paralyzed when she heard the words come out of my mouth. Then she immediately went out into the backyard and inspected the small dwelling. She began to shout and cry that she was no dog. I told her that her days of casual disobedience were over and that she would learn to be my subservient little bitch before I allowed her in the house. She threatened to leave but I just shrugged my shoulders. She protested and argued with me with every curse word she could think of. I promised her that she would be welcomed into the house but that she needed to go through a trial period first to test her willingness to totally submit. I asked her if she still wanted to move in with me. She just looked around at the luxurious space inside the house and then eyed the little doghouse in the back. She sat on the back porch for the rest of the day and pouted.

By the time it got dark, she was all cried out. I went outside and took her by the arm. She was still shouting and protesting as I led her to the doghouse. I made her strip off all her clothes while instructing her to focus on surrendering to the fact that she was now my property. When she saw me pick up the metal dog collar that was chained to the ground, her mouth dropped open in disbelief. I wrapped it around her neck, clasped it tightly and added the lock. I told her that there was twenty feet of chain if she wanted to roam around the yard. She was totally shell shocked. I went back inside to get her dinner. I had picked up sushi from her favorite restaurant. I wanted to break her in slowly and assure her that there was love at the bottom of my cruel ways.

As I was about to go back out, I saw that she was on her hands and knees crawling into the dog house to see how it looked on the inside. I brought her food on a metal tray and slipped it through the door. She was already curled up on her blanket. I had to admit that it was so kinky seeing her laying there completely naked with a dog collar around her neck. She was still pouting but she didn't outright protest her new circumstances anymore. I leaned over, kissed her on the cheek and told her good night. She picked up the chopsticks and began to eat her sushi. It was so arousing that I really wanted to take her roughly right there.

The next morning, when I went out to see her, the reality of being forced to live in a dog house had truly sunk in. She began to yell at me that I was crazy and that she needed a bath and that she needed to do her hair and that she needed a latte and that she needed dozens of other things. It was the middle of summer and it was already hot out. I told her to crawl out to the middle of the yard and I would hose her off. She was absolutely furious with me but I told her that if she didn't that I would just leave her to be dirty. I turned the hose on full blast as she grudgingly crawled onto the lawn. I washed her from head to toe and then brought her a towel. I told her that if she needed to wash herself from here on out, she could crawl to get the hose.

As I was about to go back inside, she looked up at me and it occurred to her that I was really going to keep her like this for as long as I saw fit. I asked her if she was having second thoughts and she didn't say anything. She just crawled back into her dog house. I knew that on one level she hated being treated like this, yet on another level, she got off on the dehumanizing perversity of it all. She later told me she masturbated every night she was kept like that.

Over the next week, she began to mentally break down from her normal demeanor. I spent most evenings having deep discussions with her about her past and about us. I knew that she had a lot of unresolved issued about being adopted and that she carried those issues into every relationship that she had ever had. She had constructed this imaginary world in her mind where she could control how everything in her mind worked out, only it didn't exist in reality. She had to let go and be forced to decide if she really wanted to wholeheartedly give into me without any reservations.

Her protests, her crying and her temper tantrums became less and less frequent. After another few days, there were none at all. She learned that this was the only path I was giving her and that she was going to have to show me how absolutely submissive she was to me if she wanted to be let in the house.

One morning, I came outside to find her perched at the doorway of her dog house with a slight smile on her face. She wished me a good morning and told me she was ready for her bath. I washed her down and dried her off as if it was all completely normal that I was treating my naked girlfriend like a pet animal. After several more days of the same response, I realized that she had learned her lesson. I formally notified her that she would be allowed into my house but to never forget her place. I told her I had no problem putting her back in the doghouse. She was ecstatic when I removed her training collar. She pranced into the house and immediately took a shower. She was traumatized over the whole experience but she never forgot it.

She later told me that she hated being out there chained up all alone but at times she got a deviant thrill out of it. She said that in retrospect it perversely aroused her being kept like a naughty dog, but that she never wanted to be there for days at a time again. I had taken her list of rules and posted them in a frame on the wall. I had a professional printer make them to look like an antique relic so visitors would think that it was just some humorous memento from the past. There was nothing humorous, though, about the rules. At the bottom of the list, there was a small imprint of a dog house to remind her on a daily basis what would happen if she broke any rule.

Our relationship slowly evolved into a world of its own. As far as our neighbors know, we are this regular suburban couple who likes to have dinner parties, get involved with all kinds of cultural happenings and go on road trips. Behind closed doors, our exchanges are as deviant and taboo as they get. She loves to mouth off just so I'll slap her across the face or put her over my knee and spank her bare butt. When she gets too sassy, I'll put a ball gag in her mouth, strip off her clothes and make her clean the whole kitchen with a tooth brush. When she gets really disobedient, I put her in a cage that I had installed in the basement. Our whole dynamic truly feeds on her being the extreme naughty brat and me being the disciplinary dictator who is enthralled by his depraved power over her.

It's strange to say, though, that I never really want her to totally submit to me every second of the day nor does she want to. She just likes to be dominated and I like to keep reinforcing the fact that I have the unyielding upper hand. Our sex life is even kinkier now…lots of rough sex, rope bondage, spreader restraints, forced deep throating, pussy slapping, caning…even various kidnapping fantasies and heavy humiliation. We both love it. She is my smiley housewife, my naughty girl and my owned slut all in one.

A couple years after she moved in, our relationship was progressing deeper and deeper into the ownership mentality. To say we have a very unique connection is a vast understatement. On a daily level, part of her inhabits a very regular suburban lifestyle. She has a small business as a caterer, she loves to bake, she's really involved with foodie culture, she finds interesting places to go to in the city and she tends to her organic garden in our backyard. On a relationship level, we have an incredibly complex dynamic. I interact with her as a traditional loving soul mate, yet I also regularly discipline her in the most strictly patriarchal ways, subject her to the most physical rough and kinky acts imaginable and always let her know that I completely own her in an ever-present way.

After a number of years, I came to a point in which I wanted to "mark" her as mine. We had talked about it before but had never acted on it. After we attended a friend's wedding, though, the desire to visually illustrate my ownership of her kept running through my mind. I thought about a tattoo but I decided that the nature of our relationship called for something more extreme, so I elected to have her branded. At first she was conflicted about the idea, but the more we discussed it, the more enthralling the whole vision of her being marked like a true slave became to both of us.

I did the research and found someone in Montana who was into the lifestyle and had real expertise in branding. He had learned to do it with cattle, but he had also branded a number of woman in the BDSM community. I discussed everything with Selene and we planned out the details. The specific design would be a Korean symbol for loyalty, along with my first initial above it. It was a perfect fit for her. It would be done on the right cheek of her ass so as to remain largely hidden. I also insisted that we have a small ceremony in which we both profess our vows of faithfulness before the actual branding was performed.

I'll never forget that moment. It was not only a significant affirmation of our love and of our particular way of extreme living, but the event itself was incredibly surreal and inexplicable powerful. We invited a number of individuals, total strangers really, who were involved in D/s relationships but also just wanted to watch like voyeurs. The only rule we had for them was that they couldn't take any photos. We had the ranch house where it was to take place decorated like a wedding scene...lights strewn on the ceiling, silky white ornamentation from wall to wall, a black carpet to the branding alter...it was truly epic in the most deviant way.

The professing of our vows seemed to go by in a flash. Both of us were so nervous about the final event that we were just in a dream-like state. As the rancher heated the branding iron that he had designed, a number of the onlookers helped me secure Selene. We used leather straps to tie her to the metal hooks that had been crafted into the wooden wall of the ranch so she couldn't move a single inch. Just to make sure that she didn't shift in place, we held her down as the rancher move towards her with the iron. When he pressed the red-hot piece of metal against her flesh, it seemed like time slowed to a standstill. She gritted her teeth, there was a wisp of smoke and then he pulled the branding iron away. It was the wildest thing I'd ever seen. I stared at the little oriental symbol as if I was in a trance while the rancher attended to the aftercare. I can still picture the whole scenario in my mind, second by second, to this day.

We both love to look at it and remind ourselves of the entire ceremony. It was such a simple act but at the same time so completely perverse. It felt like we were part of some illicit cult. In retrospect, I think the strangest thing about the branding was the day we came back home from the ranch and casually waved to the neighbor as he was watering his lawn. He had no idea that that smiling woman in the passenger seat had the flesh of her ass singed just a couple days before. She was irrevocably mine. Or let me correct that, she is irrevocably mine. Until death do us part.

Chapter 9 – Discipline

"Right discipline consists, not in external compulsion, but in the habits of mind which lead spontaneously to desirable rather than undesirable activities." –Bertrand Russell

"Discipline is based on pride, on meticulous attention to details, and on mutual respect and confidence. Discipline must be a habit so ingrained that it is stronger than the excitement of the goal or the fear of failure." –Gary Ryan Blair

"Without discipline, there's no life at all." –Katherine Hepburn

Discipline is typically an essential element of a relationship between a man and the woman he owns. It sets a solid foundation of consistency that allows a woman to develop faith in her owner's concern, care and desire for her. It can be used to enforce rules, change behavior and mold a woman's personality and body. Discipline can include corporal punishment, verbal chastisement, corner time, restriction of freedoms, humiliation, sensory deprivation and any other action with a goal of negative reinforcement. The only instance where these are not to be used as negative reinforcement is when the woman is masochistic and enjoys pain. With such a woman, a man should consider these disciplinary actions as rewards and he should use them as positive reinforcement.

It is rare, though, that even a masochistic woman does not consider at least one of the above actions as a negative consequence of her behavior. There is always some personal freedom or possession that a woman prizes. At the very least, a man can put her in isolation from others or himself for extended periods. The human mind naturally detests solitary isolation for long durations of time. Even masochistic-tending women will break down at a certain point and will remember its effects when they consider repeating the offense.

There are some basic principles of discipline that should be followed. First, it is important to match the punishment to the infraction. Minor disobedience should result in minor discipline. Extreme disobedience should result in extreme discipline. Secondly, administer the punishment immediately following the offense. The woman should mentally associate the two in the precise moment of time. By making the inevitable discipline predictable and properly done, the woman will respect her owner's word. She will understand that if he tells her that she is going to be disciplined, she will indeed be disciplined. On some occasions, she will know precisely why she is being disciplined by a simple look from her owner. At other times, a stern lecture and reprimand is necessary before or during the disciplinary session. Some couples like to use safe words, which are used by the woman to indicate she has reached a bad breaking point, instead of a good breaking point, and needs the man to stop. These are generally used in "session play" where the man does not know the ins-and-outs of the woman's personality but they can certainly be used if boundaries need to be set.

There are innumerable types of disciplinary implements. Some are made for discipline while others are made for entirely different purposes but make perfect punishment devices. A man should be creative and particular when choosing disciplinary implements. Consistency is important but the spirit of the action should be kept lively and spontaneous. Natural implements include the bare hand, belts, paddles, straps, rulers, whips, floggers, canes and crops. Belts can be hard, soft, new, old, thick and thin. Paddles include BDSM leather and wood paddles, fraternity-style paddles, ping pong paddles, paddle ball paddles, butter paddles, cotton-combing paddles and many other objects that are made in a paddle shape. Straps include BDSM leather straps, prison straps, razor straps/strops, equine straps, cattle straps and many other objects used as straps for other purposes. Rulers and yardsticks can be thick, thin, new, vintage and made of various woods. Canes can be made of wicker, bamboo, fabric and many other types of wood. There are vintage canes from English boarding schools, disciplinary canes used in foreign countries and modern canes made specifically for BDSM use. Other disciplinary implements include carpet beaters, spatulas, hair brushes, pieces of birch or willow branches, hickory sticks and switches taken from certain plants with long, hard vines or twigs. A man should make full use of the broad spectrum of implements and constantly keep an eye out for objects that might be well-suited for punishment purposes. Online auctions, garage sales and second-hand stores are excellent sources.

When punishing a woman in any way he decides to punish her, it is of vital importance that a man knows what he is doing. If he is not an expert spanker, he should start slow and easy. Learn how to use the implement. Practice striking her in specific spots and varying the degree of force. Be aware of her reactions. Get a sense of her pain threshold. Ask for her feedback. Certain implements can be very dangerous if not used correctly. Don't let one's emotions get out of hand. Enjoy perfecting the skillful use of an implement over time.

A man can either be very ritualistic with the punishment or do it spontaneously. He can send the woman to a special place or room to wait, causing an extra period of anxiety to think about what she is going to get. He can make her bend over to touch her toes or wrap her hands around the back of her calves. Objects to bend her over include chairs, sofas, workbenches, spanking benches and desks. There is also the traditional over-the-knee spanking. The man can be as consistent or as varied as he likes. He can make her count the spankings or repeat a phrase such as the traditional, "Thank you, sir. May I have another?" He should make full use of his imagination in creating a very particular and memorable disciplinary session.

It is also vital that the woman does not enjoy the discipline. It is natural that most submissive-tending or owned women enjoy the sensation of being spanked or physically disciplined to some degree. There is a fine line between pain and pleasure. It is important that an implement is used at a severe-enough intensity that it causes real pain and discomfort for the woman. If the woman acts out or "brats" purposely to get a spanking, the punishment should be altered to truly affect her behavior and discourage her desire to be disciplined. A man should distinguish pleasurable spankings from disciplinary spankings. At no point should the discipline become abusive or result in negative personality traits. In a sincerely committed ownership situation, the woman should never fear the man in a manner that she deeply does not like or causes resentment over being in the relationship. Fear is a very valuable tool of an owner but it is a means to an end. The end should always be a positive result for both the man and the owned woman.

Other physical punishments include face slapping, hair pulling and striking of the palm with a ruler. Face slapping is particularly suited for punishment for talking back, forbidden language and attitude adjustment. There is also the traditional mouth washing or placing a bar of soap in the woman's mouth during corner time punishment. There are many types of soap that can be used, some more distasteful than others. Experiment to determine what type is most effective.

A vital element of the punishment is instilling the acceptance of the punishment in the woman's mind. While certain situations inevitably result in a bratty-type kicking-and-screaming session as she gets her panties pulled down and spanked a bright shade of red, this should generally not be how a scene plays out. She should accept the punishment because it has been earned. The attitude with which she accepts her punishment is just as important as her attitude in daily life. A refusal to accept a punishment is even grounds for a secondary punishment session. One can be given immediately and a secondary one can be given before bedtime. There is also the option of putting her "on restriction" that includes daily spankings during the duration of her grounding.

Mental punishment can often be more effective than physical punishment. Verbal chastisement and humiliation, if used in the right way, can get to the core of a woman much more quickly than physical discipline. A man should understand how a woman views herself. He should know her insecurities as well as her real aspirations. A man should never belittle or humiliate a woman in a way that causes her to form a negative or self-loathing image of herself. The proper words or phrases should communicate a feeling of disappointment or disapproval. Expectations should have been previously discussed. The owned woman should know precisely who she is expected to be in her personality, her behavior, her physical shape, her adherence to rules and her performance. There should be little or no difference between how the man conceives of her and how the owned woman conceives of herself.

Sensory deprivation can also be an effective punishment. A woman can be tied up and blindfolded. She can be placed in restraints such as a full body spreader, handcuffs, shackles, a straight-jacket, armbinders or other devices. Antique slave devices such as heavy metal collars and wrist or ankle shackles are very effective as well. Some men like to use a cage to fully restrict the woman and to make her mentally feel like an animal. One can use a standard cage manufactured for a large dog or he can have one manufactured to his specifications. If using a cage, make sure to monitor her regularly, particularly if she has been restrained with a ball gag as well. A woman can be kept in a cage for a few hours or for much longer periods. If kept in a cage for an extended period, make sure to provide for nourishment such as a bowl of water and regular feeding times, as well as toilet needs. Other men like to go to the extreme of building separate slave quarters such as a locked room in a basement. There is also the option of putting the woman in a dog house in the backyard. If any of these more extreme measures are taken, there should already be a deep level of trust developed in the relationship.

The removal of freedoms, privileges and normal amenities is also a very effect means of discipline. This should be something that the woman especially prizes or needs. This is entirely up to the man and he should be imaginative in his discipline. She can be forbidden to use her car and be made to take the bus to work. She can only be allowed to eat a type of food she dislikes. She can be forbidden any sexual pleasure. She can be forced to get a demeaning second job. The options are endless.

Other punishments include sentence writing, essay writing, BDSM-oriented devices such as butt plugs and chastity belts, cleaning the floors with a toothbrush or old-fashioned hand brush and public humiliation such as scolding in front of a friend or a spanking within view of strangers.

In the end, the disciplinary action should result in the desired effect of the man. There is endless pleasure in disciplining a woman but it should not cause the woman to enjoy it to the point of it being ineffective. There should be a joy in helping the owned woman achieve a goal or alter her personality in a positive way. A man should reward her properly when she does as she is told, breaks a bad habit or meets his expectations. He should take pride in what he owns and she should feel the pleasure of administering correction. The world of discipline can be bound up with many conflicting desires, fears, pleasures, pains and thoughts. There is a certain spiritual, psychological and metaphysical sensation of feeling alive at the heart of the act but the man should control the fine line between this potent sensation and the real purpose of the punishment. If the man is sadistic, or the woman is masochistic, the world of discipline operates in a completely different sphere. These dynamics are addressed in the chapter on sexual gratification training.

Pride in Service

An owned woman should never serve as if it is a chore. Pride in service is the term used to express the quality of deriving pleasure and satisfaction from serving a man in the precise way he likes to be served. A woman should focus on what she is doing as its own end instead of as a means to getting something for herself. If she is required to clean the kitchen floor until it is spotless, she should take pride in the fact that she can do an impeccable job at being a floor cleaner. It is a partial mental separation between serving to please the man and serving to be a good server. Pride in service adds to the woman's sense of self-worth in her place as an owned human. It is akin to the pride a military soldier maintains in being a soldier. The attitude is as important as the action. It does not matter if she is making breakfast, taking charge in a work situation, sucking cock for an hour without stopping or reading a book she is told to read. There should always be a prideful pleasure interwoven in the act and in its completion. Failure to maintain pride in service or doing something with a bad attitude can always be corrected with proper discipline.

Case Study 9.1

"The Disciplined Hotwife"

Matthew and Georgina

Matthew: I have always been into disciplining my significant other in both strict and pleasurable ways. Even as early as high school, I would spank my girlfriend for being naughty or getting bad grades or just because her cute little ass was there and my natural impulse was to smack it until it turned a deep shade of red. I love the sharp quickening of emotions that happens when my palm strikes that female flesh.

When I met Georgina, though, I was really able to take it to the extreme. I think she might enjoy it even more than I do. She had been raised with spankings so she had her own conflicted issues with it. She told me at the beginning of our relationship that she used to hate getting disciplined, but as she got into her twenties she began to fantasize about it in a sexual manner more and more. She told me that she would ask her boyfriends to spank her, but it was never that good because they really weren't into it nearly as much as she was.

Yet, just as we were fully getting into spanking in all its endless variations, the whole thing unexpectedly evolved into something much, much more than just vicious slaps of her ass. It took us on a journey down into a whole new substratum of kink that I never expected to be so uncontrollably stimulating. It became like a drug addiction and Georgina was my gateway to harder and harder sexual dope.

I actually spanked her the very first time I met her. It was a very unique situation. I had just purchased a duplex in Los Angeles and was looking to rent out one of the apartments. She was the last person that day to come to see it. She is a baby-faced blond with a very distinctive look of innocence and has these deep russet brown eyes that make her look as if she had come straight out of a Margaret Keane painting. She had come to Los Angeles to be an actress, as females from all over the world tend to endlessly do. I found out later that she was not a natural blond at all. Her father is from Latin America and her mother is from was Kentucky. She has a nice perky spankable bottom that she must have gotten from her Latin side.

After I showed her the apartment, she asked me about the rent. I told her the rate and then I added that it was due on the first of the month without exception. She jokingly asked me what would happen if she was late with the rent. Normally, I'm not so explicit about my enjoyment of discipline, but something inside me told me to just be open with her right away. I've learned that if you are overtly expressive about being into spanking with someone you have just met, either they will quickly signal that they are into it as well, or they will think you are just kidding. Either way, there is nothing to lose so I told her that if she was late with rent by a single day that I would whip her bare butt on the spot.

She laughed at me, at first assuming I was joking and then repeated back my comment, asking me if I really would spank her for it. She was wearing a pair of baby blue shorts and I just couldn't resist. I walked over to her, grabbed her lightly and gave her a hard smack over her shorts. Then, I asked her, "What do you think?" I guess it was fortunate that she was into it or she probably would have just up and left. She thought I was a bit crazy for doing that, but I could tell she was definitely suppressing how much she liked my audacity to do it.

I asked her if she wanted to go ahead with the paperwork. I gave her an intense look and she smiled self-consciously before glancing away. She muttered a yes as she shyly giggled. I told her she had 30 minutes to get me the first month's rent and the security deposit. She asked me, "Only 30 minutes?" I replied to her that I have a leather strap upstairs that I would take to her if she was one minute late. She raised her eyebrows at me. I looked at my watch, repeated the disciplinary promise and then led her out.

She returned 45 minutes later and knocked on my door. She pleaded that there was a long line at the bank. I simply told her to go wait in her new apartment while I got my strap. She couldn't believe I was serious but the whole vibe of the exchange was more playful than anything of a true disciplinary nature. When I entered the apartment, she was standing there fidgeting in the empty living room. She asked me if I was really going to spank her and I told her, "Absolutely." I motioned for her to go bend over the kitchen counter. She was grinning the whole time as she sauntered over to the tile counter and rested her arms on it. She glanced back at me teasingly as she extended her legs taut and arched her back. Her shorts were so short that the curve of her butt was exposed when she bent over. She looked like a picture-perfect naughty ingénue.

I wasted no time in swatting her ass with the vintage leather strap. After the third one, she glanced back at me again and I noticed she still had a smile on her face. She was enjoying it a little too much, so I took a harder swing and aimed at the bare strip of flesh just below the bottom of her shorts. I struck it soundly and she suddenly gasped. I took aim and repeatedly strapped her on the same place over and over. After a half-dozen of those, she was on her tip-toes trying to get away from the force of the strap. After a few final hard swats, I stopped.

I took the keys to the apartment out of my pocket and set them on the counter next to her. She stood up, turned around and glared at me. I could tell by the look on her face that the spanking ended up being harder than she thought it was going to be, but her cheeks were flush with arousal. I told her I was going to get the lease for her to sign and she mumbled, "Okay." On the way out, I noticed a small hook that was built into the wall next to the door. I hung the strap on it before I left.

It only took a couple of weeks before we started having a fling. I would run into her almost daily and we quickly got to know one another. As I was passing by on my way home one afternoon, she invited me into her new place to show me what she had done with it. She was unpacking groceries and had bought a couple bottles of wine. We started drinking, one thing led to another and we ended up in a flurry of kisses and groping on the floor. The sex was very raw. I had her on her hands and knees while I furiously spanked her. When she orgasmed, it was incredibly vocal. The dramatic actress in her delivered her lewd lines right on cue.

As we started to get involved, she began to tell me much more about herself as well as all her dreams and visions about making it as an actress. Anyone who has spent any amount of time in L.A. knows you could fill stadiums ten times over with such naïve star-struck thespians. She didn't really know anyone but was adamant how driven she was on becoming a serious actress. I typically roll my eyes at such proclamations but there was something special about her that made me bury my cynicism. She asked if I knew anyone that could help her out, but I didn't really know more than a handful of people who worked in the middle management realm of the industry. I told her, though, that it wasn't really a matter of who she knew. I explained to her that she just needed to do great acting work and be pathologically disciplined about everything she did. When I said the word "disciplined", she looked up at me and smiled. She asked me if I would help her stay focused. We both knew exactly what that meant and I readily agreed.

I became like a strict mentor to her and used a wide variety of implements to discipline her. I set her schedule for what time she got up, what she ate, when she went to the gym, which acting classes she took and which films she auditioned for. I was working from home developing various real estate deals at the time, so it was very easy for me to look after her. I would knock on her door at eight in the morning and she was expected to have showered and be ready for me. I instructed her to answer the door totally nude. The first thing I did was inspect her body to make sure she was fulfilling her workout regimen and keeping perfectly fit. If I was not pleased, she would be made to get on her hands and knees, and then I would spank her with a small paddle.

After inspection, she would provide the details of her plan for the day to me. This included attending acting classes, going to work, applying for parts, working out and running errands. At the end of her day, before we had dinner together, she would report the outcome of her day. Once again, if I was displeased with any of it, she would receive repeated strokes of the paddle. Occasionally, I would have her record her performance in her acting classes, give her feedback and discipline her for any mistakes. Because she loved to be spanked so much, though, it was hardly ever punishment to her. It was more about having someone completely there for her every single day. The spanking was simply our own physical affirmation of that bond.

After a couple months of this regimen, I began to make more demands on her. I required her to submit to a certain number of roles and actually get a certain number of parts in quality films. At first, she protested that she had no control over who would actually cast her. I simply told her that she better raise her level of acting craft then. Each Friday afternoon, she reported her results to me. If she did not meet the goals I had set for her, she would be strapped with this thick vintage strap. It was an antique prison strap with a wood handle I had purchased at auction. It had been formerly used on prisoners in Scotland during the early part of the twentieth century. It was very stiff and, according to her, it hurt like hell. After a few weeks of getting her bare ass thoroughly spanked with it, she miraculously began to get more and more roles.

One evening we went out to attend the premiere of a short film in which she had played the lead. When I saw her do her thing on the big screen, I was completely blown away. I knew she had solid talent but she was a bona fide natural. Her presence in every scene was intoxicating. She possessed such a girlish look but her aptitude for visual detail made her seem seasoned far beyond her years. I couldn't believe I had not truly noticed it before that moment. I like to think that the strict discipline had something to do with it, but the truth is that it probably only accelerated the flowering of her raw capabilities. I glanced over at her in the dark theater and realized I was starting to fall hard for her.

As we were walking to the car, I told her in the most heartfelt words I could muster that she was really something special, both as an actress and to me. I was muttering a bunch of other words when she started to cry and then lunged over to hug me. It was such a tender moment that I will never forget it, especially after I had fallen into the rhythm of being so strict with her.

After that night, I was suddenly more and more motivated to bring out the very best in her. I was like a cruel but kinky teacher. She protested often, but she never asked me to stop and she was always ecstatic when she made real progress. I would also always reward her efforts and her accomplishments with both praising words and surprise gifts such as a vacation to some exotic locale. I not only loved to see her achieve real success, but I sincerely enjoyed being such an intimate part of her flourishing on a daily basis. There was nothing like seeing her bright little face first thing each morning when she opened her front door to me, completely naked, in expectation of her inspection and detailed preparation for the day.

As time went on, our relationship started to get more and more serious. My investments in real estate were going exceedingly well and I told Georgina that she could live in her place rent free as long as she continued to meet my expectations. She was absolutely ecstatic. It gave her complete freedom to pursue her acting career without any unnecessary financial worries. We began to develop a deeper level of trust, explored some really taboo fantasies and got to know each other inside and out. We share a similar sensibility in movies and books so we spend a lot of time at old theaters and independent book stores. Sometimes that means browsing up and down the book aisles together, other times that means me secretly fondling her cunt in the corner of the store before I take her to the gentlemen's room to get fucked. We not only have a similar appreciation for the more pleasurable things in life, but our dynamic feels like we are old friends who can tell each other absolutely anything. The connection has always been very open and exploratory in spirit from the very beginning.

Our relationship, though, is always intertwined with her development as an actress. Even when we have sex, I will sometimes give her a certain role to play. Sometimes I will tell her to act like a very pretentious actress and then spank the arrogance right out of her. Other times I will order her to act like a giggly slut and then face fuck the bimbo right out of her. I will even make her speak with a particular accent or pretend to be a certain character. It's like having a hundred different women in one.

There was one night in particular, though, that her role playing set the relationship off in a whole different direction. She was joking around with me in a flirtatious way when she started to pretend like I was the director of a film in which she wanted to get the lead role. She was speaking to me in a very lascivious manner, asking me if she could suck my cock to get the part. It was such a turn-on that it lingered in my mind for days. I had always had vague fantasies of telling a girlfriend to be flirtatious with another guy, but I had never explored any of it in real life. The thoughts of her being with another man generated this extremely arousing mixture of obscene pleasure and outright jealousy in me that I couldn't get out of my mind.

When we went out, we would sometimes go to industry-type parties brimming with producers and directors. A couple of weeks after she pretended that she was giving me a blow job in order to get an acting role, we were at a party in the Hollywood Hills. There were a lot of well known celebrities and successful producers there. Georgina pointed out one in particular who she told me was producing a major film that was currently being cast. It was when she mentioned, though, that he was married that the idea clicked in my mind.

I pulled her to me and whispered in her ear about how much it turned me on when she sucked my cock the other night. I motioned toward the producer she had pointed out and told her that I wanted to see her do the real thing. Her eyes opened in stark shock at the idea and she asked me if I was serious. I told her I was absolutely serious and that she needed to do it right now or I wouldn't let her go out for the next month. She pleaded that had never done anything like that which only made me want her to do it that much more. I told her to gulp down her drink and get her little slutty ass to work. After more anxious protests and one more shot of vodka, I ushered her off toward the guy. Just as she was walking away, I told her she better do a good job or she'll be paying for it later.

I watched her as she casually lingered around the guy. When he strolled over to the bar to get a drink, she immediately followed and perched herself right next to him. I was intensely jealous just watching them talk, but the fact that I was the one who had initiated her flirtatious intentions gave me some feeling of control over the spectacle. Georgina did everything she could to make her desires obvious. She smiled and laughed at everything he said. She casually touched his arm and brushed her body against his. She stared at him like she wanted to fuck him on the spot. Finally, she leaned over and said something to him. He laughed and said something back to her. A moment later, he casually walked away as she followed him. She looked over in my direction and gave me a knowing smile. I moved to follow them as they both disappeared out the front door.

When I got outside, they were climbing into his car. I couldn't believe it. I took out my phone and sent her a text message, asking her where they were going. A few seconds later she sent me back a text that read "somewhere private". I raced to my car and sped off to follow them. A couple of minutes later they pulled off of Mulholland Drive onto a scenic nook that overlooked the city. I pulled my car off to the other side of the road and watched them. I could just barely make out their dark figures in the car. I quickly sent Georgina a text telling her that I wanted to hear everything. A moment later, my phone rang and I answered it. She didn't say anything, but I assumed that she had called my number and then hid the phone.

After a few moments, I could hear them talking. She was telling him how much she loved to give head and would love to be his official cock sucker on the set of his next film. He laughed and then told her it was going to be a long shoot.

She replied that she better get her lips in shape then. I squinted in the direction of their car just as I saw her silhouette bend over and disappear. The next thing I knew the sounds of her slurping, sucking and gagging on his cock radiated into my ear. It was such an uncontrollable turn-on to hear her being so sexual with someone else. I could hear the man begin to moan as she furiously sucked him.

All I could do was sit back in my seat and listen to the show. It seemed to go on forever. He began talking dirty to her, telling her to deep throat him and that she better suck it harder if she wanted the part. Finally, I heard him sound out a series a moans as he had an orgasm. I could only imagine Georgina taking in all his cum into her mouth. I realized I was not only furiously jealous, but my cock was rock hard. It was one of the most unexpectedly arousing things I had ever experienced.

On the way home, she recounted all the details to me. I asked her if she liked doing it and she replied that it made her feel so dirty. I asked her again if she liked it and she guiltily confessed that she did. She told me, though, that she would never have done it if I hadn't ordered her to do it and if I wasn't close by the whole time. When we got home, I spanked her for being such a dirty girl and made her go down on me. Watching her wrap her lips over the head of my cock after she had just done it with someone else drove me wild. She really does have such an incredibly innocent and girlish look to her so when I saw her act so downright slutty, the contrasting blend did things to me that I can barely explain. I took her that night with such ferocious force that even she was shocked by how much the whole thing had turned me on.

After that night, I felt like I was born a new man as far as my sexual being is concerned. I didn't even know that getting turned on by your girlfriend being with other men was an explicit kink that many others enjoy. I guess Georgina would be considered what people call a hotwife, but we're not even married and that term does not even touch upon the depths I like to take things to. She brings out what I like to call my absolutely pure "slut love". She is my slut. I love her as a slut. I love to make her do the sluttiest things imaginable. I have taken her natural desire for attention and turned it into relationship pornography.

While at first she was hesitant at that initial experience, she has now embraced the shameless debauchery of her body for my own pleasure as well as for hers. She gets turned on by how much it turns me on, but she can't hide how much it brings out deeper urges in her. She has always craved the spotlight and now I have switched on all the kinky lights at once. When she goes out, with or without me, she strives to dress like a coquettish harlot of iconic proportions. This means scantily clad in tight little shorts and braless tees while running errands. This means obscenely revealing dresses while out at night. This means the tiniest of v-string bathing suits at the pool. This means being exhibited at all times as my beautiful naughty piece of ass starving for the attention of every attractive male on earth.

Her life as my disciplined actress coming into her own as a veritable starlet has now become interwoven with her life as the center of my slut love. It has been like an extravagant erotic game with no end. I still keep her on a strict schedule to further her career as an actress but I have given her a secret second life that keeps her constantly busy satiating my adulterous demands.

The oddest thing is it never gets old unlike many other fantasies do once I've explored them. I think the simple reason is because of how Georgina truly looks doing it all. It's her blond-headed innocent face, her perky lips, her baby doe eyes...all her girlish gestures. They are completely betrayed by her sexual doings the moment she crosses that line. Her protruding Latina ass and her round bouncy breasts take center stage. The second she opens her mouth to take in a cock or she wraps her naked body on top of a man's lap is pure visual ecstasy. Even to hear about it enslaves my deviant mind. It would actually be selfish of me not to share such a rare female specimen.

I could go on for pages and pages detailing it all but just to provide a sampling...

Georgina has a new agent with strict orders to orally service him anytime he wants her to. Sometimes this is at his office. Sometimes it is when he stops by and I order her to do it right in front of me. Sometimes he just texts her that he's trying to get her cast in a certain film and I tell to text him back to ask him if she can come over and suck him off. He knows to keep it all a secret, especially from his wife.

Her liaisons with other men are unforgettable. I initiate them all. I sometimes have friends over to watch some sporting event and Georgina frolics about is some skimpy get-up until I chastise her for teasing all of us and order her to strip down. She then spends the rest of the evening serving us drinks and servicing our bodies until we ultimately end up pounding away at her in every configuration.

Her trips to the gym are epic. I put her in all white: skin tight yoga pants so thin they disappear into the depths of her ass cheeks, a white thong pulled taut to show off her camel-toed cunt and a snug white top to exhibit her little nipples. I can lift truckloads of weights while I ogle her working out in front of me. Nearly every man in the place is falling over themselves to get a glimpse of her or to try to get a word in between sets. She glances over me as I shake my head at each one until the right one comes along and I nod. Sometimes it is because he has that look that makes me think he'll just sexually maul her in the right way. Sometimes he is that black guy with a huge cock that I happened to have seen in the locker room. Once it was the gym owner who she convinced to take her into the men's shower room after hours.

The possibilities never end.

I make sure though not to completely overdo it, especially when it comes to work, as I don't want her to seriously develop the reputation among people in the industry. I will typically only allow her to be with men who are married, not only to keep things safer, but I know they wouldn't want anyone else to know. There are certainly exceptions to this as many times the moment is just too perfect. She is also required to get my permission to do anything at all. This usually means her calling me on the phone and formally asking me if she can do something terribly naughty with someone I know or someone she just happened to meet. It is a perpetually arousing dynamic of which we never tire. Afterward almost any foray, I always go through the ritual of spanking her for being such as dirty girl and then pummeling away at her with all my pent-up kinky jealousy. It was my way of "reclaiming" her over and over and over. She loves that.

Miraculously, her oral favors really did get her roles in prominent films. Later, when I watched the movies and saw her, all I could think about was her going down on the guy who produced or directed it in between shooting those very scenes. Eventually, she built up such a strong reel that she didn't have any need to sexually service anyone. Yet, she still did simply for our own perverse pleasure. Our relationship, also, has gotten more serious. She has moved in with me even though I keep her apartment open for her to have a place to have her flings while I watch via the hidden security cameras. Apart from all the naughty antics driven by my insatiable slut love, I sincerely do love her. I can't imagine how my life would have turned out without her. Even apart from the kink, there's nothing else I enjoy more than lounging around with her on a Sunday morning or wandering around the neighborhood hand in hand.

Chapter 10 – Body Modification

"If anything is sacred, the human body is sacred" –Walt Whitman

"The human body is the best picture of the human soul." – Ludwig Wittgenstein

"Anatomy is destiny." –Sigmund Freud

There are many different female body types but the overall look of it can be altered in innumerable ways. Body modification includes physical fitness routines, weight control, food control, tightlace waist-cinching, hair removal, maintenance of physical appearance, piercings, breast augmentation, butt implants, tattooing, branding and cosmetic surgery. A woman's body image is tied up in many personal and social psychologies in how she should look. It is important for an owned woman to understand that it is not her body from which to form an image. It is his body to mold to his satisfaction. At the same time, a man should not create unnecessary negative images in a woman's head. He must be both realistic and focused on the positive possibilities in crafting a woman's body to his liking. Permanent physical changes should be made only after serious considerations of the psychological and physical implications in the near and distant future. A body is a dynamic thing always in a state of change. There is no ultimate rule forbidding it from being changed in particular ways. Social ideals are all relative and susceptible to constant change.

Yet, there is nothing more important to a man, at times, than a woman's body. A man loves to endlessly ogle a woman's body at every occasion, in every state of dress and undress, at all times of the day and night. It is vital for an owned woman to create and maintain the body that he wants.

The first thing a man should do is take an initial evaluation of his woman's body. Make her strip down to be examined. Take photos of her. Weigh her using either a traditional scale or one used for livestock. Make her understand that she is her owner's piece of meat. Take her measurements including her waist size and chest girth. Write down the basic qualities that are satisfactory and the parts that need alteration.

A man should create a plan for a woman's physical fitness. He can send her to a personal trainer, develop his own fitness routine for her or order her to develop a physical regimen that is to his satisfaction. Clear goals should be established as well as a daily, weekly and monthly fitness schedule. If a man elects to control her food intake, meal plans should be developed. The progress should be measured using specific measurements and photos. The goals should be realistic but the discipline for not meeting the goals must be strict and consistent.

Each man has a specific vision of how he would like to mold his woman. The general desire of most men, though, is a body with a toned physique, sizeable breasts, slimmed waist and a developed ass. Some men simply want a woman to be in shape while others like to use extreme means to achieve extreme results. The woman must be made to understand at all times that it is not a matter of her owner being unhappy with her body but purely a desire to create the body he desires to create. Negative reactions to or conceptions of body image by an owned woman should be addressed immediately.

Tightlace waist-cinching is the process of using a corset or waist-cincher to physically alter the size of a woman's waist. It should be done with extreme care and regular monitoring. A man should educate himself in the process and seek out the guidance of successful tightlacers. Extreme body modification using corsets should be avoided as it causes the body's posture and muscles to become dependent on wearing such clothing. Depending on the silhouette desired, the shape of the ribcage may be altered as well. Wearing a corset can also change the bust line, by raising the breasts upwards and shaping them, flattening the stomach, and improving posture. Tightlacing should never replace physical fitness as a means to shape a woman's figure. It is merely used to further train the body in gradual degrees.

To begin tightlacing, a woman should ideally be measured for a custom corset. This can either be done by the corset maker or by taking the woman's measurements according to the maker's needs. Since the corset will be worn daily, and perhaps at all times, a man should put great care and creativity in choosing the style and look of the corset. The woman should be given the task of researching the history of corset styles and present sample images to determine what he likes. She should locate the best corset designers in the country to decide who is best suited for her owner's taste. Some corsets makers are familiar and in favor of tightlacing while others are not. Corsets with waist measurements four inches smaller than the woman's natural waist size are generally recommended. Once the corset is in hand, it should be laced tightly to the point of causing a firm feeling of constriction around the woman's waist but not so extremely tight that it causes shortness of breath, faintness or indigestion.

The corset should be worn daily, starting with an hour or two and building up over time to greater and greater durations. As the woman's body grows accustomed to the amount of constriction, it should be gradually laced tighter and tighter. The process of tightlacing is a long-term practice and should not be forced. It should feel constrictive on the woman but not to the point of causing her harm. To accomplish a reduction of the waist by multiple inches, it must be consistently worn and tightened to ever smaller sizes. Some women are given the goal of wearing it at least 12 hours a day while others are expected to eventually wear it at all times apart from the necessary times to bathe.

The length of time it will take to reduce the waist size and to get used to this reduction will vary depending on her physiology. The diminished waist and tight corset reduce the volume of the torso. This is sometimes reduced even further by styles of corset that force the torso to taper towards the waist, which pushes the lower ribs inwards. The smallest waist ever recorded is 13 inches, a reduction of over ten inches, but such achievements are extreme and very unhealthy for the woman.

Another consideration in the woman's body appearance is the trim of her cunt hair. A woman can be made to have it trimmed in a certain way, such as a Brazilian style, or have it shaved bare at all times. A man can also have her get it permanently removed through electrolysis or laser removal. Another option is for the woman to vary the trim in the same way she might vary her hair style. It can be trimmed in varying degrees, shaved bare or even trimmed into the first initial of her man to signify her ownership.

Permanent altercation of a woman's body should only be made after serious deliberation about the body a man desires for his woman both in the present and in the future. Regular women of all shapes, sizes and flavors modify their bodies every day but the choices they make are clouded in a world of gray moral values. On one end of the spectrum, women get breast augmentation and cosmetic surgery of all sorts because they dislike the bodies with which they were born. They are too internally insecure to live with their own particular physical composition because they deem it socially inferior and unattractive. At the other end of the spectrum, women understand that the world is governed by the survival of the fittest and the most physically fit on the exterior will usually attract more attention and success. They accept the realities of human beings and choose to act in their own best interest.

The studies Body Image Concerns of Breast Augmentation Patients (2003) and Body Dysmorphic Disorder and Cosmetic Surgery (2006) reported that the woman who underwent breast augmentation surgery also had undergone psychotherapy, suffered low self-esteem, presented frequent occurrences of psychological depression, had attempted suicide, and suffered body dysmorphia, a type of mental illness. In the same study, post-operative patient surveys about mental health and quality-of-life, reported improved physical health, physical appearance, social life, self-confidence, self-esteem, and satisfactory sexual functioning. It is a double-edged sword. One can either try to treat the internal or change the external. Both, or neither, can work.

A man who owns a woman must consider both ends of these spectrums as well as his own desires and pre-conceived ideas about what constitutes an attractive woman. He should not conform to society for the wrong reasons. He is taking her mental health and physical appearance into his own hands.

Cosmetic surgery has evolved to the point where a doctor can do just about anything to a woman's body. Yet, there are limits to what alterations look both natural and attractive to other people. The simplest of people can often tell when a woman has had "work" done to her face or body.

A man who owns a woman is, in a sense, an artist and creator of her body as it exists and changes over time. He can either leave it unaltered or modify it according to his own vision. She is his woman and he will be the one looking at her day-in and day-out, year-in and year-out. If he decides to alter her, he should thoroughly research the choices and possibilities of the particular body modifications he desires.

Implants can be added to a woman to accentuate the size, form, and feel of a woman's natural breasts. There are three general types of breast implant device, defined by the filler material: saline, silicone, and composite. All three have their advantages and disadvantages. A man should not only seek out the top physicians who perform breast augmentation but he should thoroughly research photographic examples of women whose breasts are similar in shape and size to his own woman.

There are many directions to go with the body of a woman. A man can choose to replicate the desired symmetry that underlies most conceptions of feminine beauty or he can pursue more pronounced lines that accentuate extreme curves. Some men desire soft curves while others want big tits and big curves. Aesthetic plastic surgery involves techniques intended for the enhancement of appearance and is specifically concerned with maintaining normal appearance, restoring it, or enhancing it beyond the average level toward some aesthetic ideal. Besides for breast augmentation, there are lip enhancements, butt implants, tummy tucks, liposuction, laser skin resurfacing and nasal surgery. A man who owns a woman should generally never consider liposuction as physical fitness achieves the same results in healthier ways. For lip enlargements, a man should make sure not to change a woman's lips to appear unusually large in an obvious way as this tends to make them look very disfigured as she ages.

Butt implants are popular in Latin American countries and with Latin American women in the U.S. A man should consider the alternative option of a physical fitness routine that increases the size of the woman's buttocks. If this does not produce the desired results, implants that create the "big booty" shape are sometimes considered but should be weighed against the inevitable changes of age. Some women are born with very pronounced features, such as large noses, which are deemed to be deviant from the dominant norms of beauty. In the end, it is up to the owner to decide what choice to make, but he should thoroughly discuss all the physical and mental implications of any final decision with the woman. He can either pursue the path of cosmetic surgery or he can use discipline and positive reinforcement to modify the psychological disposition of the woman toward her appearance. Every procedure has its benefits and costs. Reason should drive erotic desire and emotion. Create the woman you want and live to enjoy those decisions.

Body piercings can be both attractive ornaments on a woman's body and a signifier of ownership. A woman can be pierced on just about any part of her body, including her tongue, lip, belly, clit, nose and ear. If a man wants the woman to display a sign of his ownership of her, he should consider having a custom piercing made for her. The piercing can signify his name, the universal "O" ring or any design that he creates. If properly done, a piercing can be a powerful signifier. A metallic design of his initials displayed on her tongue, her exposed belly or her clit commutates a raw, simplistic command of her body.

The final considerations concerning a woman's body is how a man marks her to show his ownership. This is generally done when the couple gets married or officially consummates the ownership with some type of ceremony and contract. Some men do not care to physically mark a woman at all. Others desire to tattoo her or brand her with a cattle-style iron. A tattoo can be a number that marks her as a member of the popular Slave Registry or it can be more personal in nature. Possible word markings include "slave", "property of x", "owned", "queen", "loved", "taken" and "slut". The options for tattoo designs are, of course, infinite and there is no shortage of quality tattoo artists. The tattoo can be placed anywhere on the body. Popular places include on the small of the back, above the cunt, on the upper arm and on the inside of the mouth. Some tattoo aficionados like to use multiple tattoos or tattoo the woman's whole body. In all cases, the man's sheer creativity will dictate the designs on his owned woman's body.

Branding is the process in which a mark, usually a symbol or ornamental pattern, is burned into the skin of a woman, with the intention that the resulting scar makes it permanent. If a man desires to brand a woman, he should educate himself on the proper way to do it. The process uses the physical techniques of livestock branding on a human but it has been used for many centuries to designate slaves. Ancient Romans marked runaway slaves with the letters FUG (for *fugitivus*). American colonial slaves were often branded with the sign of the particular European crown, the symbol of the private owner or the sign of the cross after Christian baptisement. Brands are typically placed high on the outer thigh, on the belly just above the woman's cunt or on the buttocks.

Some men still heat branding irons in a wood or coal fire while others use an electric branding iron or electric sources to heat a traditional iron. Regardless of the heating method, the iron is only applied for the amount of time needed to create a permanent mark. If a brand is applied too long, it can damage the skin too deeply, thus requiring treatment for potential infection and longer-term healing. A man should know what he is doing or consult with a qualified brander who can train him or is willing to do the procedure.

Case Study 10.1

"Matter over Mind"

Liam and Bailey

Liam: I am attracted to all female body types, but I've always been more attracted to a particular type of body over all others. I like to call it the *perfect* type. I know. Of course there really is no truly perfect body, but to me the ideal figure is one with dramatic curves, full breasts, a tiny waist and a round ass. I think the human eye is naturally drawn to symmetry and movement in a woman. When my woman struts down the street, I want to see her hips sway and her breasts bounce.

When I met Bailey, she already had a really nice body. She was gifted with good DNA and worked out regularly. We actually met at this new Crossfit-type gym that we had both just joined. I don't want to say that both of us our on the superficial side of things, because it's not really true. Yet, we are both definitely more about physical pursuits and fitness and living the good life than we are about sitting around reading Nietzsche asking each other about the meaning of life. That's not to say I don't enjoy quality conversation and good art, I just prefer to be out making money so I can fly on a jet to Buenos Aires with a nice piece of ass by my side. And Bailey was certainly a nice piece of ass, and a good woman to boot.

I had gotten the idea of "owning" a woman from a previous girlfriend I had dated many years ago. She was really into the BDSM scene and told me she wanted to be an owned woman. I had no idea what she meant at the time but later became very attracted to the idea of considering your loved one as your own personal property. I had nothing in common with that girlfriend, and it was a short melodramatic relationship, but I have her to thank for introducing me to the idea.

After Bailey and I got to know each other and started seriously dating, I in turn introduced her to the notion of a man owning a woman. A grin immediately spread across her face. I couldn't believe it when she told me that she was completely familiar with the whole dominant and submissive world. She had been in many relationships in which she started out from day one as the submissive.

It was such a strange twist of fate that we came together randomly like we did. There was no outrageous shock over being introduced to that deviant kind of extreme bond. We both wanted it. I was looking to own a woman and she was looking to be owned. It was simply a matter of having the right chemistry and mutual interests and all that bullshit and we definitely had all our personal and kinky stars aligned.

We clicked in all the right ways that a normal, healthy couple should click. We were bluntly honest with each other and we both enjoyed the simpler things in life like good food, good wine and good sex. The first year of our relationship was probably the best year of my life.

Bailey had always really enjoyed getting attention in an exhibitionistic way so she was completely open to letting me make her body look exactly like I wanted it to look. It became the focal point of our D/s dynamic. The first thing I did was put her on a strict workout regimen with the goal of accentuating what she already had. It consisted of a mixture of swimming, running, Pilates and weight training that aimed to keep her toned and flexible while building on her insanely curvaceous ass.

Each aspect of her body was regularly inspected and all infractions resulted in strict discipline. She was forbidden from exceeding a certain body fat percentage at all times. If she ever did, she was punished by being made to crawl on all fours anytime she was in the house and I would refer to her as my "naughty little pig". She was made to do an intense routine of such exercises such as squats, lunges and extensions that would give her a nice, toned bubble butt. I would inspect it often by making her squat fuck me with her butt facing toward me. If it wasn't to my liking, I would make her spend an additional hour, after we had sex, squatting up and down in the corner.

To check her flexibility, I would have her do the splits completely naked on the edge of the couch before I came up behind her and fucked her with her legs spread open the entire time. After several months of this regimen, natural workout routines had pushed her body to its maximum beauty. I finished off the basics of her new look by having her get the hair between her legs permanently removed so she would always be bare. It also served to display the tiny black "owned" tattoo I would end up getting for her when we got married. It was inked in just above the slit of her cunt.

Bailey had always enjoyed wearing corsets, but had never worn them for the purpose of reducing her waistline. I wanted to give her body a truly hourglass figure, so I took her to a custom corset maker to get her measured. I ended up purchasing several designed specifically for her body. At first she only would wear one when she came home from work, but she gradually built up to the point where she was wearing one nearly 16 hours a day. After she got used to its constriction around her body, I would make it tighter and tighter, constantly pushing her to the limit of what she could handle. At times, she would grow faint in public and I would allow her to loosen it up, but she generally bore the extreme demands on her body very well. The few complaints she would make quickly disappeared when I took her out in a tight evening dress and men couldn't take their eyes off of her.

The final major modification of her body was made by augmenting her breasts. I wanted to give her a nice full C-cup that still looked natural. I had her research every plastic surgeon in the country to find the best doctors. When she narrowed them down to a short list, I had her provide me with sample photos from each one. After a number of conversations and consultations, I finally settled on one doctor and had the procedure done. After a few weeks of recovery, we decided to celebrate her new body with a vacation in the south of France.

When we weren't having deviant sex and showering each other with bottles of Chateau-harvested Rosé wine in our hotel room, I spent the entire time exhibiting her body to the extreme. At the beach, she wore a tiny white G-string that was transparent when it got wet. If someone was looking closely, they could actually see the little calligraphic-styled "owned" tattoo above the visible curves of her cunt. I paraded her up and down the beach as she clung to my arm. As we passed in front of the crowds, men stared, women eyed her up and down in jealousy and couples got in fights when the men turned to get a better look. At night, it was more of the same. Bailey would wear skimpy, tight, see-through dresses that exposed her body in all its glory. She was my primo human property and she loved every second of attention she got.

All I can say at this point is that life is terribly short and all of our bodies are going to decompose to dust. Carpe diem and carpe noctem because that's all you got in this Sun-circling existence.

Chapter 11 – Oral Training

"I've given guys blow jobs just because I've run out of things to talk about." – Anne LaMott

"For sure, even the worst blow job is better than, say, sniffing the best rose . . ." – Chuck Palahniuk

"Blow as deep as you want to blow." – Jack Kerouac

Teaching a woman to suck good cock is one of the supreme joys of training a female and also an excellent way to build her self-confidence in being able to pleasure her man like no other woman in the world. The same can be said of intercourse. She knows, or it should be communicated to her, that a man has no reason to stray when any sexual experience with another woman will be absolutely second-rate compared to what is experienced with her. Apart from teaching a woman how to fuck when she is on top during intercourse, schooling a woman to be an expert cocksucker pays off dividends for years to come for her owner.

Sexual training in general is one of the phenomenal aspects of Dominant/submissive relationships that set it apart from typical relationships. It frees a man from being locked into any mediocre sexual dynamic with a woman. It allows him to take hold of the problematic negotiation process of what a woman is customarily willing or knows how to do and transforms it into mind-blowing erotic bliss. His only true limitations are his imagination and his own ability to seduce, to dominate and to perform.

It should be noted that before a man jumps into the endless pleasures of getting good head, he should take into account his own skills at orally pleasing his woman as well as the sheer time he puts into it in light of her oral regimen. It is true that what is of fundamental importance in a D/s relationship is the man's gratification, yet it is also true that the more attention a man puts into the woman's pleasure, the more she will strive to gratify him. If a man does not know how to lick good pussy, you should immediately learn how. A deep online search will provide you with countless techniques.

The method of giving a man a good blow job is akin to the three acts in a dramatic theatrical production. There is the approach, the sucking and the finish. Each one must be taught to the woman as distinct acts. There are also the facial, attitudinal, psychological and physical considerations through which a man must guide his woman.

Even before the approach to giving the man head, there is foreplay, ritualistic decisions and elements of spontaneity that must be learned. Some men desire that their women ask them if they would like their cock sucked at specific times or particular parts of the day such as upon waking up or after coming home from work. A woman can be given instructions to ask her owner such as:

> *"Would you like to be sucked off before you get up?"*
> *"Do you need some good head?"*
> *"May I give you a blow job, please?"*
> *"Are you in the mood to fuck my face?"*

Other men just prefer to be woken up with his woman's mouth wrapped around his cock or for her to get on her knees when he walks in the door after work.

A woman can also be instructed to regularly ask a man if he would like oral sex throughout the day or during the course of the week. A man can tell her to strive to spontaneously ask him if he would like it sucked in order to please him when he would not otherwise expect it. She can lean her head over to him while driving, whisper a request while out shopping or politely ask to be taken to a restroom at a restaurant or bar to get on her knees. If she fails to remember to ask her owner regularly, he should discipline her as a reminder and follow it with a hard face fuck.

Other possible rituals include making the woman touch her hand to his cock throughout the day to see if he would like it taken out and sucked, forbidding a woman from touching it at all without asking and requiring a woman to wait on her knees with open mouth at the time he gets home or when he is ready to go to bed. The possibilities are endless.

Training a woman to give good head begins with teaching her how to approach a man's cock. She should be instructed to get the man sexually excited with an erect cock before she ever touches her lips to him. Each man likes the approach different but the woman should have a large repertoire of words and actions. She can beg on her knees or from across the room, using such phrases as:

"God, I want your cock in my mouth so bad."
"You're making me so horny. May I give you some good head?"
"Will you please fill my mouth hole, Sir?"
"Can your babygirl come get her naughty little face fucked?"
"Would you like to gag this slut?"
"I'm so hungry. Can I suck the cum out of you?"

A woman should know how to tease a man from a distance by the way she looks at him, by how she is dressed, by how she reveals herself, by how she undresses and by how she moves her body in provocative ways. She can be made to crawl to her owner with her mouth open and her tongue out. She can be told to prep her mouth with plenty of saliva for a sloppy blow job. She can beg over and over for a man's cock. She can be spanked repeatedly until a man believes her desire to suck. If a woman does not naturally have a strong craving to give head that shows overtly in the expression on her face and in her attitude, she should be given strict lessons until she does. This can include both positive and negative reinforcement, including brainwashing and cock worship sessions. An owned woman should want her man's cock like a hungry, salivating animal. If she shows any lack of urgent desire to suck, harsh discipline should be meted out and additional attitude training should be used.

When a woman's lips are at the point of touching a man's cock, she should not simply start sucking like it is a rote action. There are dozens of ways she can accentuate her man's excitement before she begins to suck. She should be taught to use her eyes in a teasing manner, looking from a man's eyes to his cock and back again. She should be taught to extend her tongue to touch the man's pre-cum and play with it teasingly as it strings from his cock. She should be taught to touch her finger to the man's pre-cum and rub on her lips like lip gloss or rub it on her bare nipples. She should be taught to extend her lips to only the pre-cum and suck it out of him. There are many possibilities but the overriding intent is to teach her to perform according to what excites her man. She should be an artist of cock sucking from the very first moment.

It is important to train a woman how to use her own saliva. A man should explain to a woman how wet he likes her to get his cock and how sloppy he likes his blow jobs. Saliva play includes drooling profusely on a man's cock and sucking it back off, gagging on his cock to make herself salivate, letting the saliva run down her chin, positioning her body so the saliva falls onto her breasts, filling a glass with extraneous cock sucking saliva for the man to use when he fucks her and covering his balls and asshole with copious amounts of saliva. If a man likes it, he can make her spit on his cock. He can also spit into her mouth to give her more saliva to use on him and as a sign of her submissive physical place. Other possibilities include making her wait on her knees with a ball gag in her mouth as she drools all over her body, only letting her lick him with her eyes closed and her hands behind her back and using sex toys to train her mouth to stay open while she takes it deep and salivates profusely.

Once a woman begins to suck a man's cock, there is a plethora of ways for her to give good head. It is just as important for a woman to always try to vary her performance as it is to give a good performance. A woman should be made to understand what motions and techniques a man likes, how long he likes her to do each motion and when she should change to a different rhythm. She should know how to combine hand stroking and cock sucking into a perfect cadence of pleasure for the man. Techniques include:

The Lipstick Trick: With the man lying back and his cock stiffly pointing upward, the woman holds the base with her fingers to steady him. She should brush her closed lips against the head of his cock, rubbing it across her wet mouth as if she were applying lipstick. Vary the motion by having her open her lips a bit, rubbing his head between them. She should occasionally take the whole head in his mouth, then go back to rubbing the tip against her lips.

The Circular Suck: She takes him deep into his mouth as she looks him in the eye. She presses her tongue firmly against the underside of his cock and as she very slowly pulls off of him with sucking rhythm while her tongue, in circular movements, she moves up and down his shaft.

Stroke Orchestra: The woman strokes the man's cock with a broad variety of pressure, speed and alterations as she sucks. She should move her hand up and down the shaft with the same thought of a conductor directing an orchestra. She can stroke it long and hard, fast and easy, roll her palm over the head and vary the rhythms to keep him on edge. She should always make sure that his cock is thoroughly wet so it doesn't caused the man discomfort.

Super Suck: The woman clasps her lips tightly around the man's cock and sucks it as hard as she can several times in a row before returning to a normal amount of pressure.

Cherry Popping: As her mouth ascends from bobbing up and down on his cock, she takes the head into his mouth and gives it a hard suck as she pops it out of her mouth. She repeats the motion over and over, popping the head out of her mouth with a loud sound.

The Backstroke: The woman uses the underside of her tongue instead on the frenulum, the super-sensitive spot located below the head of his penis in the center of the underside of the coronal ridge. She should hold the base of his cock and rest her chin on the underside of his shaft for stability. Have her place the underside of her tongue on this sweet spot and quickly swipe it from side to side like a windshield wiper.

The Ice Cream Lick: She should make her tongue completely flat, and then slowly run it along the length of his cock from base to tip as if she was taking a long lick of an ice cream cone. She should take her time, licking it up and down, and then continuing all the way down to the man's balls.

Rhythmic Bobbing: Rather than just bobbing up and down at a constant speed, have her start with ten slow bobs, then move to a few slow bobs and a few fast, then three slow and two fast, and so on. She should learn to get a feeling for how much each rhythm pleases the man, repeat the combination and then change it up once again. A man can instruct a woman with speed orders to maintain control over her sucking. He can also spank her when she doesn't respond correctly or with a quick enough reaction to his words.

Ice Cube: Have her put an ice cube in her mouth before going down. The heat of her mouth combined with the occasional flashes of chilliness will keep the man in a state of anxious sensual tension.

Mint Mouth: Have the woman suck on menthol-flavored candy such as Altoids or cough drops. The menthol that causes the tingling in her mouth should cause the same tingling on the skin of a man's cock. She can also use carbonated drinks such club soda or champagne and swish it around her mouth as she sucks in the cock.

Upside Down: Make her lie on her back on the bed or a couch with her head leaning off the edge and tilted backward. The man stands with his cock at her mouth and penetrates her in and out. Either she can be made to remain still or she can be told to bob up and down on it. Angle her head so the cock can slide in a straight line down her throat. This can be an excellent position to teach the woman to deep throat. She can be made to gag or the man can hold it in deep for a prolonged period. Another option includes making her hold on to the man's ass cheeks and pull his body toward her mouth in a desired rhythm.

Ball Sucking: The man should teach the woman how he likes his balls sucked. He can make her lick them all over, suck them delicately into her mouth or have her take a quick hard suck as she pops them in and out of her mouth. The woman should learn to lick underneath his balls as well in the sensitive area between the base of his balls and his asshole. Make her lick there while she strokes the cock.

Hummer: Make her hum while she sucks. She can do a sexual moaning hum or she can be made to hum whole songs.

Sideways Suck: Have her move to either side of the cock and wrap her lips around the shaft in a sideways manner. With her lips tucked around her teeth, make her use the pressure of her jaw to clamp up and down on the cock firmly and then move up and down from the base to the tip.

Cock Dessert: Have her eat dessert off the cock. The woman can use chocolate syrup, whipped cream, honey, sugar, caramel or anything else she likes or the man wants her to eat.

Standing Face Fuck: Make the woman squat down with her back and head against the wall. Stand opposite her with the cock placed at the level of her mouth. Hold her by the hair and fuck her mouth in and out as if it was her cunt. This is an especially good position if the man wants the woman to gag as she cannot move her head backward. Vary the rhythm and depth of the cock in her mouth and throat.

Deep Throating: The ability to deep throat is one of the most essential qualities of a good owned woman. Though some women have particularly small mouths and throats, all women should be able to deep throat to some extent, depending on the size of the man's cock. If a woman doesn't already know how to deep throat, she should be placed on a practice regimen to help take a cock deeper and deeper into her mouth. There is both a psychological and a physical element to deep throating. The woman must not only want to deep throat, she must want to strive to train her body to take the entire length of the cock. There are limits to what the human body can do but it is just like any other physical feat. Where there is a will, there is a way.

The woman can be made to practice on a daily basis, aiming to go down further and further on the man's erect cock. She should aim to control her gag reflexes and get used to the feeling of the cock in her throat. She must focus on the feeling of opening her oral cavity to her man. On a mental level, she must convince her man that she wants it there and be disciplined if she does not change her attitude. She can be given rewards each time she makes progress as well. If a woman has not deep throated before, she must be guided through the adjustment periods and pushed toward the ultimate goal of touching her lips to the base of a man's cock. If necessary, a man can have her use a large dildo to practice on when he is not there. She can also be given pornographic videos of deep throaters to watch and replicate. A woman can either deep throat a man or be face fucked in a deep throat way. An elite deep throater can lie on her back and allow the man to fuck her at any depth of rhythm he chooses. He should be able to smack his balls against her face with ease. Once a woman learns to deep throat, she should practice on slipping her tongue out of her mouth to lick a man's balls.

Ass Licking: An owned woman can be trained to love to lick a man's ass. He should shower and thoroughly clean himself before the woman starts to lick him. Giving oneself an enema is the best way to be completely cleansed and made fresh for her tongue. Some women are hesitant about licking ass but are more willing once they have been assured the man's ass is ready to be licked. The woman can either kneel in blow job position or the man can sit on her face to get his ass licked. If he desires, he can make her extend her tongue to a taut position, spread his cheeks over her face and bounce up and down on her. If a man is trying to make his women feel especially dirty, telling her to lie down to tongue-fuck his ass will usually work very well.

For all techniques, variety and spontaneity are the key elements of good cock sucking. A woman should know when to go from one technique to another and back again, and feel what each does for her man. There are a myriad of other little techniques a woman can use, given that every owner has different proclivities. If allowed, a woman should ask a man what he loves during oral sex.

Cumming Techniques: When a man is ready to cum, there are options for both how he cums and what the woman does with the cum. A man can simply cum on her face or on her body. She can be told to leave it there for a certain duration of time or she can be ordered to wipe it off with her fingers and put it in her mouth. If a man decides to cum into her mouth, he can make her hold her mouth open for any duration of time while he strokes his cock to ejaculation or he can have her suck him to completion. In either case, she can either be made to swallow or be told to keep the cum inside of her mouth.

Some men like the woman to perform some cum play for him. Cum play is the process of playing with the man's cum with her mouth and fingers. She can be made to let the cum slide out of her mouth back onto his cock, and then lick and suck it up once again. She can be made to do this multiple times. She can also take the cum from her mouth or face with her fingers and lap it teasingly with her tongue. If the man desires, she can be made to hold the cum in her mouth for a long duration and not be permitted to swallow until he tells her to. In any case, cum play is a performance for the man and the woman should engage in it eagerly with a desire to insatiably please her owner.

If a woman doesn't not like the taste of his cum, a man should try adjusting his diet. According to the Kinsey Institute, fruit (especially citrus, pineapples, bananas, and papayas), spices (cinnamon, nutmeg, and peppermint, among others), parsley, wheatgrass, and celery up the flavor of semen. Cigarettes, caffeine, drugs/medications, dairy products, red meat, onions, high sulfur foods, processed fast food and garlic make it taste worse. Also make to drink plenty of water.

The environment in which the man's cock is sucked is also fundamental to his overall pleasure. While sometimes he just wants to come home and be sucked off, at other times he wants to make an experience out of it. Memorable places to have his women suck him include at a movie theater, in the car in broad daylight or in rush hour traffic, in a gas station restroom, in an airplane seat under a blanket, in an alley, in a dressing room, at the library and in a hotel room next to the window.

Cock Worship

The practice of cock worship is the process of elevating a man's phallus to a near-religious symbol that saturates every thought in a woman's mind. In ancient religions, the phallus was viewed as the source of life, creativity and energy. A man can be defined with many descriptions but the essential thing that separates a man from a woman is his cock. The raw worship of the cock is the woman's testament to the male urge to dominate, penetrate and seed the fertile cunt he owns. It is a good idea to incorporate cock training when a woman is broken in. It is not generally meant to be done as a regular practice but as an initiation ritual or a training technique.

The precise activities to use for a woman's worship of his cock depend on the man's personal preferences. In general, a woman should be made to think of the man's cock and the sucking of it at all times of the day. It should begin at the start of the day. A woman should wake up before the man and then proceed to wake him up by taking his cock into her mouth. She should be given a certain duration of time to suck him as well as precise directions on how it is to be sucked. After she is finished, there are numerous options. A man can use a penis-shaped gag that she is required to immediately wear. She can be made to write sentences or an essay on cock-centric subjects. She can follow the man as he gets ready for work or his day, kneeling to suck him as he eats breakfast, showers and gets dressed.

Cock worship activities will depend on work routines and the weekly schedules. If a woman is required to go to work, she can be assigned tasks to keep her mind focused on his cock. She can be made to call him or send him text messages/emails at regular intervals with specific phrases repeated. Such mantras can include:

"I want your cock so bad right now."
"I want you to come face fuck me in front of my boss."
"I need to suck cock all day and all night."
"I was made to suck cock."
"I am a cocksucker and everyone knows it."
"I want to suck cock before I am allowed to speak."

A man can also make a woman tell him during the day how she wants to suck his cock at that moment. She can be given a dildo to take to work and take regular breaks to go to the restroom to suck it for a certain duration of time.

If a woman is at home, it can be taken to the extreme. She can be made to spend the whole day doing nothing but sucking a man's cock, practice sucking using different objects, wearing a cock-shaped gag, repeating worship mantras and writing essays about the practice and belief in cock sucking. A man can use intense disciplinary sessions in which he scolds and slaps her in an interrogatory fashion until she professes her love for cock to the level of satisfaction the man desires.

An alternative method of cock worship, if the man likes to make his woman be with other men, is the married-man cock-sucking regimen. When the woman is out of the house at places such as the grocery store, a shopping mall, a café, a bar, a restaurant or any other place, she should strive to find married men, flirt with them and aim to seduce them on the spot in order to suck their cocks. She can suck the cocks at a hotel, in the car and anywhere else. She can even be made to have the men record her sucking their cocks using the camera on her phone. She should only be permitted to talk and be with married men in order to minimize any transmission of STD's. The man can also use a group of friends who he knows but are not in his tight circle of real friends. They can be permitted to call her at any time to have their cocks sucked.

A woman practicing cock worship should always end her day by going to bed with her owner's cock in her mouth. She can also be made to wear a penis-shaped gag during the night.

Cock worship can include the placement of ancient phallus-shaped icons and sculptures at certain places in the house. The woman should be made to get on her knees at certain times of the day or night to recite her cock prayers. Here is a sample extended recitation:

"As a cocksucker, my place is between the legs of my owner. I love cock and can't get enough of it in my mouth. My sexual fulfillment depends on the pleasure I give my owner and his generosity in allowing me to please him. As a cocksucker, I realize my only real sexual organs are my mouth, tongue, and throat. As a cocksucker, my only need is to pleasure my owner. When I am at my true place between his legs, I have no other needs. As a cocksucker, I solemnly vow, without hesitation or regret to possess a willing mouth, know I belong on my knees in the presence of my owner and accept my owner's cum in any manner he requires. I will maintain such focus on his cock and his pleasure that it becomes the center of my universe. I will learn when he needs me to suck, swallow, gag, stroke, and choke without having to tell me. I know my

place in the world and love and embrace being a cocksucker, as this is the only way I can perform to my owner's satisfaction. I accept that my owner is allowed to say whatever he wants or call me whatever he wants while I am pleasuring him.

I will show my addiction and need for my owner's cock and cum by begging for it if need be, for a cocksucker has no pride. I will make my mouth a willing and anxious hole for his cum and wear the cum on my body with pride. I will learn every nuance of his cock and what pleasures him the most. I will surrender to deep throating, to face-fucking, to multiple cocks or to being used in any way. It will never stop until my owner is finished with me and truly satisfied. I will be ready for my owner at any time, or multiple times. As a cocksucker, my sexual identity is tied to the cock of my man. I know that in life I will only achieve fulfillment through the graciousness and charity of my owner and hereby vow with all sincerity to service my owner to the best of my ability and strive to improve my technique. The consequences in breaking this contract will result in my spiritual, sexual, and physical punishment. I love cock. I love cock. I love cock. I love cock. I love cock."

Chapter 12 – Sexual Gratification Training

"Men just aren't viewed as sex objects in the same way that women are. Women don't think about men being naked in the same way that men think about women." –Janice Min

"Instant gratification is not soon enough." –Meryl Streep

"Sex is good. Everybody does it and everybody should." –Robbie Williams

A man who owns a woman wants to fuck her like her wants to fuck her, but he also wants her to sexually gratify him when she is made to be more of an active participant. In addition, he wants to be sure that what he does to her sexually drives both her mind and her body absolutely wild. Some couples prefer that the D/s dynamic in their relationship is limited to sex play. They see it as an escape from the demands and doldrums of daily life to a world of erotic freedom. Sexual gratification training, though, as opposed to the larger realm of erotic play, is about teaching the woman how to please the man. It should only be done once the relationship has been established and there is undeniable mutual attraction. It can include teaching her various sexual motion abilities, how to actively fuck, how to role play, altering her sexual personality and controlling her jealousy.

When dominating a woman sexually, she should respond according to how her owner wants her to respond. Training one's woman consists of using a regimen of exercises, assignments, rewards and punishments to get the results one wants. There are certain qualities to instill like eagerness-to-please and assertive physical desire for the man but she can also be expected to do a number of other things at different times. Even in the very act of it, she can be made to moan softly, moan loudly, grunt, talk dirty, beg, ask for more or even be quiet. An owned woman can be told to ask her owner if he would like to fuck or be fucked at certain times of the day or night. She should know what he likes to hear, use variety in her approach and always be searching for new ways to please her man.

The process of "edging" can be used to keep a woman in a constant state of arousal. Some men prefer that their women are always in a mode of eager horniness and lust, desiring sex constantly like a crazed animal. When a woman is edged, she is sexually stimulated to the very edge of having an orgasm but not permitted to actually climax. Either she can be told to masturbate at certain times of the day or the man can stimulate her himself. As she is edged more and more while being forbidden final orgasmic satisfaction, she will naturally grow hornier and hornier. A man can keep her in this state all day long or for multiple days. The constant arousal and denial will alter her overall mental state and her very consciousness. The underlying desire for sex will radiate through everything else she does during the day and night. She will go utterly mad with her craving for release and be willing to do anything to get it. When she is finally permitted to climax, the pent-up need for an orgasm will transform average sex into outright savage fornication.

A vital element in sexually training a woman is the teaching of her to be an active participant in the various motions and erotic positions that are possible. A man does not always want her simply to spread her legs and take his thrusts. At the very least, she should learn how he would like her to use her vaginal muscles while he is inside of her. He might want her to keep them tightened around his cock as much as possible or just as he is about to cum. He can also sternly order her in the act to constrict her muscles with a phrase such as "keep that pussy tight for me, baby" or give her a slap on the face along with a command to "tighten up, you little slut". Overall, she should learn to vary the way her vagina is relaxed or constricted to keep her man constantly satisfied.

Secondly, a woman should learn how to use her own body during intercourse. This can be as simple as learning the various motions and rhythms of her hips to enhance the movement of his cock going in and out of her.

More importantly, she should be taught how to take an active role when she is on top of the man. Some woman can be shy or insecure about being on top and need to be guided through it all step by step so it is stimulating for both of them. She should learn the myriad of positions and techniques that are possible in taking charge of giving pleasure during intercourse. It takes time for a woman to truly master taking an active role. A man should be patient and fully aware of what is going on in her mind and with her body. At the same time, there should be a certain level of strict expectation that she is constantly learning to perfect her skills. There are entire books such as the *Kama Sutra* as well as many contemporary sexual position manuals that should be used for complete instruction and for inspiration. There are also pornographic videos galore online that can be used as visual aids. A few of the positions include the woman astride, the face-off, the cowgirl, the reverse cowgirl, the cowgirl's helper, the reverse missionary, the champagne room, the Om, the lazy man and the pretzel dip. Yet, there are hundreds and hundreds more.

A favorite on-the-top position is the squat fuck, a form of the cowgirl/reverse cowgirl position. The position allows the man to freely admire his owned woman from the front or from behind. It is the physical incarnation of the woman's worship of the male phallus with her own body. This position entails a woman placing her feet next to the body of the man and squatting on his cock repeatedly. She can either be facing him with her hands on his chest or turned around so the man can ogle her ass as it squats up and down. Wearing high-heeled shoes often assists her in maintaining the correct leverage. She can also be made to bend over in front of the man as he sits, place her hands on the floor and squat fuck him like that. This position requires the woman to actively use the muscles in her thighs and ass. If she cannot squat fuck her man as long as he would like, she should be sent to the gym to increase her physical fitness. She can do squat, lunge and leg extension exercises, in addition to running, on a weekly schedule until she can squat fuck for as long as her owner desires. Hard spankings during a squat fuck will also aid in invigorating her motions.

A dominant must also not forget that it is his responsibility to please his submissive as a reward for her good behavior and as an expression of his profound love and desire for her. A submissive can be allowed the pleasure of her wildest fantasies, even if they consist of her taking on the role of the sexually dominant one. A dominant man should know how to cultivate the deeper needs of a woman to feel truly wanted and appreciated. There is nothing wrong with a dominant man spontaneously getting down on his knees and licking his woman's cunt while she has orgasm after orgasm. A man should thrive in giving pleasure as much, or nearly as much, as he demands getting it. On a nonsexual side, there are also the options of rewarding the woman with such pleasures as cooking for her, massaging her, catering to her shopping desires, running errands for her or doing anything else that she would welcome as an unexpected pleasure.

A man should also know the ins-and-outs of his woman's body and how it responds to pleasure. Some women can only orgasm from clitoral stimulation. Other women easily climax from vaginal sex. Some women can even climax from nipple stimulation or from intense pain play. A man should know the basics of a woman's anatomy if he doesn't already. The glands of the clitoris and the urethra are located just above the vaginal opening. The clitoris is the small round-shaped part at the top of her cunt (a word used generically to identify her genitalia). It is highly sensitive to being touched, fondled, flicked, licked and slapped. The fleshy folds around the vagina are the labia majora and the labia minora. The G-spot is another sensitive area located on the front interior wall of the vagina. The A-spot is a third sensitive area at the deepest part of her vagina where the vaginal wall connects with the cervix.

A dominant man should aim to become an expert in knowing how to stimulate his woman. The ability to quickly bring her to the point of orgasm can be used as one of his methods of control. He should know how to stimulate her clit in a variety of ways. This comes with practice and being aware of what precise motions and stimulations arouse her. The same goes for fingering her, licking her clit and fucking her. The surest path to getting a woman to eagerly submit in the moment is the knowledge of how to bring her to such a deep place of arousal that she is willing to do anything he tells her to do.

Bondage Play

Bondage play and bondage sex are one of the four pillars of BDSM. Nearly every woman has some fantasy about being tied-up. There are certainly endless ways to constrain a woman from tying her to the bed with a scarf, to hogtieing her like an animal, to blindfolding her and gagging her, to elaborate Shibari rope techniques. The abstract feelings of controlling and being controlled are made very physical in the world of bondage. The submissive is restrained, made to surrender, exhibited and sometimes even humiliated. It is also her affirmation of trust in the dominant. She might find a certain deep level of peace by completely letting go and giving in to his power and control in being bond.

Bondage can be a very powerful tool in both restraining a woman and using it for sexual gratification. A man can tie an undressed woman to a chair at the kitchen table, place a vibrator between her legs and leave it there while she tries to eat in a proper manner. He can take off his belt, use it to bound her arms behind her back and fuck her roughly from behind. He can restrain her in elaborate rope bondage so her mobility is completely limited and then bring her to the edge of orgasm without letting her have one. He can blindfold her with her own stockings, put her in a metal spreader and let other people watch him have his way with her. He can restrain her while he spanks her to her breaking point. He can collar her neck and chain it to her ankles behind her while he deep throats her to a gagging frenzy. He can deprive her of all her senses using a blindfold, earplugs and headphones while he teases and torments her from head to toe. He can pretend to kidnap her and restrain her with duct tape while he forcefully has his way with her. The possibilities are endless.

Bondage can include using cuffs, Japanese bondage, suspension, chastity devices, predicament bondage, rope bondage, mummification, mental bondage and even confinement. Its implements can be anything and everything that will keep a woman bound. These include scarves, rope, stockings, ties, leather restraints, metal cuffs, bondage mitts, chastity belts, collars, leashes, tape, arm binders, corsets, sleep sacks, body bags, spreader bars, straightjackets, cages, bathrobe belts, leather belts, cling wrap, BDSM leather restraints, handcuffs, sports wraps, latex, rubber, yarn and duct tape. Note, even if you are practicing consensual nonconsent, make sure to establish a safe word for bondage play. It can be impossible for a dominant to determine if a woman is having serious blood circulation issues. Also, keep a pair of scissors handy as well as an extra key if one is using a lock to secure the bondage gear.

Japanese rope bondage (Shibari) is a world unto itself. Consult *The Ashley Book of Knots* for extensive knowledge on tying knots as well as *The Seductive Art of Japanese Bondage* by Midori. If you are just beginning to experiment with rope bondage, take things very slowly. Start with short ropes, 10-20 feet in length, made of cotton, raw silk, hemp or bamboo. Make sure what you are tying it to, such as the bedposts, can endure the full strength of a woman's force when she begins to pull on it and thrash about. Also, consider safety issues such as rope burns, circulation problems, limiting breathing or harsh pressure on her neck.

Rough Sex

Taking a woman roughly opens up the doors of perception to another realm of dark kinkiness. It is paramount that you know your woman very well before engaging in rough sex. If you don't, communication, consent and limitations should be thoroughly discussed. If she has any emotional triggers from past traumatic experiences, take this into account. Playing rough can be extremely intense, especially if taken into the more taboo areas. Mainstream society typically condemns treating a woman roughly, but at the same time, men and women are bombarded by rough play in movies and television. One should never confuse reality with fantasy, yet no one should tell a healthy couple how to limit their sex lives.

There is a balance between talking out scenarios of playing rough and simply giving into primal urges. If a woman knows exactly what is going to happen, the power of rough play is diminished. A man should be keenly aware of a woman's personal psychological triggers and her sensibilities. He should be firmly in the moment, constantly ingesting feedback from the woman's physical, vocal and emotional reactions. Each of their conceptions of what consensual nonconsent actually means to them should be discussed. For rougher sex, she can be spanked on her ass or cunt, her face can be slapped, her hair can be pulled, she can be spit on or into, any part of her body can be clamped and she can be manhandled in a harsh physical way.

Breath play and choking can be performed during an intense kissing session, while having oral sex or during intercourse. There is nothing like the feeling of pressing a woman forcefully against the wall and holding her by the throat while you have your way with her cunt. It is important, though, to move slowly into this territory. You do not want to end up in the emergency room or in a jail cell trying to explain to the authorities that you were just "playing rough". During breath play/choking sessions, stay vigilantly aware of the amount of pressure being applied, the hand position and the duration that a woman's breath is being restricted. Learn about the practice in depth before you try it. Never apply intense pressure on the trachea. The proper technique is to place the hand underneath the jaw towards the ears and press upward on the carotid arteries, thereby reducing blood flow to the brain. Once again, start slowly and don't try to take things too far. If one is into serious breath play, take a course with a local BDSM organization before jumping into things.

The style and variety in a man's rough play is entirely personal. More intense sessions can include rape play, intense face and breast slapping and hardcore deep-throating. Specific samples, ideas and techniques can also be found in various topic-specific BDSM books, online kink videos and fictional novels. A dominant man's imagination should have no precise limits.

Impact Play

While bondage can include a good spanking, there is a wealth of possibilities in impact play by itself. The types and tools of disciplinary action that was elucidated in a previous chapter can also be used as a means of pleasure. For almost all women, a certain amount of pain is pleasurable. A sudden smack on her bare ass gets her adrenaline going and a few more painful ones might be the beginning of a "pain high". Powerful endorphins, those morphine-like substances residing in one's own body, get released and all that tingling, stinging and throbbing radiate through her body.

A man can use spanking, caning, strapping, paddling, slapping, flogging, whipping, birching, switching or any other action that causes impact on a woman's body. The important element to master is knowledge of the grey area between pleasure and pain. For some women, certain implements cause incredible pleasure while others are just nightmarish pain. A soft slap during sex might be very kinky but a hard one that includes a severe scolding might cause an outpouring of tears. Awareness and communication is vital when determining what is turning on a woman and what is hurting her. A man should typically begin slow and soft and work his way up to faster, harder strokes. This is the best practice whether he is using his hand, a paddle, a cane, or any other implement. Accuracy and intensity set the tone of control and punishment. Secondly, causing a woman pain might be a turn-on for the dominant. Impact play is one of the most direct roads into the psychology of masochism and sadism.

Some men and some women are also into bruising. The very sight of the black and blue marks creates arousal in them. The woman feels owned in a very real and memorable way. The lingering pain serves to amplify this. If one bruises easily, take precautions not to overdo it. A woman should not take any blood thinners such as aspirin, antihistamines or medications which cause blood to thin as a side effect. Make sure to drink lots of water after heavy impact play.

A close cousin of impact play is sensation play. This includes using clips, clamps, clothespins and zippers, as well as pinching, hot wax play, electricity play, knife play, fire play, tickle torture and any other activity that involves using a foreign object to produce a sensation on a submissive's skin or body.

Masochism

Masochism is the desire and ability to become sexually aroused, and perhaps even climax, while experiencing pain and discomfort. If a man determines a woman is a partial or total masochist, this will completely change the sexual and disciplinary dynamic. Many or all the disciplinary acts are turned into moments of pleasure for the woman. If this is the case, pain should be withheld from the woman and only given as a reward for good behavior. Many masochistic women also risk getting into violent relationships, allow themselves to be exploited, harm themselves and have difficulty controlling their own lives in a healthy way. They might cut themselves, practice bulimia on a regular basis or try to instigate a man to beat them out of anger. If a man becomes involved with a masochist, communication is vital and psychological therapy should be considered to determine if there are unresolved issues from the past.

That being said, each human being is wired very differently and a hardcore masochist might be the perfect match for a man who loves heavy impact play and the doling out of pain during sex. The dominant might also see pain as a vital element of showing his ownership of the woman in a physical way. For some men, there's nothing like rough sex play in which the woman gets her face slapped, her ass spanked, her hair pulled, her back shoved against the wall and her mouth roughly engorged with his tongue, all the while telling her such things as: "That's right. You're mine, bitch! You're *my* slut! Tell me how badly you need it. Beg for it like the needy whore you are. Kneel! Get down! Suck it good before I fuck your little mouth hole. I own you and don't forget it."

Masochistic play can be enhanced not only by good vocal delivery, but by the establishment of the scene in advance. While some masochists might get off any time you pull out an implement and strike them in the right spot, creating a powerful setting and psychological environment can take the experience to another level. A woman can be blindfolded, taken into a room that has been prepared as an interrogation chamber, restrained like a prisoner and psychologically tormented while she is repeatedly punished for *wrong* answers. All her senses can be controlled, including what she sees, hears, tastes, smells and feels.

Sexual stimulation can be alternated with administering of pain in greater and greater degrees until she is high on pain and on the verge of an orgasm. She can be made to beg for more pain and to be allowed to climax. A man can tell her to feel exactly what he wants her to feel. He is the owner of her pain and her pleasure. For some women, the feeling of pain can accumulate to higher and higher levels of pleasure and emotion that makes them feel that they have entered an altered state of consciousness. It can be a strange emotional experience in which they disconnect from the pain, or even a spiritual experience in which they thrive in the deeper atonement with human suffering and existence. Communication following the end of such sessions is vital for both the man and the woman.

Sadism

This is a set of activities involving the physical, emotional or mental suffering of another that is sexually arousing for the one doing and controlling the activities. Some people see sadomasochism as the two halves of pain play combined, but that is not necessarily true. A sadist, in the strict sense of the word, gets pleasure from another's pain and discomfort. If the recipient finds that pain to be pleasurable, then the sadist is not inflicting true pain. It can be a complex dynamic if the man has sadistic inclinations and the woman has masochistic inclinations. It needs to be determined what is truly painful and what is not.

If a dominant man is a true sadist, the sadistic activities he does should not necessarily produce sexual excitement for the submissive. They are turning on the man for his own pleasure. For any man wired in this way, it is vital that he communicates his true intentions and the times he is being sexually sadistic. He cannot misuse his sadistic leanings as an excuse to abuse or mistreat a woman. He must be restrained in how and why he torments a woman for his pleasure, and he must be sincerely honest with his feelings. A submissive woman should also understand that she is serving his needs to submitting to his pain. It might not give her any pleasure in the immediate moment, but it should generate a feeling of satisfaction and pride for her obedience and service in the long term.

Role Playing

Role playing serves to create variety and fulfill fantasies in the sexual lives of owners and their submissives. It is the process of letting the imagination go wild. Role playing is one the best ways to reinvigorate a couple's sex life and the D/s bond. One can explore fantasies taken from realistic situations or one can delve into the dark recesses of one's mind to experience alternate realities and play with psychological elements that might not be at the forefront of one's personality. It can be a means of both getting fantasies fulfilled and engaging irrational fears. Each person can bring ideas and fantasies to the table. Before engaging in any intense or taboo role play, the man should discuss with the woman any previous traumatic experiences or negative emotional triggers.

Role playing can begin spontaneously or it can be planned in advance. Some people are very good at improvising while others need to rationally plan out details or even need the safety of knowing the situation in advance in order to feel safe in letting go. A role playing session can start with a man suddenly walking through the front door dressed like a cop, nightstick in hand, shouting at his woman to get on the floor. It can start with a simple text message from the submissive confessing that she has been a naughty little girl at work.

Flashbacks to a previous time in one's life or to a traumatic experience can serve as the base for intense role playing sessions. If one grew up in a morally or socially repressive environment, re-enacting those moments as they occurred or as revenge fantasies can be quite powerful. If a woman was raised to act very proper and made to fear being promiscuous, playing the dirty whore who is taken to a public place dressed like a slut, and then taken home by her man as if he is a stranger, can be highly arousing. If one is in a racially mixed relationship, race play can be taken to some very dark places that include objectification, dehumanization, racial slurs, humiliation and impact play.

Age Play

Age play is often a very powerful allure for certain couples. There is a taboo feel to it, especially if one is exploring forbidden and illegal intergenerational relationships. There is also a sensation of escapism to it. One can imagine a time in which life was simple and without the stresses or responsibilities of adult life. One can also be conjuring up a wonderful or traumatic memory. Perhaps a woman witnessed a childhood friend being spanked when they were growing up and it was the first moment that she became aware such activities even existed. Fantasy age play can include anything from the woman pretending to be a baby to the dominant pretending to be an older man. The woman can take on the particular personality of a young child that she never had a chance to explore, such as the naughty brat or the spoiled princess. A man can pretend to be older than he is in order to take on an air of seasoned authority.

In any case, age play should be openly discussed between a dominant and his submissive. They should agree that they are consenting to explore potentially very taboo territory and be honest about their feelings and desires.

Taboo Play

Taboo scenarios can be anything that is seen as not socially acceptable in mainstream society or as forbidden in the regular dynamic of a personal relationship. It takes one to the dark side on an emotional and psychological level. Doing bad things can be seen as good pleasure. A certain amount of controlled violence can be an expression of love and desire. Taking and giving up control becomes erotically charged on a whole other level of transgression. Both the dominant and the submissive are opening themselves up to desires and needs that require immense trust by both participants. A rape-play or a force-play session can uncover real desires to rape or use force in unacceptable ways. Communication and feedback before and after this kind of play is vital.

Certain taboo scenarios can uncover feelings and fantasies in both participants that they never realized even existed. It is vital to come to this territory already having a strong awareness of one's personality and the negative aspects of one's behavior. One must be grounded in a healthy reality in everyday life in order to truly explore the darker dimensions of taboo play. If that is made vividly clear, the ideal state of mind, when beginning a taboo scenario, is just to let go and see where things take you. The use of powerful language is paramount to creating a realistic scenario and getting deep into someone's mind. Letting go of any normal judgment is the key to seeing what exists beneath the surface.

Taboo scenes include coerced rough sex, full-on consensual nonconsent rape play, hate play, force play, incest play, cheating play, race play, public humiliation, blackmail play, D/s role reversal play and anything else that might exist in the dark recesses of your imagination.

Bimbofication

A particular kind of role-playing is bimbofication. This entails making a woman a dumb, giggling sex object through the way she acts, how she dresses and the shape of her body. It is a fetish that involves turning a woman into a mindless sex machine using physical transformation and mind control. There are many types of bimbos from the blue eyed, blonde-bobbed vixen to the big-titted brunette with high heels and long eyelashes. There is a certain excitement of taking an intelligent, career-minded woman and turning her into a total airheaded sex object either as role play or for real. Every man has a different idea of how a bimbo should look but popular attire includes tight revealing tops, gaudy heels, choker necklaces, hoop earrings, Stepford style sundress, tops with pink ribbons and bows, "tacky" clothing and ruffled miniskirts. The bimbo mindset is typically enforced by never allowing the woman to engage in intelligent conversation, making her profess her simple minded thoughts in casual conversation and having her display her body at all times in an exhibitionistic manner.

Some men like to take bimbofication a step further and have the woman get breast and/or ass implants and other cosmetic surgery such as face lifts or lip enlargement. Many women choose this as a full-on lifestyle before they ever get involved in a serious relationship. Their bimbo fetish turns into an all out lifestyle that revolves around constantly modifying their bodies at the gym and at the plastic surgeon's office and dressing provocatively at all times in public and in private.

Personality Alteration

An owned woman generally has her personality modified in some way by her man but personality alteration can also be used in a temporary way. A man might want his woman "to be someone else" as a fantasy or to keep things interesting in the relationship. She can be made to be extremely proper or nerdy, take on a foreign accent and demeanor, act like a constant flirt or cultivate her intelligent and bookish side.

Humiliation and Degradation

Humiliation and degradation play can be especially powerful with an owned woman. The desire to be humiliated and degraded is a popular trait in some women who desire to be owned. A man should make sure to understand that the urge is best kept in a setting of play and fantasy. Humiliating and degrading a woman in a real way is not only unhealthy for the woman's mental state, it will cause other emotional problems that the man must handle. Once this is understood, it allows both the man and the owned woman to take humiliation play to greater depths. Nearly every woman has a potent emotional urge hidden in some part of her mind to feel sexually overpowered. There are many scenarios that create a raw sexual excitement such as treating a woman like a piece of meat with three holes for her man to fuck. Adding a racial and gender-based element can even further enhance the role playing.

Some women completely thrive on the idea of existing in a lower caste of human being. They see themselves authentically as nothing more than property. They love to go to the deepest spheres of sub space in their minds and remain there. They bask in the emotional power of living as a real slave. They love to obey in an absolute manner. While every owned woman should feel like she is a man's possession, some women prefer to see themselves as nothing more than that. They exist as property and their fantasies often revolve around being treated like an inferior person.

Other common role play scenarios include boss-secretary, doctor-nurse, daddy-girl, teacher-student, cop-suspect, prison guard-prisoner, stranger-woman on the street, boss-naughty executive, kidnapper-abductee, owner-dog and customer-stripper. Other major categories of role play include animal role play, interrogation, objectification and force play. As with any sex play, costume, props and location can always dramatically enhance the experience.

Anal sex

Anal play can be a very potent realm of kinky pleasure and satisfaction. For some men, taking a woman up the ass has a certain taboo feel to it. They might have learned that good girls don't take it up the ass. For others, it is another door into domination and submission. It also is convenient in that one does not have to worry about pregnancy, if that is a concern. The raw pleasure in anal sex is thrusting one's cock in a tight hole. The psychological pleasure is that the woman is some kind of dirty slut who takes it up her ass.

If a man desires anal sex or anal play, the woman should be properly clean and be ready to be penetrated as the man desires. She should give herself an enema either just before the act or as part of her daily ritual. Some men set rules or time windows for when they might want to have anal sex, or sex of any kind. During these time restraints, the man expects that the woman be squeaky clean and the woman should prep herself accordingly and be ready to take it up the ass at any given moment. Anal positions tend to be a replication of regular sexual positions but certain positions allow for the comfort or discomfort of the woman. Placing a pillow under her belly while she is facedown might allow her to relax. Making her get down on hands and knees on a hardwood floor might force her to relax.

Anal play typically requires a gradual build up to full penetration. One can use lube or repeated application of saliva to ease the friction. One can begin by inserting one of two fingers and slowly pushing them in and out to begin the process of opening her up. A man's fingers should be clean and free of cuts, and his nails should be trimmed very well. Vocal coaching is extremely helpful with anal play. This can be anything from an encouraging "just relax" to a more assertive "open that ass up for me, slut". A man can also tell his woman to open herself up with a dildo or butt plug and be ready to take his full cock upon arrival. If he is opening her up himself, he should continue to penetrate her with a couple of fingers until she can take them all the way in. Women's physiology varies, as does the length and girth of a man's cock, so one should get a feel for what is comfortable and what is physically possible.

When he feels she has been prepped enough, he should slowly push the head of his cock into her ass. Ease it in, inch by inch, slowly pushing it in and out while building up to deeper and deeper penetration. One can give the woman the option of placing her hand on the man's torso, or even on his cock, to help her relax and maintain control of how deep it goes. Some women can take it all the way in while others cannot. There might be a certain amount of anal training required over the course of the session, or even over a longer duration of time, to get her to completely open up to full penetration. Keep her well lubed at all times.

Anal training can consist of many techniques. A man might simply need to teach her to be able to take the full length of his cock or he might want her to submit to the pleasure of a rough ass fucking session. He can make her wear a butt plug under her clothes before he is to meet her. He can use an anal hook and a rope to keep her bound and ass-ready. He can train her to keep her ass relaxed and open so it does not instinctively constrict closed when he pulls his cock out during sex. He can train her to ride his cock from the top. There are also the options of using a butt plug, a dildo or one's fingers to create the feeling of fucking a woman in both holes. One can always bring in another man, as well, if he wants her to be double penetrated. Just make sure he is tested for STD's and he is a good performer.

Vaginal Fisting

The attraction to vaginal fisting resides in the extremity of the act. A woman is not made to easily take a man's whole hand, or even most of his hand, into her vagina. She must work physically, emotional and psychologically to take it. In a way, it is the physical act of surrendering to total submission. The sensation of having one's hand fit tightly inside a woman's cunt, feeling her heart beat through the cavity walls and making her completely open herself to his control can be highly arousing. Also, most women most likely have never been fisted. It creates an emotional scenario of losing one's extremeness virginity. Saving the act for when a woman is "broken in" should be considered.

When, or if, a man decides to fist his woman, it is vital that he has an in-depth understanding of the physiology of her vagina. The vagina is the muscular canal connecting the cervix to the exterior of her body. The vaginal walls are made to stretch for the obvious child-bearing purposes, but the precise ability for them to stretch depends on her specific bone structure. Some women are made with greater capacity to take it while others are not. Other factors that might affect her fisting capabilities include hormone levels, previous surgeries, previous child birth and previous experiences being fisted. Estrogen levels are one factor of the elasticity of the vagina and a man should communicate with a woman regarding this. Lower estrogen levels mean thinner, less flexible walls which are more likely to tear. If she has had surgery to this area, one might want to forgo the entire idea of fisting.

The crucial aspect underlying a powerful fisting experience is the woman's sheer desire to be fisted. She must want or be trained to crave a man's hand inside of her and she must be coaxed moment by moment as she takes his fist. Secondly, while taking an entire man's fist is the ideal experience, one should not be disappointed if this is not physically possible. Four fingers or even three might be enough to create an erotically charged moment of really opening up a woman's cunt.

The commencement of a good fisting begins with the appropriate positioning of her body. A man should consider both her comfort and his fantasies. Positioning her on her back with legs up or on her side is more likely to allow her to relax. Putting her on all fours is more likely to be visually and metaphorically stimulating. As a man begins fingering her in and out, communicating what is working and what is not is vital. Also, using a good lube is typically an important necessity. The best lubes are generally silicon or water-based and should be glycerine and paraben free. Oil-based lubes can trigger yeast infections. Other recommended preparations include gloves (either latex or non-latex, purchased at the pharmacy or from a BDSM outlet) and a towel underneath her body. A man can also keep her restrained or even simultaneously stimulate her with a vibrator.

As a man slides his fingers into her at greater and greater depths, turning his hand around and around to open her up, he should guide the entire experience with vocal delivery. Depending on the tone he wants to create, possible expressions can include: "That's it. Just relax. Open up to me." "Spread those legs and take it like a good slut." "Beg for my whole fist. Beg for it to be inside of you." "Open up. I own this cunt." "Gonna' fist fuck you good and deep like you need to be fist fucked." "This hole is mine. I want this hole completely open."

He should guide her to take deep breaths, continue to relax her muscles, thrive in the emotional experience of the moment and keep pushing into her to reach greater depths. When she finally reaches the point in which your hand can enter her past the knuckles, curl your fingers in to make a fist. Slowly guide the fist in and out of her. Let her know she is being fisted. Thrive in the experience, use greater force if desired and take her to those climactic highs where she wants to be taken.

As a side note, fist fucking is a very potent experience and demanding to a woman's body. While a small amount of blood is not a rare side effect, there should never be profuse bleeding. There should also not be any burning sensation or sharp pain. If any of these things occur, stop immediately or consult a doctor.

Polygamy

While most relationships between men and owned women are monogamous, some men prefer to engage in affairs or own more than one woman. Sometimes this is called a "polyamorous household". Unless the woman has come into the relationship with the understanding that it will be polygamous or her owner will be with who he pleases, a woman must be trained to accept and desire for her man to have other women. For most owned women, it comes down to the fear of the man finding a woman he likes more than her and deciding to leave her. The man must be sure that he is being honest and committed to owning his woman for the long-term. Just as he has cultivated his own self-control to advance his life, he must use self-control with his emotions when being with other women. Strict precautions must be taken against STD's as well.

If a man desires other women, there are many options. He can take on regular lovers, be with whomever he wants, take on another owned woman or be with another woman during set periods of time. If he wants to own more than one woman, he must decide if both women will have equal power, rights and responsibilities or if one woman will subjugate the other to her authority. He can also alter the order of power between the two women on a weekly or monthly basis depending on who has earned it through their service to him.

There are really no absolute rules but a man must be thoroughly capable of owning multiple women. He must have the financial resources for keeping them in his household, but more importantly, he must have a thorough understanding of how the female mind works. He must be confident in his ability to control their jealousies, keep them in check and maintain their feeling of value to him and to themselves. Consult more detailed resources of living a polyamorous lifestyle if this is truly desired.

Case Study 12.1

"Submitting to the Very End"

Gavin and Lola

Gavin: The only thing Lola and I had in common when we met was that we had both made a sprawling mess of our lives. We had each married young, divorced bitterly and squandered years and years drinking away our troubles night after night. I used to fantasize about an alternative sexual universe of my younger days in which I already had pocketed the hard-learned wisdom of my own age, yet still retained all the cavalier brashness of a teenager. To think of all those bratty snobs I would have spanked, how many of those wayward vixens would have fallen madly in love with their "daddy", all that mad rough sex that would have been had with those straight-laced prisses I had no idea were just begging to be manhandled.... The snapshots of lost moments haunt me. It's like they say, live and love and fuck ferociously because all of this ends.

Those early years are gone and there's absolutely nothing I can do to get it back. But what is here is Lola. Lola came along and slapped the past out of me. She inspired me to stop living in a ruminating world of charades and give her the hard dicking she was craving and be the colossus of a man I was born to be. She is my muse of all muses. She so thoroughly invigorates my imagination that I think I have now lived out the sexual adventures of ten lifetimes. There is no end to the whorl of spontaneity once you just let go of the all the regrets and realize that we will all have to give up the ghost one day.

We met at an Alcoholics Anonymous meeting we had both been forced to attend. I had stepped outside to spare my ears from all the victimizing dribble that they were pouring down my throat. No one wanted to hear my domineering rants about alcoholism not being the disease, that society was the disease. People attach a great sense of guilt to drinking, but I never shared that guilt. I love to drink. I had just never found anything apart from my art work that was all that much better than a good bottle of pinot noir or a bone dry Riesling. Lola followed me outside a few minutes after I had left. We had already exchanged coy glances numerous times. I could tell she liked my tirade against the 12 steps. She walked up to me in the parking lot and asked me without the slightest reservation if I wanted to take her out for a drink. I knew right then that she was my kind of woman.

Her gunmetal blue eyes and her sassy mouth got me the moment I met her. Her tightly-dressed curvaceous figure and the sharp upturned curve of her nose gave her the look of an English nanny to me. I don't know why, but it did and was tremendously arousing and I wanted to have my way with her right there in the bar. I was explicitly candid with my dominant swagger about treating my significant other as my one and only prized and loved possession. Fortunately for me, even though we were both bourbon-bombed, she was much more of a lady who made me work for it. She had a general distrust in men and she insisted that I prove my worthiness to her.

After a few weeks, though, we were irreversibly entangled. She brought out the madman in me. As an artist, I constantly need inspiration and intriguing encounters. She insatiably craves attention and won't stand for a single day of boredom. We're as near to a perfect match as they come. Yet, it took quite a bit of fits and fights until she really gave into my rough-hewn ways.

In fact, even after I had been seeing Lola for nearly a year, she had a difficult time letting go and trusting me. She works as a teacher of wayward youth, but used to work in law enforcement and has a master's degree in forensic psychology. She has always been surrounded by people who were trying to get over on her. With me, she was initially always on the lookout for evidence that I had done her wrong. Not only that, her previous husband had cheated on her and she took revenge on him by being with someone as well. She reacts in a fury of vengeance at times. It is one of the vital reasons why she was attracted to dominant/submissive relationships. She desired absolute commitment and trust from the other person.

Yet, ever so slowly, we reached a point where she became confident in sincerely believing that I had no intention of deceiving her whatsoever and that I had never met anyone like her. There was never a reason why she should have thought otherwise. I am always bluntly honest with her to a fault and communicate everything to her, even if the thoughts that pass through my mind sometimes come out of my mouth sounding unfiltered, lewd and outrageous. It was what really drew her to me. I am completely an open book filled with nothing but uncensored urges and genuine honesty. When Lola realized that I hid absolutely nothing from her, or even myself, she really began to open up and give more and more of herself.

After a certain point, each of us had learned to let go of all the baggage and hang-ups of our past and just be ourselves. The mutual candor and loyalty to one another made everything else in our relationship blossom like a field of wild poppies. All our energy and efforts went into the sheer enjoyment of life in and out of the bedroom. Moreover, we are both very kinky individuals and just want our time away from work to be nothing but sheer uncomplicated pleasure. We don't have any of that heavy-handed sort of strict Dom/sub vibe. We are just both hedonists at heart. She loves that I do things to her. I love that she does things for me.

Lola also has the most extraordinary set of sexual skills and she is always craving to expand her repertoire. I am incredibly lucky how erotically giving she is. Whether it's her sloppy deep-throat blow jobs or her riding me long and hard reverse cowgirl-style, she likes to feel like there is no one better in the whole wide world at what she can do. It's like I never have to teach her how to submissively please me. She just eagerly does anything and everything better than any other woman I've ever met.

Even well before I officially made Lola an owned woman by way of marriage and the gift of a silver choker necklace that she wore at all times, we had a riotously good sex life. We did everything from naughty trysts on the side of the road to ball-gagged and hog-tied BDSM debauchery at home. As our relationship progressed, though, we wanted to continue to expand the vitality of our erotic dynamic in ever more imaginable ways. I've learned that once you are married, simple kinky play just doesn't do the same thing for you. You have to go deeper and deeper into unchartered territory.

We mulled over all sorts of new ideas and read numerous sex books. At first, I wrote notes to her in the morning about what I wanted her to do that night and posted them on the refrigerator. Sometimes it was as simple as telling her to be waiting naked for me at home on the living room floor in a doggy-style spreader. Other times, it was something more extravagant like having her watch the most popular porno of the day online and then making her repeat the exact performance for me.

Our new escapades were thrilling at first, but the fact that I knew what to expect took away the sheer spontaneity of good in-the-moment sex. So, I decided to write out about 50 different detailed ideas on small pieces of white paper and put them in a wooden box that was placed on the counter. I also made Lola do the same. Then, for the next month, we would both add numerous ideas to the box on a daily basis until there were several hundred collected. I also ripped out various passages from sexually tinged novels and other kinkier books. I added another hundred blank ones which meant that we would not have sex at all. I mixed up the whole container of little white notes and told Lola to pick one out each morning without looking and not tell me anything about what to expect.

It worked even better than I had imagined. I never knew if I would be getting one of my deviant fantasies fulfilled, if she would be offering some naughty act of her own or if there would be nothing at all. In the first month, we had sex in front of a few of our friends, she came to my studio without any notice dressed in a business suit asking to be fucked on top of my desk, she served me a seven course dinner while sucking my cock in between each course, I watched her take off her clothes at an amateur stripper night in a distant town, she wore a butt plug when she had to give a work presentation in front of a large audience and I even once had a friend dress up as a cop and come arrest her, handcuff her and then strip search her before I walked in to take over her shocked and naked body.

It was that last adventure that sparked a conversation the next night. As thrilling as our sexual antics were, I felt like nothing is truly thrilling unless you are actually taking risks with your own fears and fantasies. It's got to be real. It can't just be concocted thrills. I brought up the idea of her being with another man and asked her if she had ever thought about it. She told me that she had read things about it but

281

that she had never really considered it because every guy she had been with up to that point would be way too jealous. She said she would also be terrified that it would end up ruining the relationship.

"What if it made the relationship better?" I replied.

She glared at me intriguingly but she was still apprehensive.

"Do you think you could really handle that?" she asked me.

I divulged that I had already fantasized about it many times in the past week. She raised an eyebrow and then paused for a moment as if the idea made her think about something else entirely.

"Well, since we are in a confessional spirit, I wanted to tell you something," she hesitantly said.

"So tell me," I said, curious that there was even anything that substantial that she hadn't yet revealed to me.

"Well, after I divorced my ex, I had a disturbing dream about being made to watch him be with that other woman. I think it was just a way for my mind to deal with the fear and self-doubts. But when I woke up I was inexplicably turned on."

I was in disbelief how this impromptu conversation had unexpectedly triggered both of us to share our pent-up fantasies. Yet, in retrospect, that is just what makes our relationship so rare and unusual. We both need and want the ultimate extreme bond that comes with dominance and submission, but we also both crave that this exclusivity includes being free to explore all our dark fears and perilous urges.

"Now I know I can handle you being with another man, but could you seriously risk the emotional repercussions of me with another woman?" I demanded to know.

She thought deeply about it for a moment.

"I think that if I can't, I could never really fully trust you," she responded. "I know it sounds strange but I want to watch you with someone else and then still know your feelings for me are completely unchanged."

Now I was the one who was unsure about it, even with the thrill of being with another woman was dancing around in my head.

"You really want to?" I asked again.

"Yes," she said, "I think maybe it even might turn me on to see my man be totally desired by another woman, but in the end it's only me who really does it for him."

We looked at each other and seemed to simultaneously sense how arousing this might really be.

"Will you do it?" she urged me. "I want you to do it."

My own perverse urges were now being put on the backburner.

"Say please," I told her.

"Please, baby. Please go have your way with some little slut and make me watch every second."

We both laughed and kissed each other deliriously. I stood up to pop open a bottle a wine. My mind was already reeling with the possibilities.

Ironically enough, a few months before this night, I had met a woman at a charity event and there was a very raw sexual attraction between the two of us. She was looking for a fling and was very candid about it. I told her that I was married. She said she didn't mind, but I told her that I did. She gave me her business card and that was the last time I saw her.

I told Lola about it and she insisted that I call her right away. I couldn't believe this sudden turn of events was happening so fast. I immediately called the woman the next day and asked her if she remembered meeting me as well as what she had suggested at that meeting. She said she certainly did. She wanted to know if I had suddenly changed my mind about it all. It was then that I broached the idea to her. I told her that I was still very happily married by that I had told my wife about her and that she not only was okay with it but she wanted to watch.

The woman nearly started to laugh, but then said, "Hmmm....that sounds possibly interesting. She just wants to sit there and watch?"

She was suspicious and I hadn't really thought about the exact details yet.

"Well, would you want her to do more than watch?" I inquired.

"I just wouldn't want to meet you and be some side bitch for your thrills. I like to be one who has been sexually satisfied when it's all said and done."

"Understood," I replied. "Well, she is very open-minded. I can make it crystal clear to her that you are to be the center of attention."

She suddenly warmed up to the idea. She asked me a few more questions and then the conversation went silent as she pondered it all.

"Alright, why not? I'm not committing to anything but take me out to dinner and we'll see where it all goes from there," she firmly proposed.

I sensed that the woman almost had a dominant streak in her. I immediately agreed to her conditions and we made plans for the coming weekend.

I called Lola and told her. She was even more excited then I was.

I spent the rest of the week trying to think of how I was going to pull this off. How was I going to create a casual situation in which Lola would be there watching everything? When I got home I told her that I wasn't so sure this was going to work. She told me in her typical way not to worry and that she would make it happen. I asked her how she was going to do that but all she would say is that it would be a surprise. The tantalizing anticipation along with the fears of the night going terribly awry swirled in my head.

I met the woman the next evening. She really was stunning and voluptuous as a woman can be. Her jet black hair, her hungry dark eyes and her skimpy black dress was the spitting image of a wife's worst nightmare. Lola was going to go mad with jealousy, I thought. We flirted the entire time during dinner and were casually fondling each other by the time we were leaving the restaurant. I made sure to plaster her with cocktails. She asked me if I wanted to go somewhere else for dessert or a drink and I suggested that we just go straight to my place for that. I think she might have had a plan to lure me away for herself.

"So your nice little wifey is just patiently waiting for us at home?" she skeptically asked me.

"Yep," I responded. "Don't worry. You won't be disappointed." I felt like I was channeling my wife's words.

"Okay, let's go," she said as she wrapped her hand around my arm and giggled to herself.

I sent a text message to Lola to let her know that we were on our way and that she should prepare a dessert and drink menu for us. When we got to my place, I cautiously opened the front door, not knowing what to expect. Just as I entered with the woman, Lola strutted out from the kitchen. She was wearing a very slinky French maid's outfit with black stockings and high heels. The white frills on the bottom of the outfit barely covered the tops of her thighs. She immediately greeted me.

"Good evening, sir. Welcome home."

She glanced at the woman and I could see the raving jealousy in her eyes. Lola looked so incredibly arousing, but when the other woman got a look at her, she looked at me in astonishment. I was nearly as shocked as she was at her get-up and didn't even know what to say. I ushered her swiftly into the living room and told Lola that I would call her if we needed anything.

The woman immediately asked me if she was going to join us.

"Well, I think she is just fine at the moment. She is very good at serving. Do you not like to be served?"

She grinned at the reality of her being in this situation with this kinky couple.

I told her with a grin that my wife is more like a servant and she knows that she is always to dress to please me. She laughed at our audacity and wanted to know more about the deviant lifestyle that we seemed to be living. I told her a few vague things, but I didn't give her time to inquire further into the situation. I simply grabbed her and pulled her on top of my lap as we fell onto the couch. We began to kiss and after only a few minutes, we were ravenously fondling each other in a fit of sexual emotion. Out of the corner of my eye, I noticed Lola perched at the edge of the kitchen watching it all, looking as if she was ready to come tear us both to pieces. I paused for a moment and asked the woman if she still wanted dessert and a drink.

She smiled and replied, "Sure, why not?"

I called for Lola and she scurried out of the kitchen in her racy little outfit. I told her in a very formal manner that the lady and I would like dessert and drinks.

Lola tried to bury her raging emotions and responded in key.

"Of course, sir. I'll bring you a menu right away."

Lola disappeared back into the kitchen and then quickly returned with a leather-bound menu with a number of items printed on nice linen paper. She had really gotten into this. I took the menu from her, but when she turned to leave, I told her to wait until we were ready to order. As I was looking at the choices on the menu, the woman eyed Lola, who was standing patiently in front of us with her arms behind her back.

The woman beseeched me again to tell her what kind of relationship we really had and I told her that she serves me any way I want her to. I asked the woman if she wanted to see her do something for us. She raised her eyebrows, utterly mystified by what I meant. I looked toward Lola.

"The lady would like you to get on your knees in front of her and give her a nice licking before she enjoys her dessert."

The woman glared at me in utter shock but she didn't even have a chance to respond. Lola gave me a deviant grin.

"Certainly, sir."

She bent down on her knees as I rolled the woman off of my lap. Lola looked up at the woman and asked her politely if she minded if she lifted her dress up. She smiled at Lola, and at me, and then told her with a delirious laugh that she didn't mind at all. I could see she was starting to get a thrill out of this spontaneous depraved stunt.

Lola methodically lifted up the woman's dress, pulled her panties to the side and buried her head between the woman's thighs. I excitedly watched as Lola casually lapped her tongue up and down the woman's cunt. After a few moments, I grabbed her by the hair and pulled her head up to chastise her.

"Unless you want to be dismissed for the evening, you need to lick it properly," I warned her. "Is that clear?"

"Yes, sir," she obediently replied.

I pushed her head firmly between the woman's thighs and she started licking her in a wild flurry. I told the woman not to hesitate to give her a firm spanking if she wasn't licking her the way she wanted her to. The woman smiled at me, still a little unsure of the situation, but certainly enjoying the oral pleasure. I took the woman's hand and placed it on the back of Lola's head. After a few moments, the woman was readily directing Lola to exactly where she wanted to lick her.

"Oh, yes. Right there, you good little bitch," she instructed her.

Just as the two of them were really getting into it, I informed Lola that I was ready to order. She casually pulled her head from between the woman's thighs and stood up in a very formal manner. I ordered a pair of cognacs and a chocolate fondant that Lola had put on the menu. Lola nodded to me, her lips now glistening, and left to get the order. The woman giggled again and told me how much she was starting to enjoy this. She was astonished at the whole situation but she was also very aroused at the fact that I had a wife so eagerly ready to serve. I leaned over to her and told her very suggestively that the maid will do absolutely anything we want.

I grabbed her and pulled her back on top of my lap. We fell into our rhythm of kissing and aggressively fondling each other once again. Just as we were getting heavily into it, Lola returned carrying a silver tray with our drinks and dessert. I didn't stop from kissing and pawing the woman for a second, but I glanced over to Lola to see her standing there with a look of raging jealousy on her face. I continued to give the woman deep, passionate kisses and made her patiently wait beside us.

After a few more minutes, I finally paused and said to the woman, "Why don't we have the maid feed us and provide us with sips of cognac?"

A naughty smile spread across the woman's face before she told me that that was an excellent idea.

Lola, trying her best to suppress her intense anxiety, lifted one of the cognac glasses to the woman's lips and she took a sip. Her hands were subtly shaking. She repeated the act for me and then began to feed each one of us bites of the chocolate fondant. I kissed the woman once again. The taste of cognac and chocolate filled our mouths as our tongues locked together in a swirl of intoxicating arousal. I was suddenly so turned on that I ran my hands underneath the woman's dress and pulled off her panties. By the time they were off of her, she was already unbuckling my belt.

Lola eyed every little act but continued to provide us with sips of cognac and bites of chocolate as we stripped off all of our clothes. With the mutual awareness of Lola, dressed as a naughty maid beside us, we were both getting uncontrollable horny. I pulled the woman to the floor and moved her mouth onto my cock. She eagerly sucked it in and furiously stroked it up and down with her hand. I looked over to Lola. She gave me a sharp glance and she seemed as if she was ready to throw the tray at me. I immediate gave her a stern look and ordered her to go get a condom "so I could properly fornicate with the lady." It was so unbelievably intense.

Lola marched off to get one as the woman continued to bob her head up and down on my cock. When she returned, I pulled the woman's head off of me and ordered Lola to prepare me. Her hands were visibly shaking with a kind of resentful fury as she opened up the package and then unrolled the condom onto my hard cock. The woman sat beside me in a kinky state of excitement as she watched the whole charade. As Lola stood back up, I pulled the woman back on my lap and eagerly slid my cock up inside of her. She began to ride me slow and deep. Lola stood there, almost frozen in her spot, as I fucked the woman in front of her. The woman was really getting into it and started bouncing up and down on me in a fit of sexual pleasure. I was savoring every moment of the scene and I even made Lola continue to provide me sips of cognac while the woman fucked me.

After what seemed like an eternity of time had passed, the woman finally reached a climactic orgasm. When she began to let out a series of moans, Lola could barely keep her composure. To see her standing there so obediently in her little French maid dress with her black stockings barely covering her thighs was as strangely pleasurable as the actual sex with the other woman. When I was ready to have an orgasm, I casually pulled the woman off of my lap and set her down beside me. I ordered Lola to get on her knees in front of me.

The woman watched in voyeuristic glee as Lola bent down between my legs. I pulled off the condom and began to stroke my cock to the final climax. Lola obediently opened her mouth and waited. After a few more strokes, my cum began to stream through Lola's lips and she eagerly took it in. After the final drops fell into her mouth, I told her she could swallow it. She took a deep gulp and then opened up her mouth to show me. The other woman was in amazement the whole time. I told Lola that I was finished with her services for the evening and that she was excused. She dutifully stood up, glared at me with a suppressed rage in her eyes, straightened her dress and strutted out of the room.

I turned to the woman and kissed her again. We played with each other for a while longer as she kept asking me how often I did things like this. I told her that it was the first time. She didn't believe me, but she still said she thoroughly enjoyed it. A little while later, we both got dressed and I drove her home.

When I returned, Lola was waiting for me in the living room. When I walked over to her she stood up and went to slap me. I caught her hand and held her.

"You didn't have to be so goddamn into her like that," she yelled.

I could feel her arms and body shaking uncontrollably.

"Baby, I was the one playing along. I couldn't help it after the way you were dressed and spoke to me when we got back from dinner," I tried to explain.

"And you didn't tell me how fucking hot she was. You could have warned me," she said.

I held her in my arms for a moment.

"So you didn't like it?" I asked her.

"I loved it," she immediately uttered. "That was so intense."

I was shocked. I leaned my head back to look at her to make sure she was serious.

"I mean I was so out of my mind with jealousy, but just being there and watching you be with her while you pretended like I wasn't drove me wild. It was like I had no control over it but at the same time I got so aroused when you made me serve the both of you. I didn't expect that at all," she confessed.

I was relieved I hadn't pushed things too far.

"So it really turned you on?" I wanted to know.

"God, yes. You acted like such a stud. Seeing how much she was into you totally unhinged me."

"I was just really trying to take you to the edge, baby. It wouldn't even have been a bit of such a wild turn-on if I was alone with her," I professed to her.

She abruptly looked at me directly eye to eye.

"Is that the honest to God truth?"

I grinned at her question.

"That's God truth," I told her. "Do you know how lucky I am to have a woman who lets me do something like that?"

She smirked and gave me a kiss.

"You better feel lucky, mister." She told me. "I mean, mister sir," she quipped.

She was still wearing the sultry little maid outfit. I reached down and pulled off her panties.

"Lola, baby. Come smother your naughty cunt all over my face. I want to hear you orgasm to the thought of what just happened," I playfully ordered her.

I slid to the floor and pulled her on top of me. She was already wet and when I started to lap my tongue across her clit, she instantaneous began to moan and purr and writhe all over my mouth. She closed her eyes and I licked her furiously, wondering what moments she was envisioning. She drew it out for a long time and climaxed in a fits and shakes on top of me.

It wasn't too long after that night when we talked about her being my "cuckquean". I never even knew that there were women who get sexually aroused from watching their man be with another woman. I mean men are animals. They all love to be with other women. But it is an entirely different thing when it is what a woman wants as well, and a very delicate dynamic. If it wasn't for how we are with each other, it would have never come about. Lola is not only a special woman in her own open-minded right, but her experience with her ex somehow altered what turns her on and made her feel like it is what she needs in order to completely let go with me.

Yet, Lola took the experience to heart in a way that I had never expected. She was unusually quiet and deep in thought for weeks and weeks after it happened. I wasn't really sure what she was going through so I asked her directly.

She began to ramble on and on about how there can never be any ultimate trust between two people because each of them is in constant state of change and the very meaning of trust is always emotionally elusive.

I suddenly thought that night had changed things in a terrible way, but she insisted it was not that at all. I asked then what it was that was affecting her so strongly.

"I just saw everything in its own light. I am Lola the person. I am Lola the wife. I am Lola the submissive woman..." she carried on before pausing.

"And?"

"And they are all masks I have been putting on," she told me with an odd dreaminess in her tone.

For a moment I thought she might be having a mental breakdown, but she kept at it.

"And all these wild sexual adventures and inventions and trials we have are in the end just another step towards our own end," she blurted out with a succinct sense of finality.

We talked more and she continued to ramble on to my counterpoints, but what had changed inside her was beyond words.

For weeks, and probably months, I spent many hours trying to digest it all and figure out what had triggered these thoughts and what they even meant. I initially began to regret not only our threesome of sorts, but also all the contrived sexual adventures that I had considered as nothing but pure pleasure. Yet, another part of me just accepted them as the inevitable course of our relationship and had potent memories of each one.

Yet, Lola was set on a much deeper expedition and I knew well enough to step back and let her be her.

Over the following months, she underwent such a heavy transformation of character that I could see it in her eyes. She became not only profoundly submissive to me, she became profoundly submissive to the world. We would be out and about at night and she would wander off and I would find her talking to some random homeless man in the street, or buying drinks for strangers, or even cozying up to another woman in a moment of intimate seduction before inviting her to go home with us.

There were many more moments and events that transpired until I fully accepted that she had departed on some new expedition of submission and she had completely given up her old identity. There was nothing I could do to dominate her that would stimulate her new being. I became just a spectator in her act of submission to a world of personal reckonings and mindfulness and Christ-like giving and breathtaking love.

She did not stop being submissive to me. On the contrary, she was extreme submissiveness in the flesh. She would do absolutely anything I wanted at any time of the day or night no matter what it was. Yet, it was not a regular personal submissiveness but some sort of existential submissiveness that engulfed me as part of its mission.

At first I did not know what to make of it, but I just let it be and let it become what it was meant to become.

A lot of time passed with the two of us in this strange state of affairs. It almost became something I got used to. What ultimately snapped her out of it was when she got in a car accident. It scared the hell out of me when I got the call but it ended up being only a minor thing. It woke her out of her strange daze and she started to act more like her old self, though she is still a very changed person to this day.

It was a great relief when she asked if we could start doing some more playful antics like we had once done all the time. I readily agreed and we returned to picking fantasy ideas out of the box on the counter. Everything is much more free and whimsical now. There is no more intense drama in any of our adventures. I have been with other women in front of her again and she has been with other men, but neither one of us harbors any jealousy or resentment. It is now more about sharing what we have together with others. It is all very relaxed and unforced. Neither one of us feels utterly driven to rejuvenate our sex lives in any way. If something happens it happens, if it doesn't it doesn't. We had many spontaneous adventures over the past year, but that kink is really just a smaller sliver of our irreplaceable bond. We could let each other do anything at all and we both know at such a profound level that what we have together is absolutely irreplaceable.

Chapter 13 – The Owned Woman Lifestyle

"No man or woman who tries to pursue an ideal in his or her own way is without enemies" –Daisy Bates

The act of "owning" a woman truly happens spontaneously as a natural consequence of a man getting to know a woman over time within a serious Dominant/submissive dynamic. A dominant man who completely falls for a woman will do everything he can to understand her, possess her, eroticize her, care for her and make her *his*. A submissive woman who completely falls for a man will want to feel like *his* in a deeply intimate, possessed way. One can either formalize the ownership identity with a contract, a ceremony or a serious discussion, or one can simply affirm its existence through daily action and constant awareness.

If one is more on the side of formalizing the D/s identities, the ownership of a woman can be made "official" in multiple ways. A couple can have a traditional wedding that includes a vanilla ceremony along with a private exchange of vows which pertain to the real ownership of the woman. This can be as elaborate or as simple as the couple desires and the man envisions. If the man desires to have his woman marked, it is a good idea that she be tattooed or branded during this time period.

Many couples elect to create a "slave" contract that binds the woman to the man as personal property. Although such a contract could never be enforced as legally binding, it is a good way of affirming both the man's and the woman's belief in the nature of the relationship. It is also a means of stating the financial agreement between the couple as well as any limitations of the owner's power. In pre-modern times, a woman who was truly owned as property was traditionally forbid to own any personal belongings. All assets including financial holdings, personal income and material goods were said to belong to the owner. The woman was typically given an allowance for her expenses or required to ask permission for any expenditures. A couple should put serious thought into such a contract. Although all couples getting married expect to spend their lives together, the reality is that half of marriages end in divorce. A couple should consider a pre-nuptial agreement that details the distribution of assets in the event of an unforeseen permanent separation. A proper attorney is better suited to advise them on the specifics of such agreements as well as provide guidance on the laws of their particular state.

Although any woman is generally advised to protect herself in any agreement she makes, many women who thrive in relationships in which they are owned like the idea of not being allowed to have any personal assets. It gives them a sense of being provided and cared for by their owner. It also frees them from the stresses of money management as the owner is expected to provide anything necessary for basic living needs. On a mental and spiritual level, it affirms to her that she is wholly dependant on the man and she lives with the same possessions as she came into the world and with which she will leave.

Another option for consummating the ownership is creating a video testimonial. Although a slave contract is not binding, a graphic video in which the owned woman is put on display and testifies to her belief in being a man's personal property can be more realistically binding. Unless the woman is fully public with her beliefs and practices, making such a video can be a true testament to her trust and faith in her man. A typical video would entail recording the woman naked on her hands and knees with a metal collar around her neck connected to a chain. Her slave markings should be recorded and explained. If the man wishes, he can make her perform sexual acts on him on camera. The woman can also recite her love for her man, her agreement to being his property, her core beliefs, her duties and rights as an owned woman and anything else that is pertinent to the relationship. It is all up to how one likes to create the relationship of power and identity. The man should keep the video in a very safe place such as a safe deposit box.

The relationship between a man and an owned woman can be an entirely private affair or it can be something that is shared among a group of friends, or even within a community. Some men do not care to engage in local BDSM group functions or even to tell any of their friends. Others like to fully participate in the lifestyle community via the various online connections and local groups that proliferate. There is also the option of having a separate group of friends who know that he "owns" his woman. They can either be found within the BDSM world, or they can "compartmentalize" their groups of friends. Some men do not wish that his work colleagues or good friends know his atypical beliefs. An owned woman should generally be encouraged to meet other owned women to have a support structure and social network with which she can openly engage. Online fetish sites such as Fetlife also have many groups which are tailored toward providing answers and support to fellow submissives.

If a man elects to socialize or network with other owned-women couples, there is the option of seeking "slave trades". The process of slave trading is much the same as "wife swapping" in which a woman is temporary traded for another man's woman. If a man decides to do this, there should be a clear discussion if there are any limits placed on the temporary ownership of the other woman.

In the end, a successful long-term relationship between a man and an owned woman is found on the same principles as any normal relationship- a deep, soulful connection, open communication, a desire to grow as individuals and a sincere feeling of mutual love. The only major difference with relationships driven by a male owner is that the man is the essential creator of the dynamic. He not only sets the ultimate rules and builds the dynamic according to his vision, but he is responsible for maintaining strict consistency and caring for the woman in every way. Once the woman gets to know and trust the man, she is surrendering to his vision.

Depending on the dynamic of the couple established at the outset of the relationship, she might want constant input as to her needs, fantasies and the details of every act of domination, or she might long for total submission to a man's protocol, orders and erotic force. Owning a woman can, at times, be work to get her to a place that she needs to be taken to and a man must rise to the occasion at all times to maintain respect. An owned woman typically likes a firm masculine presence not simply for the physical sensation but as a constant reminder that she is cared for and loved like no other woman.

Another road that couples elect to take is the development of a balance between a woman's submissive side and her personality/pursuits out in the larger world. While the sheer power of a D/s relationship resides in that potent dynamic between the controlling power of a man and the surrendering of a woman's ego to him, there is great potential in nurturing opposites. Existing in a state of pure property can truly amplify the urge to be oneself and desire for greater freedom out in the work world. Nurturing this balance can make the ownership dynamic that much more powerful. If a woman is encouraged to aggressively pursue her ambitions, coming home to the reality of existing only for her man's control and desire can be a very intoxicating equilibrium. Such a situation can even eroticize her own power. If she is standing in front of a room of businessmen, lecturing them in a dominating manner on how to do something, the thought that just underneath her business suit is a shaved cunt and a piercing with her owner's initials on it can be a very arousing aphrodisiac.

Cultivating Ownership Consciousness

The discovery of ownership consciousness thrusts one from proper mainstream society into a world all one's own. It is taboo, but it is undeniably powerful. The social order tells one that it is not right for a man to own a woman or a woman to be owned by a man. But one's heart, mind and sexual cravings say otherwise.

Once a D/s relationship has been established or consummated with a ceremony, it is important to cultivate the dynamic in deeper sexual, psychological and spiritual ways. While there are many schools of thought on the cultivation of erotic consciousness, the practice of tantric sex is one of the most powerful. Tantra is the ancient Eastern spiritual practice that embraces sex as a crucial element in the path to enlightenment. It revolves around the experience of subtle energies within one's sensual embodiment. Yet, on a more profound level for the man-and-owned-woman dynamic, it is the focus on accessing these energies both to enhance pleasure and to challenge one's egotism into its dissolution. The desire to increase pleasure is self-explanatory. The use of energy to dissolve one's ego can be used as a natural extension for training a woman to submit and surrender herself completely. It is cosmic submission. It is becoming aware of the supreme flow of the sacred life force of love itself. It can be conveniently labeled Tantric Ownership.

The journey to enlightenment is the process of developing awareness of one's divine connection to the universe. It is a matter of fusing mindful consciousness and erotic energy. One focuses on being entirely in the moment and using breath, movement, touch, sight and sound to move sexual energy from the genitals to the rest of the body. The greater distinction between tantric sex and regular intercourse is that the focus is not on the goal of obtaining an orgasm. It has no ultimate goal other than expanding the flow of sexual energy.

The techniques of tantra center around the slowing down of thoughts and movements in order to focus on every infinitesimal moment of an erotic experience. It can be practiced by both the man and the woman. It is a type of meditation in which the focus of one's thoughts is sexual energy. It begins by focusing on one's breath. The first step is learning how to take deep conscious breaths while concentrating on the breath itself. Depending on such factors as one's natural breathing rhythms, the stress in one's life and the degree to which holding one's breath has already been transformed into muscle memory, breathing in deep, easy rhythms might take some time. Breathing in and out through the nose is relaxing. Breathing in and out through the mouth is energizing. Alternate between the two rhythms. The important thing is to not criticize any distractions of thoughts or the inability to breathe in deep rhythms. Simply return one's thoughts to the breath.

In tantric philosophy, the body is made up of spinning spirals of energy called *chakras*. These are located in the same areas as the glands of the endocrine system (at the perineum, the lower belly, the solar plexus, the heart, the throat, the forehead and the crown of the head). One can generate erotic energy in the genitals and move it to other these areas of the body and beyond.

The physical practice of tantric sex begins with the flexing of the pubococcygeus muscle, that small muscle in the genital area that one uses to control urination. The conscious squeezing of this muscle is called doing a *kegel*. Contracting and relaxing it in repeated motions generates energy, and strengthens the power of the muscle. One can perform kegels by oneself or one can utilize them in erotic experiences with one's partner. The fundamental core of tantric sex is using kegels, along with focused thoughts and deep breathing, to build energy throughout the body. Serious practitioners of tantric sex can develop the ability to control their point of orgasm, inhabit the rich zone of pleasure leading up to the climax and have multiple orgasms over long periods of intense arousal. It is all about the power of controlled thought and relaxed breath.

If a man wants to practice tantric D/s sex with his woman, the final element is the use of prolonged eye gazing. As the windows are the eyes to the soul, they are also the energetic pathway between a dominant man and his owned woman. What is often referred to as "the look" in BDSM terminology is elevated to a cosmic level. Focusing one's eyes on each other connects erotic energies. The energy flows back and forth between the man and the woman. The nature of his gaze, whether it is intense, soft, direct, dominating or calm, creates the kind of energy he wants to channel into the woman. In the same manner, the nature of her gaze creates the kind of energy she wants to channel into the man. The options are infinite but it is a powerful means of cultivating Dominant/submissive consciousness. He is constantly and actively controlling the energy and she is constantly and openly receiving it. He is focused not on just being dominant, but participating in the eternal flow of Dominance. She is not just relinquishing herself to him. She is relinquishing her entire sense of who she is to the infinity of the universe. She realizes the voidness of all things.

Cultivation of true enlightenment takes years of serious practice and dedication. The practice of sacred sexuality is found in many other religions and traditions, as well, including Taoist, Sufi, Buddhist, Jewish, Pagan, Wiccan, Occult, Native American, and Afro-Caribbean cultures. If one is interested in pursuing these practices in greater depth, there are entire books focused on them such as *The Art of Sexual Ecstasy* by Margot Anand.

On a more immediate sexual level, tantric sex is about using genital energy to create pleasure throughout the body. It is about tapping into those vital fears of letting go and completely submitting to the experience. It is about using sexual energy to move through consciousness and get deep into each partner's memory. A man can use tantric practices to move energy to any part of a woman's body. He can utilize pain, roughness, tenderness, pleasure, restraint, strong words and even quietness to achieve rich erotic experiences that are only possibly with supreme awareness of his body, her body, her mind, his mind, her life, his life and the complex bond between the two of them.

The Long Road

The road to finding the woman to own for a lifetime is not an easy one. A man has got to love a bad woman once or twice in his life to be deeply thankful for a good one. One should neither settle nor be delusional. Some women marry men hoping they will change and some men marry women hoping they will not. Don't make that mistake. A good woman begins by resisting a man's initial advances but ends up blocking his retreat. An owned woman is a woman in love with the right man. The rewards greatly outweigh the efforts required to find the right woman and train her to be owned. Most people live lives of quiet desperation, going to work like robots and attending social functions like programmed citizens of the world's corporate mentality. The world of owned women can open the doors of perception for both the woman and the man if viewed as a creative universe of possibilities instead of a limited subculture of a few kinky minds.

In the end, human beings are all fragile creatures. Men and women are both born out of the same confusion, but men, in the gross simplicity of the universe, are physically stronger than women. The only true submission is the submission to death. What happens before then is a revolt against mortality and a testament to the opposites of man and woman. The man who is meant to own a woman and the woman who is meant to be owned by a man understand this. That is the simple truth that underlies the complex drama of a sincere ownership relationship.

List of basic fetishes and fantasies to explore:

A
Amateur stripper nights, amateur porn, anal beads, anal hooks, anal training, animalistic sex, anonymous encounters, arm binders, artistic cutting, asphyxiaphilia, ass to mouth, ass worship, auralism.

B
Ball gags, ballet shoes, bare bottom spanking, bastinado, bathroom use control, begging, behavior modification, belly-dancing, belt spanking, Ben Wa Balls, big tits, bimboification, bisexuality, biting, black men, black women, blindfolds, blow jobs, body hair removal, body modification, body worship, bondage, boot blacking, boot licking, boot worship, boss/secretary, branding, bratting, breast bondage, breast spanking, breast whipping, breast/nipple torture, breastfeeding, breath play, breeding, bukkake, bullwhips, burlesque, butt plugs.

C
Caging/confinement, candle wax, caning, catsuits, chastity, cheerleading uniforms, choking, clamps and clips, cling film, clit spanking, clothespins, clover clamps, cock milking, cock worship, cocksucking, collar and lead, consensual nonconsent, corner time, corporal punishment, corset training, costumes, covert bondage, crawling, creampie, crops.

D
Daddy/girl roleplay, deep throating, degradation, shaving, dildos, doctor/nurse play, dollification, domestic servitude, double penetration, douching.

E

Edge play, electrical play, electrotorture, emotional masochism/sadism, encasement fetish, enemas, erotic photography, ethnic play, exhibitionism, eye contact restrictions.

F
Face fucking, face sitting/smothering, face slapping, fetish wear, figging, filthy mouths, fire play, fish hooks, fishnets, fisting, flirting, food play, foot massage, forced intoxication, fucking machines.

G
Gagging, gags, gangbangs, geisha, genital piercings, glory hole, gloves, golden showers, Gor, group sex, gun play.

H
hair bondage, hair pulling, hairbrush spanking, handcuffs, handjobs, head shaving, Hentai, high protocol, Hojojutsu, hoods, hook suspension, human furniture, humiliation, hurting the ones you love, hypnosis.

I
Ice cubes, impact play, impregnation fantasy, incest play, interracial sex, Interrogation.

J
Jerking off sessions.

K
Kidnapping roleplay, kitchen sex, kneeling, knife play.

L
Lactation, latex, leaving marks, lycra/spandex.

M

Maid Uniforms, makeup control, making home movies, masks, massages, medical play, medieval devices, mental bondage, military role play, mind control, mummification.

N
Needle play, Nyotaimori.

O

Obedience training, objectification, old guard slavery, orgasm control, orgasm denial, orgies, otk spanking, outdoor bondage, outdoor sex.

P
Paddling, pet play, piercings, piggy play, pigtails, pinching, play rape, pony play, posture collars, predator/prey, predicament bondage, prostate massage, public humiliation, public play.

R
Religious play, remote-control devices, restraints, riding crops, rimming, rope bondage/suspension, rough sex.

S
Sacred sexuality, sapiosexuality, scarf bondage, scarification, schoolgirl roleplay, scratching, sensory deprivation, strip tease, sex fighting, sex with strangers, sexual objectification, sexual slavery, shackles, shibari, single tail whips, slave bells, slave tattoos, sleep assault, sleepsacks, spanking, speculums, speech restriction, spiritual bdsm, spitting, spreader bars, squirting, suspension bondage, swallowing, swinging, switching.

T
Talking dirty, tantra, teacher/student, teasing, threesomes, tickling, tit fucking, tit slapping, tongue sucking, triple penetration.

U

Uniforms.

V

Vaginal stretching, verbal humiliation, vibrators, Victorian lifestyle, vintage lingerie, voice play, voyeurism.

W

Wartenberg pinwheels, water torture, waterboarding, watersports, wax, webcam control, whipping.

Z

Zentai.

Random Kinks, Fetishes and Turn-ons: a man in a tuxedo with his cock in her mouth in the bathroom at the opera, a vintage corset previously worn by a Victorian woman, fucking on the kitchen floor covered in sugar and flour, falling into a kinky love-spell at 40, barely legal liaisons, a wooden spatula on a bare butt, putting a naked housewife in a cage, a hard slap for a foul mouth, tender love after rough words, a white woman with a big black cock gagging her mouth, a Latina squatting in reverse cowgirl, an Asian mistress wearing only English riding boots while strutting on Italian marble, a Japanese schoolgirl in intricate rope knots, a rolled cigarette going into a man's mouth, driving through the desert at 120 miles per hour with her mouth bobbing up and down on his cock, staying kinky late at night after the kids are in bed, holding hands while strolling down quiet, rainy streets, a man who is willing to fight for his life to make it happen, branding a woman's flesh because you love her and want her to know she's yours, being there for a woman when she needs you badly, being there for a man when he needs you badly, breakfast without utensils, fresh squeezed juice from turning oranges on firm breasts, fresh baked bread in two mouths, feeling love and pain and pleasure in the same moment, frolicking on the beach in late summer, watching a woman walk down the beach in the skimpiest of attire, naked midnight sex on a foreign beach, a metal collar so heavy she has to struggle to make it through the day, an eloquent evening dress on a woman who likes it rough, simple white panties on a woman who needs to be held, making her lick all the salt off a cocktail glass, making your kinks last as long as your years, living the age you feel, fucking any age you want to fuck, saying fuck-off to images of beauty and getting lowdown dirty, a woman changing a tire, a man who can talk to any stranger, making her shave your face, sending devastatingly kinky text messages with simple words, writing a letter with an fountain pen, calling her a good whore, ripping off the clasps on her garter belts, slapping her across the face and looking her in the eye, ripping the back of her nylons open, that early-morning, tingly warm feeling in bed when endless images of kinky acts flood the mind...

Recommended Reading:

BDSM
Sm 101: A Realistic Introduction – Jay Wiseman
The Topping Book – Dossie Easton and Catherine Liszt
The Bottoming Book – Dossie Easton and Catherine Liszt
The Pleasure's All Mine: Memoir of a Professional Submissive – Joan Kelly
The Seductive Art of Japanese Bondage – Midori
Justine, Philosophy in the Bedroom, and Other Writings – Marquis de Sade
Venus in Furs – Leopold Ritter von Sacher-Masoch

The Intellect
The History of Sexuality – Michel Foucault
Emotional Intelligence – Daniel Goleman
Beyond Good and Evil – Friedrich Nietzsche

A General Introduction to Psychoanalysis – Sigmund Freud
Brainwashing: The Science of Thought Control – Kathleen Taylor
The Development of Sadomasochism as a Cultural Style in the Twentieth-Century United States – Robert Bienvenu
Partner selection, power dynamics, and sexual bargaining in self-defined BDSM couples – Bert Cutler
Verbal Behavior – B.F. Skinner
The Prince – Niccolò Machiavelli
The Art of War – Lao Tzu
A History of Genius – Darrin M. McMahon
The Wisdom of the Heart – Henry Miller

Sex

The Kama Sutra – Vatsyayana
Blow Him Away: How to Give Him Mind-blowing Oral Sex – Marcy Michaels
The Art Of Seduction – Robert Greene and Joost Elffers
The Phallus: Sacred Symbol of Male Creative Power – Alain Daniélou
Philosophy in the Boudoir: Or, The Immoral Mentors – Joachim Neugroschel
The Art of Sexual Ecstasy – Margot Anand
The 50 Greatest Love Letters of All Time – David Lowenherz
Come As You Are – Emily Nagoski, Ph.D
The Little Black Book of Sexual Positions – Dan and Jennifer Baritchi
Passionista – Ian Kerner, Ph.D
101 Nights of Great Sex – Laura Corn

Appearance

The Corset: A Cultural History – Valerie Steele
Tight Lacing – Peter Farrer
Westmore Beauty Book – A Complete 1950s Guide to Vintage Makeup, Hairstyling and Beauty Techniques – The Westmores
Amy Vanderbilt's Complete Book of Etiquette – Amy Vanderbilt

Miss Manners – Judith Martin

Fiction
Delta of Venus – Anaïs Nin
The Story of O – Pauline Réage
Carrie's Story: An Erotic S/M Novel – Molly Weatherfield
The Sleeping Beauty Novels – Anne Rice
Bared to You – Sylvia Day
The Lover – Marguerite Duras
Crash – J.G. Ballard
Belle de Jour – Joseph Kessel

A Small Sampling of Vendors:
Coco de Mer
The Stockroom
L BAR M Ranch Products
Lovesick Corrective Apparel
Extreme Restraints
Honey Birdette
Thistle and Spire
Marie Mur
Agent Provocateur
Creepyyeha
Restrained Grace
Sub-Shop
Lovehoney
Kink.com
FetLife.com
Home Depot

Other Titles from American Taboo Press

Strict Women – Annabelle Watson

American Taboo –Madison Ava Jones

Actress: Unauthorized Memoirs of a Hollywood Slave – Madison Ava Jones

Force Me – Madison Ava Jones

The Black House – Madison Ava Jones

Spanked: Real Stories – Gabriella Luciano

The Slut List – Gabriella Luciano

Made in the USA
Columbia, SC
27 February 2021